Allison Forbes was born in Edinburgh and brought up and educated in Salisbury, Wiltshire. She taught classical ballet and folk dance for twenty three years, including, in 1986-90, on the Performing Arts course at the Italia Conti Academy in London.

On moving to Manchester she worked as a residential caretaker in a tower block for Manchester Housing until her retirement in June 2004. In the latter years she studied Law with the Open University and was awarded her LLB in December 2004. She hoped to go on to qualify as a barrister, and although this did not happen she is a Student Member of Middle Temple.

She has two grown up children and is proudly owned by two resident felines.

*To Pauline
with every good wish
from
Alison Forbes*

TOWER COURT

Tower Court

ALLISON FORBES

Willow Bank

WILLOW PAPERBACK

© Copyright 2010
Allison Forbes

The right of Allison Forbes to be identified as author of this Work has been asserted by her in accordance with the Copyright, Designs and Patents Act 1988

All Rights Reserved

No reproduction, copy or transmission of this publication may be made without written permission.
No paragraph of this publication may be reproduced, copied or transmitted save with the written permission or in accordance with the provisions of the copyright Act 1956 (as amended).

Any person who does any unauthorised act in relation to this publication may be liable to criminal prosecution and civil claims for damage.

A CIP catalogue record for this title is available from the British Library
ISBN 978-1-906166-24-3

All characters in this story are fictitious and any resemblance to any person either living or dead is purely coincidental.

Willow is an imprint of
Willow Bank Publishers Limited
www.willowbankpublishers.co.uk

First Published in 2010
By
Willow Bank Publishers Ltd
e-space north
181 Wisbech Road
Littleport
Ely
CB6 1RA

Printed and bound in Great Britain.

– Prologue –

The tall, thin man drove into the car park of the faintly seedy-looking tower block. He looked for a space to park and found one between an elderly van and a rusting wreck of a car which had obviously been there for some time, judging by the leaves and general debris that had built up under its wheels. He noticed, absently, that one of its tyres was flat. He nodded to himself; he had been told that the block was rundown, and this was clearly the case. It looked as though it would suit his purpose well enough.

To his extreme annoyance, not to say rage, he had found himself in the position of having to shift his headquarters. Who would have thought that the bumbling officers of the Met would have got so lucky? Or had one of his "members" squeaked? He shook his head, they all knew the penalties too well. Still, the officious officer responsible for the thin man's abrupt departure north had not lived to realise his success. He remembered with deep pleasure the splash when the weighted, but still living, body had been thrown into the canal. There had been no record that it had been found. The thin man did not usually attend an execution, it offended his fastidious soul, but this had been an exception.

So far so good; it was time to investigate further.

The thin man waited, and soon his patience was rewarded. He watched as two elderly women approached the main door of the block, laden with shopping. He contrived to arrive at the door at the same time as they did and politely offered to help them with their bags. They accepted gratefully, and the thin man passed into the building with them. He was unaware that the little meeting had been watched by the security officer. His name was Phil, and he was pleased that the Williams sisters, who were favourites of his, had been given help. He grunted approvingly as he watched the little party cross the foyer and enter the lift.

The thin man parted cordially from the ladies who had so obligingly facilitated his entry into the building and continued up in the lift to the top floor. He looked round briefly, noting the general feeling of neglect, and wrinkled his nose at the sour smell that seemed to pervade the block. He wondered if there was a caretaker, or resident cleaner. If there was, he seemed to be pretty negligent. So much the better. He found a scratched and battered door that said "s-air-", opened it, and found himself at the head of stairs that wound their way down, presumably to street level. There was the same air of neglect and decay that he had seen in the rest of the building, not to mention evidence of filth that had been inefficiently cleared up. He went all the way down and out into his car. Really, it was very satisfactory and would suit him admirably, once he had installed one or two of his henchmen as residents. That should not be difficult, given the state of the place, would-be tenants were hardly likely to be beating a path to the door. He decided to call in few favours.

    The thin man drove away, well pleased with the results of his little expedition.

– Chapter One –

I looked with a mixture of awe and trepidation at the fifteen-storey block of flats soaring above me. It was now my responsibility – mine. It was called Tower Court, my first reaction was that it looked decidedly more tower than court.

I had been delighted, and not a little surprised, to be appointed; after all, jobs for 50-something females do not grow on trees. Now faced with the reality, coupled with the rueful knowledge that I had been given absolutely no training, I felt close to panic. I controlled myself. It was only housework on a rather larger scale – wasn't it?

I placed the fob I had been given on the key symbol beside the big glass and metal door and went inside. There I came face to face with an elderly lady, rather stooped, who looked me up and down. She eyed my very new-looking uniform.

"The new caretaker, are you? About time. How long will *you* last, then?" She seemed to imply that caretakers lasted weeks, not months, and the turnover rate was high. "This is a very dodgy area, you know." She then disappeared into the lift while I was still getting my breath back. Rather hysterically, I felt I could almost see a puff of green smoke as she vanished.

Before I could lose my nerve completely, a door on my left marked "Security Office" opened to reveal a large, heavy-built, cheerful-looking man, smartly dressed in an immaculate uniform. He looked me up and down.

"So you're the new caretaker." He sniffed. "It's not right. Caretakers are men."

"There are quite a few female ones now," I said mildly. "Times change." In fact, there had been no other females at the interview but I didn't see the need to labour the point.

"Not 'ere they don't." He was positive about this. "It can be dangerous, and the work is far too heavy for a lady like you."

Oh, my public school accent; it always seemed to be getting me into trouble.

"I'll just have to prove I can do it, then," I smiled. "Er – who are you?"

"I'm Phil, Phil Johnson; me and Fred do week about, day shift. Geoff and Rob do nights. Fred's not going to like this. He's a man's man, he is." Having got this somewhat obscure remark off his chest his manner thawed slightly. "This is the Security Office. You'd better come and have a look if you really are the new caretaker." He peered at my name badge, all shiny and new. "Fran – ces – ca. Oh no, that won't do. We'll call you Frankie. You're not from round here, are you?"

I followed him meekly into the office and blinked at an array of computer screens showing various aspects of the building and car park, as well as pictures of the surrounding area.

"We serve part of the estate as well as the tower block," Phil explained. "The whole place is pretty well covered by CCTV." He was obviously proud of the set-up. "Not much gets past us. And we control the main door, you can only get in through us unless you have a fob as a resident."

Privately I wondered how true this was as I made admiring noises.

"By the way, how did you get in?" Wordlessly I held up my fob.

"That explains it. For a moment I was worried." He waved me to a chair and settled down for a gossip. "For example, the old dear who spoke to you just now. She's Joan Foster, lives on the 7th floor. Been here forever but scared of everything, she is, and nasty with it. Don't mind her. You listen to me and you'll do just fine."

Clearly I was to be taken under his wing. I ventured a comment of my own.

"Isn't watching all those screens day in and day out deadly boring? You seem so cut off from the outside world."

"There's ways round it. You can have good chats with people." At that moment a buzzer sounded sharply, making me jump. "That's the Williams sisters, look. Live on the 2nd floor and always forgetting their fob. Nice pair, but vague." He indicated a screen showing the main door and two white-haired ladies beside it, laden with shopping. "Hello, girls. Forgotten our fob again, have we?"

"Sorry, Phil, yes. But you will let us in, won't you?"

"Don't know about that, don't know what you're up to, do I? And I've got the new caretaker here. Got to show her what's what, haven't I? Oh well, seeing it's you. Take care."

***

Phil watched as the new caretaker went out. On the camera he saw her go up to the Williams sisters and then accompany them into the lift.

He sighed as he watched. He had been in the job a long time, seen several caretakers come and go. Some had been really good to start with, then had either got lazy or demoralised, then left. None had stayed long. He thought about the last one, Rich.

"Waste of space, he was," he said to himself. "And a thief. How did he expect to get away with flogging off all them stores? And then to try and embroil me – *me* – in his scams." Even mentally, Phil was disgusted. He had been with the security firm, Safeashouses, for many years and was proud of it, and of his job. He wouldn't do any thing to jeopardise it.

Phil's life had not been easy. He had been at rock bottom when he was given a chance by the brand new security company calling itself by the unlikely, and to him, ridiculous name of Safeashouses. A man he had actually met in prison, who had contacted him when Phil came out and was desperately looking for work, had started it. Phil's wife had dumped him as soon as he went inside, for a moment of madness when he acted as lookout and driver for a pair of singularly ineffective would-be bank robbers. They had all been caught with contemptuous ease by the police, imprisoned, and there he had met up with Jed Rochester, inside for a con, which even to Phil's innocent ears sounded ridiculous. However, it had proved to be a wake up call for Jed, who swore to Phil several times while their sentences coincided, that he would never, ever, go off the straight and narrow again.

To his surprise, when Phil had followed Jed into the outside world, he found that his friend had been as good as his word. Not only had Jed started this security firm but he contacted Phil to offer him a job. Phil was stunned. Privately he wondered where the capital had come from to enable Jed to go into business, but he knew better than to ask. As far as he could see, this was a legitimate offer in a legitimate business, and he had enough problems in finding work, any work. He accepted with becoming gratitude.

"It's like this," Jed had said, at what passed for an interview. "I know what you've done, you know what I've done," (More or less, added Phil mentally) "so we can trust each other. I am never, ever, going to stray from the straight and narrow," he added earnestly for the umpteenth time.

"What, not even to beat the tax man?" Phil joked.

Jed answered with complete seriousness. "Not even that. It's not worth it. Now, are you with me? I trust you to be just as keen to keep out of prison as I am." He was suddenly deadly serious. "Everyone who works for me must be squeaky clean."

"I'll not let you down," promised Phil, with equal seriousness. He too had had enough after his, he hoped, only taste of prison life.

It had all worked out very well. He had been put into this tower block; he and a friend of his, Fred Davidson, shared the daytime shifts, week about, and two others, Geoff Wilson and Pete Forrest, shared the evenings. Fred had also had a chequered career, but had managed to keep out of prison; Phil suspected that the same might be true of the other two.

"A right case of poachers turned gamekeepers," he said to Jed.

"Works, though, doesn't it?" And Phil had to agree that it did.

As time went on he found that not only was he grateful for the opportunity, he actively enjoyed the job. He liked getting to know people, and knowing what was going on in the neighbourhood. He enjoyed the repartee that passed between him and some, at least, of the tenants. So far, he had not been able to form much of a working relationship with the caretakers, but he had a feeling this might be about to change. He thought about the new one.

"Could be a right asset," he thought. "Bit different from the rest, might even want to *work*!"

***

I went out to meet the sisters who introduced themselves as Mary and June. I offered to help them with their shopping and we travelled companionably up in the lift to the 2nd floor.

They dropped the bags on the floor with a combined sigh of relief. "Sorry we can't ask you in just now for a cup of tea but perhaps later, when we've settled ourselves. We find that shopping rather takes it out of us nowadays." The elder of the two, Mary, was clearly feeling weary. "What's your name, dear?"

"Francesca." I indicated the name badge.

"Oh dear, that won't do." Unconsciously she echoed Phil. "What about Frankie? Less formal. You're not from round here, are you?"

So Frankie I duly became, while wondering just how long it would take to overcome my foreign-ness.

***

Mary and June entered their flat thankfully. They hated to admit it but they were beginning to find even such an ordinary task as shopping was becoming more and more difficult. They went into their spotless little kitchen, where June, the younger, immediately put the kettle on.

"Go and sit down, dear," she said kindly. She looked a little anxiously at her sister, who was leaning against the worktop. She did look alarmingly pale.

"I think perhaps I will," said Mary. Now June was really worried; her sister seldom took any kind of rest without argument. She was relieved when the kettle boiled. She made the tea and took it through to the living room where Mary was leaning back in "her" chair with her eyes closed.

"I really do think you should be checked out by the doctor" June said. "Perhaps I should be too. We're not getting any younger."

Mary roused herself. "Nonsense," she said. "I'm not eighty yet. Nothing at all these days. Anyway," she said, changing the subject. "What do you make of the new caretaker, this Frankie?"

"She seems very pleasant," returned her sister. "I liked the way she came to help us. And it's good to see she has taken the trouble to speak to Phil."

"She probably didn't have much choice there," Mary smiled. "You know what Phil is, he always has to know what's going on."

"Good thing too," June snorted. "Rich wasn't going to do anything, even when it happened right under his nose. The whole block is looking really neglected now, and, you have to admit, it smells."

"Yes, it does" agreed Mary. "We're well rid there. Do you know, I couldn't even remember his name? And he's not been gone that long – has he?"

"There you are then," said June, triumphantly if a little obscurely.

Chatting companionably the sisters settled down to enjoy their well-earned cup of tea.

***

I debated with myself whether I should be a good caretaker and inspect my new responsibility or visit my own flat first. Nesting instinct won and I descended in the lift to the first floor, and to flat 3 that was to be my personal domain for the foreseeable future. There was a caretaker's office on the ground floor but that could wait. I needed to see my home.

As I emerged from the lift I nearly fell over a man, rather younger than myself, who was engaged in tenderly watering a feeble-looking fern outside his front door (at least, I presumed it was his).

"Oh, hello," he said, looking up but still stooping over his patient. "Are you the new caretaker? We heard that one had been appointed – at last. Do you know anything about pot plants? My name's Julian." And he shook hands with an abstracted air.

"No and yes," I replied, taking his questions in reverse order. "It seems that we are to be neighbours."

"Oh, are you moving into flat 3? Good, it's been empty for a while. So is flat 4" - he indicated the flat opposite mine - "and Magda Benjamin lives in flat 2 opposite us. It's an odd arrangement, odds together opposite evens. Drives new posties mad."

"I can well imagine it. I'm Frankie." I had accepted my new persona.

"Nice to meet you. I'm Julian Fry and my partner, Ron Peters, is inside. You must pop in when you're settled." And with a final smile he vanished into his own flat leaving me to open my own, new, front door.

***

Julian closed the door carefully behind him and wandered into the living room. Ron, tall and lanky, with a mop of unruly dark hair, was draped over an armchair with a ginger cat fast asleep on his chest.

"Wake up, sleepyhead. The new caretaker's arrived."

Cat and man opened a sleepy eye apiece and shut them again. "So what?"

"So it's female," retorted Julian ungrammatically, and dropping into a companion armchair. He surveyed his partner's lean length affectionately. "There's nothing to choose between you and Furball in your propensity for sleep."

Ron condescended to open both eyes. "Female, eh? Well, she can't be worse than that layabout they finally kicked out. What's her name, and what's she like?"

"Frankie, she said, though it's Francesca on her name badge. Seems alright, looks you in the eye, nice firm handshake."

"That, at least is something. That other twerp never looked you in the eye. Real shifty, he was." Ron was a firm believer in 20 – 20 hindsight. "I don't think I ever shook hands with him but I'll bet it was of the wet fish variety. Does she do cats?"

"No idea, but she doesn't know about pot plants. I think that one at the door's had it. Did Lucy Locket try to eat it?"

"Don't know. Ask Furball." And Ron prepared to resume his interrupted slumbers.

***

Julian wandered into the bedroom and sat down on the bed. Thoughtfully he removed his shoes, always the first thing he did on returning home. He thought about the new caretaker; she seemed to be a vast improvement on her predecessor. Yet she made him feel vaguely uncomfortable, slightly uneasy. He wondered why.

He was back, mentally, some twenty years before. He and his twin brother, Paul, were about to celebrate their joint twenty-first birthday, they were looking at the car given to them by their father: a bright red mini. It was not new, but they both fell in love; while Paul just stood and gazed, Julian, flamboyant as always, gave a wild whoop.

"I'm in love," he shouted.

They looked at each other. "Who's going to drive her first?" said Julian, uneasily. He knew the answer; he was the younger by fifteen minutes. Sure enough:

"I am, of course – junior."

"Actually, neither of you can, until tomorrow, it's not insured until then." Their father, Bernard, had come out of the house and was standing behind them; they were both too engrossed to notice. He looked at them with pride, his two tall, good-looking boys. Though it was apparent that his eyes lingered longest on the elder. Paul was indeed the more striking of the pair, though quieter; there were times when the ebullient Julian seemed almost to be a pale copy, painted in Paul's left over colours. Bernard went on, "I mean it, both of you. I was a bit late setting the insurance up for the two of you as named drivers and it doesn't come into force until tomorrow morning."

Paul's face fell. "Surely, a few hours early? Just round the block?"

"No." His father was firm. "In my position, no member of the family can go against the law. You know that perfectly well." The twins looked at each other and grimaced, this was a well-known record. Their father was a magistrate, the twins often wished that he wasn't, it had often seemed to interfere with their, to them, innocent pleasures.

"That's fine, we can wait. Thanks tons for giving it to us. We never expected it." Julian remembered his manners. "But when we can –"

"I shall have first drive."

Julian grinned at the memory, then paused. What was it about the new caretaker that had put it into his mind? He tried not to think about his brother, even after all these years it was too painful. He went back into the living room to join his sleeping partner, then paused again. How would he have coped then without Ron? He resolved to remember more often what Ron had done for him.

***

I closed the door behind me and surveyed my new – currently empty – home. I was to commute initially from the other side of Arkchester to here at Heathfield. It was not a prospect that appealed but I could live with it for now. The flat appeared to be reasonably spacious: living room, kitchen, bath and two bedrooms, thank goodness. I resolved to import a couple of chairs until I could move all my goods and chattels in. I hoped the Office would allow me some time off to do this.

I thought back over how I had arrived at this point.

I had arrived back in England after a traumatic time. A serious accident had robbed me of my current career and a plane crash had robbed me of husband and children at the same time. I had recovered, more or less, from the accident; I could move freely again, and I had no doubt that looking after a block of flats was well within my capabilities. Recovering from the plane crash, however, was another matter. That was still a long way off.

I had discovered the advertisement for a caretaker for Tower Court by the merest chance. I had found a discarded newspaper in the bus and the advertisement had leaped out at me, almost as if it was meant. Mesmerised, I took down the particulars and applied for the job. I hardly felt surprise when I was called for interview. Though now I was here, well now, that was a different kettle of fish altogether....

Taking my courage in both hands I set off on my first block inspection.

The block consisted of fifteen floors, with four flats on each floor. Two lifts stopped on alternate floors, even and odd and stairs ran down each side. It seemed confusing but doubtless I would become accustomed.

Shock, horror! Did my predecessor not do *anything?* I gathered that he'd been gone a good while and reliefs came in to cover the block cleaning, but they didn't seem to do much either. The stairs were indescribable, litter everywhere – and worse. Heaven knew when they'd last been mopped, the whole place smelled sour and musty and I didn't care to attempt to identify the various components. After two flights I went down to the Security Office in search of a plastic bag; at least I could pick up the litter if nothing else.

On my way down I met a young man with an air that seemed strangely furtive. He seemed to be in his mid twenties, thin, shabby and, I thought, Asian in appearance. As I opened my mouth to say something polite he seemed to give my uniform a horrified look and bolted down the stairs as though pursued by the Furies. I wondered what on earth could have scared him; surely I was not that alarming? I gave a mental shrug and continued on down the stairs and on to the Security Office.

I felt that Phil was an old friend. "Have you, by any chance, a plackie bag?" I asked him. "The stairs are knee deep in paper, tins and worse."

"That'll keep you out of mischief for a while. Here you are. Bins are out the back." He handed over the required plastic receptacle. "How are you off for stores? Only, I did hear the old caretaker used to sell them off at car boot sales."

"Goodness knows, I haven't dared look. First things first." And I departed to wrestle with what I felt promised to be a Herculean task.

Some time and several bags later I was able to congratulate myself that at least the stairs, all of them, were clear of litter, and I was exhausted. I wished I could just collapse in my own flat; instead I tottered out to the car to drive what felt like miles across town.

***

My immediate boss, Roger Knight from the Office, finally came to see me on a welcome visit. At last I now had some stores; I had ordered a long shopping list over the phone and he brought some of it with him. My flat being still very minimalist in its furnishings I entertained him in my caretaker's office on the ground floor. This was equipped with a desk/table, two chairs and a cupboard, so was hardly more welcoming than my flat. And the only cupboard was empty.

"Why is there so little in the way of stores?" was my first question. After Phil's comments about my predecessor I was curious as to what Roger would say. Sure enough:

"Your predecessor had a useful sideline going in flogging his stores off on the estate. We only discovered it when we sacked him for long-term idleness and incompetence, apparently it had been going on for years. It's very difficult to get rid of an established caretaker," he added ruefully. "It was only when his negligence actually began to pose a danger that we were able to do it."

"What is this area really like?" Question no. 2. "I've had some disturbing reports."

"About what you would expect. A bit rough in parts but nothing really bad." Such as rape and murder? Only a little gentle mugging I supposed, nothing to get upset about. "It would help you to get on terms with the police. I'll see if they can drop in on you." A mixed blessing: do I need a bodyguard?

I felt I was making good progress with sweeping and mopping the stairs - though I admit to concentrating on the bits that showed, the lifts and the foyer – as best I could without cleaning materials. But the block was beginning to look a little better, a little more cared for, and, I thought, was decidedly less smelly.

The stores having finally arrived, and armed with a brand new mop and bucket and a gallon of liquid polish, I started on the foyer floor. So I was not best pleased when a boy on a bicycle came through the main door and cycled blithely across "my" clean floor en route to the lifts.

"What do you think you're doing?" I roared above his earphones.

"Oh, sorry," he looked taken aback. "Wasn't thinking." He dismounted sheepishly and tiptoed into the odd-side lift. Which reminded me, I needed a list of tenants; I made a mental note to ring the Office when I'd finished the floor.

It was evidently my week to meet monosyllabic tenants. I was doing my daily block check and was on the 13th floor when the door to flat 51 opened a crack and someone peered out. I couldn't really see who it was; the light had gone (I replaced it that afternoon, my first repair). "Is he there?" a voice whispered hoarsely, then: "Who the hell are you?" and the door slammed before I could introduce myself. Yes, I definitely needed a list of tenants.

The following week I was given time off to move into my flat, much to my relief. I was well fed up with commuting. It would be a while before it was as I wanted it but at least I now had a proper base.

***

Ron looked up from feeding the cats as Julian came in.

"She's moving in," Julian announced, flinging his coat on a chair.

"Who?" Ron spooned Whiskas into the bowls as his customers weaved around his feet and tried to climb up his leg. "Ouch! Get down, Lucy. It's coming, and will be all the quicker if you don't interfere."

"Frankie. The new caretaker, though she's not quite so new

now, is she. I think she's going to be alright, don't you? I mean, the block looks better already."

"Anything would be better than that waste of space, Rich. Or almost anyone. Do you remember how he tried to flog us that floor cleaner? Blatant, or what. And do hang up your coat. I'm always telling you."

"Sorry. Do you think we should ask her in? Being neighbours and that."

"Good idea." Ron put the bowls down to the ravening cats. "There you are. That's twice you've been fed this month – count your blessings. Let's wait and see. She might be another Rich, though I doubt it."

As he fed the delighted cats his thoughts returned to the past and another, very special, cat.

***

Ron Peters, a scrawny, undersized five year old, was huddled in his favourite, and, indeed, only, hidey-hole. This was the space between the fence and the shed in what passed for a garden in the children's home, where he had lived for almost all his short life. Because of his stature and general skinniness he was a prime target for the bullies among the bigger boys; so far, they had not been able to reach him in this sanctuary, though, to be sure, he suffered for it later when they did spot him. Added to his lack of inches and general weediness he was taciturn to the point of muteness. Sometimes he did not speak for days at a time. The staff at the home wondered about it occasionally, but as the home was hopelessly under-funded and consequently extremely short staffed, they did nothing.

Cuddled up with Ron was the only creature in the whole world that he loved, and who, he firmly believed, loved him. This was a large tabby and white cat called Mouser; presumably this was intended to remind him of his duties, but Mouser, at best, was an indifferent hunter. Now he was curled up in Ron's arms, purring rather sleepily.

This mildly idyllic scene was interrupted by one of the bigger boys, Jimbo, whose greatest pleasure in life was tormenting anyone and anything smaller than himself. In this category both Ron and Mouser scored high points.

"Come on out, I know you're there," he bellowed, having decided that a little torture would serve as an appetiser before tea.

Mouser, a veteran, leapt out of Ron's arms and up a convenient tree. His hunting might be weak but he could climb for England, a necessary accomplishment. Ron felt bereft, but at the same time glad that Mouser was safe. He wondered which was the lesser of the two evils: to stay put and be sure of harsher treatment later, or to come out and add to his collection of bruises straightaway. Few of these showed, Jimbo was an artist and took a pride in his work. The dilemma was answered by the tea bell; with a parting "You wait, I'll get you!" Jimbo hurried off to be first in the queue. Food was important. He needed to keep his strength up for the pleasure to come, didn't he.

Ron followed slowly, having first made sure that Mouser was safe. He did not really care about tea, the food was pretty bad, and not to say sparse, but there was safety in numbers under the – fairly – watchful eyes of the few staff. Perhaps a miracle would occur to put off the evil to come, he had not quite lost a spirit of optimism – yet.

He lingered in the dining room as long as he could after tea, unwilling to leave its dubious safety. But all too soon one of the staff came up to him.

"Come on," she said, not unkindly. "Go and play in the garden. I've got to lock up."

All the rooms were kept locked when not in use.

Silently, as always, Ron went out into the garden. His spirits lifted, he could see no sign of Jimbo. Could he have gone out with somebody? It seemed unlikely; perhaps, after all, miracles did happen.

"There you are, you little runt. Punishment time." Jimbo stepped out from behind the hedge, near the road. Then Ron saw, to his horror, that Mouser was clutched, squirming, in Jimbo's ungentle arms. "This is what you get for hiding from me," Jimbo shouted, and flung the cat, paws flailing, into the road. There was a shriek, which Ron was to hear in memory for many years, a squeal of brakes, then silence, which seemed to last forever. Then the sound of a vehicle driving away.

Ron was frozen, rooted to the spot. Then, with a demoniacal howl of rage, he snatched up a large stone and launched himself on the astonished Jimbo. So sudden and ferocious was his onslaught that Jimbo went down before him as though Ron was twice his actual size and strength. Falling on top of his enemy Ron kicked, bit and lashed out with his stone, screaming out imprecations, which mingled with Jimbo's yells of surprise and pain. Authority was soon on the scene, managing, not without difficulty, to disentangle the combatants.

"What on earth's going on here?" demanded Jean, one of the care staff. "Have you been bullying again, Jimbo?"

She knew him of old.

"Though it hardly looks like it," she added, surveying the pair. Jimbo was a pitiable object, covered in dust and bleeding copiously from a deep gash that Ron had opened up over his right eye. He was crying more loudly than any of his previous victims, she was interested to see.

"He just *attacked* me," Jimbo sobbed, pointing at Ron who stood, flushed and breathing heavily, the stone still in his hand. "I wasn't doing *nothin'*. He just *attacked* me."

"Is this true?" asked Jean incredulously. She looked at Ron, half Jimbo's size, but clearly the victor in this bout. She felt rather pleased, she didn't like Jimbo.

"He killed Mouser," said Ron, unusually loquacious. "He *murdered* him."

"Didn't. Stupid moggie ran into the road," whined Jimbo.

"You – threw – him. Threw him over the hedge," Ron glared at him.

"That's no excuse for attacking Jimbo," the second carer, Frank, took over. He was considerably less sympathetic than Jean, he didn't like cats. "Though if you did throw the cat over the hedge, Jimbo, that was very cruel, very cruel indeed."

Neither of the adults, though kind enough, and as conscientious in their duties as they had time and energy to be, had the faintest idea of the catastrophic effect the incident was having, and would continue to have, on Ron.

"Come inside, both of you, and we'll get you cleaned up. You've not heard the last of this," Frank added ominously. The little procession passed into the house, Jimbo still wailing, and Ron returned to his usual silence. What was the point of saying anything?

One good thing, though, the older Ron smiled grimly to

himself. Jimbo never laid a finger on him ever again, and was left with an interesting scar over his eye that would probably be with him for life.

***

Blissfully unaware of the reservations about me on the part of my neighbours I started to tackle the block seriously. Living on the premises I found made a big difference. I was much encouraged as people passing through the foyer started to comment favourably.

"The place looks a lot better now – and smells better."

"It's a treat actually to see the caretaker. You could never find the old one when you wanted him."

I glowed.

Then, one day, when I was polishing the lifts (much needed, I might add), a tall, heavily built man with an air of one who had gone to seed came in, looked at my efforts and snorted.

"New broom, eh? That won't last. Didn't with me, I soon found out how to beat the system." I looked a question. "I'm Rich. The last caretaker. Could we have a word in your office? Morning, Phil" to Phil, who had emerged, quite suddenly, from the Security Office.

"Sorry, I'm busy." While I appreciated the chaperon I was not going to waste time on this interview.

"Could put a bit your way. Could double the money the stingy Office gives you, easy." By selling off my stores, presumably. "Could help you make some real money if you get my meaning."

By drug dealing? I wouldn't put it past him. I wouldn't trust this specimen as far as I could throw him – and that wasn't far.

"Sorry. No. Got to go." Thankful I was in the lift I pressed a button – any button – and was whisked, rather slowly, away. As the doors closed I heard him saying, presumably to Phil, "Silly woman. Some people won't be helped." Safely back in my flat I peeped out and watched him swagger – there was no other word for it – out of the car park. And, I hoped, out of my life.

***

After a brief chat with Phil, who ended the conversation by going back into the Security Office and shutting the door with unnecessary firmness, Rich stalked out of the building, head high.

He admitted privately to himself that he bitterly regretted losing the caretaker's job. It had been a nice, cushy way to earn a living, with plenty of perks. The sale of stores had been a very profitable sideline; he felt only contempt for the powers that be that they took so long to realise that he couldn't possibly use up new products so quickly. Then he made sure that every little favour he did for tenants had its price; there was no way he was going to do something for nothing, was there?

But, with hindsight, he realised now, too late, it had been unwise to try and run his flat off the communal electricity. Though, there again, it had taken them long enough to find out…

He sighed and went on his way. Surely some easy, profitable work would turn up soon. It didn't even have to be strictly legal.

***

Soon I had my first set-to with the bin men. The bins, which were either parked at the back of the block or put in the bin room where the rubbish chutes ended, were, I had learned, collected every Wednesday. The chutes ran from top to bottom of the building with openings on each floor, where moderate sized bags of rubbish could be deposited to fall down into the bins at the bottom. So, with sixty flats, even these large bins were filled pretty quickly and needed to be changed (by me, like nappies). Then came the week when the filled bins were not collected. I'd put them where I thought they should go, lined up at the back, but the decidedly supercilious young lady who answered my irate call said that was wrong.

"Where should they go, then?"

"I've no idea. It's not my business. Probably round the front. But the bin men can't haul them all that way." I, presumably, could. Seething, I managed to persuade her to send the men out again. The next day, when they arrived, I was still fuming. And had dragged all the bins round to the front.

"Why ever did you drag them all this way? You should have left that to us."

I explained about the supercilious young lady.

"Oh, you don't want to listen to *her*. We don't. Do you know, the other day she sent us right over to the other side of Heathfield to empty bins she swore blind we'd forgotten? It's not even our area.

And, would you believe, the bins had gone, not been emptied but gone, the place was down for demolition. I ask you. What a wally. No, luv. You put them where you like and we'll pick 'em up. Up in the sky if you like. We didn't come yesterday because we were full up, see? You're not from round here, are you?"

We agreed that I was not and sorted out exactly where we wanted the dratted things to go. Round the back....

I'd also had a call from the local police in the person of one Sergeant Robin Lutterworth. He promised to drop in as soon as he could "to have a chat about this and that," he'd said cosily. What, for heaven's sake? Is this area as bad as I am beginning to suspect?

I decided to visit Phil in the Security Office and casually mention Sergeant Lutterworth in the course of conversation. Phil was very scathing about the police force in general.

"Never there when you want them, always there when you don't. They don't care tuppence about us. Think I can manage on my own. How can I when I can't leave here? And that Rich was worse than useless. No, I don't know this Sergeant Lutterworth. Don't want to."

No help there, then.

Rather to my surprise Robin Lutterworth did turn up two days later. His visit was an eye-opener. I thought at first that he was winding me up.

"I'm afraid this is a dodgy neighbourhood and we have our eye on several of the flats here. I don't think you're in the slightest danger but we would appreciate your help." They didn't say anything about *that* at interview.

"We would like you to make a note of anything strange going on and let us know. And we'll give you a special emergency phone." Not scary at all. "Look out particularly for these car registration numbers." He handed me a list. "If they come in call us at once."

This was definitely the down side of living over the shop. I could never escape. Thank goodness we had security on the premises.

I debated whether to mention flat 51 which, having received a list of tenants, I now knew to be occupied by Bonzo Ray. I felt his behaviour did come under the heading of something strange.

"Oh yes, we know him. He's one we're watching. As a fence." Wow.

"What about the ex-caretaker, Rich?" I asked. "I think he's approached me for drug dealing."

Robin looked wistful. "Very probably. You don't have an address for him by any chance? We were just going to pick him up when he was sacked and vanished into the wide blue yonder."

Sadly, I had not.

"Make sure any communication with us is by phone, we don't want to alert any plug-uglies with an added police presence."

No, we don't. Kind of them to think of it. Oh well, if it gets too exciting I suppose I can always leave. Flee the country. Disappear. Oh 'elp!

As he was leaving Robin seemed to think that he had perhaps gone a bit too far and their carefully selected caretaker might after all vanish into smoke. "You really don't need to worry," he assured me. "We'll keep a good watch on you and we are only a phone call away."

Was that supposed to be a comfort? Evidently my face showed what I felt as he came back into the flat.

"I really do mean that. We'll see you are perfectly safe – and anyway, there's nothing pending as far as we know. We need you to tell us when it is."

I tried to gather my social skills together. "I'm not in the least worried." (May I be forgiven.) "Goodbye, and thank you."

Alone, I collapsed into the nearest chair. What had I let myself in for? What on earth would happen next?

– Chapter Two –

Ron was putting the finishing touches to his to-die-for goulash when Julian, hung around with photographic equipment like a Christmas tree, crashed through the front door, late as usual.

"Can't you do anything quietly?" asked Ron, resignedly, from the kitchen.

Julian looked injured. "That was quiet – for me. Anyway, never mind that, Magda's back."

"Oh good, would she like some goulash? There's loads."

"There always is with you. I'll go and ask."

Five minutes later he was back, accompanied by a tall, slim, stylishly dressed 30–something brunette, her looks clearly stating her Israeli origins. She kissed Ron with enthusiasm.

"It's good to be back. Rome was fantastic but too hot, even for me." Magda's surprisingly high-powered job as a fashion editor took her all over Europe, usually at a moment's notice. Friends and acquaintances, puzzled by her preference for an uninspiring flat in an uninspiring neighbourhood were kept in ignorance as to how much of her, admittedly high, earnings went to support a large extended family in Tel Aviv. Ron and Julian were the only ones to know this.

Magda turned to Julian. "Who's been under your lens today?"

"Nothing much, just publicity shots for the Rosealba School. Usual young hopefuls done up to the nines for tap, modern and ballet. But next week, all being well, I'm off to shoot the Gressington Ballet down south at their school. Now, that should be good." Julian adored his work as a photographer specialising in dance, and his growing reputation was beginning to harvest enquiries from professional companies as well as from local dance schools and hopeful parents.

Ron appeared from the kitchen. "We've got a new caretaker," he announced.

"I know, I told you," said Julian patiently, "And I thought the place looked better."

"She's just moved in next door," Ron continued. "We should ask her round, make her welcome. Any excuse for a get-together. Do you think she'll be sociable? Any attachments?"

"Impossible to say, but she seems friendly enough. We'll just have to see. No sign of attachments so far." And Ron retired back into the kitchen.

"What about trying her after dinner?" Magda suggested, never one to hang back. "I've got some duty free bottles. Let's check her out."

"Why not?" Julian responded. "Any excuse."

***

I was dozing in front of the television, thankful to be in my own flat at last and not facing a commute, when I was surprised by a knock at the door. I glanced at the time, nine o'clock; ah well, a penalty of living over the shop. But when I answered the door there was Julian, grinning at me.

"Fancy a drink?" he asked, "and I don't mean cocoa. Magda in No 2 is back from Italy and has duty frees shouting to be drunk."

"I'd love it," I grinned back, unwittingly earning myself several brownie points. This would beat TV any day, and it was Friday, so no early morning start.

I found Ron and Julian's flat a big contrast to my own not-yet-lived-in quarters and made a beeline for two magnificent specimens of cathood reclining on the sofa. "Who are these?" I breathed. My own flat felt horribly empty without a resident feline, I had always been owned by cats in the past.

"The ginger gentleman is Furball, he's always getting them with that long coat, and the white and tortoiseshell is Lucy Locket, no one quite knows why." I flopped down on the floor to make friends but was recalled to better manners. "And this is Magda Benjamin, supplier of wine and just back from Rome. Red or white?" Julian, still grinning, held a bottle in each hand.

I blushed. "Sorry, I didn't mean to be rude but I do so miss having a cat."

Magda was laughing. "Don't worry. Nothing will endear you more to these two than a passion for cats. I have it too, but I am away so much it wouldn't be fair, so I share these two. How are you finding the block? And the job?"

I sat more appropriately in a chair and accepted a large glass of red wine. "There's an awful lot to do. Did my predecessor do *anything?"*

"Not much. We kept this landing as we wanted by doing it ourselves, at least Ron did it mainly. He writes cookery books, and on food generally, and works from home, so he fits in housework as and when. He says it clears his brain. I'm not arguing, his food is to die for and he's always trying new recipes. I'm the gardener; the balcony plants are fine but pot plants don't like me as you have seen."

"Perhaps there's not enough light on the landing," I suggested.

"Good point. I'll try it on the balcony, or at least in here." Julian looked pleased.

"I cadge a meal whenever I can," laughed Magda. "Ron really is an amazing cook."

"So are you," Ron protested.

"Yes, but only Israeli food Mama taught me. You can cook anything."

"What is this area like?" I asked. "I've seen Heathfield, of course, but I've not ventured into the town proper yet."

Julian took up the sing-song voice of a tour guide. "Arkchester gets it's name from the fact that it was a soldiers' camp on a bend of the river Ark. The river has changed its course over the years but can still be seen as part of the Manchester Ship Canal – though you have to be both quick and sharp-eyed to see the notice," he added with a grin. "And Heathfield has grown up as a suburb of Arkchester."

Ron took up the tale. "The settlement became a village, then nothing much happened," he blithely skipped over several centuries, "until the industrial revolution, when six magnates discovered the Ark water to be especially good for the manufacture of cotton goods. These six joined forces, built mills and harnessed the water from the river, which was still a viable river at this time, and brought Great Prosperity to the town, which grew rapidly and haphazardly. Not that their workers would have appreciated it," he added feelingly. "This was a time of great hardship as well as prosperity, and the workers were little more than slaves. The Six, as they came to be known, ran the whole area exactly as they pleased, with very little regard to legislation and the outside world. They say that Arkchester was the last place in England that had education available to the children, they were needed in the mills, you see, and too much education puts Ideas into the Minds of the Workers."

"You must have made quite a study of this place," I said, impressed. "Did The Six do any good things?"

"In fairness," Julian answered, "they did lay the foundations for the Arkchester of today, which is somewhere between a town and a city. They built that amazing Town Hall as a monument to their generosity, also a marvellous theatre, which still tempts major companies here today. There is a strong cultural element in the town, which they did a great deal to initiate. We are proud of our orchestras, choirs, etc, and, of course, the University."

"I didn't realise there was a university here," I said, "What is it like?"

"According to the locals, Oxbridge can just close down," Magda joined in the discussion. "I believe it is good, though, and has a fine reputation. It was also founded by The Six, so they weren't all bad."

"You'll meet several of the students here," Julian informed me. "This is quite a favourite place for them to live during their university career."

I settled back in the chair with my wine, as the conversation became general. If this was what being a caretaker was all about I was all for it.

As I sat there, relaxing for the first time since I took up the job, I was glad to let the conversation flow round me. Magda was talking about her Rome trip, it sounded like hard work rather than glamour. Ron was saying very little; I felt that this was usual with him. Then Julian, answering a question from Magda, woke me up.

"Yes, it's a definite invitation, I am to go down to the Gressington School next week and do a series of photographs of the School, and of the company before they go on tour. It's what I've been after for months."

"Do you often get invitations like that?" I found myself asking.

"Not nearly often enough," laughed Julian. "I'm a general photographer but I like to specialise in dance and it's mostly local schools looking for advertising, or doting mothers with their 'talented' children plus trophies. At least I don't have to watch them dance. But enough about me. What did you do before you came here? Have you always been a caretaker?"

"Oh, this and that." I hoped I sounded casual. After all, I had only just met these people, much as I enjoyed their company, and I valued my privacy above all else. "Tell me about this company, the Gressington? Are they good?"

Julian was easily diverted. "They have a reputation that compares with the Royal and the English National and entries to the school are literally fought over. I went to an audition once and two mothers nearly came to blows."

I tried to look puzzled. "The Royal? The English National?"

"The Royal *Ballet,* the English National *Ballet.* They both have schools, the Royal Ballet School at White Lodge in Richmond and the Senior School in Floral Street, Covent Garden, and the English National School is in Kensington."

"Oh yes, I've heard of them." I decided that too much ignorance was as bad as too much knowledge. "And the Northern Ballet school in Manchester. Is there a company too?"

"Yes, though it's nothing to do with the school. I can see we must take your education in hand, or perhaps you don't like ballet?"

"I like ballet." Julian looked relieved. "Only I've not seen much." May I be forgiven.

"Anybody hungry?" Clearly Ron had had enough culture for one evening.

Much, much later I negotiated a path back to my own front door. As I turned to wave to Magda outside her door I blessed my good fortune in meeting up with these people; I was sure they would become true friends. As I shut the door I was highly relieved I didn't have to get up in the morning.

***

"She'll do." Ron yawned. "But she's not saying much about herself, is she?"

"No, but it's early days yet." Julian was philosophical. "A few more nights like this one and we'll have her whole life history."

"That I very much doubt," Ron told the glasses as he loaded the dishwasher.

"Do you think she has had anything to do with dance?" Julian asked suddenly as he put the cats' biscuits into bowls.

"Whatever gives you that idea?" Ron responded. "She didn't seem to know anything about the major companies."

"No, I know. It's more the way she stands and moves, as though she is used to having her body completely under control, you know what I mean?"

"Yes, I do know what you mean, and I think that she knew far more about what you were saying than she wanted us to realise. Oh well, it's her business. If she wants us to know about her past life she'll tell us when she's good and ready. And I'll bet you anything you like that it's nothing discreditable."

Julian looked shocked. "Oh no, I didn't think anything like that. It's just my 'satiable curiosity. You know what I'm like."

"I do indeed. Come on, Elephant's Child. Bed!"

***

Magda returned to her own flat in a thoughtful frame of mind. She was remembering when she had come to England from her native Israel....

She stood outside Heathrow and looked around her. She was shaking; she had escaped from one danger and wondered what lay in store for her now. But she had made it, she had escaped. Feeling that she was at last taking control of her life, she picked up her bags, shook her long, dark hair back – a characteristic gesture when she had made up her mind to a plan of action – and made for the underground. She would get herself into London and take it from there.

Magda Benjamin came from a large, extended family, mainly living in Tel Aviv. Since her parents' simultaneous deaths in a plane crash when returning from visiting yet more relatives in England she had been living with an aunt and uncle. Unfortunately, her uncle, taking advantage of a lengthy stay in hospital on the part of her aunt, had started creeping into his pretty niece's bedroom for a "chat". Rather than upsetting the entire family, Magda, having dissuaded her uncle from further activities with a shrewdly aimed kick, decided that it was time to spread her wings and fly the nest. Hence her arrival, quite alone, at Heathrow.

Three weeks' later she found herself, somewhat to her surprise, settled in a small flat which she shared with a distant cousin, and working as a dogsbody in the London office of a magazine where another, even more distant relative, had an interest. She reflected that being part of a very large family had distinct advantages. To be sure, it was not entirely what she wanted to do but it was a start, and she could get her breath and earn money. It meant that she wasn't using her degree in Art and Design, obtained with much sweat, blood and tears from the University in Tel Aviv, but that would come in time. She had made a start.

With a rare and rather pleasurable feeling of nostalgia Magda settled further into her favourite armchair and continued enjoying her memories of her early time in the U.K. It was very late and she should have been going to bed, but she still felt on a high after her successful Roman trip so she decided to indulge herself.

She had hardly settled at her desk one morning (a very small desk, rammed into the corner of the big, open-plan office in a space between the photocopier and the coffee machine, as befitted the most junior and insignificant member of the workforce) when Wendy, her immediate boss and occupier of a far larger desk on the other side of the room, came hurrying over to her.

"Are you capable of stringing two or more words together?" Wendy demanded, skidding to a halt and only just missing the coffee machine. "In writing, I mean?"

"Yes," replied Magda composedly. "I did some freelance articles before I left Israel."

"Thank heaven," Wendy heaved a heartfelt sigh of relief. "You must go over to Hammersmith, to this address, and write up what you find there. Julie's off sick with a bug. *Now,* not next week!" And she positively pushed the startled Magda out of the office.

Outside, Magda took a moment to get her breath and see where she was meant to be going. She was relieved to discover, from the A to Z that was her constant companion, that the street was near the tube; her destination turned out to be a very new, very trendy boutique. It was divided into two distinct halves, one side aimed at the late teens-early- twenty-somethings and the other, apparently, at a thirty-plus clientele. She decided to look at younger age group first; accordingly she pushed open the door of the that half and went in.

Strolling around she found that she liked the clothes but she thought that the sales room was tatty, the music too loud and not sufficiently up to the minute and the service appalling. Two young girls were gossiping and giggling in a corner; Magda thought at first that they were customers until one vanished into the back regions and returned with two mugs of coffee. She turned her attention back to the clothes. These she really liked on a closer inspection, and phrases began to form in her mind as she began mentally to shape her article.

When she went into the other half she found it rather better designed, but, conversely, the clothes were not as interesting. The décor was obviously aimed at the older clientele, the music was quieter and less would-be trendy. Magda suspected that this had been the original shop and that the younger branch had been opened on its back, as it were.

A well-dressed woman looking to be in her mid forties came forward as Magda started to prowl.

"Can I help you?" she asked, with a practised smile.

"Yes," said Magda, deciding to jump in at the deep end. "I've been sent by my magazine to have a look at your shop and write it up."

"Oh, yes, you must be Julie. They said you'd be along. Come into my office and we'll chat over coffee. I'm Fiona, I own the shop."

"Thank you," said Magda, "but, in fact, I'm not Julie, I'm Magda. Julie's off sick." Then, feeling that one good turn deserved another she added: "You might like to chase up the girls in the other shop. They paid not the slightest attention to me when I went in, just stayed gossiping in the corner, then brought out two mugs of coffee."

"In the shop?" exclaimed Fiona. "I'll kill them. That's strictly forbidden in case of spillages on the clothes, as well as looking so unprofessional, as well they know. Oh, they're on borrowed time, those two." She stormed off into the other shop, returning a few minutes later, still fuming.

Magda and Fiona settled down in the small, rather untidy office, situated where Fiona could keep an eye on the shop. They were interrupted several times by customers, Magda gathered that this side, at least, was doing well.

Fiona agreed. "This is fairly steady all week, the other side goes mad evenings and weekends. I'm quite pleased with the way it's all going. The young side is new, and I've not long taken over this part. I bought out the owner, who was a friend of mine, when she wanted to retire. I hope you'll give me a good write-up."

"I'll do my best," Magda laughed. "Good luck."

On the way back to the office she was weighing up phrases in her mind and settled down to write as soon as she was installed at her desk. She had just finished when Wendy rushed up, in a hurry as usual.

"There you are. Did you find the place alright? Be a love and write it up as soon as you can."

Silently Magda handed her the neatly typed copy. "You didn't say how many words but here you are."

Wendy gaped at her. "You can't have done it already – can you?"

"I can and I have. Now, I'm off for a sandwich, I haven't eaten all day." And she swept out of the office, leaving an awestruck Wendy gazing after her.

From then on Magda's progress through the magazine's hierarchy was rapid – and she was moved out of her tiny desk between the photocopier and the coffee machine. Then she began to be sent out to cover shows, first at home and then abroad, accompanying more senior staff. She was even able to move into her own small flat, bidding a cheerful farewell to her distant cousin. Things seemed to be set fair for her; after her trauma at home in Israel she hoped it would last.

Magda grinned reminiscently and stretched. She glanced at her watch. It was now definitely well past her bedtime!

***

I came down the next morning to find a major flood in my nice clean foyer. It seemed to be coming from a cupboard I'd not really noticed before; on investigation I found it awash with very smelly water, apparently coming from a large pipe in the corner running from the floor until it disappeared through the ceiling.

"Oh, that's the soil stack," said Roger airily when I managed to catch him at the Office. "It carries all the water and - er – waste from the kitchens and bathrooms. Which side is it?"

"The right hand side as you come in," I said faintly.

"The odd numbered flats then. Just mop up, I'll be round as soon as I can."

I surveyed my new indoor lake and fetched mop and bucket. I mopped with vigour, but it took forever. Even Roger looked sympathetic when he arrived late in the afternoon, especially when I informed him, somewhat acidly, that I had so far mopped three times.

"I'll get you a wet and dry," he said, then seeing my obvious bewilderment, added indulgently: " vacuum cleaner that sucks up water and dust."

Somewhat to my surprise he was as good as his word; a well-used but operational machine arrived the next day. At least I could now keep the water level down but it still needed doing at least twice daily. I could have done it every hour on the hour had I not rebelled. And no news as to when it might be repaired.

"This is always a problem in tower blocks," Roger said cosily when I tackled him about it. "We have to find where the leak starts, then we can repair it."

Yes, so what about looking for the dam' thing? I thought, but did not say.

"Yes, soon, soon." Roger was thinking aloud. "We'll have to write to all the odd numbered flats. We know that your one and the void are safe, we'll just have to look above." Fine. Wait a minute, the void was no 4, an even number. I pointed this out. "But no. 3 is my neighbour and he is often in during the day."

"Good. We'll try there this afternoon."

However, the fates took a hand: the foyer ceiling collapsed. Luckily no one was hurt, and it was only plaster, but it rang instant litigation alarm bells in the Office. I've never seen people move so fast. I say no-one was hurt, but Tony Barnstaple, the cycling student from flat 17 had to leap for cover. I forgave him for cycling on my clean floors (of distant memory) when he helped me to clear up. I asked him what he was studying.

"Oboe, at the University's Music School. It's affiliated to the Royal Northern College of Music in Manchester," was his somewhat surprising reply. Were there no "ordinary" tenants in this block?

"How do you practise?" I asked. "No-one's mentioned it, and we can't all be passionate about oboe music."

He grinned. "I have a silent piano in the flat which I play with headphones. Piano's my second instrument. And I practise oboe at the Music School." He loaded a final spadeful into the bucket. "That should do for now. Beginning to pong though, isn't it?"

This, of course, was the signal for the builders to come in to make safe – and, also of course, make more mess. Tony vanished into the lift, I wished I could have joined him. By the time the work was "finished" – it didn't look finished to me – it was way past signing off time. I cleared up, yet again and trailed, grumbling, to my flat. No overtime, this was why I lived on the premises in a rent free flat.

***

Jacquetta Meyer stood at the window of her flat on the 10th floor and sighed. She was heavily pregnant but the baby was not due for another six weeks. She felt like a beached whale, and her husband, Joshua, was away visiting relatives in Israel. "I'll be back in plenty time for Junior's arrival," had been his parting shot as he left.

She turned back into the room and a sudden pain stabbed at her back. She sighed again, what bliss it would be to be able to move easily once more. She wondered whether she could call down to her friend Magda on the first floor, but she knew that Magda was not long back from Rome and decided not to bother her.

"Don't be such a wimp," she told herself sternly. "Dozens of women cope with pregnancy on their own. And it's not an illness. Perhaps Josh will ring soon?" She tried to work out the time difference in Israel but it was too much bother.

Her backache eased and she settled down with her knitting to watch television. But she nodded off almost at once as she so often did nowadays, even in the bath, though her size precluded any danger of drowning.

Suddenly she awoke with a cry. The television was talking to itself but she had no idea what was on. The clock showed the time to be nearly 2.30am. Then she felt a sharp cramp low down and clutched protectively at her bump. Surely the baby couldn't be coming, it was too soon. She waited; then again, an unmistakeable cramp. She grabbed the phone, never far away when she was alone, and punched in Magda's number. A drowsy voice answered at the fourth ring.

"Magda, quick, please, the baby's coming!"

"No! It's too soon. Are you sure?"

"Pretty sure, though it's not like last time." Jacquetta had had a previous pregnancy that had ended tragically in a stillbirth and was booked in for a hospital delivery because of it. "But it's so early!" she wailed.

"Sit tight, I'm on my way up."

***

I was blissfully asleep when a loud knocking on the door dragged me out of bed. Cursing I struggled into my dressing gown and found Magda on my doorstep.

"My friend Jacquetta in flat 37 seems to be having labour pains. Josh, of course, is away. Can you come up with me?"

"Yes of course, just let me get some clothes on. You go on up."

I hauled on the first available garments and sallied forth. I remembered seeing a heavily pregnant girl in the lift and foyer but had only passed the time of day with her. I hoped the lift, often temperamental, would not choose this moment to stick.

In flat 37 I found Magda and Jacquetta keeping calm by a major effort of will. Jacquetta was clearly terrified; after all, the baby was early by nearly six weeks, and I presumed it was her first.

"How far apart are the contractions?" I hoped I sounded as though I knew what I was talking about. "Are they regular? Have the waters broken?"

"We're quite sure this is it." Magda was positive. "The contractions are about ten minutes apart so there's no mad rush. I'll call an ambulance."

"I'll do that, you stay with Jacquetta." I dialled the magic 999 and informed the impassive but not unsympathetic voice that I required an ambulance.

"That could be a problem. What seems to be the matter?"

"We have a lady in labour with her first, contractions ten minutes apart, no other signs."

"Good, no immediate hurry, then. There has been a major incident on the motorway and we are very short of vehicles and paramedics in consequence. We'll come as soon as we can, about half an hour, probably. I don't suppose anyone could drive her to hospital, could they?"

"No, there's only me, my car is too small and I daren't take the responsibility."

"Fair enough. Half an hour, then."

That didn't seem too bad, I thought as I relayed the news. "About half an hour, incident on the motorway," I reported. The baby, apparently, heard this as things promptly speeded up alarmingly. Magda and I got Jacquetta onto the bed then Magda hunted out sheets, towels, blankets, anything she could think of to help two very inexperienced and nervous midwives.

"Do you know anything about this?" Magda whispered as we burrowed in a drawer for towels.

"Only from having two myself," I hissed, taking an armful from her and going to put on kettles for the hot water so dear to authors' hearts.

In the end it all happened surprisingly fast. By the time the ambulance turned up, an hour after the call, a furious baby boy was exercising a very fine pair of lungs as he shouted his rage at the transition into an uncaring world. His mother gazed at him adoringly, the amateur midwives sat limply, slumped in chairs, hoping they had got it right.

Mercifully we had, even to the extent of not cutting the cord (what with? Unsterilised kitchen scissors? The carving knife?). We got brownie points for that. The experts duly cut and tied the cord and delivered the placenta (which I had completely forgotten about) then whisked mother and son to hospital and rather more orthodox treatment.

"You've done a good job there, girls," the paramedic complimented us. We nodded weakly, returned to Jacquetta's flat, and with one consent decided to leave the clearing up till the morning. As we adjourned to my flat for restoratives I reflected that no one had mentioned in my interview that midwifery training would be an advantage. Magda broke it to me that Jacquetta should have had a hospital delivery because of a previous stillbirth.

"I'm thankful I didn't know that at the time."

"Lucky you. I did. But I didn't see the point in both of us panicking. Good thing the lift didn't break down, too. It's getting really temperamental."

"I'll say. I'm shattered. We did good, though, didn't we?" On which heartening thought we separated, Magda hauling herself reluctantly to her feet and departing to her own flat. I was left to make the most of what little remained of the night.

My final thought was that I must remember to tell the Office that they had a new tenant.

***

Magda went into her own flat; she felt exhausted, and she knew that it wasn't only the excitement and drama of assisting at the birth. Her mind went back into the past again, this time with considerable reluctance.

She had been at her job in the magazine for about six months, with a meteoric rise through the hierarchy. Surprisingly, the other girls showed no signs of jealousy about this, possibly due to Magda's own straightforward approach to it. She was also now ensconced in a small basement flat ("Garden Flat" according to the landlord) in a large Edwardian house on Frognal Lane in Hampstead, which had access to the back garden of the house and to the communal gardens serving all the surrounding houses. She was not sorry to have her own premises; living with her cousin had not always been easy.

Magda was sitting at her desk, immersed in research on her computer when she became aware that Edward Martin, part-owner and editor of the magazine, was standing beside her.

He smiled kindly at her. "Am I right in thinking that it is your birthday?"

She nodded speechlessly, taken completely by surprise.

"What is it now, twenty-four, twenty-five?"

She found her voice. "Twenty-five." In fact, she was only twenty-two, but she had been afraid that she would be considered too young at twenty-one so had lied on her application form.

"Then I think I should take you out for a drink to celebrate your quarter century. Six o'clock suit you?"

"Y-yes. Thank you." She stared after him, bemused, as he

sauntered into his own office. It must be unheard of, she thought, for such an important man in the office life should pay attention to such a junior member, even if she had achieved a great deal in a very short space of time. She shrugged; if he wanted to act strangely it was up to him. She returned to her research and failed to notice the significant glances exchanged by the other girls. Beddy-Eddy, as they had dubbed him, was famous among them for latching on to new girls, the younger the better. Indeed, they wondered that it had taken him so long. As he was an extremely handsome man, as well as important in their small world, he seldom met with a rebuff.

"Should we warn her?" asked one of them when she and Wendy were closeted in the cloakroom.

"Oh, I think she can look after herself," replied Wendy. She was not exactly jealous of Magda but she was very aware of how rapidly the other girl had progressed. "It won't last long. She's not Beddy's type."

"No, you're probably right," said her friend.

The birthday drink was followed by others, and the occasional dinner; all perfectly harmless, but Magda found that she was feeling a little uneasy. Although Edward was punctilious about bringing her back to her flat after each outing, she was careful not to invite him in for coffee. She used the excuse that the flat was too small for entertaining and he seemed to accept that. Unknown to her, the other girls were watching events with rapt attention, even running a book on how long she could hold out. They felt she was doing rather well and hoped it would continue.

One evening in November, Magda was home early. She had been doing some interviews and had gone straight home rather than struggling through the rush-hour to return to the office and then go home. She was curled up in her favourite chair with a mug of coffee and a book when she was astonished to hear the unmistakeable sound of a key in the lock of her front door. She sat frozen; the landlord had sworn that the locks had been changed when she moved in, he said it was his regular practice. She knew that she hadn't given a key to anyone, so what was happening?

To her stupefaction Edward appeared at the door. "I don't know why you said this flat was too small for entertaining," he said breezily, looking round and advancing into the room. "It's quite big enough for a little drink *á deux*."

"How did you get in?" asked Magda, indignantly.

"Easily, with a key," said Edward. He smirked. "You will leave your things lying around at the office so it was simple to get a copy made."

"How *dare* you meddle with my possessions and invade my privacy!" Magda was furious.

"Oh, don't make such a song and dance about it," said Edward impatiently. "You ought to be grateful that I've been paying attention to a little thing like you. I'll bet the other girls are seething," he added complacently. "Now calm down, and let's have a little drink together. I take it you've got something we can drink? Something interesting, that is, not tea or coffee."

"I have not," said Magda emphatically, "and I wouldn't offer it if I had. I want you to leave immediately. Go on, get out."

"Oh, I don't think so. You owe me for all the food and drink I've put down your neck. Extremely expensive food, in extremely expensive restaurants. Now it's pay-up time."

Before she could move he was on her, pinning her arms by her sides and forcing his lips on hers. She fought wildly, but he was a big man and controlled her easily. Then he became impatient.

"Keep still, you little fool. I'm going to have you, so you may as well enjoy it. I'm told I'm rather good," he added smugly.

At that Magda screamed and struggled even more until he struck her two tremendous blows across the face, which left her sick and dizzy. Only half conscious, she felt him carry her into the bedroom where he threw her onto the bed and coldly raped her.

"Next time, you'll see it my way," he said as he got off her. "It's quid pro quo, not that you're likely to know any Latin," he added contemptuously. "Don't be late in the office tomorrow. I'll let myself out."

Alone, Magda lay quite still. Then reaction set in and she started to shake. She managed to crawl to the bathroom where she ran a boiling hot bath and stayed in it for a long time, trying to wash everything away. It didn't occur to her that this was the last thing she should have done; anyway, she didn't think anyone would believe her if she did go to the police. There was no sign of a break-in, and the story of how he had copied her keys sounded incredible even to her.

At last she pulled herself out of the now tepid bath and returned to the bedroom. The sight of the tumbled bed sent her running for clean linen. In frantic haste she stripped and re-made the bed. Only then was she able to crawl into it, but it was long before she finally slept.

She became aware of the insistent ringing of the phone as she struggled hazily back to consciousness. She hauled herself out of bed and went to answer it, as much to stop the noise as to find out who it was that was ringing. In fact, it was a rather agitated Wendy.

"Where on earth are you?" she demanded before Magda had a chance to speak. "It's chaos here. Beddy-Eddy's like a raging bull and you're so late. What's up? Are you ill?"

"You could say that," Magda answered quietly. She had decided, at some point during the long night that she would say truthfully what had happened if she was asked. "Edward came here last night and raped me."

"*What?*" There was a gasp at the other end of the phone. "You stay right there and I'll be over. And if Eddy asks me why I'm leaving the office, I'll jolly well tell him – and enjoy it!"

Magda smiled wanly as she put the phone down and crawled back to bed.

An incredibly short time later Wendy was not only at the door but inside the flat. "You left the door unlocked," she said accusingly.

"Not me, Eddy," said Magda. "He evidently didn't bother to lock it when he left. He's got a key."

"You never gave him one." Wendy was shocked.

"No, of course I didn't. I've never even asked him in after we'd been out. He stole my keys at the office and got them copied. Apparently I owed him for the 'expensive food and drink' he'd given me."

"The…" Words failed Wendy, perhaps fortunately. She had a ripe vocabulary when she was roused. "How are you, though?" She had her first look at Magda's battered face and gasped. "Did he do that to you?"

Magda nodded, then wished she hadn't, it hurt too much.

"You should see a doctor, hospital, even. Have you called the police?"

"No, what's the point. They'd never believe me. Not with no sign of a break in, and the key copying is so unlikely. Except that it happened."

"Yes, I suppose you're right. It's a man's world where rape's concerned. What are you going to do? Pack it in at the office? I hope not, you're really good."

Magda smiled gratefully. "I don't know. I can't think straight. You do believe me, don't you?"

"Oh, yes. Why do you think he's called Beddy-Eddy? He always tries it on. It's the first time he's gone this far, though. I wish now we'd warned you. Pippa wanted to but I thought you could handle it. I'm sorry."

"It's not your fault. It shouldn't be a problem."

"No, you're right there. Look, I'm going to phone in, say my old gran's sick again. Useful old bird, she is. Pity she's dead, really, I can't use her funeral as an excuse. But she enjoys very poor health." Wendy grinned. "Then I'll get a locksmith out to change the locks – we'll charge it to the mag, Eddy won't dare complain – then we'll dream up a plan of action."

True to her word, Wendy first brought Magda a much-needed cup of tea then set to work. Having dealt with the office and the locksmith she collected Magda's key and departed to do some urgent shopping. Magda, promoting herself to her dressing gown and a blanket on the sofa began to feel much better, and very angry.

"You know, I don't want just to run away from the job," she said, when Wendy returned. "I did that last time, but that was to spare the family." She had already confided in Wendy the reasons for her departure from Tel Aviv. "I don't want him to think he's beaten me."

"Good for you. I hoped you'd say that." Wendy beamed at her with proprietary pride. "If you'll let me, I'll tell the girls, and he'll have to cope with all of us. They all like you and have never been that keen on him, even if he does pay our wages. Not too generously, either," she added feelingly. "Now, we'll have a quiet, girlie day. Do you want me to stay the night?"

"I wouldn't mind," said Magda gratefully. "Even with the locks changed I'll feel scared."

"No problem. I'll just give Pippa a call, she lives near me and can bring in a pair of clean knickers for the morning." Magda laughed. "That's better," said Wendy approvingly, and beaming at her. "By the way, where's that layabout locksmith got to?"

At that moment the doorbell rang, and did indeed prove to be the locksmith. Magda settled back, feeling very much stronger, and determined not to give in.

The next morning they went into the office together. Then Magda retired to the cloakroom, where she checked that the make-up she was wearing did not do too good a job of covering up her bruises. Wendy and she had decided that vanity must give way to embarrassment – for Eddy. She still ached, but that merely made her more determined not to give in. Then Wendy came in, grinning broadly.

"Just as I expected, we're all right behind you. You've no worries, Eddy, on the other hand, has plenty. Come on, let's get you settled before he comes in."

In the office Magda found that she had been moved to a desk in the middle of the room, with girls all around her, making a protective phalanx. She sat down at it and smiled round, noting that they all, without exception, smiled back.

"Hey Mags," one of the girls called out. "You coming for a drink tonight, after work?"

"Sure will," she called in reply, seeing Edward Martin's shadow through the glass panel in the office door. He seemed to hesitate, then came in.

Wendy shot a quick glance behind her, then spoke as though she hadn't seen him come in. "Pippa, did you see that story in the paper about the boss who raped one of his own employees?"

"No!" said Pippa in pretended shock. "What a dreadful thing to do. Oh, hello, Mr Martin, I didn't see you there." Edward Martin swept through the office like a tornado and slammed his office door. The girls giggled over his discomfiture.

That set the pattern for the days and weeks ahead. The girls rallied round Magda as she recovered from her experience. Edward continued to keep his distance from her, and, indeed, from all the girls. She began to feel relaxed and happy once more, enjoying her work and the companionship of the other girls.

She was so busy that she failed to notice that a certain regular occurrence was unaccountably absence. It was only when she had to rush to the cloakroom to be sick that she began to feel uneasy. The second time it happened she found that Wendy had followed her in.

"You alright?" Wendy asked, concerned.

"Yes, I must have eaten something."

Wendy looked at her steadily. "Are you sure? Have you missed – you know?"

"Of course not." Then the penny dropped and Magda looked horrified. "Oh God, no! Not for some time."

"I think you should go and buy a test," said Wendy, gently. "Pop out to the chemist now. I'll cover for you."

Magda hurried out to the chemist nearby that all the girls used regularly. She felt that the assistant's face was unnecessarily expressionless as she chose and paid for the pregnancy test kit. Back at the office she vanished into the cloakroom.

Twenty minutes later Wendy came to find her. Mutely Magda nodded.

"It's positive." It was a statement, not a question.

"Yes."

"Poor old you. I take it it's because of the rape?"

"Oh yes, there's no doubt of that."

"If you want to get rid, and I know I would, I'll take you to see my doctor. Unless you've got one you could go to?"

"No," said Magda. "There never seemed to be time."

"As I thought. Don't worry, leave it all to Auntie Wendy. She'll see you through."

Sure enough, a couple of weeks later Magda found herself back in her flat, sore and shaky, but relieved of what she could only see as her burden, given the horror of the conception. Wendy was a tower of strength throughout, and Magda said so.

"Nonsense, you'd have done the same for me." Wendy grinned at her. "Now, I know it's early days, but have you any thoughts about the future?"

"I don't think I can go back to the office this time," Magda admitted. You've all been wonderful, but I think I've shot my bolt there."

"No, I'm inclined to agree with you," Wendy said, sympathetically. "I've had an idea, a plan, really, that I've been mulling over for some time. How would you feel about moving away from London and starting up with me in our own magazine?" Magda gaped at her friend in astonishment. "Yes, as I say, I've been thinking about it for ages but didn't want to go it alone. Now, I think we make a good team, don't we?" Magda nodded. "I've got a good friend in a place up north, Heathfield. It's a suburb of Arkchester, and really rather a nice place. I've visited a few times and it seems to have quite a lot going for it. I think we could start up there. Are you on? With the general idea, anyway? We can settle the details as and when if you are."

Magda rose, went across to Wendy and hugged her. Wendy hugged her back. "That's a yes, then?"

"That's a yes."

Which was how, in the fullness of time, Magda had come to live in flat 2, on the first floor of Tower Court.

Magda sighed and stretched. She felt, for the first time since the abortion that a burden of guilt had been lifted from her. Helping to deliver another child into the world had eased her. Even though the venture with Wendy had succeeded beyond their wildest dreams, and their friendship had also continued to grow, there had always been that nagging ache at the back of her mind. Now, for the first time, it was gone.

– Chapter Three –

No sooner had I recovered from my plunge into midwifery than I was again disturbed when "off duty", this time at about 10.30 when I was fondly contemplating my bed. An almighty racket broke out in the car park. I peeped cautiously out to see a right *West Side Story* rumble going on. No weapons were in use as far as I could see, but plenty of fists and yelling. I called Security; Geoff, one of the night shift security officers, was on duty but too busy to help.

"Call the cops," he ordered. "They'll come more quickly for you than for me anyway."

I duly dialled 999 (again) but either someone was quicker than I or the police were already on their way for a squad car and a couple of vans arrived in minutes, and the battlers were loaded in and driven away with great dispatch. Putting on some clothes I went down to confer with Geoff.

"Come in, come in," he said cheerily, clearly not averse to having company. "Want a brew?"

I accepted coffee and settled down for a gossip on the grounds that I was far too wide-awake to sleep and might pick up some useful information.

"What did you mean, the police would likely come faster for me than for you?" I wanted to know.

"They hear from me too often," he answered. "I keep an eye on the surrounding houses as well as the block," he indicated the screens showing houses, mostly dark and – presumably – sleeping. "I'm expected to cope, even though I can't leave here." I remembered Phil had said much the same thing. "We used to have a mobile patrol and that was much better. But they stopped, cost I suppose. Most things are." He seemed to be quietly resigned to the situation.

"What was that battle all about? Does it happen often?" was my next, rather anxious question.

"Not that often," Geoff said comfortingly. "Don't you try and do anything, just call out the cops. They'll come if they can, they're not too bad that way. If they don't, make a note of any damage, report according and we'll match it up with the CCTV. How's your coffee? You're not from round here, are you?" Obviously this was still a serious lack on my part and I wondered how many more times I was going to be asked this question. But I agreed that no, I was not, the coffee was fine and asked him how long he had been in the job.

"Nine years, give or take. Me and Pete, we're a team, see? Same as Phil and Fred on days. We're left alone, pretty much. Suits us. We know who's who and what's what. Sort of."

Clear as mud.

"But what was the riot all *about*?" I insisted.

Geoff shrugged. "No idea," he said airily. "More coffee?"

I declined, but thought I'd try and clear up another little mystery.

"I keep seeing shabby young Asians on the stairs," I said. I saw one on my first day here and he seemed to be terrified by my uniform, I don't think he looked at me. Any ideas?"

Geoff looked startled. "No," he said, " but then, if they're on the stairs we wouldn't see them. No cameras," he pointed out.

I got up. "Oh well, doubtless all will be revealed in time. Thanks for the coffee." I returned to my lair feeling completely bewildered.

The fates must have taken pity on me as the very next morning they deposited a friend in my path in the shape of a small, very young, very frightened kitten. She (I thought, though she was too young to be sure) was jet black all over, and her eyes were still baby blue. I scooped her up as the car park was far too dangerous a place for such a scrap, and we departed to the flat for food and cuddles. I determined to do the decent thing and ask around but I would dearly like her to stay. In a very short time she had me wrapped firmly round her diminutive paw. She told me her name was Sophie and she had quite determined to stay. I hoped she was right. Dogs were not allowed in the tower block but cats were so I hoped for the best. Furball and Lucy between them had made me feel quite broody. After signing off I got her some proper cat food from the shop, she said it was delicious. I did wonder if she was weaned but she seemed to be able to cope. I also procured a large packet of cat litter; I hoped she was with her mother long enough to be house-trained...

The police duly came round to ask me about the rumble in the car park, sending Sophie behind the sofa in high dudgeon.

"Did you happen to see how it started?" asked the officer, pad and pencil at the ready.

"No, I didn't, I didn't look out until the racket started. I was on my way to bed."

"Security said it happened quite slowly." He seemed reproachful. Obviously I should keep vigil at my window all night, just in case.

"Maybe so, but I was off duty so I didn't look out until it got really loud. And as I said, I was going to bed." He still seemed to be reproachful so I made a mental note to pay more attention to odd noises outside, particularly at night. Perhaps Sophie would help? As a sort of watch cat? When she was bigger, of course.

I went next door to Ron and Julian when I came off duty; as accredited cat people I took Sophie with me but was prepared to whisk her away if Furball and Lucy Locket, as senior in age and residency, objected.

"What a little poppet." Julian was instantly enslaved. "Where did you find her? Or is she yours? I assume she's a she, she looks every inch a female even at that size."

"I found her cowering in the car park," I answered. "I shall have to ask around but I really want to keep her. Like you, I'm pretty sure it's a her."

Julian investigated. "Yes, probably," he agreed. "Do you want a vet? Ours is good and into cats. I think he would like to look after the big ones, lions and cheetahs and the like. Put her down and see what Lucy and Furball make of her. Have you given her a name?"

"She told me, Sophie," I said with a tinge of reproach.

"Yes, I see what you mean, definitely Sophie."

Nervously I put Sophie down and a certain amount of routine spitting and glaring followed which we studiously ignored. Ron and Julian clearly had the same attitude toward cats that I had, that they were personalities in fur coats. Any one listening would think we were quite mad.

Me: Sophie tells me she likes my flat, plenty of chairs.

Ron: Yes, Furball's the same, he approves of the balcony. Good for keeping watch and plenty of game [pigeons]. Not that he or Lucy have ever caught anything. Still, they live in hopes, even though a pigeon is nearly as big as Lucy [who is small and dainty].

Julian: You should see Lucy when the telly's on. She loves show jumping but won't let us watch football. She says it's boring, no animals.

And so on.

After that I did pay more attention to noises in the car park but nothing else alarming happened. I continued to clean the block, which was now looking quite respectable, and generally settling myself in. I felt quite an old hand at the game!

***

The interlude with Frankie and Sophie reminded Julian of several similar exchanges that he and Ron had shared in the past, though until Ron had come into his life he had not been particularly interested in cats. Other things were far more important....

He remembered when Paul and he were in the car together for the first time. His brother was driving, rather too fast for Julian's peace of mind, along a winding lane that led, as both the boys knew well, into the outskirts of a small town, and thence to their favourite pub.

"This is the life," crowed Paul, drawn out of his usual taciturnity by the thrill of driving his first car. He conveniently forgot Julian's co-ownership. "She handles like a dream. I can't wait till I can really let her out."

"Not here," said Julian, quickly.

"Of course not here. What do you take me for. On the motorway. I don't know, though – " and simply to taunt his twin he accelerated, making the little car leap forward.

"Careful!" shouted Julian, as the hedges streamed past at, to him, frightening speed.

Paul laughed, but consented to slow down – fractionally. They were approaching the junction that took them into the main road and the pub. "I can't wait to take Chrissie out in this. She'll love it."

"Ch – Chrissie? Chrissie Lucas?" Turning in his seat Julian stared at his brother. "But Chrissie's *my* girl. You know she is."

"Didn't she tell you? She promised she would. She's mine now. We're an item." Taking his eyes off the road Paul looked at his twin.

"I'm sorry. She promised me she'd tell you. Let you down lightly."

Something snapped in Julian's brain. Paul had just taken that which was his once too often. He became aware that he was shouting at his brother, screaming. The car, still moving much too fast, swerved ominously. He was aware of passers-by staring at their headlong progress, of a wavering figure beside them, that seemed to bounce off them, a dark mass ahead of them, a dreadful noise of screaming metal and –

He swam up out of the depths in a haze of pain. It was centred in his right leg, and he seemed curiously immobile. He moved his head, frowning, and found that his mother was sitting beside him.

"Where am I?" he asked her fretfully.

"In hospital, but you're going to be alright."

"Where's Paul?"

"He's here too." His mother was uncharacteristically brief.

"That's alright, then." He drifted away again, unaware that the tears were streaming down his mother's face.

When he woke up again he was alone. The pain seemed to be less, and he could move about in the bed. A nurse came up, picked up his wrist, checked his pulse.

"What happened?" he asked her.

"Car crash," she said laconically. "You've been very lucky. Do you remember anything?"

He shook his head. It hurt. "Nothing. Except – Paul was driving. Our new mini. He's the elder, so he had the first drive." It seemed important to explain this. "How is he? Is he here too?"

"Yes. Now I must fetch the doctor." She hurried away. Julian dozed.

Sometime later heavy footsteps approached Julian's bed. Julian opened his eyes, his father was standing at the foot, glaring at him. "We've just switched off Paul's life support machine," he shouted. "Paul's dead. It should have been you."

"No, no, you mustn't say that!" Julian's mother, Angela, crying, clutched at her husband's arm. "You don't mean it."

"I do mean it," Bernard said furiously. "The wrong son is dead." And he stamped heavily away, shoulders slumped. Angela fluttered after him, leaving Julian frozen with horror.

He lay there, absolutely still, staring at the ceiling. He felt numb, but dreaded how he would feel when this numbness abated. He was aware of the nurse approaching but could not move.

"Are you alright?" she said. "I heard what your father said. Try not to worry, people say awful things when they are in grief and shock. He wouldn't have meant it."

"He meant it, alright," Julian whispered. There was a pause. The nurse stayed quietly beside him, waiting. "Could I see him?"

She pressed his hand. "I'll see what I can do."

Soon she was back with a wheelchair. "It's really far too soon for you to be out of bed, but under the circumstances – John, could you give me a hand?"

Another nurse came up. "Frances, are you mad? There's no way this patient should be moved. He's far too fragile."

"He wants to see his brother. You know?"

"His – oh yes, that case." Together they carefully manoeuvred Julian on to the chair and placed his plastered leg on a support. The room swam dizzily, but with a massive effort of will Julian managed to stay conscious and the little procession made its way slowly to the lift.

Paul was lying still and straight behind curtains in the Intensive Care Unit. Frances wheeled the chair up to the bed. "We'll be just outside these curtains," she said. "Take as long as you like. We'll see that no-one disturbs you." She went out, closing the curtains softly behind her.

Julian could hear her arguing with someone outside who seemed to want to move Paul. Then the voices died away and he was able to concentrate on his brother. He looked at him, unfamiliar in his absolute stillness, yet so very well known, well loved. Whatever injuries he had were hidden, he looked to be peacefully asleep. Julian sat there for a long time, almost as still as his twin. At last he moved, and Frances, clearly on the watch, looked in.

"Are you ready to go now?" she asked gently.

"As ready as I'll ever be," he replied. "I still can't believe it."

"No, it takes awhile," she answered, wheeling him expertly back to the lift.

Back in his bed Julian fell suddenly into an exhausted sleep, helped by the merciful numbness.

A few days later his mother came to see him. "Your father's

still raging," she said, in answer to his question.

"Why is he so angry?" asked Julian. "Why does he blame me so much? After all, I wasn't driving."

Angela looked disconcerted. "He's convinced you were," she said. "He thinks that Paul would never be so silly as to crash."

But I would, or could, thought Julian bitterly. Then he remembered how he had shouted and screamed at his brother just before the crash, in his fury at what he saw as Paul's theft of Chrissie. Yes, he thought. I was to blame, even though I wasn't driving, and I didn't touch Paul, though I felt like strangling him.

His mother was speaking again. "The funeral is on Tuesday, but your father has forbidden you to come."

"That's not fair!" Julian burst out. "He's my twin. I must be able to say good-bye."

Angela shrugged. "You may not have been driving but he still has to blame you for the accident." Otherwise he has to blame himself for giving the twins the car in the first place she thought, though loyalty to her husband prevented her from saying it – yet. "But you'd not be well enough to come anyway, would you? Be reasonable. Hopefully, he'll come round in time, but it won't be soon." She got up. "I must go, he frets if I'm out too long. Try to understand." She smiled at him, rather distantly, and left.

For the first time since Paul's death, as Julian lay quite still, slow tears squeezed out of his closed eyes.

"I say," the rather faint voice came from the next bed. Julian turned his head away, but the voice continued. "I say, it wasn't your fault. It was mine."

Julian's eyes snapped open and he turned to look at the next bed in amazement. "How can it possibly be your fault?" he demanded. "You weren't even there."

"Oh yes, I was. I'd been in the pub, I was blind drunk and I think I tried to cross the road. I'm not very clear, but I remember being thrown out of the pub and straying towards the road, then a big bang and nothing more until I woke up in here. Broken leg, broken ribs, broken arm, you name it, it's broken. And if your brother hit the truck swerving to avoid me, that makes it my fault. I've been trying to pluck up the courage to tell you for days. I'm Ron Peters, by the way. General waste of space."

Julian smiled faintly. "I'm Julian Fry, also pretty broken. In many ways. Thank you for telling me. I think we're all to blame. I was screaming at Paul who'd just told me he'd pinched my girlfriend. But he was driving much too fast. Oh well, let's hope my father calms down before too long. I always knew that Paul was his favourite son, but not that he actively disliked me."

"Who dislikes you?" Frances, the nurse, came up. "Time for your pills, both of you. Are you talking about you father, Julian? I told you, people say all sorts of things in the heat of the moment. He'll come round, you'll see. Just give him time." She smiled at them. "Anyway, if the funeral is on Tuesday there is no way on this earth you would be able to go, even if Mr Prentice doesn't decide to have another go at your leg as he's threatening to."

Julian looked alarmed. "An operation? Is that likely?"

"*Another* operation. Yes, it is. He had a go at you when you first came in but he's not altogether happy with you. He's going to decide tomorrow." Briskly she smoothed their sheets. "I'm glad you two have made contact. Now, try not to fret. Just get some rest. I'll see you tomorrow, I'm going off duty now. Bye bye."

Back in the present, Julian suddenly realised why all these memories were coming back to him. Frankie reminded him of Nurse Frances.

***

Mercifully, there was no repetition of the uproar in the car park; whatever it was all about, and whoever had been involved, they seemed either to have settled their differences, or to have given up. I hardly cared which.

Not that I didn't have other problems. I was becoming increasingly concerned about the lifts. They had been temperamental for quite some time, all the time I had been in the block I now realised. They seemed to me to be slower than ever, and to be becoming increasingly bumpy and noisy. I gathered that they were pretty old, as lifts go, and I decided to have Strong Words with Roger about them. So far no one had been stuck in them, not even me, though I was in and out of both of them in the line of duty several times a day. I felt that this happy state could not last but I hoped nothing too drastic would happen.

I took the opportunity of sounding out Roger when he came in to do one of his infrequent block inspections.

"I am becoming very concerned about the lifts," I informed him bluntly. "They are breaking down, and getting stuck, more and more frequently, and the lift engineers complain that it is becoming progressively more difficult to get spares. Is anything going to be done about it?"

"The short answer is no, not at the moment." This was not what I wanted to hear. "They say that there just isn't the money available just now, and while they can be repaired, they must be." He looked at me sympathetically. "I know that's not what you wanted to hear," (Too right, I thought.) "but that's all I can say."

"But they're becoming increasingly bumpy and noisy," I said despairingly. "Surely there have been complaints?"

"Not really, no," he said. "And no one's been stuck in them, not even you."

And with that I had to be content. Which I wasn't, not by a long chalk.

***

On the 14th floor, Lottie Maynard was looking forward to the visit of her two little grandchildren: Julia aged seven and Fiona aged five. That this also meant that her daughter Susan was included she tried to discount. She had never been on particularly good terms with Susan, the middle one of her three children, the only girl and the pet of her father. Her daughter's marriage, as far as Lottie was concerned, had only increased the gap between them. She couldn't stand her son-in-law; to her mind he had increased Susan's propensity for self-dramatisation and whining. She was amazed that the children were turning out so well.

Mentally she shook herself, she really should not be so uncharitable. But at nearly eighty she felt she was allowed to be truthful, to herself at least. She sighed and went to the window to see if she could see the distinctive yellow 4x4 monster her daughter affected, another bone of contention. Susan hardly drove anywhere, why on earth did she need such a large, ostentatious vehicle?

Returning to her seat Lottie must have dozed off, for the next moment there was a thunderous knocking at the door and shrill voices calling: "Granny! Granny! Hurry up, it's us! We're here!"

Moving with surprising ease and agility for her years Lottie hurried to open the door and welcome her beloved granddaughters, both in a high state of excitement. Visiting Granny was a highlight of their rather regimented lives.

Predictably, Susan was already grumbling as she presented a cool cheek for her mother's dutiful kiss.

"That lift is rumbling more than ever. One day it will break down and then what will you do, perched all the way up here? You should move nearer to us so we can look after you." This was an old complaint; the last thing Lottie wanted was to be removed from her comfortable flat where she had lived for so many years. She had all her friends nearby, friends who had known her husband as well, she certainly did not want to live with strangers in her daughter's orbit, she would feel she was living in a straightjacket. Still less did she want to be "looked after" by anyone, least of all by Susan and her husband.

She replied soothingly as usual and responded to the girls' clamour for their favourite games.

The afternoon passed all too swiftly for her and at five o'clock on the dot her daughter rose to leave. Heaven forbid that Philip's supper should be delayed by so much as a minute, thought Lottie sadly. She accompanied her family to the lift, which did indeed seem even slower and more rattling than usual, and called "Good-byes" as it slowly descended.

***

I was just about to enter the "odd" lift to go to my flat (yes, alright, only one floor but I was feeling lazy) when I became aware of screaming from the other lift, serving the even floors. I glanced at the indicator; it appeared to be at the 6th floor. I leapt into the odd numbers' lift and got out at the 5th floor; the screams were undoubtedly louder but still above me. I returned to the lift and carried on to the 7th floor. Here the sounds seemed to be below me, the lift being stuck at or around the 6th floor, so I flew to the stairs and down to the next floor.

"It's alright," I shouted. "This is the caretaker. We'll soon have you out. How many of you are in there?"

"Me and my sister and Mummy," a scared and undoubtedly very young voice quavered. "Mummy says she can't breathe."

Mentally cursing Mummy for her lack of control, and then reproaching myself; after all, she might really have breathing problems, I called back: "Don't worry, you'll soon be out. I'm just going now to get help. Keep calm, I won't be long."

At that moment Ken and Margaret Murray, an elderly couple who had lived in the block since their marriage forty-odd years before, looked out of flat 22. "What's up?" Ken asked, looking concerned. "What's all the shouting?"

"The lift's stuck with a family inside," I replied. "Could you call the fire brigade? Then I can stay with them, they're very upset."

"Perhaps it's Lottie's family," said Margaret. "She said they were coming this afternoon, and they always leave at five. Never do to be late with Philip's tea, he's the fussy sort." She was clearly unimpressed. "We're old friends of Lottie's and the children know us. Julia! Fiona! Are you stuck?" she called up.

"Yes, and Mummy can't breathe," the young voice came back. Though Mummy seemed to have enough breath to yell with, I thought sourly.

"Don't worry, dears, it's Auntie Margaret and Uncle Ken here and the nice caretaker is going to get help." Whereupon the nice caretaker departed to call up the cavalry in the shape of the local fire brigade.

Fred was on duty at the Security Office so I explained the situation to him as I waited, having retrieved the lift keys from my office on his advice.

"You'll need the keys to the roof and the lift motor room," he instructed, "then they can raise or lower the lift so it's on a floor. Then they can open the door." Good thing someone knew what to do.

Knights in shining armour duly turned up some fifteen minutes later in two very large fire engines. They looked huge in the car park, and their crew looked equally huge in the foyer.

"Why two?" I wanted to know.

"Always two with people stuck. Now, where are they?" rather impatiently.

Recalled to my responsibilities I escorted them up to the 6th floor then took two more men up to the roof. On the way down I stopped off at Lottie's floor to reassure her. I found her concerned but not unduly worried.

"I'll bet Susan is creating and the girls coping," she said with some asperity. Clearly she knew her family. I had to say she was right. "But Ken and Margaret are there," I was able to tell her. We went down together to see how the family was coping.

By the time we arrived they had been extricated and the little girls were by now enthralled with the adventure and by being rescued by massive firemen.

"They're *enormous!*" Fiona was goggle-eyed.

"Just like *London's Burning,*" confirmed Julia. Their mother promptly collapsed into full-blown hysterics. Cravenly, I allowed Ken and Margaret to shepherd them all into their flat. The fire officers and I beat a hasty retreat to the ground floor.

"Nice little kids," said one, "but that mother – "

"It takes all sorts," said another philosophically. "You'll have to get the engineers out to fix the lift," turning to me. "I reckon they'll both need replacing before long. Cheerio!" And the whole party clattered out to their waiting engines, which by now were surrounded by all the local youth.

I had a feeling that Philip's tea would be late that night. I also felt that I didn't care.

***

Jimbo Preston stood in the car park and stared up at Tower Court as it soared above him. He wondered what the fire engines had been for, he could see no sign of a fire.

Since leaving the children's home all those years ago he had grown into a thickset, stocky figure with short, bristling light brown hair and a permanently truculent expression. As he seldom bothered to shave he looked what he always had been, a thug.

It had taken considerable ingenuity on his part, not to mention luck, to track down Ron; he had never forgiven the younger boy for giving him the scar over his eye, or the trouble he had got into over the incident with the cat. Even thinking about it, so many years later, made him seethe. "I'll get even with the little runt," he promised himself, fingering the scar. "He won't have amounted to much, living here in a council flat, sorry, housing association," he corrected himself. "I wonder which flat he's in?"

Looking at the key in his hand he went towards the main doors and let himself in. He took the lift for the odd floors and went up to the third floor and into flat 9. "This'll do," he murmured, looking round. "I wonder what did happen to that piece of shit after I left the home?"

***

The children's home was supposed to be a centre for adoptions but these rarely happened. Consequently, Ron was more than a little surprised to be summoned, as soon as he returned from school, to the Matron's office. A little older now, still undersized, still taciturn to the point of muteness, he was by now more assured. He was one of the "Big Boys" and, as such, rarely picked on. In fact, all bullying in the home had stopped as soon as he had routed Jimbo, who had left; where he went, he neither knew no cared.

In Matron's office he found a large, red-faced man with a frizz of ginger hair round what seemed to be an increasing bald patch. He was apparently having tea with the Matron.

"Ah, come in, dear," the Matron's face cracked into an unaccustomed smile. "This is Mr Jones, who is looking for a little boy to adopt. Mr Jones, this is Ron Peters, one of our older boys to be sure, but I am sure he would prove very suitable."

"Sure, sure," said Mr Jones, impatiently. "My wife wants the child, I don't want to be bothered with all the nappy and bottle nonsense, and being woken at all hours in the night. I suppose he's housetrained?" He laughed loudly at his own joke.

"Ron behaves very well and his manners are good," said the Matron, rather coldly. "Run along, dear, and have your tea. I take it your wife will be coming to see the child?" Ron heard her say as he shut the door carefully behind him. He waited, listening brazenly.

"No need. She'll take what I bring her," he heard the unlovely Mr Jones say shortly. Ron shivered. The home was hardly paradise but living with Mr Jones, who seemed to regard children in the same light as a puppy or a kitten, would surely be worse. But he knew that he would have to move on soon and he had heard rumours that the home was closing down. He heard steps approaching the door and shot off down the passage before he could be caught eavesdropping.

"Get everything ready for me and I'll come back on Thursday

to collect the kid," Mr Jones told the Matron as he left.

"Certainly, Mr Jones." But the Matron looked after him thoughtfully as he disappeared along the same passage down which Ron had scampered only minutes earlier. Are we doing the right thing? She wondered as she went back into the room. He is a singularly unpleasant man. But I don't suppose he'll actually ill-treat the boy, she comforted herself. And we do need to find homes for as many as possible before we close. She sighed; for once rumour had not lied and the home was due to close in less than six months.

As it turned out it was not so bad for Ron. Mr Jones, or Uncle Charles as he learned to call him, seemed to be totally uninterested in him, but his wife, Blanche, was, though undoubtedly a little silly, kind and caring. In fact, she was over the moon at having someone to love, albeit a child rather older than she had envisaged. In many ways, her husband was as uninterested in her as he was in Ron, so the two were brought together, once Blanche had got over her initial nervousness, in a growing bond of affection and esteem. Blanche learned to appreciate Ron's wisdom, well in advance of his years, and Ron in his turn blossomed under her unstinting love. He settled down to his new life in their little suburban semi really very happily.

To his great delight there was a cat, uninspiringly known as Tabby, for obvious reasons. She was a pretty little thing and Ron soon became devoted to her and she to him. He had never got over the dreadful death of his beloved Mouser. He blamed himself for it; if he, Ron, had not upset Jimbo, he reasoned, then Jimbo would never have retaliated by killing Mouser. As a result he cried himself to sleep for many nights afterwards, burying his head in the bedclothes to stifle the sound.

It was here, with the Joneses, that Ron discovered the joys of cooking, and that he had a decided talent for it. Blanche, though woolly in most other aspects of housekeeping, was a demon in the kitchen, and loved to invent new, and generally very appetising, dishes. As soon as she discovered Ron's interest she enrolled him as an apprentice and the pair spent many happy hours together, competing amiably as the young Ron's expertise grew.

"I wish your Uncle Charles was as interested in food as you are," she would say wistfully. "I don't think he notices what he eats at all."

Certainly, Charles Jones demolished anything placed in front of him at high speed and almost total silence, watched by the anxious cooks. Anxious, because if he did not care for it they were very soon told.

"What's this rubbish?" he would roar, pointing a shaking finger at the offending plate. "Take it away and bring me something I can eat!"

Mercifully, this happened only rarely, and Ron learned the basics of cooking, and how to be adventurous almost without realising it.

Life continued calmly, if rather lacking in excitement, until Ron was sixteen. Then Blanche, of whom he had become exceedingly fond, died suddenly. This was his first experience of death as it affected him personally (apart from the still mourned Mouser), and it was a shock. But worse was to follow. When they arrived back at the house after the funeral Charles took him into the living room (cold and bleak without Blanche's amiable chatter) and sat him down.

"Now look here," he said. "There are going to be some changes round here. I never wanted a kid in the first place, that's why I stuck out for an older one. I'll not say you've been bad, little trouble at all, really, all things considered, and Blanche was happy, but I've got my sights set on the next Mrs Jones and I want you out."

Ron gasped. "Out? Just like that? Why, if I've been no trouble?"

"I told you. The next Mrs Jones doesn't want to be saddled with a kid of your age which is nothing to do with either of us. After all, it's not as if you were regularly adopted."

"But I thought I was," said Ron, bemused.

"Oh no, it was just a little arrangement I made with the home when they were trying to clear out all the kids. Anyway, I've arranged a nice little bed-sit for you, rent paid up for the month, so you can settle down and get yourself a job. You're sixteen, so you can leave school."

"But – but suppose I don't want to?" asked the flabbergasted Ron, who indeed had ideas, encouraged by Blanche, of going to college to train as a chef.

"Tough. We can't get all we want in life. You'd better learn that right now." Charles stood up. "I'm off out" (to see the next Mrs

Jones, thought Ron savagely, sore that Blanche could be replaced so callously). "You can stay here tonight, but get packed up and be off first thing in the morning. The rent book is in the room and here's the key." Without another word he went out, and Ron heard the front door slam as he sat there, staring at the closed door with the key held in his hand.

A few days later Ron sat in the shabby room, which was all that his former, presumed, adoptive father had seen fit to provide him. He felt completely desolate, missing Blanche; desperately she had truly been a mother to him. He was also missing, with a despair that surprised, and indeed, shamed him, Tabby, the little cat who had come so close to filling the vast emptiness left by Mouser. She was growing old now, but she had been his constant companion during the years he had lived with the Joneses. He was shocked to discover that he never been officially adopted by them, merely lived in their house. On sufferance as far as Charles was concerned, it now appeared. He wondered what the children's home, that had allowed this to happen, had really been like. Perhaps it was as well it had closed. Or perhaps it had had to.

He went out into the street, anything was better than sitting moping in his depressing room. On an impulse he went into a pub. It looked bright and welcoming. He hesitated, then went up to the bar and asked for a pint. He was under age, but he knew he didn't look it. Sure enough, the barman served him without question. Pleased by the small triumph Ron took his drink outside, to one of the tables in the proudly named beer garden.

He sat there in the early evening sun; the beer slipped down a treat. He began to feel more cheerful.

"Anyone sitting here?" A young man of his own (apparent) age was standing beside him.

"No, mate. Be my guest." This was living. Perhaps Charles Jones had done him a favour after all.

"Cheers. Come here often?" The young man settled himself, swinging his leg athletically over the end of the bench that was fixed to the table.

"No, it's my first time," said Ron, truthfully.

"It's not bad, though I've known better." Clearly Ron's companion was a man of the world. They settled down to make a night of it.

Ron's life began to fall into a pattern: hunting fruitlessly for work during the day, then spending the evening drinking with his new friend, whose name was Steve. Gradually the evenings began to take over. His job search became sporadic, he took on any temporary work that would pay his rent and keep him in drink. Steve disappeared; he didn't know where or even when, his life had become a haze, punctuated by drink.

Then, one evening, he was thrown out of a pub. Of late he had become belligerent in his cups and the pub landlord was fed up. Ron staggered into the street. His wavering steps took him across the pavement and into the path of an oncoming red mini. There was a dreadful noise of screaming metal and –

He became aware of pain, all over, but mainly down his right side. Everything seemed to be encased in plaster, he couldn't move. He moaned, he really couldn't help it, it seemed to be forced out of him. A nurse materialised beside him.

"So you've decided to come back to us, have you?" she said cheerfully. "I win the bet. I said you'd come round before him." She indicated a still figure lying in the next bed. "He was in the same accident as you. Do you remember anything?"

Ron shook his head, then stopped, it hurt too much.

"Yes. Well, you've both been very lucky. The boy's brother isn't going to make it. It's really sad, it seems that they were twins. Well, I'd better get going, I'll be back soon just to check on you." With a final smile she bustled away.

Ron lay quietly over the next few days, watching the activities round the next bed. He watched as the parents came, as the father raged, and as the young man, whom he now knew to be called Julian, went off to see his dead brother. He lay completely still, trying to be invisible when the mother told Julian of his father's prohibition concerning the funeral. He jerked slightly when he heard that the father blamed Julian for the accident. As the mother left, the distress from the next bed was palpable.

"I say." Julian's head turned away, but Ron continued. "I say, it wasn't your fault. It was mine."

***

Ron didn't know why he had started thinking back over the past; it wasn't something he did as a regular thing. He believed that the past should stay where it was put, in the past. Nevertheless, when Julian came in one afternoon, he found his partner sitting in the gloom of early evening, nursing an empty mug and giving Julian the idea that he had been sitting there for some considerable time.

"Anything wrong?" asked Julian delicately, realising that Ron's unusual abstraction was not going to lift.

"No, just thinking." Ron roused himself with a visible effort. "About the past – heaven knows why."

"That's easy," replied Julian. "I've been doing the same. Don't you remember that nurse, Frances, coping with us in the hospital when we were both in bits – literally as well as figuratively?" Ron nodded. "Doesn't she remind you of Frankie? Or Frankie remind you of her? Enough to get remembering, anyway?"

Light dawned on Ron. "Yes, I do see exactly what you mean."

***

The younger Ron looked across at his friend slumped in the chair and sighed. Julian spent most of his time just sitting, mourning his brother, Chrissie and his estranged father in equal measure. Then he would jump awkwardly to his feet and limp around the room, bemoaning his loss. Ron could understand it, but it was time to put the past aside and go on. They were both recovering well from their injuries, being young and fit, but they must both find work.

"Julian, if all things were equal, what would you want to do with your life?" he asked suddenly.

Julian looked at him, an arrested expression on his face. "Do you know, I've never really thought," he said.

"No, you and your brother just swanned around, enjoying life." Ron allowed some exasperation to enter his voice. True, Julian did need a wake up call but he didn't want to be brutal.

Julian grinned for the first time since the accident. "Sorry," he said. Then he sobered. "We did exactly that. We knew we must eventually settle down, have a career, or at least a job, but there always seemed to be plenty of time. We had so much fun together, Paul and Chrissie and I –" His voice broke.

"Has Chrissie contacted you at all since the accident?" Ron

asked. He had wanted to ask this for some time, to make Julian face the fact that she hadn't been next or nigh him. He hoped he had judged it aright.

It seemed that he had. "No, she she's not been near me, not even a Get-Well card." Julian didn't seem too concerned. "Probably blames me. Just as my father does."

"Yes, well, times change." Ron was brisk. "We both need work, or training, and we can't live here much longer." He looked round the seedy bed-sit with distaste. Julian had moved in with him when they had both come out of hospital as Bernard Fry had flatly refused to have anything to do with his surviving son, but the arrangement was far from ideal. "Look, I've got to go out. I've got an interview at the Rose and Crown for kitchen work. You have a good think about what you want to do while I'm gone." He gave Julian an encouraging pat on the shoulder and went out of the room. Shortly afterwards Julian heard the front door slam and knew that he was alone.

Julian stayed slumped in his chair in his familiar misery. Then, with a conscious effort of will he sat up, then went to the minute cupboard that called itself a kitchen and made himself a mug of very strong coffee. It was a turning point; it was the first time he had ever done anything of his own initiative.

Sometime later there was the sound of hurrying footsteps, somewhat dot-and-carry-one to be sure, but undoubtedly hurrying, and Ron burst through the door looking more excited than Julian had ever seen him.

"They're taking me!" he shouted, then stopped and gazed round the room in amazement. "What the –"

"You've no frilly apron here, and your cloths leave a lot to be desired," Julian scolded, grinning broadly. The grubby room looked transformed, and somehow, larger. Although still dingy, Julian had managed to clean every surface, and to find a home for everything, or bin it, so the clutter was gone; the windows were open to the breeze so the musty smell was banished. Considering the relatively short time Ron had been gone the transformation was astonishing.

"Well!" Ron collapsed into a chair. "Can't turn my back for five minutes. But are you alright? Not in pain? I know I still feel battered."

"I'm fine, though I admit I need a break now. Sit still, I'll get us both a coffee and you can tell me All."

"And there's plenty to tell." Ron lit up like a candle at the reminder. "Thanks, I'm ready for this." He accepted the mug Julian handed to him. It crossed his mind briefly that this was the first time Julian had done anything for him, though he had done plenty for Julian. He banished it, Julian was clearly making a big effort. "I'm not sure how aware you are of the job I was going for?"

"Not very," said Julian apologetically. "Too sunk in self-pity."

"Well, you've had a lot on your plate." Ron was forgiving. "It was just a kitchen job, cleaning, running errands, preparing veggies, that kind of thing. When I got there, all hell was loose in the kitchen; one of the cooks had cut himself badly and the chef was going ballistic. In the heat of the moment he thought that I was staff, swore at me for being late, and had me cooking before I knew what was happening. Talk about a hands on job interview! That's why I took so long. Not that you wasted the time," he added, looking round appreciatively. "Anyway, when the service was finished and we were clearing up Chef suddenly realised I was a stranger and asked me, not politely, what I f-ing thought I was f-ing doing."

"So you f-ing told him," said Julian, enthralled.

"I most certainly did. Anyway, I've been taken on as an apprentice, with time off to go to evening classes, starting at once. I'm over the moon," he added, unnecessarily.

"I gathered," said Julian, grinning broadly. "I, too, have news. I took your advice and did some hard thinking as well as hard cleaning. I've also had a quick word with my mum on the phone, she's not as dead against me as my dad is." For a moment a bleak look crossed Julian's face, then he brightened determinedly and went on. "Anyway, she's going to work on my dad to finance me through college, if I can't get a grant, and I've decided to study photography seriously. I've always been interested, and pretty trigger-happy with a camera, and now I want to make it My Life's Work."

Ron grinned at the implied capitals. "Good idea. Where will you live? Do you think your parents will let you back home? Or do you intend to move right away and study somewhere else?" He looked, unaccountably, a little strained.

Julian hesitated. "If you'll have me, I'd like to stay here." There was silence for a moment as Julian and Ron looked at each other.

Suddenly, all thoughts of Chrissie fell away as Julian realised what he truly wanted.

***

Ron, as was usual now, was experimenting in their tiny kitchen when Julian came bounding in.

"Success, success!" he crowed. "I'm enrolled on the BA Honours course at the University! They've accepted my 'A' Levels, even though I am a bit older than the other entrants. So now we're both on our way. I should get a part grant at least, so my father can just stump up the rest. He needn't even see me. Just pay up!" He flopped onto a chair.

"That's brilliant," said Ron, warmly. "How long is the course?"

"Three years, and it sounds fascinating. Now I must go and meet mum and tell her. I just wanted to tell you first," Julian smiled, a little shyly.

"Now you've told me, go and see your mum, then you can try this when you get back. Can't have you doing a BA half starved." And Ron retired back to his pots once more, unconsciously setting the scene for many future occasions.

Angela Fry was waiting patiently in the little café where she had promised to meet her son after the university interview. She looked at her watch; Julian was late even by his standards. She sighed, the situation at home had not got any easier. Bernard still blamed Julian for his beloved Paul's death; in spite of evidence to the contrary he was convinced that Julian had been driving the mini. Angela was quite sure he had not been, she knew her sons and knew that Julian would have quite a job on his hands wresting the wheel from Paul – ever. The situation was not helped by Julian's guilt over his reaction to the news that Chrissie had thrown him over for his brother. Secretly, Angela was rather pleased she was well out of the picture; she had not cared for that young lady at all, and was not impressed by the way she had vanished into the sunset when it all went wrong. However, as things stood there was no way that Bernard would allow Julian to visit the house, never mind move back there. Angela hadn't dared tell him that she and Julian had met several times. She pretended that contact had been minimal, and only by phone, but she was hanged if she was going to lose both her sons because of her husband's pig-headedness.

But she had managed to persuade Bernard that he was duty bound to help Julian into further education by playing on Bernard's guilt at having supplied the mini. She felt bad about it but she also felt she had no choice, given his intransigent attitude. She just hoped it would all work out.

The door of the café flew open and Julian erupted into the shop. He pounced on his mother and enveloped her in a bear hug.

"They'll take me!" he yelled, making all the other shoppers lingering over tea and cakes look round, many smiling at his exuberance. "I'm enrolled on the photography BA Honours course at the University!" He flopped into the chair beside her, nearly sending it flying.

"Congratulations," she said, pouring him tea. "How did you do it?"

"On the strength of my 'A' levels," he said more quietly. "Thank goodness I buckled down and really worked that last year. They wouldn't have taken me with any lower grades, they said so. Now I've got to approach the grants people, though if they turn me down because Dad's so filthy rich, will he stump up? I really want to do this." He looked anxiously at his mother.

"I'll see that he does," she said decidedly, "though I think it will be at the cost of not seeing him. Could you cope with that?"

"If I have to," said Julian soberly, trying not to show how much it hurt. "I always knew that Paul was the favourite, of course, but I never realised how little I meant to him. Oh well," he shook himself. "I'll just have to prove to him that I can make something of myself, won't I?"

"I'm quite sure you will," his mother said fondly.

***

Some years later, Julian sat in their one armchair, now shabbier than ever, and surveyed the room, a glass of beer in his hand. Ron, as usual, was writing up a recipe and oblivious to his surroundings.

"I think we should move," Julian said suddenly. "What do you think?"

Ron grunted but vouchsafed no other reply.

"Hey, Ron! Wake up! What about moving? You could have a

cat," he added, cunningly.

"Just let me finish this and then you'll have my full attention," said Ron, still engrossed. A few minutes later he flung down his pen and turned to face Julian. "What were you saying?"

"I said, what about moving?" said Julian patiently. "For the third time."

"Well, I was busy. Why do you want to move? What's wrong with this place?"

"What's wrong with it? What's right with it." He started to tick off on his fingers. "1) it's too small. 2) it's too shabby. 3) it's falling apart. And 4) it's too small."

"I suppose you're right, it's not really convenient, especially now we're not students anymore. Where did you have in mind? And can we afford it?"

"Certainly we can now that we're both earning. Your reputation is growing and so is my portfolio. I thought, what about that tower block in Heathfield? A friend of mine from uni says it's so run down we should get a flat there easily. It might be worth a look."

"You're on. Now I come to look at this place I wonder how on earth we manage, though it's done us proud up to now. We owe it to ourselves. I know that block. It's pretty grotty but we'll have a look."

Three weeks later Julian and Ron stood in the middle of flat 1 Tower Court and looked at each other bemusedly. "We'll, we've done it now," said Ron.

"*Yes,*" said Julian "Now we can start living!"

"When we've got a cat," said Ron. "Or two…"

– Chapter Four –

Haidar Dalal looked at his daughter sitting on the other side of the table and sighed. She wore the demure dress of a Muslim girl but her mulish expression was entirely inappropriate for a young girl listening to her father telling her about her future. He detested these modern Western ways that were undermining the world that he knew. It had been a mistake sending her to the local school; he could see that now, though it had been his dead wife's wish. He sighed again. I must be patient, he counselled himself.

"You are fourteen now, and it is time you were considering marriage," he said firmly. "This is not the first time that we have talked about this and I am tired of your attitude. I have just the man in mind for you, in India."

His daughter, Amrita, looked horrified. "In *India!*" she exclaimed. Then, hopefully, "Is he young? Good looking?" If he was, then perhaps it was not such a bad idea, after all.

"He is of a suitable age to look after a young, giddy wife," said Haidar, repressively. "His looks are immaterial. He is also willing to take you with a small dowry, yet endow you handsomely."

"So it is all about money," said Amrita, disgustedly. She looked at her elder brother, Jahnu, who, although sitting at the table with his father and sister had so far taken no part in the discussion. "What do you think of this?" she asked. Although a good many years older than she, he had always supported her in the past and she trusted him.

"You should listen to what our father says to you and be obedient to him," he said to her severely.

They had all been speaking in their own language, which was always used within the home, but at this Amrita broke into English. "Why did you send me to an English school if you wanted me to grow up as a good Indian girl?" she asked, passionately. She leapt to her feet. "I won't do this! You can't make me!" She was crying as she rushed from the room.

The two men looked at each other. "She'll see we're right when she calms down," said Jahnu consolingly.

"I expect so," said his father, who was far from sure. "I wish, so much, that your mother was alive. She should deal with all this, not me." He sounded pettish. He brightened. "Perhaps Yasmina can make her see sense."

Privately Jahnu doubted this. Yasmina was the housekeeper and older, even, than his father. But he agreed, politely. After all, Haidar was the head of the family.

***

I had just started on my rounds one morning when I met a total stranger coming out of the odd-side lift.

"Good morning," I said politely. "Are you a new tenant?"

The stranger scowled. He was a stocky man, not tall, with very short, dirty light brown hair, and a pronounced scar over his right eye. "What if I am?" he demanded, truculently. "What's it to you?" He eyed me up and down, hopefully taking in my uniform, but clearly unimpressed by what he saw.

"Then I'd like to introduce myself," I said mildly. "I'm the caretaker, Frankie. I live in flat 3, so don't hesitate to call on me if you have any problems." As I gave him my introductory spiel I found myself hoping devoutly that he wouldn't take me up on the offer.

He seemed to make a conscious effort to be conciliatory. "Thank you," he said. "I'll remember that." Then, after a pause, "I suppose you know all the tenants here?"

"Most of them," I replied. "Now, if you'll excuse me, I must get on." Somehow, I didn't want to answer any more questions.

"Of course, of course," he said hurriedly. "I'll see you around."

It was only after we'd parted, and I was in the lift, that I realised that I'd forgotten to ask him his name.

The next person I met up with was Lottie, who could always be relied upon to cheer me up. I'd seen her about but we'd not really spoken until the lift broke down.

"When will it be repaired?" was her first question. I had to admit I didn't know but would do my best to get things moving. I was developing into a champion nagger; I didn't like it, but it seemed to be the only way to make things happen. "They say they're waiting for a part," I said. "The usual excuse." Then turning to, hopefully, happier topics: "How's the family? Got over being stuck?" I mentally reviewed Susan's high strikes with distaste.

"The little girls loved it," Lottie laughed, "But Philip was livid that he had to come out and fetch them and have his tea late. Silly man. He tries to live like a railway timetable. Life's not like that."

I agreed. "I have to admit I was not over-impressed with Mum."

"A perfect pain," said her loving mother frankly. "And her husband's no better. As well as living by a timetable he *likes* to make a fuss, even when there's no need. Never heard of keeping calm in a crisis. I blame her father for Susan; when she fell down as a dot she would run to daddy who would raise the roof, make such a fuss you wouldn't believe. Never bothered with the boys. Hopeless. Pity she was the only girl, sisters might have made both of them see sense. Still he's gone now, and I do miss him. But how the children have grown up so well is a mystery."

"Perhaps Gran has something to do with that."

"Could be, I do what I can. You're not from round here, are you?"

No, I didn't scream. Perhaps, in time they might accept me as a sort of foreign mascot.

After this entertaining session with Lottie I continued on my rounds and was somewhat taken aback when I reached the 6th floor to find a girl, little more than a child, in floods of tears outside flat 24.

"What on earth are you doing here? And what's the matter?" In my surprise I was less than sympathetic.

"Oh please, sorry, I need Chandra. She does live here, doesn't she? And Amma? Chandra and Amma Naidu? Chandra's my cousin. I've been here all night. I'm Amrita."

"Yes, they do live here." (Mentally I blessed my faithful list.) "But they are away until tonight." I knew that, they'd asked me to keep an eye on the flat and take in a delivery for them. They were clearly not expecting a descent on them by a cousin.

"I shall wait." And Amrita settled down so firmly that my instinctive protests died. I resolved to keep an eye on her during the day and provide some sustenance.

***

"Oh, I am tired." Chandra eased her load of shopping bags as she and Amma, who was equally laden, entered the lift. "Oh no, bother, it's still out of order. Let's try the other one and walk down one." Wearily they transferred to the odd side lift and rose to the 7th floor. Laden as they were going down to the 6th floor was undoubtedly easier than going up from the 5th.

"Good heavens, what on earth are you doing here?" Chandra stopped so suddenly at the sight of her cousin sitting on the floor beside their door that Amma nearly bumped into her. "Does Haidar know you're here?"

"No, no – and *please* don't tell him. Oh, I'm so glad to see you – I need such help." And Amrita burst into floods of tears, clearly not for the first time. "I've been here since yesterday."

"Come in, come in – we cannot talk here." Amma glanced round the mercifully empty landing and ushered his female belongings into the flat. He had the usual male horror of feminine tears. "Try and stop crying and tell us what is going on. Why must Haidar not know you're here? He's a good man, a good father. He'll be worried sick."

" No, no, you don't understand." Amrita was rapidly becoming hysterical. "I love Another."

Chandra decided it was high time she took charge. "Come and sit down," she said soothingly. "Amma and I must sort ourselves out, we've been away. Just sit quiet and we'll all settle down."

Her soothing manner had its effect; Amrita obediently sank into a chair and Chandra whisked her bewildered husband into the bedroom.

"What on earth's going on?" Having lived in the UK since babyhood his reactions tended to be British rather than Indian, a trait shared by his wife. "What's upset her?"

"I don't know, but my guess is that it is the question of Amrita's marriage. It's becoming a real bone of contention. Haidar insists on choosing her husband and now he wants to send her to India for an arranged marriage. He's mentioned it often before, but she feels more British than Indian; it's a clash of cultures as well as generations. Anyway, fourteen is far too young to be married for someone brought up here. But Haidar always was old fashioned and has grown more and more Indian as he grows older, and since Lakya died. She would never have approved of this."

"What are we expected to do?"

"Goodness knows, let's just wait and see what she says. But I do suspect that this is where her mother's death has made all the difference."

Together they girded up their metaphorical loins and went out to face a situation that they feared could lead to a family catastrophe if not handled very carefully. In this they were proved to be right. They found Amrita composed but pale and exhausted. Chandra's instinct was to provide food and drink and then put the child to bed but it soon became clear that Amrita's problems were way past that sort of palliative help.

"What is it?" Chandra asked instead.

"My father wants to send me to India" – Chandra shot a triumphant glance at her husband – "and I wish I was dead." Amrita showed her despair and her youth in one sentence. "Why does he expect me to be a western girl in a western school and then force me to be Asian?" she asked passionately. "He's got some horrible old man lined up for me in India and I won't go. I won't! You've got to help me."

Chandra and Amma looked at each other. Theirs had been an "arranged" marriage but they had effectively arranged it for themselves. Having met and fallen in love it was an easy matter to persuade their respective families to agree. And Chandra had not been fourteen. They had never had to face a clash of cultures like this.

"How can we help you?" Chandra stalled for time.

"You must hide me here. My father will believe you if you say you haven't seen me. You're his niece."

"But I can't lie to him, he'll be so worried about you. Where does he think you are now? And what about school?"

"Staying over with my friend. And school doesn't matter." Amrita was impatient. "And he *deserves* to worry, the way he's been. He's threatened to lock me up until he can take me to India. I only escaped by pretending to go to school and saying I was staying with my friend. My – my boyfriend helped me."

This put a totally different complexion on things.

"What boyfriend?"

"Aktar. He's Asian. It's alright."

"What do you mean, alright? You're only fourteen. Far too young to have a serious boyfriend." Chandra was really perturbed.

"He's seventeen. I'm not too young if I'm going to be married," said Amrita unanswerably. "Anyway, he and I have got to be married. I think I'm pregnant."

"What? But that's illegal." Chandra was suddenly all British.

"Only in this country. And I can't marry anyone else now, can I?"

"Did you do this on purpose?" Amma interposed sternly.

"Well, it seemed like a good idea at the time. And I didn't expect to get pregnant just like that. And Aktar does want to marry me, truly."

"Does he know about the baby?"

"Er – no. But you will let me stay here and hide me from Papa, won't you? Please? Or I don't know what I'll do."

"For the moment, I suppose so, but we'll have to sort things out and fast. Meanwhile, food, then bed for you, miss."

"Oh thank you, thank you Chandra. I knew I could trust you." And Amrita, all child again, flung her arms round her cousin's neck.

***

Sophie and I were curled up together on the sofa when Chandra came down to inform me of her family saga and to ask my advice. I told her that I'd met Amrita on the landing and had tried to keep some sort of an eye on her.

"Thanks," she said absently and plunged into her story. "I really don't know what to do," she finished. "I know Haidar, he's of the old school, his word in the family is law, especially since Lakya died. She could manage him," Chandra added with a sigh.

"I don't quite see how you can hide Amrita forever," I said. "The flat's a little small, and as you said, what about school? And goodness knows what the legal position is. What you can do, in the short term, and don't quote me on this, is have a quiet word with Security so you have warning if her father does turn up. But if he does, and asks me, or heaven forbid, if he brings the police in, I shall have to come clean."

"Yes, I quite understand." But Chandra was clearly distracted. "That's not the worst of it. You see, she thinks she's pregnant. Apparently she had some wild idea of forcing everyone's hand by sleeping with her boyfriend and got caught."

I was speechless. Amrita seemed such a child. Poor Chandra, she was such a nice person and clearly very worried about her niece and the family implications. I did not envy her.

***

I was cleaning the lift when Ron came into the foyer, laden down with supermarket bags. I went to give him a hand. "Thanks," he said. "I never understand how food items which are light in themselves weigh so much when you're trying to get them home."

"I entirely agree," I said, laughing. I spotted a familiar packet. "And cat food most of all."

"I'll say," said Ron, feelingly. At that moment the main door opened and our new tenant came in.

"Room for a little one?" he said breezily. As I moved over to make room, I felt Ron stiffen.

"Yes, certainly," I said. "By the way, I forgot to ask you your name when we met earlier, and what flat you're in?"

"Does it matter?" he asked, suddenly surly.

"No, of course not, but –" At that moment the lift creaked to a halt on the first floor. To my surprise, I found Ron almost hauling me out of the lift, together with the bags.

"Come in here," he hissed, as the lift door closed sending our sulky companion on his way. "Do you know who that was?"

"Not really," I said. "I met him this morning but I forgot to ask his name. He doesn't seem to be the friendliest of individuals."

"If he is who I think he is, then he's not," said Ron tersely. "But I can't really believe it –" He seemed to remember himself. "Look, I must think about this, talk it over with Julian. I'll see you later. Thanks for your help." And he vanished into his flat, leaving me with my mouth open.

***

Haidar Dalal was sitting at his desk when his housekeeper, Yasmina, came hurrying in. She was in a high state of excitement.

"The little one, she is gone!" she gasped and collapsed in complete hysterics. It was sometime before he succeeded in calming her down, and settled her in a chair with a cup of tea. Then, cautiously, fearing to set her off again, he began to question her.

"Surely she has gone off to school?" he said soothingly. "And I gave her permission to stay the night with a friend."

"But most of her favourite things have gone," wailed Yasmina. "It is my fault, all my fault. You gave her into my charge and I have failed you." She collapsed into another paroxysm of crying.

Haidar, completely bewildered by this time, looked up as his son burst into the room. Haidar looked at Jahnu's set face and abandoned his attempts to soothe Yasmina.

"What is it?" he asked, dreading what he might hear. "Is it about Amrita?"

His son nodded. "She has been seen going about with a young man, a boy," he said heavily. At that moment the phone shrilled, making both the men jump. Jahnu, who was nearest, answered it.

After listening, but saying nothing, he set the receiver back on its cradle. "We have been completely dishonoured," he said bleakly. "Amrita has run away with a boy. She has gone to our cousin, Chandra."

***

Chandra was busy in her kitchen when Amrita came in.

"Can I go down to Frankie's flat?" She asked. She and the caretaker had become very friendly while Amrita was staying with her cousin. Too frightened to go out she loved to go down to Frankie's flat, browse through her books and talk to Sophie the kitten, rapidly growing into a handsome cat.

"Yes, of course." Chandra was abstracted. The whole situation worried, and indeed, alarmed her. She wasn't really scared of her uncle but....

She was still deep in her thoughts as her hands automatically carried out her household tasks. She knew that her uncle was fanatical about the family and utterly convinced that whatever he decided was right. She could not see any easy way out, it was a case of deeply rooted cultural beliefs.

Suddenly there was a thunderous knocking at the door. Chandra froze, then remembered that Security had promised to screen all calls to her flat with extra care. Relieved, she hurried to open the door. To her horror her uncle Haidar and his eldest son Jahnu were standing there, glaring at her. Yasmina, Haidar's elderly housekeeper, was cowering behind them.

"Where is she? Where is the slut? I know she has come here, and the boy. I order you to produce them!" Haidar was shouting as he pushed past the terrified Chandra. He rampaged round the flat, bursting into each room, still shouting. Shaking, Chandra retreated into the living room. Jahnu followed her, standing over her as she sank into a chair, every bit as frightening as his father.

"I – I don't know where she is," lied Chandra. "She didn't come here. Is she missing? Isn't she at school? And what boy are you talking about?"

"Don't lie to me, woman." Haidar joined his son in the living room. "I am the head of the family. I know she came here. I know she is still here. The fellow at the gate said so, and probably the boy too." Sobbing Chandra capitulated, the combined force of her uncle and cousin was too much for her; generations of obedience suddenly overcame her western veneer.

"Yes, she came here, and yes, I hid her. I was afraid of what you might do to her. You must be kind, gentle; she is pregnant by this boy but he is Asian. And he's not here, never has been."

"*What?*" Jahnu screamed. He spun round and dashed out of the room. Chandra heard the front door slam behind him.

"Then we are doubly shamed." Haidar sank wearily into a chair. "Where is she now?"

Completely cowed, Chandra sobbed: "In the caretaker's flat downstairs. But you must forgive her, she's only following western ways."

"Western ways are evil. I know what I must do." And slowly, heavily, Haidar left the flat.

***

I enjoyed having Amrita in the flat and even Sophie, a high stickler, approved. We were all sitting on the floor discussing *Gone With the Wind,* an old favourite of mine, but new to Amrita, when there was a quiet knock at the door. It was after hours but I had not changed, and anyway, whatever the time, doors had to be answered.

A large Indian gentleman was revealed. He pushed past me without ceremony, shouting unintelligibly. Amrita clearly understood what he was saying and jumped to her feet. He started shaking her and she began to cry, then shouted in English: "Stop it! You're hurting me. Stop, I'm pregnant, you can't make me go to India, Papa!"

Her father hit her two tremendous blows across the face, knocking her to the floor. "Slut! Whore! You disgrace the family!"

I had stood transfixed, while Sophie, sensible cat, shot behind the sofa for her life, but at that point I moved forward to help Amrita. But as I tried to lift her to her feet my unwelcome visitor shoved me aside, knocking me into a cupboard – I discovered later that I had an interesting gash to my face and developed an impressive black eye. Then he dragged poor Amrita, screaming, from the flat and slammed the door (*my* door) in my face. I leapt to the phone and dialled 999 (*yet* again, they must be sick of me at the control centre), I could hear Amrita screaming all the way down the stairs.

"Police, *quick!*" I shouted into the phone. "There's been an abduction, there may be murder!" I didn't really believe that but I did fear for Amrita's safety and that seemed the quickest way to summon help. Then I hurried to the balcony and my grandstand view over the car park.

I saw Amrita and her father come out of the stair door, Amrita still screaming. He dragged her towards a red car in the car park just below me. Then, to my absolute horror, there was the sound of a shot and Amrita's screams were abruptly cut off. I could not believe what I was apparently seeing. The shot seemed to come from a young man standing beyond the red car. I saw him aim what could only be a gun, and fire. Then the two men bundled what I feared was Amrita's body into the car, got in themselves and raced away, tyres screaming. Incredibly, I did manage not only to see the number plate but had the presence of mind to write it down.

All this happened amazingly fast and I had just started to wonder where Chandra and/or Amma were when they arrived at my door, breathless, with an elderly Indian lady in tow.

"What has happened?" Chandra shouted, recent tears clearly visible on her face.

"Yes, what?" demanded Amma. "I have just come in, what on earth is going on? And what have you done to your face? Oh, this is Yasmina, Uncle Haidar's housekeeper."

Shaking violently from reaction I began to tell them what I had seen. Chandra burst into tears again, and when Amma had explained the situation to Yasmina she too started wailing. Into this uproar the steadying arrival of the police was a relief.

A WPC took the Naidu family upstairs while another raided my kitchen for restoratives. I managed to collect myself sufficiently to outline what had happened and to give them the registration number of the red car. Then I started shaking violently again as reaction and shock set in.

"Is there anyone who could come and be with you?" asked the officer who seemed to be in charge. "You should get that cut attended to, it could need stitching, and you are definitely in shock." I became aware that I was still bleeding copiously from my contact with the cupboard, courtesy of Amrita's father, also that it was extremely painful.

"Any one of the neighbours," I managed to croak. The WPC helped me to swallow some revoltingly sweet tea, which undoubtedly steadied me. "Not flat 4, it's empty, but either of the other two."

I lay back in my chair exhausted, and was content to let things drift.

I heard Ron's voice in the hall and the kindly police officer explaining: "She's witnessed a shooting, probably fatal, is badly shocked and has a nasty cut on her head. Can you be with her?"

"Yes, of course, she's a friend, not just the caretaker. I'll just call Magda, she's also a friend and we'll be straight in. Does she need a doctor?"

"Hospital probably, but we'll see how she does. The cut certainly needs a stitch. In my view."

"No hospital," I whispered. I couldn't face leaving the safety of my flat even protected by Ron and Magda.

"Don't worry, we'll sort it all out."

I'd not realised before what a soothing voice Ron had. I drifted away.

***

Ron and Magda looked at each other over their caretaker's inanimate form.

"What on *earth* has been going on?" Magda was the first to speak.

"Goodness knows. Perhaps the police will give us a hint. All I know is that there was a lot of shouting and screaming, here and in the car park, a bang – presumably the shot – a screech of tyres then nothing. Then more crying and wailing until the police called me in to Frankie. What a to-do. Quite ruined my soufflé."

"Let's see to Frankie first. She seems out for the count. She looks ghastly and I don't like that cut. Ambulance?"

"Since she's the only driver here we'd better, though I don't like to move her. Let's call them and see what they say. That cut needs stitching anyway."

Magda got up. "If necessary I'll go with her. She certainly shouldn't be alone." She turned as the WPC, who had been called away by her superior, returned. "We think we should call an ambulance and I'll go with her to hospital. She's badly shocked and that cut needs a stitch."

The officer nodded. "I agree, and I'll follow, just in case she can tell us more about what has happened."

At that moment the ambulance, duly summoned by Ron, arrived to join the fleet of police cars occupying the car park and Frankie's unconscious body was borne away.

***

As soon as the ambulance containing Frankie and Magda was out of sight Ron grabbed Julian's arm. "Quick, back to the flat," he said urgently, then refused to say another word until they were safely home and the door was shut and locked behind them.

"Whatever is the matter?" asked Julian, completely bewildered.

"I should have told you earlier, but I was thinking about it, and then all this blew up and I forgot."

"Ron, you're not making sense. Should have told me *what?* Forgot about *what?*"

"There is a new bloke moved in and I think, in fact I'm sure, it's Jimbo."

"Who? Ron, you've lost me. Come and sit down, calm down, and begin from the beginning." Julian was getting seriously worried, this behaviour was totally unlike the usually calm and controlled Ron.

"Sorry." Ron consented to sit down. There was a short silence while he marshalled his thoughts. "You remember, back at the children's home I had a big set-to, the only fight I've ever had, in fact, with a bully called Jimbo? I think his other name was Preston, though I can't be sure, it was so long ago."

Julian thought. "Was he the one who –"

"Killed Mouser, yes," said Ron hastily. Even after all the years the memory was painful. "I gave him a huge gash over the right eye," he grinned reminiscently, with considerable pleasure.

"Yes, well, what about him?" Julian asked a shade impatiently.

"I'd just come back from the supermarket and was laden –"

"As usual," Julian interrupted, grinning.

"As you say. Frankie was helping me –"

"Again as usual –"

"Yes. I do wish you'd stop interrupting, this is difficult enough without you ruining my train of thought."

"Sorry, sorry." Julian raised placating arms. "I won't say another word."

"Thank you. As I said, Frankie was helping me with the bags, and we were actually in the lift when this lout came pushing in. He was the right build, the right age, the right colouring, and," pausing for effect, "he had a very pronounced scar over his right eye."

"It seems an awful coincidence," said Julian dubiously. "I know we're not that far away from where the home used to be, but even so. It's so long ago, what, thirty odd years? Give or take? It is stretching it a bit. Do you know where he went after the home? He left before you did, didn't he?"

"Yes, he did, and no, I don't know where he went. But I just feel sure it's him. Especially after I saw him lurking in the car park just now. That's just like him, rubber-necking at a drama when there's no way he could help. And somehow, I'll find out for sure."

"Then what?" demanded Julian. "Are you going to bash him again? Or do you think he's going to bash you?"

"He'd have a job now," grinned Ron. "No, I don't know what to make of it – yet. But I'll do my damndest to find out. Even ask him outright if necessary." He got up. "And now, I think, coffee, to soothe my shattered nerves."

"Good idea," approved Julian. "I'll look out a bottle of wine for when Magda comes back from the hospital."

Ron looked anxious. In the ferment of memories he had almost forgotten the events of the last half hour or so. "I do hope she's alright," he said.

"Bound to be," said Julian, comfortably. "She's a tough old bird."

"You'd better not let her hear you say that," laughed Ron, departing for the kitchen "She would definitely not approve of that description!"

***

Meanwhile, in the car park the new tenant under discussion had been an avid spectator of the shooting. He couldn't care less about the unfortunate victim; the sight of the gun, followed by the get away was giving him an almost sexual thrill. He had seen the two Asian men dashing into the building, clearly very excited about something, and had waited, just in case anything else happened. He was rewarded beyond his wildest dreams.

He saw the younger of the two men hurry out again and dive into the car in which they had both arrived. He watched as the young man emerged from the car and crouched down behind it. He saw the older man come out of the building, holding a struggling, screaming teenage girl in his grasp. The watcher drew back out of sight and gave a gasp of pure joy as the girl was forced towards the car and the shot rang out.

He continued to watch as the girl collapsed and was bundled into the car, and as the car raced away. Then he realised, that if he didn't want to become involved as a witness he had better make himself scarce. He sidled round the corner, melted out of the car park and waited for a discreet interval before returning.

***

Upstairs, on the 6th floor, the WPC assigned to the Naidus family was having a hard time. Chandra could do nothing but cry,

Amma clearly did not know what had happened, and the elderly Yasmina continued to wail. The officer was not even sure what she was supposed to do, it was all outside her limited experience to date. Being a well brought up English girl, as well as a police officer, she retired to the kitchen to make tea.

Amma joined her. "What has been going on?" he asked. "My wife says that her niece has been shot, surely that's not right, I must have misunderstood?"

Thankfully the officer abandoned tea. "We can't be sure at this stage until your caretaker has recovered but it looks as though the girl was abducted by one man, possibly her father, and shot by another, unknown. We don't know at the moment whether she's alive or – not. Anyway, it's a serious incident." She remembered herself. "And you, sir. Who are you, and where were you at the time of the shooting?"

Amma explained himself. "I had just arrived in the foyer when I heard all the shouting and screaming. I was already in the lift so I came straight up here and then almost immediately straight down again to the caretaker's flat. My wife can't stop crying and Yasmina only wails so I really don't know what's happened, except that my wife's niece has vanished. Will you be here much longer? I don't want to be rude but I want to settle everyone down."

Suppressing the impulse to say she couldn't get out fast enough the WPC said she would have a word with her superior and departed thankfully. She wondered if she was really cut out for the police force.

***

I was kept in hospital overnight for "observation". Of what? Incipient mania? I wish. Magda, bless her, brought me home but to an empty flat; there was no sign of Sophie. I could only hope she had gone to ground somewhere inside. I didn't see how she could have got out, but in yesterday's general uproar anything could have happened.

Duty bound, I rang Roger at the Office. He was round almost before I had put the phone down. He was, of course, horrified. "You poor thing. You should have counselling; I've heard they're very good. Take you through it all so you don't have nightmares."

"Thanks, but I'd rather work it through on my own, if I can. I've written it all down for my police statement, that helped."

"Take some leave then, I'll sort it. Make it sick leave. Go somewhere exotic and forget all about it."

Using what for money? And what about Sophie? Assuming she planned to come back to me. Still, he meant well.

Chandra came down to see me; she looked ghastly. Apparently I was not the only candidate for the hospital, Yasmina had collapsed and had to be admitted with chest pains and palpitations. Unlike me she was still there. "She seems to blame herself for it all, goodness knows why," Chandra sighed. "I hope they're caught soon then we can settle down, or try to. And it's awful not knowing for sure whether Amrita is -" she broke off, struggling with her tears. I guessed they were never very far off.

"Where are they likely to go?" I wanted to know.

"They'll probably try family first, there are plenty of us around. They might even try to go to India, but the police say the ports and airports have been alerted. There's still no sign of Amrita but no one has been admitted to any local hospital with gunshot wounds. If only we *knew*." And Chandra again began to show how slight her grasp on the "proper way to behave" really was.

I tried to soothe her but soon realised she needed to be away; the old easy friendship between us had taken a knock. She needed to close ranks with her family and I, though involved, was well outside. I was sorry, but I understood; I would probably feel the same in her shoes.

I met Ken and Margaret when I was on my rounds, they had obviously been looking out for me. They must have been completely bewildered by the uproar on their previously quiet landing. Sure enough: "Do you know what was going on here yesterday?" asked Ken, trying to look as though our meeting was quite accidental.

I was not sure what I ought to say but I gave them somewhat curtailed version of events. "Though we're not sure how seriously Amrita was injured," I finished. "As you will realise, Chandra and Amma are in quite a state so don't be surprised when you meet them."

"Yes indeed," Margaret was immediately sympathetic. "Poor things, what an awful thing to happen."

At that moment two police officers arrived in the lift to speak to the Murrays so I beat a thankful retreat. I wondered if they would speak to me again; I hoped not. I felt I needed to put some time between me and the events of yesterday.

Sprawled inelegantly in a chair that evening I heard a rustle, then a clatter, then Sophie stalked in looking indignant. Goodness knows where she had hidden herself but we were both very pleased to see each other, especially when I sped to the kitchen to repair the Starvation of Months. I decided then and there to find another kitten so that she would have company if these upsets were par for the caretaking course.

Amazingly everything quietened down for a few weeks. The soil stack didn't flood – much – no one got themselves stuck in the lift, though they repeatedly broke down and seemed to take longer and longer to put right. "Sorry, miss. Can't get the parts" was the usual excuse. What would it take to make them replace the lifts, I wondered. These constant repairs must cost nearly as much as new ones. And they were old; they did not have metal cages but it was close, the next newest model as it were. And they were so slow! Since I was in them so often in the line of duty they nearly drove me frantic.

The next, and greatest, excitement was Ron, bearing a kitten. He knew well that I was looking for a companion for Sophie, especially seeing how well Furball and Lucy got on together – most of the time. It had been the subject of many evening discussions.

"A friend of ours has found this scrap dumped in a bin, would you believe? He looks about the same age as Sophie was when you got her, and as a male (I think), should suit madam very well. Stop her making eyes at Furball."

Sophie had indeed made her feelings about the male feline very clear with Furball. She would have to be 'done' sooner rather than later, I had already decided.

Ron put his black and white companion down on the floor and I brought in Sophie, who had been enjoying a siesta on my bed. After some preliminary skirmishing they seemed to get on remarkably well.

"Look, she's giving him a good wash. He certainly could do with it. Evidently he doesn't smell right. They're getting on really well aren't they? Just like Furball and Lucy." Ron smiled fondly at them. At that moment World War III seemed about to erupt, but I agreed that they would probably get used to each other in time as I grabbed Sophie. She was busy telling the newcomer that 'she was not that kind of girl,' when he tried to sniff her tail.

Ron, laughing immoderately, retired to his own flat where cats did not fight – often, leaving me to separate the combatants.

Soon after this I heard that Haidar and Jahnu had been caught and charged with murder and GBH. They had tried to hide among their extended family but had been given up to the police – not everyone in the family being sympathetic towards a so-called honour killing, for poor Amrita had indeed been killed outright by Jahnu's bullet. But at least the family could now bury her. I wondered how the boyfriend was getting on, and whether he knew what had happened, or about the baby. Quite possibly not, if the family closed ranks, and that information had been kept out of the papers – just. I couldn't ask Chandra, who seemed to be avoiding me now. I couldn't blame her. I wondered how long it would be before it came to court. When Robin dropped in to see how things were going I took the opportunity to ask him.

"It varies, he said, helpfully. "We've got to get all the evidence together, prove that we've got a case with a good chance of a conviction, which we have here. Then everything has to go to the CPS – Crown Prosecution Service," as I looked bewildered, "and they decide whether to continue. There is no doubt in this case, though they are both pleading not guilty and saying nothing very loudly. We have eyewitness reports, and family members have heard them talking so it should be straightforward enough. But once the whole thing goes to the CPS it's virtually out of our hands, unless something new turns up."

"But *when* will it come to court?" I asked again, patiently.

"When it does." He ducked, as I threatened to hit him. "Don't assault an Officer of the Law," he said reproachfully. "Give me a coffee, or I'll run you in."

And with that I had to be content.

– Chapter Five –

Having been lulled into a false sense of security with several weeks of peace after the trauma of the shooting of Amrita, I was consequently furious at being rudely awakened by loud music and general racket which carried on until 4am. Even worse, I couldn't be sure where it was coming from; sound can be deceiving in a tower block, I discovered. Judging by the mess I found next morning it seemed to be the 4th floor, but I could not be sure.

The next night it was just as bad so I went up to the 4th floor for a listen. It was indeed the 4th floor – my poor ears, even outside the flat – and flat 13 the culprit. I decided there was nothing to be done in the middle of the night; if I did knock I doubted that anyone would hear, so I returned to my own abode to try to sleep.

In the morning I went up to the 4th floor, full of righteous indignation. My helpful list told me that the tenant in flat 13 was one Brian Ambrose, who, I remembered, was a very large West Indian. There was no reply in the morning so I tried again in the afternoon.

In answer to my assault on the door, I was determined to be heard this time:

"Yerse?" a bleary eyed giant, clearly away with the fairies, tried to focus on me. I wondered how many of me he saw, he was clearly on something.

"The noise. At night. Could you keep the music down? Or off? I've had complaints." Yes, I had, from me.

"Wha' music? I can't hear no music."

"At *night*. Loud music at *night*. When people are trying to sleep?"

"Oh, then. That music. OK." And the door shut, ending the conversation. I left, but was not able to persuade myself that I had accomplished anything at all.

I was quite right, the noise continued unabated, even with Security buzzing them. The police, when I contacted them, were sympathetic but could not interfere unless a crime was being, or about to be, committed. Apparently nightly assault on the eardrums didn't count.

My personal back-up group was sympathetic. By some strange twist of building design neither Ron and Julian nor Magda were affected.

"Lucky you," I said bitterly.

"Perhaps it's a pirate radio. Is there a strange aerial on the roof?"

"I've no idea. I've only been up there once, I'm not mad keen on heights. I don't really know what should be there and what shouldn't."

"I'll try the airwaves tonight," Ron promised. "How are Sophie and the new kitten getting on?"

"Like a house on fire." I was glad to change the subject. "Sophie says his name is Rudi and he'll do very well once she's licked him into shape. I think she means literally."

True to his word Ron scanned the airwaves and came in to see me next morning.

"I've found it," he said, not without pride. "It's rather good, but it is loud."

"Many thanks, I'll get on to the Office and see what we can do."

I duly cornered Roger, who never seemed to be at the Office nowadays, and he certainly wasn't often here. He pooh-poohed the idea of a pirate radio until I told him that Ron had actually found it.

"I still don't know what we can do about it. I'll ask around." Not the most encouraging of reactions. No one seemed to know what to do. They were not licensed, presumably, so why couldn't they be stopped? And they were certainly tearing their tenancy agreement into shreds.

In desperation I called on Ron again, always the more practical of the two. "Would you come up on the roof with me? I wouldn't know a wireless aerial if it jumped up and bit me."

He roared with laughter. "Come on, then. Let's do the dirty deed."

Breaking goodness knows how many rules, guidelines, by-laws and what have you, I took the uninsured tenant up onto the roof. Once I had persuaded Ron that he was not there to look at the undoubtedly spectacular view - "How Julian would love this. Could you smuggle him up?"

"No."

"Pity." - we bore our trophy, one illegal radio aerial, away in triumph. I promptly contacted the police, I didn't want us to be charged with theft – though Ron remained discretely tucked up in his flat. I had Done It All By Myself, honest!

Shortly after my phone call, Robin Lutterworth turned up with cohorts and I handed over my booty. Then I had the undoubted pleasure of seeing, from my window, Brian Ambrose, still away with the fairies, being led away in company with some very large pieces of equipment, by some equally large police officers.

Peace at last!

***

Soon after the excitements of the pirate radio I was passing through the foyer, as was my wont, when a strange couple came in. Since they hesitated, looking slightly worried, I asked if I could help.

"Yes, please, if you would." This was the man, tall, thin with a slight accent I could not place. "We have been given the key to flat –" he consulted the label of the key he held in his hand - "60. My daughter is looking for accommodation while she studies at the university."

"Yes, of course. I'll take you up. It's on the 15th floor so I hope you like the view." I took them to the odd floors lift, praying that it wouldn't choose this moment to break down. It didn't, and we arrived safely at the top floor. "I hope you like the flat, it should be quiet for you to study." I smiled at the girl, who so far had not uttered a word. Needless to say I did *not* mention the pirate radio, now, I hoped, safely defunct. The father opened the door and we went in.

The flat was on the opposite side of the landing to mine so the layout was a mirror image, which felt a little strange. The view certainly was spectacular. The father looked round briefly.

"This seems to be suitable. Do you not think so, my dear? We'll take it." The girl still said nothing. She was young, about eighteen, I thought, and clearly very much under her father's thumb. I found myself wondering if she really wanted to go to university at all. For no reason that I could see, I shivered.

"I'm so glad you like it. You should go back to the Office now and settle it with them. Do call upon me if you need any help. I'm in flat 3." I had already introduced myself as the caretaker.

"Thank you. I am Victor du Cros. My daughter is Vivienne." And the strange couple left; Vivienne had not said one word from start to finish.

I let them go down in the lift on their own, I found I didn't care to accompany them again. I felt it would probably do Vivienne all the good in the world to be away from her father, obviously a very dominating figure in her life. I was glad it was she who was moving in and not he, he would probably dominate me just as easily. I mentally shook myself and departed downstairs on my lawful occasions.

***

On their way down in the lift Victor du Cros turned to his daughter.

"That flat should do us very well but you should not have been so silent. It seemed strange and we do not wish to draw attention to ourselves."

"No, papa."

"When you move in you will 'come out of your shell' now that you are away from your domineering father and be like any other young student."

"Yes, papa."

The lift stopped at the ground floor and they left.

***

This seemed to be a day for new tenants. I wondered why; I hoped it was because the block looked so much more cared for than it had before I came. Once again I was in the foyer when a woman, alone this time, came in and stood looking slightly bewildered.

"Can I help you?" I asked. To my surprise she took my arm and turned me until I was facing the light.

"I'm sorry, I am deaf. Could you say that again?"

I repeated myself, puzzled, then realised that she needed to see my face clearly so she could lip-read what I said. "I'm the caretaker. Can I help you?"

"Thank you, I want to look at flat 4."

"Oh good. That's the empty flat on my floor. We've been wondering when it would be occupied. Come on up." I was careful to face her all the time I was speaking and she seemed to be able to follow me.

We went up to the first floor, the lift, amazingly, behaved itself again, and we went to flat 4. This was exactly the same as the one on the top floor that I had just seen, also with two windows in the outside wall, on the west side. With perfect timing the sun broke through the overcast sky and shone brilliantly, making the flat a haven of space and light.

"Oh, this is really nice. I think I could be very happy here. You see, this is the first time I have launched out on my own. I feel a bit nervous." I wondered at this remark, as she was not a young woman, but thought it might have something to do with her deafness. It was far too soon to ask personal questions. Instead I said: "We are all very friendly on this landing. I have been here less than six months and I feel completely at home. But I hope you like cats, we have four between us."

"Yes I do, though I've never had one. We are not a very animal orientated family. I really like this flat. What do I do now, to take it? I am Judith English, by the way."

I told her to return to the Office to settle it and we moved out onto the landing. There we met Ron just coming in, laden with shopping bags. I pounced.

"Ron, this is Judith English. She wants to move into flat 4 and she likes cats but doesn't have one."

"We have enough between us for one floor so perhaps it's just as well. I hope you like it here."

"I'm sure I shall. Your caretaker said you were friendly and I see she was right. Thank you." She turned to me. "I shall go straight to the office and sign on the dotted line. Thank you so much for your help."

"All part of the job." I showed her where the stairs were. "The lifts can be a bit iffy," I admitted. "We are all agitating for them to be replaced but nothing's happened yet. Good-bye, we'll look forward to seeing you when you move in."

"She should round off our setup very nicely," said Ron,

unlocking his door. "Come in and have a caretakerly coffee and tell me All."

I was glad to take up his invitation; after all, I had just let two flats Single Handed and felt a pardonable glow of pride. I hoped the Office appreciated my efforts.

"That was the second flat I've let today," I boasted to Ron, removing Lucy from the sofa and sitting down. Offended, she took herself to the windowsill where Furball was surveying the outside world. "At least, I have if they don't change their minds between here and the Office."

"They probably won't," said Ron, handing me a mug of his special coffee. I don't know what he does with it but it tastes quite different from anyone else's, and very good. "Have you noticed how different it is here now since you came and took it in hand? Probably not, but flats used to stay empty for months. Now there are lots of new faces. How many empty flats do we have now, do you know?"

I thought. "Only one, on the top floor, I think. I don't know why the top floor should be unpopular. Perhaps people feel it's just too high. It didn't seem to worry the du Cros, father and daughter, though." And I started to tell him about the morning's viewing.

***

As the caretaker and her friend disappeared into flat 1, Judith hesitated. On an impulse she went back into flat 4, which she was now determined should become her new home.

She stood in the middle of the empty living room and looked round. As she had said to the caretaker, this was the first time she had ventured doing something on her own and she had to admit to being nervous, if not downright scared. Her mother was supportive and filled with the very best of intentions but she was also petrified of letting Judith out of her sight, imagining heaven knew what dangers might befall her daughter. She had been furious when Judith had announced her intention to start living on her own

Judith never forgot the time when she had lost her hearing.

She was fourteen years old and her mother was to be away for the night, an unheard-of occurrence. Judith was left in the nominal charge of the neighbours, who lived in the other half of their semi-detached house. They had promised to listen out for the young

Judith, and to give her some supper. She had gone round, enjoyed the promised supper and chat; she was great friends with the couple, whom she called Uncle Jack and Aunt Florrie. They had both been very good to her, and to her mother, over the years and she had implicit trust in them.

Supper over, she returned to her own house and settled down in her room to finish off her homework. This done, she got up to go downstairs and make herself a hot drink before bed, but she slipped on a loose rug and fell, knocking her head on the corner of the dressing table. She felt a momentary dizziness but it passed quickly and she went on downstairs, made her cocoa and returned with it to her room. Once in bed, she read her book, which was currently engrossing her to the exclusion of all else - Judith was a single-minded young person and liked to concentrate on one thing at a time – until sleep claimed her.

The next morning she woke late, but it didn't matter, there was no school. She was surprised how quiet it was. She finished her book, then went downstairs to get herself some breakfast. It still seemed to be unusually quiet; there was always some traffic noise, and a dog lived further down the road which could be counted upon to bark at the slightest thing. But she was thinking about her book, which had come to a very satisfactory conclusion, so paid no real attention.

Suddenly she became aware of a figure, which was visible through the glazed panel in the front door. How odd, she thought. Why did the person not knock? Or ring the bell? She shrugged mentally and opened the front door. To her surprise it was Aunt Florrie.

"What's happening?" Florrie demanded in bewilderment. "I've been knocking and ringing for ages. Are you deaf, or something? Is anything the matter?"

Judith looked at Florrie's mouth opening and closing, and the changing expressions on her face. She realised that Florrie must be speaking but she could hear nothing.

"What did you say?" she asked. She couldn't hear her own voice. "Aunt Florrie, I can't hear anything. Nothing at all."

Florrie looked at her in horror. "What do you mean? Are you playing some sort of trick? If so, it isn't funny."

"I can't hear you. I don't know what you're saying." Judith felt that at any moment she would realise what was happening and panic, but at that moment it all seemed unreal. She went into the little sitting room, followed by Florrie, and they both sat down and looked at each other.

"Can you hear me now?" Florrie shouted. Judith realised she was saying something but shook her head.

"I can't hear anything," she repeated.

Florrie looked round for paper and pencil but could see nothing. She looked at Judith and mimed writing.

"Good idea." Judith was relieved that a line of communication was opening up and jumped to her feet. "I'll get pencil and paper." She dashed up to her room and was soon back with the required materials, which she handed to Florrie.

"How did this happen?" Florrie wrote.

"I don't know," answered Judith. "I just woke up and couldn't hear. Anything."

"Do you think it will pass?" went Florrie's busy pen.

"Oh, I do hope so. Surely it will, won't it?"

"Hang on," wrote Florrie. "Phone. Shall I answer it?"

"Yes, please." Judith hadn't heard a thing. She watched the one-sided conversation.

"Your mother. She can't get away until this evening, and were you alright. Said yes, did right?" Florrie was developing a shorthand. She sat back, exhausted from all the writing.

"Yes, quite right," answered Judith firmly. "There's no point in worrying her, she'll be back as soon as she can be anyway. You know how upset she can get if something goes wrong. And perhaps this, whatever it is, will have passed by then, and I'll be able to hear again, and no harm done."

"Very true." Florrie's pen approved. "Meanwhile, dress, come back to mine. Bad to be alone." Mentally she quailed at the thought of the child, at fourteen she was little more, being on her own in the house and completely isolated by her lack of hearing.

"Thank you, I'd like that, said Judith gratefully. "This is all rather scary," she admitted.

"Of course it is," said Florrie, forgetting that Judith could not hear her. She gave the girl a hug instead, and pushed her gently towards the door.

The day passed rather slowly for Judith. She kept hoping that her hearing would come back as suddenly as it had gone, but she was still cocooned in silence. Jack and Florrie did their best but there was really nothing that they could do.

"Do you think we should take her to the doctor?" a worried Florrie asked her husband.

Jack thought for a moment. "I don't think so," he said at last. She seems perfectly well in herself, no loss of appetite," he grinned. Judith had just put away a large plateful of her favourite fish and chips as though she hadn't had a square meal for a month. "I think we should leave it for her mother to decide." They did not know then how bitterly they were to regret that decision.

Soon after six o'clock, Judith's mother, Belinda, returned. She went first to her own house, then remembered that Florrie had said she would probably have Judith with her and accordingly went next door.

"Hello," she said gaily when Florrie opened the door to her knock. "I take it Judith's here?"

"Yes she is," said Florrie soberly. "Come in. Now, before you see her I have to tell you something." She had arranged with Judith that she should see her mother first to break the news.

Belinda started to panic. "What? What's wrong? Is she ill? Has there been an accident? Has she done something? *Tell* me, for God's sake."

"I will, when I can get a word in edgeways," said Florrie, rather exasperated. Really, Belinda did fly off the handle so *easily.* "It's hard to realise it, but Judith has completely lost her hearing."

"*What?*" Belinda almost screamed. "Whatever do you mean? You've got to be joking. Where is she? How did it happen?"

"She's in here, and we don't know how it happened, apart from the fact that she could hear normally when she went to bed and when she woke up she could hear nothing at all. We've been writing notes to her all day," she smiled briefly. "Come in, she's doing very well but she's very frightened as you can imagine," she added warningly. She did not want Belinda going off at half cock to Judith and scaring her even more.

They went into the living room where Jack was sitting with

Judith. At the sight of Belinda she jumped up and hurled herself into her mother's arms, almost knocking her over. Shear relief that she was no longer alone brought the tears that she had been stoically holding at bay all day.

"Hush now, it's going to be alright," said her mother soothingly, forgetting that Judith could not hear her. "Has she been to the doctor?" she asked.

"No," said Jack. "We thought about it but she seemed to be well in herself so we thought we should leave it to you."

"Yes, thank you, I can see that." She thought for a moment then said, "I think I'll take her to the hospital. If it's not too crowded in Casualty we'll see someone there. If it is, then we'll wait till morning and go and see Dr Patel."

Jack and Florrie looked relieved, they had evidently done the right thing. Belinda scooped up Judith and they departed for the local hospital.

Unfortunately, when they got there they found that the A & E Department was heaving with rival football supporters who had been continuing the afternoon's battle, a local derby, with enthusiasm outside the ground after the match with any weapon that came to hand. The waiting time was announced to be five hours, and even as they hesitated, the neon sign changed to six hours.

"Come on, we'll see Dr Patel in the morning," said Belinda, again forgetting that her daughter could not hear her. She pointed to the neon sign and indicated the door. Judith nodded with some relief; she found all the bustle unnerving when it was completely silent. She also found she felt very dizzy now and then, which was equally alarming. She wondered why that was. Mother and daughter returned to the car park and arrived home, both feeling slightly shaken.

On the Monday, by dint of some anguished pleading by Belinda to a not-very-interested receptionist (they discovered later that she was under notice to leave because of her dismissive attitude to patients; at the time it nearly caused Belinda to despair), they were able to see Dr Patel at his evening surgery. By this time Judith was becoming more and more frightened as her hearing showed no signs of returning. Her mother, too, not the most stable character at the best of times, was becoming frantic. She began to blame herself for leaving Judith in the first place, though in fact, Judith had been perfectly safe, and her mother's presence would probably have made no difference to the outcome. Belinda, in her anxiety, also forgot how important it had been that she attended the meeting that had taken her away. Altogether, it was a very frightened pair that eventually sat in Dr Patel's surgery.

"Now, what can we do for you," the doctor said cosily, as he observed the pallor of the two sitting before him, and felt the tension coming off them in waves.

"My daughter has completely lost her hearing," said Belinda, baldly.

"When did this happen?" the doctor asked, reaching for what Judith mentally dubbed his ear light. She was to see many of these in the following weeks.

Meanwhile, she looked blankly at her mother. Belinda came to her rescue. "She woke up yesterday morning completely deaf. She had been fine the night before."

"Did she have a fall, an accident, the day before?"

"Not as far as I know," said Belinda. "I wasn't there, she was in the care of neighbours." She carefully did not say that Jack and Florrie were in the next house. "I'll ask her." She scribbled swiftly on the little pad that had already become almost part of her.

Judith looked up. "I did have a little slip in my bedroom," she said, "but I wasn't hurt, not even bruised."

"Ah," said the doctor. He leant forward and studied the side of Judith's head where she had knocked it on the dressing table with care. "As you say, not even a bruise." Then he spent a long time peering into Judith's ears. Eventually he sat back. "I am going to send you to see a specialist immediately," he said. "It is vital, in cases of sudden deafness like this that the patient is seen as soon as possible." *I just hope it's not already too late*, he added to himself. *Why is it that some people come to the doctor for the least little thing and others don't come near when it is really serious?* He shook his head over the vagaries of human kind. He was of a philosophical turn of mind.

Belinda called him down to earth. "Do you mean she should have been seen on Saturday?" she demanded.

"I'm afraid that it would have been better." Dr Patel was sympathetic. "We must now make up for lost time." He reached for the phone. Twenty minutes later, a dazed Belinda and a totally bewildered Judith were en route to the hospital.

Then followed a harrowing period, for Judith and her mother, of endless tests, none of which, or so it seemed to them, were getting them anywhere. Belinda was again reproached for not taking Judith to seek medical help sooner until she was ready to scream with mingled guilt and frustration. She succeeded finally in having a blazing row with Jack and Florrie on the subject, then burst into tears and apologised profusely.

"I'm really sorry," she sniffed. "I'm taking my guilt out on you. But it's the way they *look* at me in the hospital, as if I was the worst mother on record." There was another burst of tears.

"Yes, we do understand," said Florrie, patting her soothingly. "We feel guilty too." So it was patched up, but it left a coolness between them which lasted a long time.

Eventually, on the completion of the tests, the specialist saw them. "It's not good news," he said. Judith looked at him blankly. "The short answer is that we don't know what has caused this sudden hearing loss so we cannot cure it."

Belinda drew her breath in sharply. "So this is permanent?"

"I'm afraid so. Something has damaged the pathway of messages from the ear to the brain. It is unusual that both ears are affected, but we can find nothing else, no infection, nothing. It is possible that the knock on the head that your daughter suffered triggered something, even though it was such a minor injury. As I say, we cannot be sure.

"All is not completely lost, though," he continued in a heartening tone. "Science is progressing all the time, and perhaps, in due course –"

Judith interrupted him. She hated the way her mother and the doctor were carrying on as though she was an imbecile, or as though she wasn't there at all. "Will someone please tell me what is going on?" she said crossly. "It is my hearing, or lack of it that is under discussion. And why do I keep having dizzy fits?"

The doctor smiled apologetically. He drew a piece of paper towards him and began drawing diagrams and writing what he had said to her mother. "About your dizziness," he said, drawing busily but also speaking so that Belinda could understand. "It's concerned with the semicircular canals in your middle ear," he drew them. "They contain fluid that helps you to balance. Just now the fluid doesn't know where it is going, but it will settle. That is why dancers, when they are spinning, focus on a spot and flick their head quickly. It fools the fluid in the canals so it doesn't know they're turning."

"Thank you," said Judith politely. She was quite clear in her own mind how things stood. She stood up. "If this is how it is to be then I must start learning to live with it," she said with an assurance she was far from feeling. "Thank you for your explanations. Goodbye." And she marched out of the room, leaving the specialist staring after her in some amazement.

The next few years proved to be very hard for Judith. Her mother, still blaming herself for what she looked upon as "the accident", would hardly let her daughter out of her sight. In vain Judith told her mother, as the doctors had told her, that often it was impossible to pinpoint a cause for sudden hearing loss, and that she, Judith, must learn to be independent. What she didn't realise, fortunately, was that her mother, equating deafness with dumbness and stupidity, was struggling to realise that her daughter's disability did not affect her brain, and that she was still the bright, intelligent girl she had been before her hearing loss. Part of her realised that this was just ignorant prejudice, but she still could not entirely rid herself of it, and allow Judith to develop as she should.

Eventually, Judith fought, and won, a battle to attend classes in lip-reading and sign language. She became adept in lip-reading, though the concentration required was often incredibly exhausting. She became so proficient, though, that strangers often did not realise she was deaf; it became a matter of pride to conceal it.

When she finally mastered signing she was amazed at the sense of freedom that it brought her. It required less concentration than lip-reading, and she found she was automatically speaking and signing at the same time. She wished she could persuade her mother to learn it, and although Judith enjoyed the classes, and especially meeting up with other people with hearing problems, any socialising outside the classroom was forbidden by her mother. She never realised, fortunately, how much Belinda's prejudice was the reason for this.

Gradually she found that her other senses became sharper in

compensation for the lack of hearing; she found she was relying on her eyes, and learning to evaluate what she saw more accurately. Fortunately her sight had always been good; she felt that had that been a problem as well she might indeed have given up and acquiesced in what she called the no-life to which her mother seemed determined to condemn her.

She did manage to complete school and take her exams, even Belinda grudgingly admitted that she had to have her education. But as soon as the exams were over Judith was whisked off out of school and, she felt, virtually put under house arrest. Unfortunately, Belinda had a well-paid job so Judith didn't even have the excuse of needing to work to make ends meet in the household. She became more and more withdrawn into herself as time went on. The only person she could speak to about this was Florrie, and then only when her mother was safely at work. The coolness that had arisen over the start of Judith's deafness had never really gone away. In desperation Judith put all her energies into keeping the house like a new pin and cooking imaginative meals, though even here her mother insisted on accompanying her on shopping trips.

"I'm not a cripple, or an idiot," Judith would say despairingly.

"No, dear," her mother would say. "But you do have a – problem and it is up to me as your Mother" (palpable capital M here) "to keep you Safe."

At last, when poor Judith was in her thirties, and had almost despaired of ever being free, fate stepped in and came to her rescue. A notice went up in her local library calling for volunteers to help out with a view, if they wished, to go on and take their librarian exams. And, at the bottom, joy of joys, "This opportunity is particularly suitable for people with disabilities."

On reading this, Judith astonished everyone within earshot by giving a wild whoop. She went immediately to the desk to enrol; surely even her overprotective mother would agree to this? Though, in truth, Judith felt she hardly cared. The girl on the desk, who knew her well from Judith's regular visits over the years, and who had started to learn to sign with her, was almost as excited as she was.

"As soon as this came out I thought of you," she told Judith, "given as how you practically live here." Judith was a voracious reader, it was one of the few things she was allowed to do.

The forms were filled in, handed over, then Judith went home to await the outcome, though her librarian friend thought it would probably be a formality. "I'll speak for you," she said earnestly. "I think you'd be a natural at the job."

Judith planned her campaign with care. She invited Jack and Florrie for Sunday lunch, feeling, rightly, that she needed some back up. She primed Florrie privately; Florrie, as she had expected, was thrilled by the idea.

"It's right up your street," she said. "Tailor made, in fact. And it's more than time you had some independence. We'll back you to the hilt."

Accordingly, having made sure that everybody was feeling exceptionally well fed, and having made a point of joining in the conversation with great vigour and vivacity, Judith dropped her bombshell.

"I've signed up for a job at the library," she said, without preamble.

Florrie jumped in first. "What a marvellous idea," she enthused. "Just what you need, Judith."

Belinda interrupted. "What utter nonsense," she said, predictably. "Of course you can't do it. There's no question –"

"Why not, mum?" Judith interrupted quietly. "Just why am I unable to do it? I'm intelligent. I can lip-read so that people often don't realise I'm deaf. The job is specifically aimed at people with disabilities anyway. I really don't see your point."

"You've never been able to do anything since your – accident," said her mother mulishly.

With a huge effort Judith restrained herself from saying, "And whose fault's that?" Instead, she managed to stay calm and reasonable. She could feel Florrie nearly bursting to say it in her place and managed to kick her under the table. When she had subsided Judith went on: "I'm convinced that I am able to do this, that I want to do this, and that I should do this. Assuming that I'm accepted, of course."

A look of hope crossed her mother's face. "Of course," she said. "They may not take you on. Things can stay as they are, and a very good thing too."

"No," said Judith, firmly. "If I can't do this then I'll find something else. I can't stand this no-life any more." She rose and took sanctuary in the kitchen, feeling rather guilty at leaving her friends to bear the brunt of her mother's complaints. But she didn't trust herself to keep calm much longer.

As expected, Judith was taken on at the library, took and passed her exams with flying colours. She felt a different person, and even her mother admitted, albeit grudgingly, that the idea seemed to be a success.

After three more years Judith felt ready and able to take the final step to freedom. A post came up at the main library at Heathfield. Again saying nothing to her mother, Judith applied for the post, got it, then immediately put in for a flat at Tower Court, which had been recommended by the library personnel officer. Then she told her mother of her decision.

Predictably, her mother flew into a rage. "I've been expecting this," she stormed, "you ungrateful brat."

"I hoped you'd wish me well," said Judith, sadly. "After all, it's high time I was independent, and you should have your own life too," she pointed out.

"Well, of course I wish you well, you should know that." Her mother hugged her, unexpectedly calming down. "I only want you to be happy – and safe. But I don't think you should go," she added, with sudden petulance. "And you are very ungrateful. All I've done for you, given up for you." Her mouth twisted in self pity.

Judith sighed and set herself, not for the first time, to sooth her mother's ruffled feathers.

As Judith stood in the middle of the flat, remembering, a shaft of sunlight broke through the clouds and made a golden pathway across the dusty floor. Judith grinned, clearly it was an omen.

***

A couple of weeks later, when both new tenants were safely settled in their new homes, we had a drama on the top floor. Going on my rounds one morning I saw what seemed to be smoke coming from flat 57 – which was supposed to be empty. I watched for awhile, and sniffed. I could smell nothing and I could not be absolutely sure about the smoke. I resolved to check on a few more floors as usual and return.

On my second visit the smoke was undoubtedly thicker and I could smell something, though I wasn't sure what. I decided that discretion was the better part of valour and called the fire brigade. I went down to do this and alert Security – Fred this time – and returned to the top floor to warn the tenants. The smoke was definitely thicker now.

I knocked on flat 59 first, next door to the suspect smoke. Joan Stephenson opened the door; she was elderly and, I thought, not very strong. I was concerned about her.

"I don't want to alarm you," I said, "but flat 57 next to you appears to be on fire. I've called the fire brigade but I felt you should know."

She did indeed look alarmed. "Thank you," she said. "What do you think I should do?"

"Probably nothing at the moment," I reassured her. "I'm just going to warn the others."

I knocked on the doors of flats 58 and 60 at the same time. Vivienne answered first; poor girl, she'd only been in five minutes. I wondered what the domineering father would say about this. "There seems to be a fire in flat 57," I said. "I wanted to warn you."

She looked taken aback, as well she might. "Th – thank you," she said faintly.

Flat 58 came to life in the shape of John Giles. I could see his wife, Laura, peering at me from behind him. I said my piece again. "Thank you, but I don't suppose it will concern us." And the door was firmly shut.

Slightly shaken, I turned to the others, apparently hanging on to my every word. But before I could speak two huge fire officers emerged from the lift, closely followed by three more from the stairs. Dead on cue there was an explosion from the fiery flat, which blew the front door down.

"All of you, downstairs *now*." The fire officer was not going to take any argument. I stayed long enough to tell him that flat 58 was occupied and was only too glad to follow the other two down the stairs. I decidedly did not feel that supervising the aftermath of an explosion was in my job description. I invited Vivienne and Joan into my flat until we knew what was going to happen. Then, even though I had felt snubbed by that firmly shut door I added John and

Laura, who had now joined us, to the invitation. I just hoped Joan would make it but she was obviously not as frail as she looked and seemed to be enjoying the excitement.

"Well, this does make a change I must say," she said, safely arrived at my flat and ensconced in a chair. "What lovely cats. What are their names?" Sophie and Rudi had retired to the kitchen where they were regarding the invasion with disapproval. "How different this flat looks, so low down."

I asked them if they had seen anybody going in or out of flat 57; "I had it down as a void."

Joan agreed. "It was supposed to be empty, but though I never saw anyone I often heard people going in and out."

"Yes, indeed." Vivienne astonished me by speaking, she had the most delightful accent. "I, too, have heard but not seen. It is most strange, is it not? That we should hear but see nothing?"

At this point John and Laura got up hastily and said they must be going. I couldn't help wondering if they were avoiding the sight and sound issue. "We will go to friends," John said when I asked them what they intended to do. "Now we must go and see what is happening." And they hurried out.

"Tea or coffee?" I offered hospitably, remembering my duties as hostess but wondering how long my guests would have to stay. Joan visibly relaxed and settled down for a good gossip. "I'm sure they're up to something, those two, and probably something to do with that flat. They never speak, are always in a hurry, don't even pass the time of day if we meet in the lift. What do you think, dear?" To Vivienne.

"Oh, I agree. They are very unfriendly" (I remembered the door shut in my face) "and, I think, sly."

It was an hour later before a fire officer knocked at my door.

"The fire is under control," he said reassuringly, "but it's not out yet. I think flat 60 can go back but we would like flat 59 to wait. Will that be alright?"

I retired inside to confer with my guests. "Vivienne, you can go back to your flat," I told her. She looked relieved. "Thank you, I will go up at once." She disappeared, presumably back up to her flat.

I turned to Joan. "They want you to stay out of your flat for now," I told her. "Have you, perhaps, friends or relatives you could go to?"

She thought. "Yes, I think my sister might oblige. We don't get on that well but this is an emergency." She got up. "I'll go back to the flat, if they'll let me, and I'll do some phoning."

Authority, in the shape of the fire officer, was still waiting patiently on the landing. He agreed that Joan could go to her flat to phone, "but please be as quick as you can," he urged.

We all departed to the top floor, via the foyer where we took the even floor lift. The firemen had taken the precaution of immobilising the odd lift. For good? I wondered hopefully, seeing the replacement lifts coming a stage nearer.

Arrived on the 15th floor the fire officer took me aside. "We've called the police," he said, "things don't seem quite right here. Didn't you say this was an empty flat?"

I agreed that I had, when I rang them.

"Well, something started that fire and the flat seems to be furnished, not much but liveable in. We will have to investigate the cause of the fire of course but the police could well be interested, and your Office certainly will be."

"Yes, I can see that," I said. "I'll call the Office right away." And did so, as soon as I was back downstairs, incredibly reaching Roger first go. "Hello, Roger," I said breezily. "We have a fire here. It's under control, the firemen are still here but there is a lot of damage, I think." The fireman, who had accompanied me, nodded. "But it's in flat 57 which is supposed to be void."

"Good heavens, yes... I'll be right over."

"He's on his way," I informed the officer, laconically.

Back upstairs, however, things were not to be resolved so easily. Joan came from the phone to say that her sister could – or would - not take her. At the same moment the senior fire officer came up the stairs.

"No, no one can stay here for the moment," he said firmly. "It's just not safe enough. And I want to evacuate the 14th floor, too."

At this I felt like adding myself to the evacuation list but I remembered that Lottie was on the 14th floor in flat 55 and could hardly be left to fend for herself. I sent Joan down to my flat and promised to come to her as soon as I could; I felt really concerned about her, since speaking to her sister she seemed to have aged ten years and looked as though the hospital would be the best place for her. She went off down the stairs with a fire officer, who obviously shared my concern, to escort her.

I went down to the 14th floor and knocked on Lottie's door. I told her that the fire service wanted to evacuate the tenants on her floor.

"Yes, dear," she said, quite unworried. "He told me. I shall have to go to Susan now, won't I?" She grinned ruefully. "But I'll not stay any longer than I have to."

I asked her about the other tenants.

"Ivor in No 53 is away, on tour I think. He always tells me when he's to be away so I can watch out for the flat. He sings with Opera North. Millie in No 54, she's a nurse so may or may not be in, depending on her shift. Margaret in 56 is a teacher." She looked at her watch. "She should be back soon. But do you have to deal with all this? It seems a lot for you to do." I heartily agreed, and mentally cursed Roger who should have been in long ago to take on some of the responsibility. Ah well. If you want a job doing properly do it yourself. I departed to try and speak to the others, feeling very grateful for Lottie's encyclopaedic local knowledge.

In the end it could have been worse. Ivor Welsh – which came first, his name or his singing? - was indeed absent but Millie was in, enjoying a day off, which I promptly ruined, and Margaret came in as I was explaining it all to Millie. They both seemed completely unfazed by it all and both had places they could go. I left them to it and went down to settle Joan's immediate future.

I arrived at my front door at the same time as Roger, who had at last come to give me some much-needed support. Rapidly I brought him up to date and he went on upstairs to inspect for himself. I wished him luck.

No sooner had he gone than Millie arrived. "Am I right in thinking that there is an elderly lady on the top floor, Joan someone?" I agreed that there was, also that I was very worried about her. "She's at my flat at the moment," I said.

"May I see her? Perhaps we could get her into hospital, then Social Services can take over if she can't go back to her flat."

With a surge of relief I took her in. We found Joan looking very poorly, so Millie immediately rang for an ambulance. "She'll be far better off in hospital," Millie reassured me as we waited. By now Joan hardly seemed to be aware of what was happening round her.

"Thank you so much," I said as the ambulance departed. "I was beginning to feel a bit overwhelmed."

"All part of the job," said Millie cheerfully and went away to continue her interrupted day off.

Whatever next? I shook my head. Who would have thought that looking after sixty flats would be so eventful?

– Chapter Six –

Jimbo Preston sat in what he referred to as "my pad", flat 9. He had assembled enough pieces of furniture, mainly second hand, to make it moderately comfortable, but he was bored and disillusioned. "Where *is* that little runt?" he asked himself. "I've been here a month and I've not seen hide nor hair."

He had no idea that he had actually shared the lift with his quarry, Ron. He did not for one moment realise that the tall, lanky man, obviously full of self-confidence, was the undersized child he had bullied so viciously so long ago. Ron had made a growth spurt in his teens, so he was far from undersized, and his life with Julian and the success of his chosen career had given him the confidence that had completely fooled the somewhat unimaginative Jimbo. And, in fact, Ron had avoided the lift as far as possible since meeting his old adversary, so Jimbo had not met him again and, indeed, had almost forgotten the entire incident.

It had been an amazing stroke of luck that Jimbo had ever discovered where Ron was currently living. On leaving the children's home he had had a rather chequered career, including several stays in institutions at the pleasure of Her Majesty. It was during one of these enforced visits that Jimbo had met up with another inmate of the children's home, "Fingers" Billy by name, who had taken one look at him and burst into fits of laughter.

"Young Ron certainly did it for you," he crowed, leaving Jimbo with no option but to remonstrate with extreme force about this tactless reference.

When this little episode had been sorted, and Jimbo came out of solitary they had become quite friendly.

"Did you know that Ron was actually adopted?" Billy asked cautiously when an amicable truce had been agreed. Once Jimbo had established that he was not one to be disrespected he was perfectly amenable to social chat.

"No, I didn't," he said in answer to this question. "Who on earth would want *him*? And wasn't he a bit old?"

Billy shrugged. "Word was that the bloke didn't really care who he had, just wanted a kid. Dunno what happened next." And he dropped out of Jimbo's interest.

The next snippet of information came when he was sitting in Casualty waiting to have a knife gash, collected during a happy little fracas the night before, stitched. He overheard two of the staff talking about a road accident that had just come in. As he listened avidly to their descriptions of the injuries he gradually realised that one of the trio involved was none other than the hated Ron. He couldn't believe it, "coincidence or what," he said dazedly to himself. Clearly it was meant that their paths should cross once more. Unfortunately he was unable to go up to the ward to confirm the identity as at that moment, when he had decided to go up, two police officers indicated, not kindly, that they required his attendance with them. That had led to another, rather more lengthy sojourn at Her Majesty's pleasure, as his retaliation over the knife wound was deemed to be well beyond reasonable force. Pity the fool had died, but there you were. These things happened. And at least it was brought in as manslaughter.

The last piece of the puzzle fell into place when he met Ron and Julian's erstwhile landlady, who was bemoaning the fact that two such good tenants had left her. "Ever so good, they were," she said sadly. "Never no trouble and always paid on the nail. Ron had been with me years." After the other coincidences, Jimbo was hardly surprised at all to discover that his enemy had moved to Tower Court, and that he, Jimbo, had no difficulty in renting a flat there for himself. But now the trail had grown cold, just when it seemed that success was within his grasp.

Thoroughly fed up, Jimbo wandered crossly over to the window. Then, to his delight, he realised that while he had been sunk in reflection, two fire engines had arrived in the car park and were disgorging their officers.

"That's more like it," he thought. There was nothing he liked more than watching a disaster, unless it was making it happen. After watching for a while he let himself out of his third floor flat. By dint of going up the stairs and peeping into each landing as he reached it he soon discovered that there was indeed a fire on the top floor. Unfortunately for him, though, he was immediately spotted by a particularly large fire fighter and told in no uncertain terms to vacate the landing forthwith. Not that there seemed to be much happening, anyway.

By now thoroughly fed up at the way life was treating him Jimbo grumped his way back down to his flat.

***

The next day, after all the riot and rumpus on the top floor, I had a semi-official visit from Robin Lutterworth. In other words he was in uniform and investigating upstairs, but could also do with sustenance in the shape of coffee. Apparently I make it "just as he likes it," Delighted I'm sure, but as I liked him, and he didn't mind answering questions, he was most welcome.

He admitted that they had taken advantage of the turmoil to have a good look in John and Laura Giles' flat. "We have had our eye on them for months without having any excuse to do anything. We were pretty sure that they were involved with drugs but in a fairly minor capacity. We have been proved right in this but we really want the person, or people, behind them and there is no sign of that in the flat, they have been very careful. Far too careful from our point of view."

No wonder they wanted to get away when we began an awkward discussion. "Do you know where they have gone now?" I wanted to know.

"We have a pretty good idea but will wait for them to come back here before we pick them up. They will have to come back, there is too much in the flat for them just to cut and run. We will have someone waiting in the burned-out flat. Pity it takes so long for an iron door to be fitted." He grinned.

"What about that flat. Were they responsible for the fire?" I asked.

"Almost certainly, though perhaps it was accidental. We think they put their own lock on the door and used it either for confederates to live in for short periods, or for storage, or for dealing, though that seems unlikely. Dealing premises always entail a lot of mess and you would have noticed. And passed the information on, I hope. You are in many ways our eyes and ears here as you know, and many thanks for it."

"Not that I've seen much as yet but I'll keep looking." I had a sudden thought. "I quite forgot. Did Vivienne in flat 60 find somewhere to go alright? She had been told she could go back to her flat just before the evacuation and I quite forgot, in the worry over Joan, to check that she was OK."

"That's hardly your responsibility, I would have thought?"

"No, but she is foreign, French I think, very young, and in a strange country."

"Well, we've not seen anything of her and her flat is empty, we have been given access to all the flats on the top floor – but you don't know that. Needless to say, everything we have discussed is strictly confidential. Don't even tell the cats." Hearing this, both cats, who had decided he was definitely persona grata (perhaps the treats he brought with him had something to do with it) simultaneously woke up and glared at him "Sorry, chaps. Just don't talk, that's all." He got up. "Keep on looking out for those car registrations, would you? I have a feeling all this might stir something up." And he returned upstairs, presumably to organise the watch from the burnt-out flat. Who would be a copper!

***

A week later we had an official welcome party at Ron and Julian's for Judith. Magda was back from one of her flying (literally) visits overseas, Germany this time, which she found pretty chilly. I couldn't believe it was nearly Christmas, I still fell as though I'd only just arrived. After an amazing meal from Ron (which I had come to expect) we settled down for a good gossip with glasses full of duty free wine, German this time, courtesy of Magda.

"Does this sort of get together happen often?" asked a slightly awestruck Judith.

"Depends on when we feel like it," Julian responded. "Full scale meals are not that common, unless Ron is trying out a recipe, but drop-ins certainly are."

"Sounds like a soup kitchen. Tell me, how did the Gressington trip go?" I asked him. It was a while since he had been but what with babies and fires I'd not seen him to speak to for some weeks.

"Just what I hoped for," Julian's face lit up like a candle. "And more to come, I hope. Look, these are my favourites." He vanished into the bedroom and returned with a folder. We all craned eagerly to see as he spread them out on the floor. "These I took of Ella Foster. She was dynamite in her youth and is superb in character parts now. Her Carabosse in *Sleeping Beauty* is quite terrifying, I've seen it." So had I, but I said nothing. "And this is her taking class. I'm really pleased with that one, and so was she. I'm definitely going back when they return from tour."

"I'm glad it went so well." I meant it. "You've worked so hard for it."

"Nonsense!" interrupted Ron grinning. "I'm the only one who does any work round here. And Frankie, of course. You merely point a camera and press the trigger and Magda just swans around on the continent picking up a sun tan." ("In Germany? In December?" Magda, *sotto voce*.) "What do you do to earn an honest crust, Judith? Or a dishonest one for that matter."

"I work in the library, cataloguing and ordering mainly, so my hearing is not a problem. I do work at the counter as well sometimes and if I can't lip-read people just have to lump it. Which they do, quite happily I might add. But this is the first time I've set out on my own to stand on my own two feet, and I was more than a little nervous about it, so thank you for making me so welcome."

We all shifted a little awkwardly as you do when praised for so little. Ron hastened to refill glasses and the talk became general. Mercifully no one asked about the fire; for once I was glad of the segregation between the floors, it saved me from having to be careful of what I said, even to these good friends.

***

As usual, we kept it up until the small hours and I had barely dropped off to sleep when I was woken by many footsteps overhead. Remembering official disapproval when I failed to investigate odd noises in the past I went to the window to peep out. I could also hear footsteps on the stairs but, strangely, no voices. Outside I could see a large group of people, also very quiet; being considerate at that time of night, or, more likely, hoping to remain unnoticed? There was also a car, and two mini buses. I fetched my number plate list and found that the car was on it, heavily underlined, and one of the mini buses. I promptly added the number of the other to my list. How thoughtful of them to park where I could see them. As I watched I saw the crowd begin to file into the buses, still in the same rather eerie silence. More came out of the block and entered the transport until the vehicles were full to bursting and I could hear nothing more overhead. At one point I saw a shadowy figure that I thought I recognised but I couldn't be sure and dismissed it from my mind.

Next morning I made a beeline for the second floor before I started my rounds but I found nothing untoward; perhaps a little more litter than usual, but nothing I would have remarked upon if I had not watched in the night. Leaving the rest of the round to do later I went to call Robin as instructed.

Surprisingly he was round that afternoon, accompanied by a woman. Still more surprisingly, neither was in uniform.

"I wear two hats, literally," he said, seeing my surprised face. "In visiting scenes like the fire last week I can often find out more officially, as it were. This is Jill Hammond who is working with me. If you can't get hold of me you should be able to speak to her. Now, tell me all about last night, in as much detail as you can remember."

Prompted by questions from both of them I went over all the events. I was surprised by how much I had noticed and remembered. Things I didn't think I had noticed at the time, under questioning became clear. For example, I had not realised at the time how the majority of the people were men, and all about the same age; between thirty and forty, I guessed. It still did not make much sense to me but it clearly did to them. I also said that there had been virtually nothing to show on the second floor in the morning.

"No, I wouldn't expect there to be. They would be very careful. If they, whoever 'they' are can keep a group of that size" - we had estimated that there must have been between twenty and thirty men involved, the buses were very overloaded - "then keeping the place clean would be easy. Who lives on that floor? Not that it will mean much, they'll be working under assumed names."

I went to fetch my list of tenants and we pored over it.

"I think we can rule out the Williams sisters," I said. "They are elderly and have been here for ever. Flat 5 is Stefan Klimek, a Polish refugee. He too is getting on a bit and I would imagine would not do anything to upset his status."

"Which is?"

"I don't know, his English is decidedly limited. But his flat is beautiful, full of the most wonderful embroideries. I think he said they had all been done by the ladies of his family but he became excited when he was telling me and consequently incoherent."

"That would not necessarily preclude him from illegal goings on," Jill pointed out, "but I see what you mean. What about the others?"

"Flat 7, the one directly overhead where I think the footsteps were, are Richard Johnson and Mary White. I think it was from there but sound travel is odd in a tower block and I could be wrong. They seem a bit standoffish when we meet so I don't know them at all. Nor do I know Nancy Roberts in flat 8."

"At least we have something to go on now." Robin got up, dislodging Rudi, who thought he was the best thing since sliced bread. "We've been waiting for something like this."

"Is there any connection between this and the top floor fire?" I asked.

"No, we don't think so. We could be wrong, it has been known, but at the moment they seem separate incidents. Thanks for the new number plate number. Keep on looking, you're a grand observer. I'll just pop upstairs and see if there is anything new there. If there is I'll be back, if not we'll be on our way. Good-bye, and many thanks."

"And thanks for the coffee. Best I ever tasted." I seemed to have hit the spot with Jill too, with my coffee making skills.

"Well now, whatever next?" I asked my resident felines, neither of which deigned to reply. They too had had a disturbed night. We settled down to catch up on some sleep.

***

One of my less agreeable tasks as caretaker was unblocking the rubbish chutes. These chutes, running the height of the building and emptying into the big bin at the bottom, in the bin room, were quite accommodating but prone to indigestion if asked to swallow anything they considered to be too large or too bulky. Carpet ends came into this category, as did cardboard; however you may fold and beat it into submission, in the chute it triumphantly unfolds itself and you have a blocked chute. That meant that the entrance to the offending part of the chute nearest to the obstruction had to be unscrewed (by me) and the article in question either pulled up into daylight or pushed down. If it goes well it is really quite rewarding, the rush of descending rubbish is, when you have finished coughing and sneezing, very satisfying.

This does not happen every day of course, but I did check the chutes daily as part of my rounds. If the rubbish is allowed to accumulate it is a major task to shift it. And the little rooms where the chutes live need to be checked regularly; I cannot understand why rubbish is placed beside the chute when it is just as easy to put it down it but there it is. It is left for me to deal with. Evidently I do it much better.

One day, the week before Christmas, I was doing my usual checks and had reached the 13th floor. Here I found the rubbish chute immobile, the first time for several weeks. I groaned, this could, if I was very unlucky, mean opening up all the chutes down to the first floor. I descended to my office to collect the special device necessary to open up the chute. On my return I unscrewed the sunken screws and hauled out the chute cover. Sure enough, cardboard. This came out easily and I prodded hopefully with the long rod kept for the purpose (heaven knew where it came from but it worked a treat). Nothing. It was not going to be that easy. I unpacked more assorted rubbish, wishing, as I did so, that people would wrap up their kitchen waste. The entire block appeared to have lived on spaghetti and onions recently. Then, joy of joys I unearthed a small suitcase and the rubbish shot triumphantly down. How on earth did anyone think that a case could be digested by the chute? But my troubles weren't over. A large bag of flour, it must have been full, shot down the now empty chute, hit the edge and burst, sending clouds of flour all over the chute room – and me. I looked like a rather unconventional snowman. Seething, and thinking highly uncharitable thoughts of the perpetrator, considering it was so near Christmas, I sneezed violently and departed downstairs to change before tackling the cleaning up of the chute room.

As luck would have it I met Ron arriving at the first floor via the stairs as I emerged from the lift. Bad move, he took one look at me and burst into fits of laughter. I glowered at him. "It's not funny A-a-a-*chooo*!" I sneezed indignantly.

"No, but you are!" he responded unkindly. "You should see

yourself!" Then he relented. "Go and change and I'll have a pot of special coffee ready for you."

I decided to be mollified and accepted this olive branch, retiring with what dignity I could muster to my own flat. The cats, unimpressed, removed themselves from my vicinity.

After a reviving cup of Ron's special coffee (I didn't ask what was in it on the grounds that I didn't want to know, just drank) I felt sufficiently restored to go up and clean up the 13th floor. This was the floor where the mysterious Bonzo Ray lived. He intrigued me because of his, to say the least, unusual greeting when I first started. I had hardly seen him since; when he did need to go through the foyer he seemed to move very fast and then slither through the lift door almost before it was open. Strange little man.

That afternoon I was on the 8th floor, replacing a defunct tube in one of the landing lights when I met another tenant whom I hardly knew. Not that he was retiring, far from it, Ronnie Jacobs in flat 31 was loud – voice and dress – breezy and very hail-fellow-well-met. I wondered what he did, I felt it must be something equally loud and cheery, a bookie perhaps? He was almost a caricature of one.

"And what do we have here, this fine afternoon?" was how he chose to address me as I perched on the steps, trying to persuade the new tube to accept its responsibilities gracefully. As he spoke it slipped neatly into place, to my relief, and I looked round to see where I had put the cover.

"This what you want?" asked Ronnie, handing it up to me. "Good job you're doing here. Absolutely first class. Enjoying it?"

"Yes, thank you," I replied sedately, fastening the cover over the tube. The light obediently blazed forth. I was supposed to switch it off before I started but I never did, I'd be up and down the steps like a yo-yo. Nor did anyone else, as far as I knew. "There, that should do it for a good while now. They do seem to last quite well."

"Yes, indeed," said Ronnie with great heartiness. "Well, toodle-oo. See you around." And he departed, leaving me feeling slightly dazed.

***

Once again, Jimbo was in his flat, bored out of his mind. Then the germ of an idea, that he had had when the fire engines turned up for the fire on the top floor, came to mind. He hadn't tried arson before but there was a first time for everything. Picking up a bag of rubbish that had been waiting to be put out for several days, he went out of his flat, whistling a merry tune, and looking so innocent that the dimmest of his associates would have known he was up to something, he went into the room housing the rubbish chute.

Opening the cover as wide as it would go he peered down. "What would happen if something burning, or, better still, something explosive, were to fall down there?" he wondered. He giggled to himself at the thought of the uproar he hoped it would cause. "And no one could pin it on me," he thought. Better still, it might conceivably dig Ron out from whatever hole he was occupying. "I don't care what would happen to me, if I can just give that squirt what's coming to him," he thought wistfully. "It would be worth doing a stretch for that."

He returned to his flat to think further.

***

"Ron," announced Julian, "It's nearly Christmas. Time for a get together."

"Yes, alright." Ron was entwined with Furball on the sofa. "When?"

"I will enquire" said Julian grandly and disappeared to issue invitations. Ten minutes later he was back. "Magda any time. Judith any time. Frankie out. But Frankie doesn't seem to go out much so it's probably any time for her too. What about this Saturday?"

"Fine by me. Just go away and leave us in peace. Or at least be quiet."

Accordingly, three days later the five inhabitants of the first floor were ensconced cosily in flat 1, plus all four cats (in a state of armed neutrality but otherwise friendly enough) and digesting the delectable nibbles provided by Ron. An atmosphere of warmth and comfort prevailed, very suitable with Christmas only days away. This was providing the subject of conversation.

"What are we all doing over Christmas?" Julian was asking. "Judith? What about you?"

"It sounds silly, but I haven't really thought. I'm not used to being able to make my own decisions, I suppose. My mother, surprisingly, hasn't been in touch, still sulking because I wanted to be independent, probably."

"Frankie, what about you?"

"Oh, staying put, definitely. I get overtime if I stay on duty over Christmas and New Year, and since I don't want to go anywhere anyway I may as well cash in."

"Magda, you'll be with us as usual, I hope?" Magda nodded. "Well then. I propose that we all join up for dinner on Christmas Day and leftovers on Boxing Day. Ron will be in his element doing some real cooking."

"Since we're all involved and it's our landing, what about setting up a table on the landing?" I suggested. "It might be a bit cramped for all of us in any of the flats. We can decorate, have all our doors open so it should be warm, and really spread ourselves."

"All those in favour? Then the motion is passed with acclimation. Jolly good idea, Frankie."

"What can we all supply?" asked Judith. "We can't let you and Ron shoulder it all."

"Ron and I will put our heads together and issue our orders. This is going to be the best Christmas ever."

The conversation became general as the plans were exhaustively discussed, with the more wild ideas (a steel band, Julian) being firmly rejected by all, on the grounds of noise (me, with horrific pictures of sheaves of complaints) and expense (Magda, always thrifty). We were drifting into warm drowsiness and thinking of going off to our separate flats when we became aware of a low muttering and general movement outside. I went to the window.

"What's going on?" Magda wanted to know.

"Not a lot, as far as I can see. Just a lot of men, about a dozen, I think, standing around and talking. They don't seem to be causing any trouble."

Julian joined me at the window. "They seem quiet enough. I wonder what it's all about?"

"I'll just go back to my flat and have a word with Security." And I, all caretaker, went off.

"It is a shame, she's never really off duty," said Judith.

"Chiefly because she does the job properly." Magda got up. "I'm off to my own abode, it's getting late – or early, depending on how you look at it. Good night you two, and thanks for the evening."

Judith climbed up out of the low chair she favoured above all others in the flat. She had noticed that everyone seemed to have his or her own seat at these gatherings. "I'm off too," she said. "Thanks for the evening, and for the Christmas idea. Good night." And Judith and Magda departed.

"You know, it is tough on Frankie. She does do a good job. Still, we should have a good time at Christmas. I like the idea of opening up the whole landing. It'll be fun."

"Uh-huh. I'm asleep. Let's go to bed. Furball's looking reproachful." Ron made a beeline for his bed.

***

Back in my own flat I had another look out of the window: the men were still there, standing around and talking quietly. I called down to Security; Pete Forest was on, I asked him what he made of it.

"Don't know. They're not being any trouble – yet. I'm logging it and will call the cops out if they make the slightest move but so far I'm not bothered. You go off to bed, you nasty little stop out. Don't worry, I'll keep watching and call you if necessary, which it won't be."

"Thanks. Good night." I made my way to my belated bed, mentally resolving to make my own report to Robin in the morning. This definitely came under the heading of something strange.

The next morning I went down to the Security Office. Sunday or no Sunday, I felt I needed to know how things had gone during the remainder of the night. Phil was starting his week's stint; I asked him if Pete had said anything about the night's activities and how it had all ended.

"Yes, he left a pretty full report, though nothing actually happened. It's all on film too. Apparently they hung around for a couple of hours then left quite quietly. Goodness knows what it was all about but there was no trouble."

"Good. It's odd though. I hope nothing comes out of it. Oh well, I'm off to put my feet up. Have fun." I returned to my flat to resume my interrupted Sunday.

On Monday though, I duly reported to Robin, who was in a

hurry but took note of it. "Let me know if anything else happens," he said. "It's just the sort of thing I had in mind, prior warning. Doesn't matter if it comes to nothing. Thanks."

More brownie points I thought as I prepared to dismiss the whole affair from my mind.

***

Jimbo peered cautiously out of his flat. The landing was empty, he could hear nothing from the other flats. Now was the time!

He had decided to wait awhile before putting his plan for a little excitement into action. He was still no nearer to finding the elusive Ron but hoped with the luck that had favoured him until now that this might literally smoke him out.

He had decided on a good, old-fashioned Molotov cocktail as being the cheapest and most effective method of starting a blaze and he had it now, clutched in his hand. He crept into the bin room, opened the chute. So far, so good. He listened a moment, then lit the cloth protruding from the bottle, threw it into the chute, slammed the cover shut and shot out of the bin room as though the furies were after him.

For a moment there was nothing, then a satisfying (to him) "*Boom!*" and the bin room door flew open. He could hear the other doors and chute covers banging in a most satisfactory way. Grinning, he decided that "he had been in the lift when he heard this enormous bang, and thought he would be safer on the ground floor."

He gave this rehearsed speech to Pete when he met him in the foyer.

"Probably right there," Pete was abstracted. He caught sight of the caretaker emerging from the stairs. "I've called the fire people," he added.

"Good," I said, shivering. I had been in bed when I heard the bang and my dressing gown was not really made for prancing about foyers in December. "It seems to be contained in the chute," I added, more in hope that anything else. Then I noticed our new tenant, well, new-ish, anyway. I now knew him to be James Preston. "Are you alright, Mr Preston?" I asked him.

"Er – yes thanks. How did you know my name?" he asked suspiciously.

"It's my job," I replied, rather impatiently. "I try to know the names of everyone who lives here. Wait, don't go that way." I grabbed his arm, as he seemed to be heading for the lift. "Use the stairs, it's safer."

"Oh. Yes. Thanks." He vanished through the stair door.

Back in his own flat Jimbo was ecstatic. At last he knew how to find out Ron's flat. It had been worth the trouble of a little arson.

In the foyer I was conferring with Pete. Can you watch out for the fire brigade," I asked him, "while I go and put some clothes on? It is *not* warm enough for this."

"No probs," he said magnanimously. "You'll need the bin room key," he called after me.

By the time I was down again, rather more suitably clad, the fire engines had arrived and the fire fighters were waiting impatiently for me to open up. As we trooped out to the back I looked up to see if there was any sign of fire damage. I thought I saw a face at a third floor window, but as soon as I saw it, it vanished. I thought no more about it.

"Not much bother here," a fire fighter said consolingly. "We'll just stick a hose in the bin, it seems to be contained in it anyway. Good thing it was so empty."

"Yes," I said. "I only changed them today – er – yesterday. Do you need me any more?" I asked hopefully.

"No, luv. You go back to bed. I'll leave the key with Security. Night night."

I was only too happy to leave them to it. Tomorrow – today – would do for sorting out.

But tomorrow brought more problems. As soon as I came on duty I went down to see what havoc the fire had caused. But, to my surprise, when I went to the Security Office to pick up the bin room door key it wasn't there.

"Not a sign of it," said Fred, quite chatty for once. As Phil had said right at the beginning, Fred had never approved of a woman caretaker. I think he quite liked me as a person but I was the wrong gender for my job. "We've not had a fire in the bin room before," he added reproachfully. Clearly it was my fault.

I went round to the bin room to see if there was anything to see but there was no problem about that; not only was the bin room door wide open, but a fire officer was still in attendance. *And*, she was a woman, so sucks to Fred, I thought unkindly.

"You the caretaker?" she asked. I nodded. "Well, this looks like arson. Look here." She held up a blackened object that seemed to have once been a bottle. "I'm pretty sure that when this is examined we will find that it contained an accelerant. It was fortunate that the bin was so empty," she added, "or we might have real trouble."

I shivered. "I only changed it yesterday," I said, "and I nearly left the other one for another day as it wasn't completely full."

"Good thing you didn't," she agreed. "Brownie points to you!"

I grinned at hearing one of my favourite phrases. "What happens now?" I asked.

"Probably nothing," she admitted. "The police have been informed so it's up to them. See you around," she dismissed me politely, and went back to ferreting through the remaining rubbish.

I went back to work with plenty to think about.

– Chapter Seven –

Christmas was indeed "the best ever", at least as far as I was concerned. Opening out the landing into a dining room worked like a charm. We thought we'd better go a bit easy on the decorations as it was, technically, a communal area; I was a little worried lest we should inadvertently fall foul of fire regulations. But we decided that a tree was in order, and found a beauty, which we all had great fun decorating, with much feline help, on Christmas Eve.

Being the Gang, Judith now being a valued member, we did it in style. As soon as I was off duty we met on the landing, with all the flat doors open. The tree was standing quietly in the only available corner, where it did not get in the way of the electricity cupboard, or the dry riser. This latter, I had discovered, was the pipe running the whole height of the building with a unit on each floor to which the fire brigade could fasten the hose in case of fire. I had learned this vital fact when I first moved in, and had seen it in action during the fire on the top floor. We also made sure that the route to the rubbish chute room was clear, on the grounds that we would probably be needing it a good deal over the next few days.

Julian appointed himself in overall command and soon had us running in and out of our flats bringing the decorations that we had been collecting for weeks. Magda, in particular, had some beautifully painted baubles that she had picked up on her European travels, and one of the most sumptuous angels I have ever seen to grace the top of the tree.

"One of the girls at the magazine office makes them," she explained, "and as soon as we had this idea I begged her to make us a special one. We can keep it for years." Obviously this was to be an annual event, not a one off.

The only one of us excused decorating duties was Ron, who locked himself in the kitchen and forbade anyone to go in, even Julian. At intervals he shot through into one of the other flats, as all our cookers had been roped into service. It didn't look as though we were going to starve this Christmas.

The only fly in the ointment as far as I was concerned was that there was no Midnight Service locally; although the area was improving, it seemed that it was not considered safe to be out and about late at night. I regretted it, I had managed to attend most years; perhaps next year, I comforted myself.

By nine o'clock we were done; the tree was decorated, the vegetables were prepared – Magda, Judith and I had taken a vegetable each and dealt with it in our own kitchens – and even Ron had emerged from his kitchen with a tray of assorted nibbles and, of course, mince pies.

"As this is such a very special occasion I feel we should celebrate in style," I said, as we settled in flat 1, in our usual armchairs. With something of a flourish I produced a bottle of champagne that had been cooling in the depths of my fridge.

"What a good idea," said Judith, producing a bottle of champagne from behind her back.

"Isn't it," said Magda, producing hers, amid shouts of laughter. In the end we had five bottles as Ron and Julian had had the same idea quite independently. The cats, who had all decided to settle with us in flat 1, clearly wished we would make less noise as Some of Us Want to Sleep.

We settled down to start Christmas off.

***

Not surprisingly, we were late foregathering on Christmas morning. We had decided to meet up, in dressing gowns, in Magda's flat for coffee and waking up time, then we all set to to decorate the dinner table. This consisted of trestles that I had found in my storeroom, goodness knows what they were doing there, and a door, which had been put out at the back with the bins. As I had been a bit concerned about the question of a table, I knew that none of us had one that was really big enough, I had pounced on this several weeks ago and secreted it in my office on the ground floor. It did very well when covered by a sheet for a tablecloth, though this could hardly be seen when all the table decorations and candles were in place. These again had been collected by us all, and hoarded.

At four o'clock, after the Queen's Speech, we sat in state, now festively dressed, and prepared to make short work of Ron's culinary delights. So we were not best pleased when the lift door opened and Jimbo Preston appeared.

"Yes?" I said coldly. "Can I help you?"

At that moment Magda, obviously wanting to make the point that this was our dinner, broke in. "Ron," she said, "is there any more of this sumptuous gravy?"

"Sure is," said Ron, getting to his feet and picking up the gravy boat. He departed for the kitchen.

"Can I help you?" I said again, even more coldly as our unwelcome visitor showed no sign of moving.

Jimbo recovered himself. "Is this a private party, or can anyone join in?" he asked, with heavy humour.

"Strictly private," said Julian, getting up and looking slightly menacing. "Open only to those of us living on this landing. And if you want Frankie, unless it's a matter of life and death that only she can resolve, she is just as entitled as the rest of us to enjoy her Christmas Day in peace. Good afternoon." And he stood glaring as the hapless Jimbo mumbled something apologetic and backed into the lift. We watched in relief as the door closed.

***

Inside the lift Jimbo allowed a smug smile to appear. His plan had worked perfectly. He had decided, coldly, that this could possibly be the best time finally to discover the whereabouts of the elusive Ron and he had succeeded beyond his wildest dreams. Though who would have thought that the skinny child would grow to be so tall? Still, Jimbo thought, he was perfectly capable of reducing him to mush. He would get him somewhere quiet and really take him apart. And that stuck-up caretaker, too; he'd show her if he got half a chance.

The lift stopped at the third floor and he went into his flat, dreaming happily of vengeance to come.

Julian stood glaring at the lift doors until he was quite sure that Jimbo Preston had gone. "Sorry, folks," he said. "I must go and make sure that Ron's alright. We'll explain when we come back." He vanished into flat1 after Ron.

"Disadvantage of living over the shop," I said apologetically. "Though I didn't expect any interruptions today, or not till much later anyway."

"Hardly your fault," said Magda crisply. "What on earth did he think he was doing?"

"Perhaps he was just lonely," suggested Judith tolerantly. "I suggest we eat up this marvellous food before it gets cold."

Before our laden plates were empty Ron and Julian were back. "Anyone for seconds?" asked Julian, hospitably. "No? Then I suggest we clear this lot away and have a pre-pudding break. Then we'll explain what all that was about."

Plates were cleared in record time and we settled back again at the table. "It's Ron's story, really," said Julian.

"When I was very small I was bought up in a children's home," said Ron, his face suddenly bleak at the memory. "It wasn't all that bad; looking back, I think they were very short of funds and did the best they could. It closed down soon after I left. Anyway, there was quite a lot of bullying, and the arch bullier was Jimbo Preston."

"What, him?" asked Judith, indicating the lift.

"The very same. I was pretty sure when we met him in the lift that time, Frankie. Now I'm positive. I was very small and weedy then, very silent and a prime target.

"My only friend in that place was the resident cat, Mouser. We were together most of the time, though Mouser usually took off up a tree when Jimbo was around. Then one day Jimbo caught him and killed him. I may have been undersized but I had a temper, though even I didn't realise what I could do. I snatched up a stone and smashed it into Jimbo's face. I gave him that scar," he added with simple pride. "And, now he's found me, I think he's looking for revenge."

"He looks like a thug," I said, dispassionately.

"I think he probably is one," agreed Julian. "But I also think that we are more than capable of dealing with him, if necessary."

"Well, that's the tale," said Ron, getting up. "Pudding everyone?"

But before he could fetch it the lift appeared again. I think we all froze as it stopped at our floor; surely not Jimbo again? But the door opened to reveal a woman who was a total stranger to all but one of us.

"*Mum!*" shrieked Judith, nearly setting the makeshift table flying as she leapt to her feet. But Mum put a hand up to stop her, then carefully, but apparently fluently, she started signing, grinning broadly as she did so.

Judith immediately started signing in reply, the rest of us were transfixed. Finally, I stood up. "Sorry to interrupt this conversation," I said. "I take it you're Judith's mother? How very nice you were able to join us. Do come in. Julian, can we rise to another chair? Ron, have we killed off that turkey stone dead, or will it rise to another portion?"

"Of course it can." Once again Ron vanished into the kitchen, Julian collected a chair and a clean glass, and in less time than it takes to tell Judith's mother was ensconced with food and drink before her, looking rather bemused.

"Sorry, everyone, this is, as you have realised, my mother," said Judith, rather belatedly. "This is the Gang," she went on, "Ron and Julian, Ron's done all the cooking, Frankie, the caretaker, and Magda. They have all been wonderful and made me so welcome."

"I am delighted to meet you all. I'm Belinda. I've been very remiss in not coming here sooner, but I've come to my senses now and today seemed a good time to come and make amends. I didn't expect to be fed though! It's delicious, Ron. Wait a minute, Ron? Not Ron *Peters?*"

Ron grinned. "The very same."

"No wonder this is so good. I've got all your books. They're so clear, I've not had a failure yet."

Ron blushed. "Thank you, I'm glad you like them. Just a minute." He vanished again and returned with a book in his hand, which he gave to Belinda. "Happy Christmas, hot off the press, it's not out till the New Year."

"Thank you, that's wonderful." Belinda showed every sign of becoming immersed. She was called to order by her daughter.

"Mum, when did you start signing? You always said you never would."

"I said a lot of very silly things," said Belinda, remorsefully, "as Florrie told me when I was complaining about you going. Both you and she gave me much food for thought. So here I am."

"And very welcome too," said Ron warmly. "*Now,* what about pudding?"

***

We kept it up, the open house as it were, until New Year and then, regretfully, returned to normal.

On the Monday after Christmas, when I did my rounds, I found that flat 51, belonging to the reclusive Bonzo Ray, had a crude barricade over it. It seemed a little strange but possibly the door was not secure and needed temporary reinforcement. I carried on.

By the end of the week the barricade had become a substantial wrought-iron gate. This I did feel needed an explanation, especially as the Office seemed to know nothing about it. Consequently I decided to report to Robin and/or Jill, especially as flat 51 was our old friend Bonzo. I spoke to Jill, Robin being unavailable.

"Could this, by any chance, tie in with the crowd on Sunday?" I suggested.

"I suppose it's possible. We've not heard anything on the grapevine. Or it could be that Bonzo has a guilty conscience; he may have diddled a heavy and the crowd made him nervous. We'll organise some extra night patrols, just in case."

"Thank you, I'd appreciate that. I suppose I'm a bit jumpy still since Amrita."

"Hardly surprising. Don't worry. We'll keep an eye on the situation."

Whether there were extra patrols or not I didn't know; all remained quiet at night. I continued doing my normal work about the block undisturbed; Bonzo, presumably, skulked in his flat. At any rate, I saw nothing of him.

***

However, the following week, in the New Year, again in the wee small hours, all hell broke loose.

It was about midnight, I was in bed, but not asleep, when I heard noises in the car park. On looking out I saw a crowd congregating, pouring in from the road as I watched. I recognised some faces from the other night but this crowd was bigger, noisier and clearly bent on trouble. Pete was on duty again and did his best to keep them out, but eventually, through sheer weight of numbers they broke both the main door and the stair doors open. They then proceeded to rampage into the building. I called my special number,

I discovered later that Pete had already dialled 999.

"Is Robin available?" I asked. "Or Jill?"

"No, but I can deal with anything. What's the problem?"

"I'm Frankie, from Tower Court -"

"Oh yes, we know all about you. What's happening?"

I explained about the crowd entry, and that I recognised some faces.

"We've been expecting something like this. Sit tight, we're on our way. I'm David Jones."

Relieved that we had protection (I hoped) I rang off. I was worried about Pete, I wasn't sure how secure his office was but when I rang him he reassured me.

"It's alright, they went straight past, obviously not interested in me. According to the camera they are on the 13th floor. Oh, they're having a go at that gate outside no 51. The whole landing is heaving. And they've jammed the lift door open. I expect there's a lot of noise, but, of course, I can't hear, only see. It's most odd. And here come the police. Blimey, it looks as though the entire local force is here."

Sure enough, when I went to my viewpoint over the car park, police, men and vehicles, were converging. Some went in through the broken down main door, presumably to the even side lift, some to the stairs. Even so, far below I could hear some noise if I listened at my front door. I had no intention of going out. It must be a nightmare for the tenants on that floor. I made a mental note to check up on them in the morning.

At last, from my vantage point I began to see groups of men in handcuffs, with a large police escort, coming out of the building and being loaded into the waiting vans. Finally, Bonzo came down, was inserted into a car and driven away on his own. They would have a busy night at the local nick. Struck with a thought I rang Pete.

"What's happening about the doors?" I asked him.

"Can't do anything till the morning" was his depressing, but not unexpected, reply. "I'll report it first thing, of course, but it's specialist so I don't know when they can repair them, or even make it all secure. But I'll keep a good watch and hopefully the local rag-tag won't find out for a bit." And with that somewhat negative response I had to be satisfied.

The next morning I went straight to the 13th floor. As I had feared it was in a right state, bits of wood, iron bars, bricks and broken bottles all over the place; weapons, I assumed. The new gate had been wrenched off and the door itself smashed in, I wondered whether by the storming army or by the police. A sheet of wood had been roughly nailed in place over the door, it didn't look very secure but I supposed would serve as a temporary measure. There was also plenty of what I took to be blood; I would have my hands full trying to clear this lot up. I would fetch bin bags and gloves, no point in putting it off. That I should leave it all until the police gave permission didn't occur to me; I just wanted the mess cleared up.

Behind me, the lift door opened and Jimbo Preston emerged. Really, the man had a genius for turning up when he was not wanted.

"What's been going on here?" he asked inquisitively. "Is it because of that riot last night? What is it with this place? It's just one thing after another." He smirked, self-righteously.

"It is certainly the result of what happened last night," I said repressively, "though I would hardly describe it as a riot. The police had it all under control very quickly."

"Yes." He seemed almost wistful. "Who lives in that flat? The one with the broken-in door? Did the police do that or the mob?"

"I have no idea," I said frostily. "And I am not supposed to give out tenant's names." Not to him, at any rate. I had a feeling that his bullying career was far from over. "And now, if you'll excuse me, I have to get all this cleared up."

"Alright, alright, I'm going." He departed via the stairs, and I heard "Stuck-up bitch" float back to me through the door. I felt I was meant to. I shrugged and went off for the bags and gloves; he was the least of my worries.

I had started bundling the debris into the bags when a quavering voice came from flat 50. I had checked my list before I came up so I knew this was Rosa Stewart, an elderly lady (we seemed to have quite a few in the block) and plainly scared half out of her wits.

"Wh – who's there? Stay where you are or I'll shoot."

I blinked, I'd not expected this response. True, or too much TV? I decided to be reassuring.

"It's only the caretaker, Frankie, clearing up after last night. Are you alright?" I shouted. This brought Charlie Wilkins in flat 49 to his door.

"Yes," he said. "What on earth was going on last night? I didn't dare come out, and I don't expect either of the others did either. It's alright, you two," he called out. It's Frankie, the caretaker. Come and look at all this."

The doors of flats 50 and 52 opened cautiously and the occupants peered out. Rosa, in flat 50, was chalk white and shaking visibly. I hurried to support her, she looked as though she might keel over at any minute. Fiona Bryony, in 52, a young student, looked less fragile but just as frightened.

"What on earth was it all about?" she asked. "I was asleep, the row woke me, and I didn't dare look out. I did try the spy hole in the door but there was too much going on. And the racket!" She shuddered.

Charlie decided to take charge. "Why don't we all go into yours and have a brew," he suggested to Rosa. "We'll leave Frankie here to get on with the clearing up" (thanks very much, I thought) "and we'll all feel better. I wouldn't be surprised if the police didn't want to see us so we'd better get our story straight!" On this cheering note they all disappeared into flat 50 and I carried on bundling everything into the bin bags. Belatedly I wondered if I should have left everything alone and resolved to keep them in my office, just in case, also to leave washing off the bloodstains. I hoped they would not delay long before coming to investigate. Bloodstains are not part of the usual decorative features of the block. Sure enough, a team appeared just as I was finishing. They looked startled by the number of bags but assured me that they did not need them, also that I could clean up what they confirmed was probably blood.

"The tenants are all in flat 50" I told them, "recovering from all the upset. I think they could do with some reassurance," I added pointedly.

"Of course, we'll see them just as soon as we've had a look in here," indicating flat 51. "By the time you've mopped up we should be ready and you can introduce us all," one, presumably the senior officer, said cosily. Thanks a bunch, I thought as I went off to fetch mop and bucket.

However, by the time I had mopped up he and his team were back. "What's it like in there?" I asked curiously.

"Nothing for you to worry about" ("my pretty little head

about?" I thought crossly) "Would you knock on flat 50 and introduce us, please." At least he said please, I reflected sourly as I did as I was told. I hoped Robin and Jill would contact me soon, they didn't treat me as a fluffy moron.

In no very good mood I went downstairs to inform the Office of the latest happenings in their tower block. Roger was out – of course – so I left a message to contact me if he wanted to know about the latest drama.

Fortunately, before I expired with curiosity, both Robin and Jill came round to "interview" me about it. Well, Jill did have her notebook at the ready but I don't think she wrote much. I confirmed that I had recognised several faces from the other night.

"We've got the CCTV tapes," Robin said, "and will have a happy time going through both of them. Your cameras are going to be updated as a priority as things seem to be moving. Phil's ecstatic, I've just told him."

"What was it all about?" I asked. "Do we know?"

"A bit, not everything by any means. As we suspected when Bonzo put up that gate it was because he had diddled a thief, but we are not sure who or how. We are keeping him in custody, as much for his own safety as anything and are charging him with receiving. He's not getting bail, ostensibly because he's done a runner in the past. But he's been arrested so we can search his flat. Want to come and have look? Though if any uniform turn up you must vanish. This is strictly on the Q.T."

I accepted with alacrity and we ascended to the den of iniquity.

As an Aladdin's cave it was a bit of a disappointment. There were certainly plenty of boxes lying around but otherwise it was dingy and not over clean. After a fairly cursory look I left them to it and went down to see if Roger was taking any interest in our affairs. He was not, so I waited in my flat to see if Robin and Jill needing reviving with my "special" coffee (not a patch on Ron's, I might add).

Shortly afterwards they came down, looking disappointed.

"Not nearly as much in there as I'd hoped," Robin admitted. "Quite a lot of stolen goods I think but that's not what I was after. I need information, and proof. Ah well. Better luck next time. We haven't finished interviewing yet and something may turn up."

Duly revived with coffee they departed, looking happier.

**

I was relaxing in my flat for a moment, trying to persuade Sophie and Rudi that it was *not* feeding time just because I was sitting down, when there came a knock at the door. It was so faint that I was uncertain if I had even heard it, but I went to check anyway.

I found June there, the younger of the two Williams sisters living in flat 6 on the second floor. To my concern she looked ghastly.

"Come in, come in," I said. "What is it? How can I help?"

"It's my sister," she said, almost in tears. "I don't know what to do. I think she's ill, she won't wake up."

My stomach lurched, I remembered how frail Mary seemed to be, and the uproar last night might have been the last straw for her. "Let's go and see," I said to June, propelling her gently out of the flat.

Arriving at flat 6, I allowed June to precede me into the hall. The flat was immaculate, it must have been hard for two such frail ladies to keep it so pristine. In a pretty bedroom, where every flat surface had its picture or ornament, Mary was lying in bed, very still. I went up to her and felt for a pulse under the angle of the jaw. To my relief, I found one, though it was faint, but she was clearly very ill.

"I think we should call for an ambulance, right away," I said. I didn't want to frighten June, but it looked urgent to me.

"Oh please, will you do it for me? I'm sure to get it wrong. Mary is the clever one." She was shaking like a leaf.

"Of course I will," I said soothingly. I settled her in a chair and looked round. "Where's the phone?" I asked her.

"Oh, we don't have one. Sister always said it was a needless expense. There was no one we needed to call when we could write letters."

"You sit tight here," I told her, "and I'll go back to my flat and phone from there. I left her, making sure that I didn't shut the door, I placed no dependence on her letting me in if I did. She seemed to be becoming more uncertain as she became more upset. I thought that

Mary had probably been her mainstay, if not actually her carer.

I dialled 999. I seemed to be doing this more than at any other time in my life. "There's an elderly lady who seems to be very ill, in flat 6 at Tower Court, There is a pulse, and she is breathing, but I don't think she's conscious."

"Any history of heart disease?"

"I've no idea. I'm the caretaker."

"They'll be with you right away. Can you meet them? It's the tower block, isn't it?"

"Yes, I'll wait downstairs and take them up to the flat." Relieved, I put the phone down and went to tell June help was on the way before going to the foyer to await said help.

The ambulance was commendably prompt and the crew were happy to take June along too. At first she clung to me and begged me to come with her.

"I'm afraid I can't," I said. "I'm supposed to be on duty. I'll ask the Office though, and if they agree I'll come straight after you. If not, I'll come as soon as I'm off duty. Where are you going?" I turned to the ambulance driver.

"The William and Mary," he said. This was the local hospital, though goodness knows how it got its name. "Go straight to A & E when you get there, they'll sort you out. All set behind?" And he drove away, siren blaring.

Filled with considerable anxiety I went back to my flat to call the Office. After quite a lot of argument I managed to persuade whoever I was speaking to that helping elderly tenants in hospital was as much part of my duties as scrubbing the stairs, and, in my view, more important. Victorious, I departed to drive to the William and Mary

***

When I finally found June after the usual hospital hassle of finding somewhere to park, she looked as though she was as much in need of medical care as her sister. Mary was still unconscious, June told me they were waiting for a bed. At that moment a doctor came in, looking worried. I introduced myself, "I'm the caretaker of the block where they live."

"Not usually one of your duties, I'd have thought? Looking

after old ladies in hospital?"

"No," I admitted, "but June begged me to come and I managed to persuade the powers that be that it was one of my duties. Chiefly to shut me up, I think," I grinned.

"Good for you." He drew me to one side. "The elder one is very ill, she might not make it. The sister said something about trouble at the block last night?"

"There was a spot of bother," I admitted, "though they were not involved, but I can see how it could have alarmed them. Mary has always struck me as being very frail."

"She is. Advanced heart disease I think, and the younger is fragile. I'm relieved you're here, to be honest. Ah, do we have a bed at last?" as a nurse came hurrying in with a porter.

"We do, and in cardiac."

"Off you go, then." He shooed us all away with some relief.

***

We stayed at the hospital long enough to see Mary settled, then I persuaded June to come back with me to her flat. Before I left I had a word with the ward sister, telling her that June had no phone and that she should ring me if necessary. We carefully skated round what the necessity might be.

Sadly, it was necessary. At 3am I had the call and was able to bring June so she could be with her sister, who died without regaining consciousness. June collapsed completely when the realisation hit her and she, too, was admitted. Sadly I returned home, promising to come back the next day with things for June, "but not until I'm off duty," I warned her. "I don't think the Office would wear it again."

– Chapter Eight –

As if there wasn't enough going on, the time I had been dreading, the trial for Amrita's murder, was upon us. It had all gone through quite quickly, as these things go, as Haidar and Jahnu had been caught almost at once. I wondered whether I should try to see Amma and Chandra; I'd seen them about but they seemed mainly to want to avoid me. I decided not to try and force anything.

So here it was, the day I had to appear for the prosecution in the case of R v Dalal, at Arkchester Crown Court. To say that I was nervous was an understatement; I was petrified. I had no idea what to expect. I wasn't at all knowledgeable about court procedure, and this was Crown Court as it was such a serious charge. That, in itself, was intimidating. All I knew came from TV, so would I be bullied? Would Counsel be wandering about the court waiting to pounce on me, or was that only in America? So many unknowns, plus presumably meeting Amma and Chandra again. No escape this time for either of us.

Of course, it wasn't as bad as I'd expected, it seldom is. I duly arrived at court and was whisked away to join other witnesses, including Amma and Chandra, as I had expected. We were given the chance to see the court, which was a big help; at least I knew in advance where everyone would be. The Judge was in the middle, high up on the Bench, with the Clerk of the Court in front of him (or her?) and the court stenographer, with a very strange looking machine and a large tape deck, to one side. The dock was at the back, very big, and approached by a stair inside. The jury box was on the right, and other benches on the left were for the press, CPS (Crown Prosecution Service), probation officers etc. (By the time all this had been explained I was feeling slightly dazed, but doubtless all would become clear.) The rows in the middle were for the lawyers: prosecution on the left, defence on the right, with their solicitors behind them. I found it all very awe-inspiring, especially with the Royal Crest on the wall behind the judge. But then, I suppose it's meant to be. And it is only in America where everyone wanders about and shouts; I asked.

After seeing the court all the witnesses were herded back to the witness room to wait. And wait. Then we could go to lunch, then back to the witness room to wait again. Why so much hanging about? I wondered. It was not surprising that trials took so long.

At last, the prosecuting barrister, Mr Davies, came in to tell us that Haidar had changed his plea to guilty, and the judge had called for psychological reports before sentence. Jahnu, on the other hand was still pleading not guilty, so could we come back tomorrow morning. Two of the witnesses who were to appear in the case against Haidar were allowed to go home for good. I envied them.

***

Amma, Chandra and I went home separately. They were, I thought, staying with relatives, which was easier for all of us than dodging about in the tower block. It must have been awful for Chandra that her uncle pleaded guilty, though a relief, too, in some ways. So I was back home, with very little resolved, or so it seemed to me.

Phil pounced on me as soon as I was in the foyer. He knew where I had been, he seemed to know everything that went on in the block.

"How did it go?" he asked. "As bad as you expected or not? Were Amma and Chandra there?"

"Yes, of course they were there," I said, "but really, very little happened. We did an awful lot of waiting around, then Haidar pleaded guilty and we were allowed home for the day."

"I'm not surprised he pleaded guilty, he could hardly not," was Phil's opinion. "Everybody saw what he did. And what about what's-his-name, the son? Do you have to go back tomorrow?"

"Jahnu. He still pleads not guilty. And yes, I do have to go back tomorrow, but not so early, 10 o'clock. I can have a lie-in. See you." And I escaped to my own domain. I had had enough of people for one day.

***

It was back to court again the next day, not quite so nerve-racking now I had some idea what to expect. And this time we were off, not that I was in court to see it; witnesses are not allowed to enter the court until they are called to give evidence. I gather that this is in case anything they hear from other witnesses should colour their own evidence. I could see that it might. So we were kept locked away – at least, that was what it felt like.

By this time we had been moved to a room nearer the court itself. The Great Man – or rather, Woman, Elizabeth Fortescue QC, counsel prosecuting Jahnu, popped in to see us, smiled benignly and left. It was down to John Davies, her "junior" (in status, not age) to tell us what to expect. He was very nice and very reassuring, I almost felt I knew what was expected of me. I was even more reassured when I was allowed to re-read my statement. It all came flooding back – unfortunately. I was reminded only too clearly how nice – and how frightened – Amrita had been and how awful it all was.

There were six of us all told, not counting the police: Amma and Chandra, me, two family members - I think they had heard Haidar and Jahnu sounding off and threatening what they would do to Amrita when they found her - and a young man who turned out to be Aktar, Amrita's boyfriend and the father of her baby. He was very young and alone and looked awful, poor boy. He was glared at throughout by the family members (not Amma and Chandra I was glad to see, but by the others) as they muttered unintelligibly – to me, at any rate. He obviously did understand and looked increasingly miserable. After a while, he was taken away, I think to wait somewhere else. It was clearly necessary if he was going to be in a fit state to give evidence at all.

Then, first Chandra, then shortly after Amma, left to give their evidence and the atmosphere became even more tense. I suddenly remembered the old lady who had been at the flat, Haidar's housekeeper. I wondered where she was; surely she would be needed to give her evidence? I found out later that she was not well enough; after the shooting she had collapsed completely, and after a long spell in hospital was in a nursing home, and quite unable to testify. Meanwhile, the family were eyeing me with increasing hostility and muttering more and more loudly together. I wondered why; I couldn't help seeing what had happened, and goodness knows I didn't want to be involved. Perhaps it was because that I, a stranger, was involved in a family matter.

After lunch we were still all waiting, though now in an icy silence. I never want to drink coffee again (except Ron's, of course). At last we were told we could go home. I was shattered, cleaning the block was much less tiring.

***

However, I returned home to find that the relief caretaker had forgotten to put the bins out – I had left a note to say they were emptied on Wednesdays – and, not surprisingly, they had not been emptied. Everyday life doesn't stand still just because you are in court participating in a murder trial. Since I was home fairly early there was time to phone and see that they called the next day – and to leave another, rather curt note for the relief.

Back in my flat there was a note on the floor: did I need sustaining with Ron's special coffee? I certainly did and made a beeline for flat 1 and civilisation.

"Come in, come in." Ron was just what I needed; relaxation after the drama of the last two days. "Sit down, take off your shoes, metaphorically or actually, I don't mind. Coffee will be up directly." He retired into the kitchen to prepare the life-saving nectar.

"How's it all going?" he asked, returning a few minutes later. "I've never been to court, what's it like?"

"Court's not too bad," I said, "not that I've been in yet. It's all the waiting around. I've been sitting in the witness room with the family, and although they are prosecution witnesses too, the atmosphere is grim. They seem to blame me for the whole thing."

"Clash of cultures, I suppose. If you hadn't been there they could have kept it 'in the family' as it were. They couldn't have, not murder, but they probably don't see it like that." He got up. "Coffee should be ready now."

He vanished into the kitchen and reappeared with coffee and cakes on a small tray. "Try these. They're an experiment."

I obeyed. "M - m – m, yes delicious. Just what I need."

At that moment the security buzzer sounded sharply. "What on earth?" Rob went to answer it. "Frankie, it's for you." I groaned, if Phil needed to rout me out from another flat it meant trouble.

"Yes?"

"Sorry to call you out but there are kids stuck in the lift. I know it serves them right but we can't very well leave them there, sadly. You'll need the keys. I've called the fire brigade."

I cursed inwardly. "Alright, I'll come down. Why the dickens can't the little blighters stay out? It's only because they know they're not allowed. I'd like to keep them there all night." I went off to fetch the keys and find the lift.

The even side lift was stuck on the 5th floor. I went to it and waited – silently, I was hanged if I was going to be reassuring – until the fire brigade arrived. "There are kids in here," I said loudly, "who have no business to be in the block at all."

"Yes, we 'ave," an indignant voice called out from the lift. "I'm visiting my auntie"

"- my nan"

"- uncle", a chorus, this time.

"Alright, your auntie. In which flat?"

"Flat 3" triumphantly.

"That's my flat – and I have no nephews." I handed over the lift key, having effectively silenced the lift occupants, and escorted an officer up to the roof. We all knew the routine by now.

"Don't worry, we'll give them what for – and not hurry to get them out. Little horrors. And I'll bet they're responsible for a spate of hoax calls we've been having." Clearly the local youth were not popular with the brigade.

I left them to it and went to say good-bye to Ron. The only thing that would do now was my own flat and bed – preferably quite soon. However, Julian was back by now and they both pressed me to stay to dinner. At the prospect of one of Ron's delicious meals I was easily persuaded to change my mind.

"I'm so glad Judith's mum turned up at Christmas," I said, curled round Furball on the sofa afterwards. "It must make such a difference to them both to be reunited."

"I think it must," agreed Julian. "She doesn't say much, but she must have been very lonely. Perhaps we should all make the effort to learn sign language."

"He's only half joking," said Ron, coming in from sorting out his beloved kitchen. "Though her lip-reading is marvellous, it must be a strain."

Not for the first time I marvelled at Ron's sensitivity to the needs of other people. Was this because of or despite the children's home, I wondered.

A little while later, when we were all relaxed and chatting companionably, we were all taken by surprise. Suddenly, both cats, who had been snoozing peacefully, Furball on my knee and Lucy on Ron's, sat bolt upright and stared fixedly at the door. We none of us could hear anything, but something had clearly upset them. Julian, as the only one unencumbered, went to investigate.

"Nothing," he said, as he came back. "At least, nothing that I could see. But they definitely heard something, they don't wake up for nothing."

"Sorry, Furball," I said, getting up. "I had better get off, another long day tomorrow. Many thanks for putting me back together again."

"Think nothing of it," said Julian, escorting me to the door.

***

In his flat Jimbo Preston was hugging himself with glee. True, he hadn't managed to stuff the anonymous letter he had concocted through Ron's letterbox but it was a good dummy run. He wondered what had caused Julian to come to the door. Jimbo had only just had time to slip through the stair door and flatten himself against the wall at the bend in the stairs before Julian was out and peering down the stairwell. Jimbo was convinced he had made no noise. It did not occur to him that it was the two cats he had glimpsed when he barged in on Christmas Day who had given him away. He was not a cat person, he didn't know they could be so alert.

Ah well, better luck next time.

***

The next day it was back to court again and it wasn't any easier. The male family member was called in almost at once, leaving Mrs to scowl at me even more ferociously until she was called, shortly before lunch. I was alone then until I was told I would not be needed that day.

The next day: court again. I wasn't sure what the Office made of all this but there was nothing I could do about it. The proceedings started late as the judge had to give sentence in another trial. I do not understand the judicial system. Can't he deal with one case at a time? Anyway, they sent me home before lunch this time, and at least I didn't have to deal with family enmity. It was really getting me down. And it was the weekend! Two days of no court and the endless waiting!

When I got back to the block I found an ambulance at the door; June Williams was being brought back from hospital. I was really worried about her; I had visited her in hospital a few times, and while she had improved in health she seemed to be completely unaware that her sister had died. I went up with them and saw June settled in the flat, apparently Social Services would be in soon. I sincerely hoped so. I resolved to keep an eye on her over the weekend.

Accordingly, I called in on Saturday afternoon to see if she wanted any shopping, always a useful excuse. June seemed frail, but reasonably alert.

"No, dear," she said in answer to my question. "We're alright. Sister got some things in." I wondered whether she meant sister Mary, or the social worker, confusing her with the hospital staff. I hoped it was the latter.

"I'm sorry Mary's not here," she went on. "I think she's gone to the doctor's. Do you want to wait?"

"No, I won't, if you don't mind," I said. At least she was aware that Mary wasn't around. I hoped that was a good sign. She seemed in quite good spirits, that was something. Perhaps her mind was just shielding her from what she couldn't face.

Exhausted by these psychological reflections I went off downstairs.

***

On Monday I was back at court and this time it was my turn. No waiting, this time, straight in. The witness room seemed almost like home, and I was leaving it.

It all started off quite easily, John Davies (the junior barrister) merely confirming my name and address and the fact that I knew the deceased, and Amma and Chandra. I retold the story of how I had found Amrita outside flat 24, agreed that we had become friendly, and that I was also friendly with Amma and Chandra, or Chandra, anyway. Then Elizabeth Fortescue surged to her feet (she was not a small woman).

"And did you like these people?"

Yes, I did.

"More than other people in the block?"

I had become fairly friendly with them, but then I was equally friendly with others. (Here I refrained from looking at Ron in the public gallery; he had come in 'to give you moral support', and, I suspect, to satisfy a not unnatural curiosity.)

"On visiting terms?"

With some.

She then took me through my duties as caretaker in the block, and what terms, again, I was on with other tenants. It all took ages as Jahnu had decided that he couldn't speak English and it all had to go through an interpreter; no wonder the whole thing was taking so long.

After I had described my work in (to me) ridiculous detail the judge decided he was hungry and we dutifully departed to lunch. I must admit, the jury did look a bit glassy, it must have been all the translating. I wanted to go and join Ron but this was not allowed, I was still under oath and presumably might be got at. Sandwiches were produced and I ate in solitary state. I tried not to think that I might be being incarcerated for my own protection.

Back to court at two and I felt relaxed enough to take a look at the jury. There were four women, eight men; three of them were young and two clearly approaching pensionable age. I wondered what the age range was for jurors. Two were apparently of Asian origin and so should understand about arranged marriages and Asian customs. I concentrated.

The QC took me excruciatingly slowly through the events of the day of the murder. I must admit, I found it very difficult, especially when she made me describe exactly what I had seen and heard. I had to ask for water and – I confess – tissues. It was awful, and no easier for being nearly six months ago. (I discovered afterwards that this was to convince the jury that I had really seen what I claimed.) Unbelievably this went on all afternoon, with translating; I was a chewed rag when the judge gave us a break. But when we came back Defence Counsel was asked if he had many questions. Ominously, he said that he had so the judge decided to leave it until the next day. I was glad to stop but not looking forward to all those questions.

Ron, bless him, whisked me away and I was tucked up with more coffee and more "experimental" cakes almost before I knew it. He nobly refrained from commenting on the day's proceedings, and forbade Julian to question me when he came in. We passed a companionable couple of hours talking of anything except the case, until a particularly cracking yawn sent me to my bed.

The next day, back to court and a judgely reminder to me that I was still on oath. I was not likely to forget it. Andrew Wyndham QC rose to his feet, hitched his gown on his shoulders and prepared to dissect me like a fish (I learned afterwards that was his unofficial trade mark). He was tall, thin and slightly stooped, with a wig Rumpole would disdain, and a pedantic way of speaking; clearly, witnesses were a lesser breed, with little or no intelligence, and witnesses for the other side were the lowest of the low and pathological liars to boot. Elizabeth Fortescue, on the other hand, had been a large lady, apparently with a boundless belief in her fellow men. Come to think of it, I would have expected her to defend and he to prosecute. Showed how little I knew.

"I suggest that you could, in fact, see very little from your flat."

I could see very well. That was why it was the caretaker's flat (not strictly speaking true but he annoyed me from the outset).

"Much of the car park was out of your sight."

No, it was not.

"You did not look out until you heard screaming. You were, perhaps, in a back room?"

No, I went straight to the balcony after calling the police when the door had been slammed in my face. By Haidar.

"But you thought nothing of a little disturbance; you were not interested."

It was part of my job to be interested in any disturbance, but in this case I had a personal interest, and I was fearful for Amrita after her father's violence.

"Do you check up on disturbances, even after hours?"

Yes.

"Most commendable."

(Why did I squirm at this? It *was* commendable.)

"You could not see people clearly in the car park."

I could see them very clearly.

"The light was going."

The light was good.

"It was shining in your eyes?" A decided pounce at this get out.

I dashed it.

It was not in my eyes, the block faced south, and it was late afternoon so people in the car park were strongly lit from the side.

Regretfully learned counsel abandoned the light. "You could not recognise individuals, either before or after the event; the angle of sight was bad."

I could recognise people I knew easily and recognise strangers when I saw them again.

By this time I had lost my nervousness and was beginning to be annoyed; contrary to his belief I was neither blind nor an idiot.

"Did you see clearly where the people involved in this incident" (Incident! Someone *died* for heaven's sake!) "were standing?"

Yes, I could.

"Even if they were not standing but crouching?"

Yes, I was on a higher level.

"But you could not see the gun."

Yes, I could, clearly (I did not think it necessary to say that I didn't realise at first that it was a gun).

"But not who held it and subsequently fired it."

Yes. It was held by the defendant and fired by him.

"I put it to you that you were mistaken and could not see clearly."

I was not mistaken and I could see very clearly what happened.

"You were in shock."

Good try, but no; that was later. (Whoops, careful, I'm not sure what contempt of court is but I am beginning to feel it, where learned counsel is concerned, anyway.)

"Do you know the family of the deceased?"

Only Amma and Chandra as they live in the block.

"Do you know anything about this culture?"

Very little.

"Yet you presume to judge it."

No, I am only telling what I saw that day. I did not ask to come to court.

"You reject the whole idea of arranged marriages and have consequently made up the whole scenario."

(Had the old boy lost it? I don't know much about court procedure but really! Surely Perry Mason would have "Objected" by now?)

"Well? Isn't that the truth?"

I don't know enough about arranged marriages to have an opinion, and no, I did not make up the scenario, as you put it. What I have said I saw, I saw.

The learned QC glowered and sat down. Thank goodness. I looked hopefully at the judge to see if I could go, but no, I didn't realise that he could have a turn. But he seemed quite benign, friendly, almost.

"Were you absolutely certain about what you saw?"

Yes, I was.

Then they let me go, but said, ominously, that there might be more questions later. Why? I wondered. I thought that once you had been in and said your piece you were done. I retired back to my lonely room. I thought I would stay on in court and watch, but apparently not. Lunch, for once, was late; my session, plus all the translating, had taken the whole morning.

Back in my cell – sorry, room – I tried to picture the court as I had just seen it but found that I could remember remarkably little. I could picture the jury, just, but I don't think I looked at the defendant at all. Certainly I was barely aware of him; the mental picture I had was much clearer. I don't think I will ever forget seeing him aiming that gun and firing.

Elizabeth Fortescue came to see me with her junior while I was trying (unsuccessfully) to eat the sandwiches I did not want. She was really very nice, especially after the fish filleter.

"You did very well, the jury seemed to believe you implicitly" (how did she know? Experience?) "but, as the defence is doing its damndest to bring in mistaken identity, you could well be called back. Are you absolutely positive that what you said you saw was the fact, and true?"

"Yes, it was."

"And it was the defendant you saw?"

"Well, I didn't look at him in the dock but I did identify him absolutely from photographs to the police."

"Pity. I must see if I can think of a way you can actually see him before you come into court again."

"Elizabeth! Think of the Appeal Court!" John Davies sounded despairing.

Elizabeth grinned evilly. "I'll have a think. Be here really early tomorrow." And she and her frantic junior swept out, leaving me feeling completely wrung out.

Thankfully, for some reason way beyond my understanding proceedings were again halted and I was allowed to go.

I don't think I have ever felt so tired in all my life.

***

I duly turned up early as requested but saw no one. I was indeed called back for further questioning. This time I had a good look at the defendant as I went to the witness stand, and yes, it was definitely he whom I had seen shooting Amrita. I said so, over and over again as Defence Counsel tried desperately to shake my story. Apparently the defence had come up with an alibi (of sorts) – he tried hard to make me say that I had seen Jahnu somewhere else and had got the two incidents confused. But I stuck to my guns, I knew what I had seen, where I had seen it and said so. Repeatedly. As I left the stand I glanced up at the public gallery. I knew Ron was going to be there but I thought I saw someone else I recognised up at the back. But when I looked again there was nothing. Then, whom should I see, slipping in at the back and taking a seat behind Ron, but Jimbo Preston. Really, the man was a menace, forever turning up when there was drama, or even when there wasn't.

This time I was allowed to stay in court when they had done with me but very little more happened; the judge decided to defer Counsel's closing speeches and his own summing up until after the weekend. Apparently the interpreter was required elsewhere. I was relieved, I had definitely had enough, but I shook my head at all this wasted time.

***

Sitting in the public gallery Ron had found the trial proceedings fascinating. He quickly identified all the people mentioned by Frankie, and was glad to have the opportunity for a good look at Jahnu. He had found it hard to understand how anyone could do the things of which Jahnu had been accused; seeing him sitting there, the defendant in a trial for the murder of his young sister, Ron found it harder than ever. Jahnu sat completely impassive, as though the matters being discussed had absolutely nothing to do with him. He looked a little untidy, obviously being in custody had done no favours to his wardrobe. He was to learn afterwards, through overhearing conversations outside, that Jahnu's family would have nothing to do with him, and had actually refused to bring him clothes for him to wear at his trial.

Ron became aware of someone entering the gallery and sitting down behind him. He paid no attention, so was considerably surprised when someone prodded him in the back, not gently. He turned round.

Jimbo was seated behind him, grinning nastily. "Yes, it's me," he said triumphantly, in a menacing whisper. "You never thought you'd see me again after the children's home, did you. Well, I've tracked you down and you are going to get your comeuppance. I've not forgotten *this,*" pointing to the scar above his eye, "even if you have."

"This is neither the time nor the place for such a discussion," said Ron coldly. "I'll speak to you outside, later." He turned back to watch the proceedings below.

Jimbo sat back, deflated. This was not how his threatening manner should have been received. Ron should be pale and shaking by now, not coolly dismissive. Jimbo was totally unable to understand how the frightened child he had terrorised so easily had grown up like this. He decided that perhaps, on this occasion, discretion was the better part of valour and slid quietly out of his seat and out of the gallery. He would confront Ron at another time, in a place of his own choosing.

At the end of the day's activities Ron looked round for Jimbo. He was not unduly surprised, or concerned, to see that he had vanished. He went down to find Frankie and escort her home.

***

Although my part in the trial was over I decided to take time off from work to see it out to the end. So when I asked for leave 'to recover from my ordeal', they could hardly refuse as I took annual leave and didn't push my luck with sick leave. Accordingly, Monday saw me back in court, though I could arrive a little later as audience rather than as a witness. I stayed at the back, I didn't want to meet any family, especially as I had been a prosecution witness.

The prosecution speech was first (why are they called speeches, when they are merely a resumé of the case that they had already put to the court?). Again, it was slow because of the translations, but it seemed very clear. Elizabeth underlined everything that I had seen and heard, pointing out my distress at having to relive the experience. She also went over the evidence I did not know about as I had been incarcerated elsewhere. I did not see how the jury could fail to convict.

That took us to lunch, then it was the turn of the defence, and even I began to have doubts as I listened to the fish filleter, and I had been there! I felt like jumping up and shouting that I was sure of what I had seen and heard as again and again he cast doubt on my evidence. I almost wished I had stayed away.

Two speeches with translations and the judge had had enough. He told us he would sum up and hand over to the jury tomorrow and whisked into his back quarters. I went off home, a prey to very mixed feelings and many thoughts.

In spite of everything I was back at my post the next day. I had to admit, even without my personal involvement, the whole set up was enthralling. I decided that I would attend court more frequently in the future. I glanced around the public gallery but there was no sign of Amma or Chandra, or the family witnesses I had met, in fact no one that I knew at all. Then the judge made his appearance and I settled down to listen

The judge's summing up was masterly. He started by explaining that the jury's task was to decide on questions of fact, his only to offer guidance on questions of law. A not-very-bright child would have understood. Then he took all the strands of the case, shook them and straightened them out. I had never heard anything more clear in my life, I was very impressed. It all seemed, suddenly, to make sense, and at last I felt that my evidence was believed. Indeed, he even had praise for the way I had stuck to my guns. He did not go as far as to say that I had been bullied, but it was close. I glowed.

With translation this took nearly all day; we finished early, and the jury would retire to consider their verdict tomorrow. His Honour (I felt I was beginning to learn the terminology) reminded them that they must not discuss the case except among themselves (how can they avoid it when speculation about it has been plastered all over the papers since the trial started?) and to come in as usual for 10.30 when ushers would be sworn in to look after them and they'd be on their own. Suddenly I did not envy them; I realised for the first time what a huge responsibility they carried.

***

Back at the block I went to my usual bolthole, flat 1, for restoratives. Unusually, Ron was out, so I tried Magda's flat. She was in and welcomed me with open arms.

"Come in! Judith's here, we can have a nice girlie gossip. How's the trial going?"

Relieved that the embargo against talking about the case didn't apply to me I prepared to unload my conflicting feelings.

"It's weird," I said. "Yesterday I listened to the prosecuting Counsel and was convinced the jury would find him guilty. Then I listened to the defence and was equally sure they would acquit. I even began to doubt what I had seen."

"That is their job," put in Judith. "Since the trial started I've been doing some reading at intervals in the library. It's amazing, reading what some of the great advocates say."

"I admit, I'm getting really interested in the whole set up," I said. "Then today the judge summed up and everything fell into place again. I think they'll probably convict, but the defence was very persuasive."

"Have a glass of wine and relax," said Magda hospitably. "The sun must be over the yard arm somewhere in the world."

I duly relaxed as bidden and the conversation became general.

***

I went in at the usual time; I had toyed with the idea of going in later but I was glad I had not, it was quite impressive. The two ushers duly promised not to let anyone approach the jurors and they trotted out. The judge also swept out to his lair back stage. I listened in as the counsels started chatting; to my surprise they all seemed to be on the best of terms. Evidently, law has strong links with the theatre, they both put on performances! Elizabeth was due in another court so I decided to follow and watch.

To my surprise she spoke to me as I sidled into her court behind her.

"Hello there. Want to find out more about what we get up to?"

"Well, yes. I'm finding it surprisingly interesting."

"This is a fraud trial that has already lasted three weeks and will go on a lot longer," she explained. "My junior has been coping while I have been in the other court. I'm defending, this time, rather different."

"How is it going?" I asked.

"Slowly. Look, why don't you go to court 7. Sandie Wilson, the junior defence barrister in your case, is appearing for a sentencing. I think you might find that interesting, the last stage, as it were."

I thanked her and went off to Court 7. I found Sandie waiting outside and she made me equally welcome.

"Our Tony gave you a right going over, didn't he?" she said sympathetically. "You did well to survive, many don't. Are you here to look on?"

I explained that Elizabeth had suggested I might find it interesting.

"Come on in then and see what my idiotic client gets. Lord, what a fool that man is." And she led me in to yet another court.

In fact, her idiotic client got three years; she was relieved. "I fully expected five. I must go down and see him, he's quite likely to want to appeal and there are absolutely no grounds. He should count his blessings. Look, I doubt your jury will be back today, why don't you have a wander round the shops and look in at tea time and see what's cooking?" I decided to take her advice. The jury were still out when I returned at teatime, so I was not sorry to take myself off home.

The next day I went in as usual, visited some courts, but it was not the same as when I knew some of the participants. I had lunch in the court canteen and at 2 o'clock the PA called for " all persons

- 153 -

concerned in the case of R v Dalal to attend Court 5." I duly attended.

The same scene, with judge, jury, defendant and counsels but somehow a slightly different atmosphere. The defendant was told to stand, then the foreman of the jury.

"Have you reached a verdict upon which you are all agreed?"
"Yes."
"Is the defendant, Jahnu Dalal, guilty or not guilty of murder?"
"Guilty."

That was it, then. Amrita could rest in peace. Sentence was deferred for two weeks for reports; it was a mandatory life sentence as it was murder, but a minimum term had to be fixed. Jahnu remained completely impassive throughout, as he had during the whole trial. I said good-bye to my new friends among the barristers – even Anthony Wyndham appeared suddenly human and said I had done well to stand up to him. "I wish all witnesses were as steadfast as you," was his parting shot. Well!

I hoped Amma and Chandra were pleased. And I wondered how that poor boy Aktar was. I got more dirty looks from the family, who had returned in force for the verdict. Perhaps it had not been wise to return but I did want to know the outcome.

***

It did prove to be unwise; the very next day someone, I think one of the defence witnesses, came at me in the car park of the block when I was unloading shopping from the car. He shouted something unintelligible (probably just as well) and socked me one, sending me sprawling. He then jumped on me and things might have got really nasty had not one of the tenants jumped on *him* and hauled him off. All this right under the cameras, silly fool. But he clearly wasn't thinking straight as I pointed out when the police wanted me to prosecute. I refused to press charges, I felt the family had enough to bear without that. Security called police and ambulance, both of whom arrived with commendable promptness, and I was borne away. There was in fact nothing wrong apart from shock and bruising and I was allowed home.

I had to admit though, the next day I felt incredibly shaky and averse to going out but I found that I had forgotten cat food (how I could! Clearly I was not in my right mind even before the assault) so back I had to go to the supermarket. There I keeled over and fell, I do hope gracefully, right next to the delicatessen counter. Most embarrassing. But I did manage to get myself home, *with* the cat food and took myself firmly off to bed, much to Rudi and Sophie's delight. They do like me to stay put.

– Chapter Nine –

As a special treat, after the trial I was allowed a couple of peaceful weeks with only the soil stack and the lifts to disturb me. Even the lift situation may be improved; Roger told me that they were definitely going to be replaced, the only problem was when.

Then, having been lulled into a false sense of security, on my rounds I found the 5th floor in a right state. Rubbish, including empty bottles and drink cans, was everywhere. I was rather surprised, it didn't seem like ordinary late night party rubbish. Then Roger phoned and all seemed to be explained – unfortunately.

After polite enquiries after my health he got down to it. "What is the state of the 5th floor?" he asked.

"Not bad normally, but very bad today," I informed him. "Lots of rubbish, bottles, cans etc."

"Yes. You may have trouble on that floor. Keep an eye on it."

I wanted to know more, it wasn't like Roger to be cryptic.

"I've heard that one of the flats is being used for immoral purposes."

So now I have a brothel on the premises. Charming. I decided to go to the fount of all wisdom in the block, Phil.

"Yes, it's very possible" was his depressing reply to my question. "Naturally the night shift know more than I do, I should have a word. But there was trouble a couple of years back when a flat was being used as a place of ill repute" - with sudden delicacy - "and it was cleared out. Perhaps it's back again." Not what I wanted to hear.

I remembered my friend with the bicycle was on the 5th floor so I "happened" to be busy in the foyer at about the time he usually returned from college.

Sure enough, dead on cue he came through the doors. I interpreted his bemused expression as being due to the headphones, which clearly shut him off from the world. I pounced.

"Could I possibly have a word? It could be important."

"Be my guest. More ceilings collapsed?"

"No, it's nothing like that. Could we go to your flat?"

"Of course." He politely held the lift door open for me as we, plus bike, inserted ourselves. I took the opportunity to look round the landing rather more carefully as he juggled with keys for the door to flat 17 but all seemed to be quiet – and tidy.

"Come in – excuse the mess. I've got exams pending and housework doesn't seem very important. What can I do for you? Sit down - oh, just a minute," and he gallantly swept an armful of sheet music onto the floor. I sat.

"Is anything unusual happening on this floor?" I saw no point in beating around the bush.

"The brothel, you mean?" I blinked, I hadn't expected our suspicions to be confirmed quite so bluntly. "At least, that's what Drew and I call it. He's in flat 18 opposite. We're mates. We're probably quite wrong but there have been a lot of men coming and going so we reckoned that it was either a brothel or an opium den." He seemed quite unperturbed at the thought. I felt a little envious. "It has been getting worse, though. We were beginning to wonder if we should say something. After all, it's not much fun for Sylvia in flat 19. She hardly ever comes out now and looks scared stiff when she does."

"It begins to look as though you are entirely right." I got up. "I'll have a word at the Office and see what we can do."

***

The next day I duly rang the Office – to find that Roger was on holiday. I was surprised he hadn't mentioned it when I spoke to him the day before. I suppose he's entitled but he does choose his moments. I suppose it will all have to wait till he gets back. However, I needed to report to someone, though no one seemed to very sure who was in charge of the block in his absence, and having got precisely nowhere on the phone I decided to call round in person. I caused a small sensation; I was clearly not welcome, evidently caretakers were supposed to sit tight and take care of their properties, not wander in and disturb them at the Office.

After much patient nagging, and making it crystal clear that I had no intention of moving until I had a satisfactory answer, they referred me to Amanda Scott – who was on her lunch break and out of the office.

"Please tell her I called," I said, feeling slightly envious; I could never be sure of an undisturbed break. "I will come back this afternoon," I added, ominously.

"Perhaps it would be better to phone?" suggested a minion, hopefully.

"No, I'll call in person," I said, firmly. There was no way I was going to be fobbed off on the phone. If I were there in person she would have to see me, sooner or later.

Hoping I looked more authoritative than I felt, I duly returned at two-thirty, having carefully calculated that the elusive Amanda would be back from lunch but not yet off for a tea break.

"Sorry, she's in a meeting," said the minion, smugly.

"I'll wait." I was not prepared to give up. I found a chair and sat, with the air – I hoped – of one who was not Giving Up, whatever happened. I watched with interest as the office life flowed round me.

It was the first time I had spent any time in the Office. Generally, I conferred with Roger over the phone, or spoke to him when he came to the block, which was not often. Consequently I hadn't met any of the other workers, even though I had been at Tower Court for nearly a year, now. I knew that the Office was responsible for the tower block, obviously, but had little idea where else its duties lay. It appeared, from a large-scale map on the wall, that its efforts covered a substantial amount of the surrounding area. I began to realise why Roger was so elusive.

"Does the Office look after properties all over this area?" I asked a minion having a breath of air at the window beside me.

He – it was a male minion this time – looked astonished. "Oh no," he said. "Only this part." He traced a far smaller area at the edge of the map. "It's quite small, really. Only fifteen hundred properties, I think. Sometimes it seems to run itself." He drifted away.

I stopped feeling understanding about Roger.

After waiting for nearly an hour Amanda Scott duly appeared. "Sorry to keep you so long," she said, smiling. "That was a very difficult property. Frankly, we want to evict, but the tenant knows all the loopholes and exploits them mercilessly."

I was prepared to give battle, especially after watching the decidedly lackadaisical work ethic in the office but she succeeded effortlessly in smoothing down my hackles. We went into her office.

"It's about the brothel that seems to have started up in the block." I went straight to the point. "I take it Roger told you about it before he went on leave?"

"No, he didn't." She looked surprised. "I thought you had the block pretty well under control." She seemed quite reproachful. My hackles stirred again.

"It has only just started," I said, "I found more mess than usual on the 5th floor. It was Roger who said it was a brothel, and one of the tenants on the landing confirmed it. He is a young student and not bothered by it, but one of the other tenants is scared stiff." I was not going to let her slide out of her duty of care.

"Well, Roger said nothing about it. Leave it with me; I'll make enquiries and see what can be done." She rose. I sat still.

"I'm told this is not the first time it's happened," I said, firmly. "What happened last time? How was it dealt with?"

"I have no idea," Amanda said, still standing. "As I said, I'll make enquiries and ring you. You don't need to come in again."

Reluctantly I, too, stood up. "I'd appreciate it if it could be resolved quickly," I said. It was my turn to be reproachful. "It's not very pleasant to have to deal with it." I stalked out of her office. I tried to persuade myself that I had been Forceful and Determined, but I had a nasty feeling that I had actually achieved very little.

***

Not a lot happened for the rest of the week; I had more cleaning to do on the 5th floor but nothing drastic. Then on the following Monday I was just back from my rounds when Julian came out of his flat and accosted me.

"I've been lying in wait," he said. "Come in a moment."

I followed him in and took up my accustomed place on the sofa – with Furball's permission.

"What's happened with Security?" was Julian's sufficiently startling comment. "I'd forgotten my fob and a total stranger answered and was bloody rude." The normally placid Julian sounded seriously ruffled. "Is it a new company, or what?"

"I've no idea. I'm only the caretaker, no one tells me anything. Certainly nothing has been said about any changes. Look, I'll go down and see. It's something I ought to know about."

"Do, and I'll have coffee on the go when you get back."

Sure enough, a total stranger answered my knock at the door of the Security office, a not very friendly stranger, at that.

"Yes?" he barked.

"Hello, I'm the caretaker. Have the security officers been changed?" He did not seem the type to indulge in social chitchat so I got straight to the point. "Where's Fred? Or Phil?"

"No idea. I'm here now. See?"

"What about the night staff, are they changed too?"

"Yes. Now clear off. I've got work to do if you haven't."

Clearly I was to have no help from that quarter whatever happened. I returned to flat 1 in a very thoughtful frame of mind.

"It looks as though the whole set up has changed," I told Julian, "and not for the better. Just when we seem to be having a spot of bother, too."

"What do you mean?" asked Julian, handing welcome coffee.

I explained about the supposed brothel on the 5th floor.

"Yes, I remember we had something similar a few years ago but it settled down. How odd it should start again just when the guard has changed. And that nobody told you."

"That's not in the least strange," I retorted. "Especially as Roger is away. I don't think I've spoken to anyone else in the Office since I came here, until the other day, that is. Then I went over to try and see about said brothel and got nowhere. At least, no one has been back to me. And nothing was said then about a change in security staff. He probably just forgot, and I suppose Amanda, the one I spoke to, assumed I knew. Communication is not their strong point at the Office. Oh well, I'd better get on. I have got work to do as that blight in Security reminded me."

After that it seemed to go downhill all the way. The mess to clear up got steadily worse; either flat 20 was getting more popular or the clientele was going down-market. I began to find used condoms and, to my horror, needles, in the chute room. It seemed that sex was not the only thing on the agenda. And even, appallingly, a bloodstained jacket.

I had approached the chute room with some trepidation; nowadays I didn't know what I might find. I saw the jacket, lying where it was apparently thrown, near the chute itself. Gingerly, I picked it up. It seemed to be wrapped round something, and as I handled it, the jacket opened out and a long knife fell out, nearly spearing my foot. The jacket, where it had been, was heavily bloodstained. This, I decided, warranted police attention and I removed myself rapidly to my flat to report. But while I was waiting for the lift the stair door opened and Jimbo Preston came onto the landing, positively quivering with curiosity. How on earth does that man know when something untoward happens? I asked myself.

"What have you got there?" he asked inquisitively.

"Just something I found in the chute room," I said dismissively. I hoped that none of the bloodstains were showing. I had re-wrapped the knife in the jacket, I didn't want to charge round the block brandishing a large kitchen knife. Mercifully the lift arrived just then and I shot into it, thankful to escape more questions.

I caught Robin Lutterworth just as he was going out.

"Everything seems to happen in your block," he laughed. "Take the jacket and the knife into your office. I'll send someone round."

I was only too happy to shift the responsibility. But I was also worried about Sylvia McKenna, flat 19 on the dreaded 5th floor. I decided to go and have a chat. There was no answer when I knocked so I put a note through her door, promising to call again.

***

Up on the 8th floor, Barbara Desmond was having a battle with herself. She looked round the pleasant flat; her mother had helped her furnish it when she had moved in six months ago. Now she looked round it with a calculating eye: what could she sell?

For Barbara was a heroin addict. Not of very long standing, but long enough to become dependant, though she did try, more and more despairingly, to fight it. Just now she was longing for a fix and had just enough left for one injection. She was putting it off as long as possible.

Barbara had been brought up in a loving family, well educated, given every opportunity to 'make something of herself.' That was part of the trouble; she felt suffocated by the love that surrounded her and terrified of failing the high hopes centred on her. As an only child of older parents, though her father had died some years before, she knew herself to be the centre of their world and she could not cope. Then a friend had persuaded her, at a time when she felt particularly desperate, to try a shot of heroin. "Just once can't hurt you." Immediately her fears and worries had drifted away on a warm sea of security, even now she could remember the effect that first adventure had had on her. But it was not 'just once.' The obliging friend had come to her aid several times until Barbara was firmly hooked; Barbara had no idea that the 'friend' was one of a group of small dealers dedicated to selling for a 'master' and like all salesmen relying on increasing their customers.

Barbara looked round the room again. That picture could go, she would hardly miss it and, more to the point, neither would her mother when she visited. "I must start persuading her not to come so often," she thought. "A new job, anti-social hours, that should do." She looked at her watch, it was time. She injected herself, the syringe was ready. The sea of warmth and peace flowed over her.

***

As if our resident brothel was not enough we had another drama last night, or rather, early evening. In broad daylight! A joy rider in a stolen car careered into the car park and systematically crashed into every single car, he didn't miss one. I was having tea and a gossip in Judith's flat when I heard the first crash.

"What on earth's the matter?" she asked in astonishment as I leapt to my feet and made for the window.

"I don't know, but come and see." She joined me at the window and we watched amazed as our unwelcome visitor crashed into another car. There was not the slightest attempt at concealment, just systematic vandalism. With a jerk I remembered my duties.

"Excuse me, I must go and phone," I said. "I must call the police." Really, this seemed to be one of my main tasks these days, I thought as I hurried into my own flat. Meanwhile, the joy rider just went on bashing. It took so long that the police did catch him red-handed, but not until the last car had received his attention. I went down and peered at the scene through the door, I reckoned it was too dangerous to go out. I could see that there were two of them in the car, a girl and a boy, aged about fifteen as far as I could judge. I think the boy was out to impress his girlfriend, but I don't think it worked; she was crying her eyes out and shaking like a leaf when she finally got out of the car. They were duly carted off by the law to explain themselves. I was left to clear up the mess. Story of my life.

Afterwards I rejoined Judith.

"There was not a great deal I could do," I said, in answer to her question. "They even seem to have managed to damage every windscreen, goodness knows how. A windscreen repairer should take a block booking. I hope it doesn't up all our insurances at one go."

"Was your car badly damaged?" Judith asked sympathetically. She knew how I relied on my 'wheels'.

"Same as all the others," I replied gloomily. "I'll have call the garage in the morning. I hope it's drivable, I haven't dared try it."

Meanwhile, in the car park an indignation meeting was convening as outraged owners came out or returned to see their vehicles wrecked. The offending vehicle sat despondently at the end of the car park in a worse state than any of them. I presumed that the police would remove it in their own good time. I went down to join them.

"Unfortunately I don't know much at the moment," I said as I was pounced on by owners, all talking at once. "It seemed to be a couple of kids joy-riding but I have no idea why every car was targeted. As soon as I know more I'll tell you."

"Bloody kids," growled Charlie Wilkins (flat 49, 8th floor). "I'd lock 'em up and throw away the key until they grow up to be civilised." Although he was retired I knew he relied on his car to do odd joinery jobs and to visit his daughter in Yorkshire. This would be a big blow to him.

There was a rumbling chorus of agreement, then we all dispersed – presumably to study our insurance documents.

***

The next morning I went to clear up the 5th floor as usual and knocked again on Sylvia McKenna's door. This time it opened a crack and I could just see an eye in the gap.

"*Please* g – go away," a voice implored. "It's not this flat, I keep telling you. It's that one opposite. *Please* go away and leave me alone."

"It's alright," I tried to reassure her. "It's Frankie, the caretaker. I just wanted to know how you were."

"Prove it," the voice said more strongly. I held up my nametag. The door opened a bit wider, revealing, as I had expected, a lady whom I judged to be in her fifties. When I had seen her going in and out she had appeared to be well in control of her life. This was wearing a bit thin now. She was very pale and seemed to be shaking slightly.

"How are you coping?" I asked her anxiously. "I've spoken to them at the Office but nothing's been said to me so far. I know Tony next door is worried about you."

Sylvia looked a bit brighter. "Yes, he's a nice boy," she said. "If it wasn't for him and his friend Drew I don't think I could cope. It's the noise, you see, and punters knocking on my door at all hours."

"Very upsetting," I said sympathetically. "I'll go on nagging the Office, and don't hesitate to call the police if you feel in any danger. I'll have a word with Security, too, when I go downstairs. They shouldn't be letting these people in." Though privately I doubted I would get very far there.

True enough, when I did call at the Security office I got very short shrift.

"You do your job and I'll do mine," he said, sourly, before I'd even opened my mouth.

"This is my job," I answered sharply. "There are many undesirables going in at all hours –"

"So what?" Rudely. "Can't people have parties now in this precious block? As I say, you do your job and I'll do mine." The door was slammed in my face. I returned to my flat, fuming.

***

The next day a new police officer, Sheila Vine, came to see me about the joy riders. I fed her coffee and we settled down for a good chat about it.

"This is not new," she said. "There has been a spate of these car park sprees all over, though we don't know yet if it's all the same people or several copy-cats. I'd give them something to do." I swear I saw "picking oakum" (whatever that is) floating over her head in a balloon.

"It would seem that these young horrors did the windscreens first, though it's strange that no one heard anything. Even your security didn't seem to know anything. After all, it was you who called us, wasn't it?"

I agreed. "Not that that is surprising. This is a new lot and they don't seem to see or hear anything. Are there any CCTV tapes?"

"Yes, good ones, though they were caught at the scene anyway." She got up. "Thanks for the coffee. I'll let you know if we find anything further."

She was as good as her word. Two days later she rang me.

"This is not part of the other crimes," she said sadly, "just a copy-cat. The girl, Sarah, is the niece of a tenant evicted some eighteen months ago" (before I started I thought, with relief) "and she has harboured a grudge ever since. Why it has taken so long, and why it has taken the form of damaging private property goodness knows. I don't think she is over-endowed with brains. The boy, Ian, was just showing off and has a passion for other people's cars. It's not the first time we've met him. He's keeping the crime figures up single-handed."

"Pity someone can't start some sort of learner driving off road for under-age drivers," I said. "They might manage to satisfy their passions legally."

"Not a bad idea at that. And we still have to catch the gang, if there is one. Oh well. Thanks for your help."

"Any time." And we rang off, well pleased with each other. I suddenly remembered the 5th floor problem and wished I had thought to consult Sheila over it. Oh well, perhaps it was a little too soon to call in the police over it. After all, it might still just die down of its own accord.

***

With all the excitement, the fact that the lifts were finally to be renewed passed almost unnoticed. Then I received notification (for once) that the work would start on the odd floor lift the following week. That will be interesting with the brothel on the 5th floor....

That there has been no let up in that situation was brought home to me when I was visited by a distraught Sylvia McKenna. It was clear today that she was rapidly approaching the end of her tether over the situation, she was in a far worse state than when I had seen her last, just after the car park raid.

"I'm beginning to be too afraid to go out of the flat, especially at night." She was close to tears. "You wouldn't believe what goes on on our landing," she said, obviously forgetting that I had to clean up, "and the knocking on my door is worse than ever."

"I suggest that you get on to the Office right away," I said. "The more complaints they have the more they will have to do something. And have a word with Tony and Drew. You know they are concerned about you and will do all they can to help. If you are really frightened, call the police and say that you fear for your safety. Then they'll have to come."

"Thank you, that does make me feel less alone," she said gratefully.

"You should also keep a diary of all noise and nuisance incidents. It could be used as evidence if there is a prosecution."

She brightened. "I hadn't thought of that. At least I'll feel I'm doing something. Thank you again." She departed, I hope somewhat reassured.

But that evening major trouble started and continued into the night. I suspect it was fuelled by both drugs and alcohol, and I was aware even on the 1st floor of more movement than usual into the building; out of it as well, but mainly in. As a formality I tried to contact Security but they were not answering, or, as far as I could see, making the slightest attempt to keep anyone out.

At around 10 o'clock, I heard afterwards, an almighty fight boiled up on the 5th floor, that was audible even on my first floor. I went out on the landing to listen but did not dare go up in the lift to investigate. *Not* in my job description! I did go up to the 3rd floor but then the fighting seemed to be about to come down so I retreated hastily and dialled 999. I reckoned that this was a definite emergency and prayed that none of the other tenants on that floor would become involved.

***

Tony Barnstaple was in Drew Conway's flat watching television and sharing a six-pack of beer when they realised that the noise of which they had become dimly aware was not, after all, part of the film.

"What's going on?" Tony cocked his head as the decibel level rose. There appeared to be several males outside, all of them yelling. Then there came a tremendous crash and Drew's front door shook.

"This could be fun," responded Drew gleefully. "A fight, and us on the side of the angels. Are you game?"

"You bet." The two young men rose as one and erupted into the melée that was raging outside and on the stairs. Such was the enthusiasm of the participants that the battle soon overflowed the landing and continued unabated down the stairs and burst out into the car park.

***

I saw the rush of men coming into the car park from the block and watched as they were swiftly joined by others until it seemed that the whole area was a heaving sea of bodies. I glimpsed Tony and someone I recognised to my surprise as Drew – he was normally very quiet and reserved, yet here he was shouting louder than any of them. They both soon disappeared under a pile of kicking bodies. I wondered whether I should call up ambulances as well, then decided the police could cope.

There was a knock at my door, which I nearly ignored, then realised that it was Julian.

"I say, are you alright? What's going on?"

"I'm fine," I said, opening the door. "Come and have a grandstand view."

Both Ron and Julian were outside, looking anxious. On being reassured as to my complete safety they both came in and we ranged ourselves at the window to watch.

"I think it is dissatisfied clients from the 5th floor," I said. "Only Tony and Drew, who live on that floor have got themselves involved. I hope they don't get hurt."

"Is one of them the young lad with the bicycle?" I nodded. "Don't worry, he looks as if he can take care of himself." Ron grinned. "He's probably having a ball. A legitimate fight, what more could a lad ask for?"

"Quite," Julian agreed. I began to wonder what these two had got up to when they were younger.

At this point the police arrived, took one look at the situation and hastily called up massive reinforcements. Julian was in stitches.

"Look at that one, barking into his radio and keeping well out of the way. No one has even noticed him yet. What did you say when you called them?"

"Only that there was a fight, it hadn't turned into a war then." Luckily, the reinforcements turned up with commendable promptitude and the police, fortunately all large and more than capable, began disentangling limbs and bodies. We watched as the combatants were loaded into vans, including Tony and Drew - I was relieved to see that they were apparently unhurt – and peace once more prevailed as they were driven away.

"Whew!" We looked at each other. "I'd better go up and see what on earth it's like upstairs," I said reluctantly.

"We'll come with you," chorused two knights in shining armour, promptly. I firmly pushed away the thought that curiosity was probably uppermost in their minds and accepted the offer with becoming gratitude.

As expected, the landing was a mess with the door to flat 20 firmly shut. I doubted that there would be any more business – of any kind – transacted that night. I knocked on Sylvia's door and called reassuringly through the letterbox but there was no response; either she was not answering, and who could blame her, or she had gone away. I decided to leave her till the morning.

"Which flat is it?" hissed Julian. I indicated flat 20 and he gazed at the shut door. I felt he was just as curious about it as I was.

"I don't think I need do anything here till the morning," I said with relief. "It could have been a lot worse. And I am not looking at the stairs tonight. Let's go down and pretend it hasn't happened."

We returned to the first floor to find two more police officers waiting; as I had made the original emergency call they wanted to know what I could tell them. Ron and Julian faded tactfully into their flat as I led the two upholders of law and order into my flat and produced tea and coffee.

"The trouble seems to have started a few weeks ago when I began to find unusual amounts of rubbish on the 5th floor landing," I started my explanation. "The situation got steadily worse, with increased rubbish in the chute room and on the stairs, and including needles and other drug evidence. Yesterday I even found a blood-stained jacket and a knife in the chute room."

"Did you inform the police?" one officer wanted to know.

"Yes, I called Robin Lutterworth," I was pleased to be able to say. He nodded. "But before he could do anything this fight broke out. One of the tenants on that landing is scared out of her wits."

"You have had a time of it," said the younger of the two sympathetically. "I'd have thought that caretaking was a pretty quiet sort of job."

"Not here it isn't," I said feelingly. "It's been straight on since I started, and very little of it was in the job description."

His colleague got up. "We'll go up and have a word with flat 20," he said. "What would you say was probably going on? Not evidence of course, just your opinion."

"A combination of drugs and prostitution," I said promptly. "And the tenant's name is Susan Smith."

There was a combined snort from the officers of the law.

"There must be legitimate Susan Smiths around," I protested.

"That's as maybe. We'll see you again after we've been upstairs." And the two departed to see what they could find. I wondered if I would ever get to bed tonight.

They returned very soon; Susan Smith had been all injured innocence and sleepiness. "Nothing we could do," they said regretfully.

I made a mental note to scrutinise anything I found on that landing very carefully as I saw them off the premises and made a dive for my bed before anything else happened. The cats had long since put up affronted "Do Not Disturb" notices. We slept.

***

Only a week later than expected the engineers arrived to start installing the new lifts. They chose to start on the odd-side one first, cordoned it off, stopped the lift motor – and left. They were to work from the top down so would need to dismantle the old motor and then put in the new; why they shut off the old lift before they were ready to start on the new was beyond me. I made a mental note to check up on all my more vulnerable residents regularly – daily if necessary.

I went up to the 5th floor to clear up and to inspect the stairs. As expected, there was plenty of debris of various kinds to deal with but none of the more obnoxious. Apparently war had broken out before drugs and sex had got going. There was a good deal of damage in the car park; I hadn't realised that several "weapons" had been liberated from the dustbins. I presumed that anything needed as evidence had already been removed. I hoped so; anyway, I was clearing up. I was not having my car park looking like the set of *West Side Story* any longer than I could help. Bashed up cars were bad enough.

Roger turned up, much to my surprise.

"They've called me back from holiday to cope with all this," he said, clearly annoyed. "Can't you keep your block in order?" I felt he was only half joking.

"Now you are here," I said, trying not to sound caustic, "Sylvia McKenna in flat 19 is being driven frantic by all the goings-on in flat 20, even before last night's battle. I'm really worried about her."

"Yes, yes, something must be done," he said vaguely.

"Won't you come up and see her?" I asked.

"No, not just now. I must be off. Do what you can." And he departed hastily. To see a paying customer with fewer problems, I thought resentfully.

I went off to try and rouse Sylvia, without success. I hoped she was alright. With Tony and Drew absent from duty she was very alone.

Tony and Drew duly returned, somewhat subdued after a night in the cells.

"But it could have been worse," Tony said buoyantly. "When they heard that we were tenants on the landing they gave us an unofficial warning and shooed us off home. It was a grand fight."

Feeling I would never understand the young male, I sent them upstairs with instructions to look out for Sylvia and to keep out of trouble – if they could, and they departed grinning. I could see the pair were going to become inseparable, evidently mutual arrest makes you friends for life, especially if you had been 'mates' to start with.

Between us we managed to coax Sylvia to open her door and found her in a dreadful state. I left Tony and Drew with her and went to call her doctor, who, mercifully, was my own admirable practitioner. He came very promptly and whisked her off to hospital by ambulance. As if the fear was not enough it seemed that she had a weak heart. I thanked the boys very gratefully for their help.

"Think nothing of it," said Drew magnanimously. "Come in and have a brew." I was glad to, it had been quite a day.

"How did all this start?" I asked them when we were ensconced with large restorative mugs of coffee.

"I didn't really notice," said Tony. "I'm doing bar work to keep body and soul together while I'm at college."

"I'm a musician, too," said Drew, "but I'm spending most of my time trying to find rehearsal rooms that don't break the bank." I gathered that brothels on their doorstep didn't figure very highly in their scheme of things. "We'll do what we can, but it's not much, that's legal, that is."

I hastily assured them that I wanted them to keep within the law, but their night in the cells had bred in them a healthy respect for the forces of law and order and I was reasonably certain that they would keep within bounds.

No 20 was still very much open for business – unfortunately. There seemed to be nothing that anyone could do about it, a question of proof, I suppose. Though I would have thought that action could have been taken on the grounds of disturbance and noise being antisocial. But what did I know? I was only the caretaker. But I was beginning to feel very bitter at the lack of action from the Office.

Another fight in the car park was broken up very promptly by the police. I think Tower Court is becoming a crime hotspot. The cats were becoming seriously annoyed by all the noise and were threatening to pack a spare mouse and leave. I wished I could go with them.

***

"I really am in despair," I said to the Gang when we forgathered that evening. "No-one seems to be able, or willing, to do anything about the situation. I don't understand why the Office, as landlords, can't just go in and see what's happening."

"Freedom of the individual," said Julian wisely. "Sale of Goods Act – I mean Human Rights Act. Sanctity of the home, and all that."

"Somewhat muddled, legally speaking," I laughed, "but I see

what you mean."

"Is Security doing anything?" Magda spoke up.

"Absolutely nothing, as far as I can see. I'm not convinced that they are not actually encouraging them to come in. They certainly aren't stopping them. And if I approach them for anything they are either incredibly unhelpful or downright rude, or both. I've given up." I was feeling really depressed.

"Poor old thing." Judith was very sympathetic. "Perhaps we should do something to cheer you up, go out or something. One good thing, the lifts are going to be replaced. When are they actually starting work? Do you know?"

"The short answer is no," I replied. "That's another thing to depress me. I feel sure it's going to be as awkward as possible."

"You *are* in the dumps. Let's ban talking about the block for the evening. Ron, are those nibbles you promised ready?"

"Julian, you only think of your tummy. Coming up." Ron vanished into the kitchen and we settled down to sample his latest recipe.

***

The situation was resolved a couple of weeks later, but not by any action on anyone's part. "Susan Smith" did a flit. I had thought that there were fewer people visiting so presumably the place had become uneconomic. Then, when I went on my rounds one morning I noticed that the door of flat 20 was ajar and that there was no answer when I called, admittedly not very forcefully. I did *not* go in, far too scared, but hurried downstairs to phone the police and the Office. The police won and I escorted them to the flat, and, since they were from our local nick, went in with them. Well, they didn't tell me to go away so I didn't.

The flat was in chaos, broken furniture, spilled cosmetics everywhere, and as I said later to the enthralled Gang, "Don't ask about the bathroom. Thank goodness that sort of cleaning is not my responsibility. Strangely, the kitchen was clear."

"Probably didn't use it." Ron was scornful.

"One door was locked, and when they had broken it open they seemed to realise I was there and shooed me out." I was slightly regretful, though, after the bathroom, perhaps I didn't want to know.

I lay in wait for Roger, but his deputy, Ian Turner came instead. I suppose Roger had resumed his holiday. Ian didn't say much, I felt that I would have got more from Roger.

Two days later I received a bombshell. Far from being on holiday Roger was suspended! "Apparently he was behind the brothel," I told an equally flabbergasted Magda, the only one in at the time. "There was a load of incriminating evidence in the flat involving him and Susan Smith, whose real name, by the way, is Patricia Marsden Bell."

"I'm glad we had an up-market prostitute on the premises," snorted Magda.

"And Roger had the nerve to imply that it was my fault," I remembered, furious. "I felt at the time he was only half joking. The rat-bag!" I stormed off ostensibly to continue working but in reality to find out more if I could, leaving Magda to regale the others when they came in.

Downstairs, to my surprise, Phil popped out of the Security office.

"Phil! What's this! Are you back?" I was delighted.

"Yes, we were all transferred to another site to make room for that -" he remembered to whom he was speaking and the epithet disappeared into a bass rumble. He was always watchful of his language with me and I was grateful for it; I had heard him in full flow and he had a ripe vocabulary.

"Who was it who took over, then?" I asked. "They were most unhelpful, and so rude. They upset everybody."

"No idea. They just turned up, said we were to go to this other site, call the Office if we were bothered. At the Office we got Roger, who must have organised it."

"It certainly seemed as though they weren't making any effort to keep people out," I mused. "In fact, they seemed to be letting them in."

"So they were. Official doorkeepers. Keep the locals off their backs by being rude and there you are, a cosy little set up."

"Well, thank goodness you're back," I said feelingly. "You've been missed!"

***

I thought that was the end of the brothel saga, especially when Sylvia came home and I was able to tell her all was quiet, but not a bit of it. I got the shock of my life one night when I was just about to go to bed. There was a knock at the door, so soft that I was not sure if I had heard anything or not. But when I opened it, cautiously at that time of night, I found, of all people, Roger Knight on the doorstep. I thought he had left the country long since as nothing had been seen or heard of him. He was in a terrible state, had lost weight, was untidy, and wearing that hunted expression you read about in books.

"Please let me in, I'm desperate," he said. He kept looking round and jumping slightly at every sound; as it was Friday night there were plenty of those. Somewhat dubiously I let him in and supplied him with coffee, which did seem to calm him down. After a moment he burst out: "It was all her, she blackmailed me into letting her have the flat."

I wondered what she had got on him, and I suspected, rather dryly, that he probably had a tidy share of the profits. Who was using whom?

He gulped more coffee then burst out again. "I'm desperate. You've got to help get out of the country. You *got* to!"

"How on earth can I?" I asked him disgustedly. "And, to be honest, I don't want to. You two have put us all through hell the last few weeks. Why in blue blazes should I lift a finger for you? I'm not mad keen to appear in court again but I will, I don't owe you anything. And your girlfriend always was standoffish; I suppose she didn't want to be too friendly with the natives."

"Please, I'm begging you. There must be something you can do, you're so bright and clever –"

At that moment there was a thunderous knocking at the door which made us both leap like startled kangaroos (his nervousness was catching) and sent the cats, who decidedly did not approve of this late night to-do, into sanctuary behind the sofa. I had to open the door before a) it was broken down and b) the entire block was woken up. In rushed Susan/Patricia in a fine rage.

"Where the **!** have you been?" she screamed.

I was shaking like a leaf, heaven knows the effect it was having on Roger.

"What the **!** do you think this bitch can do to help?"

Now I certainly wasn't going to, even if I could.

"She's bound to tell the cops." You bet. "Here, you tie her up and then we'll get out of here."

The precious pair then tied me to my own chair and departed. Trussed like a chicken I was more relieved than I can say when a cautious face, belonging to Julian, who was closely followed by Ron, appeared round the door; apparently the fugitives had forgotten to shut the front door in their rapid departure. Not surprisingly they had been roused by Susan/Patricia's assault on my front door and had come to investigate.

"What was all that about?" demanded Julian, while Ron immediately started to untie me.

"Never mind that now, fetch the brandy, this is beyond coffee. There," as Julian departed, "do you want to come to our flat or shall we stay here? And who did this?"

"Roger and his girlfriend, the brothel keeper," I said bitterly. "He wanted me to get him, at least, out of the country, heaven knows how."

Here Julian reappeared, bearing restoratives and closely followed by Magda. For once Judith's deafness was to her advantage, at least she was undisturbed. I left Ron to explain while I called the police, thinking, as I did so that they must be well fed up with this block. I was told that someone would call me back, so we settled down and I filled them in more fully with the situation.

Eventually the police did call me back. "Is the situation urgent or could someone come and see you in the morning?" a plainly harassed officer inquired. "Only there is a major disturbance in the town centre and we're well over-stretched."

"Two of your suspects for the brothel are in the process of doing a runner," I told him and explained what had happened.

"Fine, I'll deal with it at this end and someone will come and see you in the morning for a statement. Good night." He rang off, leaving me feeling that Roger and Susan/Patricia had probably quite a good chance of getting clean away.

Here, I might add, I maligned the officers of the law; they caught my pet hates en route to the south coast where Roger evidently had a boat. Why, in that case, did he need my help? Unless he hoped to get away without Susan/Patricia. Serve them both right, I thought, savagely. After being tied up in my own flat I had no time for either of them.

This sentiment was echoed by Judith when I brought the Gang up to date that evening. She had been regaled with the tale of the night's activities by the others before I arrived.

"And I missed it all!" she wailed.

"You were lucky," I said, feelingly. "Still, at least the 5th floor might stay clean for a bit. And I wonder who will take us on now that Roger's gone? I'm still livid that the Office did so little, but with Roger running it I suppose there was precious little that anyone could do."

"I do hope you didn't become a caretaker because you wanted a quiet life," Julian said, solicitously.

I grinned. "If I did, I was well wrong. Ron, could I have some more of that cake? It's amazing even by your standards."

Conversation became general and I relaxed.

– Chapter Ten –

With the problem of the 5th floor sorted I settled down to cope with the next: the lifts.

However, there was another more immediate problem, which I discovered one morning when I was finishing my morning block inspection.

I was just reaching the second floor when I became aware of a figure descending the stairs below me, going very slowly, and rather shakily. Hurrying down, I found it was June Williams, in her nightie. It was definitely not the weather to be parading round the block without even a dressing gown so I hastened to overtake.

"What's the trouble?" I asked.

She smiled sweetly at me. "Hello, dear. I'm just going to meet Mary, she's been shopping. Do I know you? Are you Cousin Ruth?"

"No, I'm the caretaker. Don't you remember? Look, Mary will be coming up in the lift. I think we should go back to the flat and wait for her there. It's a bit cold out here."

"Yes, dear, if you say so." Thankfully, she allowed me to escort her back to her flat, the door of which was wide open. I settled her in a chair, *in* her dressing gown, with a cup of tea, then went back to my own flat to ring social services. I took the precaution of locking June in her flat before I left her.

I was fortunate in being able to contact the social worker who was looking after June, right away.

"I am really worried about her," I said. "She was wandering on the stairs in her nightie, she didn't realise Mary had died, or who I was. I'm afraid I locked her in her own flat. We have the lift engineers in and it's just not safe for her."

"I'm glad you did," was the reassuring response. "I'll try and send someone straight away, could you stay with her till someone comes?"

"I'll try," I said dubiously. "But I have got the whole block to see to."

"Yes, I appreciate that. Just do what you can, after all, it is our

- 177 -

responsibility, not yours."

Thankful that was understood, I returned to see what June was up to. Mercifully she was still sitting in her chair and seemed to have fallen into a light doze. I had to admit I felt guilty about her, even though she was not technically my responsibility. Since she had come out of hospital, several weeks after Mary died, I had seen a succession of carers coming in and out of the block to see her, but there seemed to be very little continuity and I was wondering how June was coping with it all. Each time I had seen her, and it was rare, she had seemed more confused.

I also felt bad that I had not attended Mary's funeral. I had had every intention of doing so, and had asked the Office to let me know when it was. But a distant relative had come down, saw to everything in a flash; it was all over before the Office even knew it was arranged. She then departed, presumably for good. Certainly no family members ever visited June.

Fortunately, I had very little time to wait before a carer arrived.

"I'm afraid that this time it means going into a home," she said. She was brisk, but not unsympathetic. In a very short time she had phoned a home, which was obviously half expecting the call, then an ambulance, and had whisked June off to start a new life. I felt breathless, but June seemed quite happy to have her life arranged round her. I found out where she was going so I could visit and waved her away, a prey to very mixed feelings.

"I hope she'll be alright," I said to the cats, as I treated myself to a reviving cup of coffee. Or would she even notice, I wondered. Sophie opened a tolerant eye at me, then resumed her slumbers. Rudi ignored me.

***

Work was now well under way on the replacement lift, with attendant noise, dirt and inconvenience. Apart from only having one operational this inconvenience was confined, so far, to the top floor and the roof, but I was anxious about Joan Stephenson in flat 59. She had seemed to become very frail after the fire and to have aged suddenly. I went up to see her.

"Oh no," she said in answer to my query. "I'm fine. Rather enjoying it, if the truth were told. I am also getting rather hard of hearing so the noise doesn't bother me a bit."

"What about shopping?" I asked. "You do have to carry it up two flights of stairs now."

"In fact, I very rarely do," she laughed. "There are so many stalwart men around that I am very unlucky if I have to carry anything at all. I think they'd carry me as well, if I asked them."

I went on my way, much relieved.

As I arrived in the foyer I met Vivienne du Cros coming in. I had seen very little of her since the fire. I was glad to see she was looking blooming and she greeted me with a huge smile.

"How are you?" she cried. I blinked; was this the subdued girl who had arrived, apparently completely under the domination of her father? I wondered what du Cros père made of the transformation.

"I'm fine," I told her. "How are you coping with the lift work?"

"It's not too bad," she replied. "It's in the evening when I need quiet and they've gone then. And it will be good to have reliable lifts."

I wholeheartedly agreed.

Once again, I was lulled into a false sense of security by several weeks of nothing major to worry about. Though there did seem to be far more filth to clear up than usual. I couldn't understand why, but perhaps there was no real reason, just unpredictable human nature. And the weather was getting colder. Then the block jinx struck again.

***

I was peacefully doing my rounds when I arrived at the 12th floor. I went to check the chute – they periodically suffered from indigestion – when I froze. There was a large, dilapidated bag in the middle of the floor where it seemed to have been thrown from the door, just like the bloodstained jacket. I started forward to look inside then paused, remembering the bloodstained coat had contained a knife. If this was really suspicious I thought I should probably be well advised to leave it alone. I went downstairs to call Robin Lutterworth instead. I hesitated over leaving the bag unattended; not for the first time I wished I could lock the doors if necessary, especially with the nosy Jimbo around. I was quite surprised he hadn't turned up, he usually did.

I rang the police then returned to stand guard in the chute room as they had instructed. And, sure enough, there was Jimbo on the prowl as usual. But even as he opened his mouth to ask questions two officers arrived, neither of whom I knew.

"Which of you two called us?" asked the larger of the two, rather brusquely, I thought.

"I did," I replied. "I'm the caretaker."

"So who are you?" to Jimbo.

"I – er," for once Jimbo was at a loss.

"If there's nothing you can tell us, off you go." The officer waited till Jimbo had gone and then turned to me. "Now, what have you got to show me?"

I showed them the bag, which they immediately opened to reveal bloodstained clothing again, with, this time, a hammer and a chisel. An accident at work? Or something more sinister? I started to comment but was speedily interrupted.

"This is nothing to do with you, now, leave it to us. If it happens again, call this number" - he handed me a card - "and leave it alone. Now off you go."

Exit self, feeling about six years old and thoroughly snubbed.

"You try finding things and not feeling involved," I muttered as I trailed back to my flat. Then I remembered that Sheila had left me her mobile number. I would ring her and have a grump about her colleagues. So I did, doubtless breaking all sorts of rules. I didn't, at that moment, care.

"I'll have a look round the office and the computer," she promised. "Put the kettle on and I'll pop in after work." She, at least, doesn't look down on me as a lesser breed.

True to her word she arrived in the early evening, looking thoughtful. "It's rather odd," she said when we were settled with the obligatory coffee. "You must keep this well under your hat, it's strictly classified. First, did you happen to take note of the officers' collar numbers?"

I gave them to her. "You've trained me well, between you."

She looked even more perplexed. "That doesn't sound like our lot at all," she said. "I'll check up tomorrow. What is strange is that there is no record of your call at all on the computer. The report on the jacket was there at first, then when I referred back to it I found it had gone. It is most odd, almost as though we have a very selective hacker."

"Does Robin know about this?" I asked. After all, it was he who started me on this 'watch out for everything' lark. "I must admit, I called you, probably quite wrongly, because I was so cross at the way the officers treated me, as a rather annoying child. I'm not used to it!"

"I should think you're not!" Sheila laughed. "We value your eyes too highly. As it turns out it's a very good thing you did call me, there is definitely something not quite right here." She got up. "I'll keep you posted, and keep on looking out."

I went to the door with her and returned, feeling very thoughtful. "What *is* going on?" I asked Sophie. She yawned.

***

Barbara Desmond looked round her flat. It looked very different from when she had moved in. She had sold the picture she had selected, but that had been followed in quick succession by other pictures, small items of jewellery and now the furniture was on its way out. She no longer tried to control her habit, just let it take her where it would. She had managed to stop her mother's visits by the simple expedient of not answering her phone calls and letters and by pretending to be out when she called round.

Thinking of this the tears rolled slowly down her cheeks. She felt that the one thing she wanted was to feel her mother's comforting arms around her and her mother's voice telling her that all her problems would go away.

The phone rang, making her jump. She checked the display; it was not her mother so she lifted the receiver.

"Y-ess?" she quavered.

"Listen to me carefully," a rough, strange, male voice barked at her. "If you want your next fix, this is what you must do...."

***

The next evening we foregathered in flat 1 for one of our regular get-togethers. For once, I didn't really want to go, I was feeling really depressed at all the things that seemed to be happening in the block. Then I felt it would be unsociable just to stay away.

"You'll enjoy it once you're there," I told myself sternly, as though I had miles to go instead of just next door.

The others were already settled when I finally dug myself out of my gloom and went. I thought Ron, usually sensitive to other people's moods, looked at me pretty sharply as I settled myself but he said nothing. Furball, also seeming to sense that I needed comfort, jumped onto my lap and curled up, purring loudly. Insensibly I began to feel better.

Magda was in full flow about some customs officer she had had a passage of arms with.

"He was a complete blight," she snorted. "I told him over and over that these were trade goods and showed him the paperwork – which he refused to look at – and if Joe hadn't been there and given him an earful in his own language we'd have been there yet."

"In the sun instead of here with winter approaching," said Julian with a touch of acerbity.

"Exactly," laughed Magda. "And just at this moment I know where I want to be. What are you giving us, Ron? It smells wonderful."

"Just you wait and see. It'll be worth it, I promise." He turned to me. "Come on, Frankie, what's up? You seem really low tonight. Furball knows you're not yourself and he's never wrong. Expound."

I felt a little embarrassed, I thought I had covered up, socially speaking. I should have known I couldn't fool these good friends for long.

"It's silly, I know, but I can't help thinking of all the things that have happened in the block since I started. It's not quite eighteen months and we have had" (I started to count on my fingers) "the soil stack and lifts – oh, I know I can't be blamed for those, or have done anything to prevent them" as Julian opened his mouth to protest. He subsided, and I went on. "The baby was a good thing," (Magda nodded) "so I'm not counting that. But we have had two riots in the car park and one joy rider doing no end of damage. We have had a pirate radio," (Ron looked wistful, he had enjoyed that) "the fire on the top floor, Amrita's murder and the brothel. All those you know about." I made a sudden decision. In spite of police caution, I needed support, and I felt that these friends could help. "There have been other things going on too, and this is in the very strictest confidence." I explained about the jacket and the bag; I didn't mention the suspect police as I had been told specifically to keep quiet about them. "The strange security guards, too, they seem to be involved. While I know that I am not responsible for these things happening I can't help feeling I should do more to prevent them, and that perhaps they are happening because I am a woman and seen as a soft option." I ran down and took a reviving gulp of wine.

There was a thoughtful silence as I stopped speaking. Then Judith, who had been following the conversation closely, spoke. "You might have a point there," she said, "but it's not necessarily a bad thing. I have been watching how people react to you when I can't see what they are saying" (with a momentary sense of shock I remembered her deafness, it was so easy to forget) "and they all relax slightly when they speak to you. I think that, far from things happening because of you, you might have stopped other things happening. That sounds muddled, but do you see what I mean?"

"I think you're right," said Magda, looking at Judith with respect. "And no one knows when you are likely to turn up, either; in working hours, or out of them for that matter; you must be a perfect pest, forever bobbing up unexpectedly. It could be that you have prevented more suspect packages being dumped."

I felt considerably better for this vote of confidence. "I must stress the hush-hush element," I said, "but you all see things going on in the block as well as I do. Perhaps we can pool our knowledge and I'll pass it on as All My Own Work. That'll get me brownie points."

"It's good to see you smile again," said Ron paternally. "Anyone hungry?"

Suddenly we all were.

***

Clearing up when the others had departed, Ron was thoughtful. "You know, Frankie's right," he said. "There has been a lot going on recently. And I can't help feeling that it might not be since Frankie came. I'm sure there's more upsets than when we first came here."

"What do you have in mind?" asked Julian. "Or, rather, who?"

"Our old friend, or, perhaps *my* old friend would be more accurate, Jimbo Preston. He always seems to be around, though he tends to scuttle out of sight when I see him. I'll bet he has a prison record as long as your arm. I think it's time I tackled him. After all, he tried to buttonhole me at court. Now it's my turn."

"What do you intend doing?" asked Julian with interest. "Violence? Or just verbal?"

Ron grinned. "I'm not sure, yet. Hopefully inspiration will strike. It all depends on where I can corner him."

"Oh well, good luck. Now, what about a spot of bed? I'm whacked."

***

An opportunity for Ron to corner Jimbo occurred sooner rather than later. The very next afternoon Ron spotted his quarry ambling through the car park and was able to nip down and intercept him before he reached the lift. He did not beat about the bush.

"Now then, Jimbo," he said, quietly, but with a certain menace, "Just what are you up to?"

"What do you mean? Nothing. I just live here."

"Then perhaps I should warn you, before you do get up to something, that I am no longer a frightened child for you to bully. And I watch out for my friends."

"I'm not doin' *nothin'*."

Ron was astonished at how quickly the erstwhile bully was collapsing. He decided to drive the lesson home. "Just remember, if you do *anything* to me, or to my friends, I will have no hesitation in calling the police. After all, I don't have a criminal record."

The bow he had drawn at a venture succeeded beyond his wildest dreams. Jimbo paled visibly and made a dive for the lift. Unfortunately he forgot that the odd floor lift was out. He swerved to the other lift and waited trembling till it came down and disgorged some passengers. Then he shot in, clearly relaxing as the door closed and he left the arena.

Ron made no attempt either to follow him or stop his departure. He watched the lift go then went to the stairs to climb to the first floor. When he reached his own flat he was grinning broadly.

"I never thought it would be so easy," he said later to Julian. "I mentioned the police and he nearly fainted. Whatever has he been up to since childhood?"

"No good, by the sounds of it," replied Julian. "Congratulations on slaying the dragon, St George!"

***

I felt much better after the session with the Gang; perhaps I was doing the job right after all. Then I was abruptly reminded of earlier problems, via the list of car numbers given to me for my attention by Robin and Jill.

Things had been very quiet for quite some time; no brothel, no drunken orgies, not even a murder. Then I began to notice that the car park was always full to bursting. It was brought to my attention by residents who suddenly could not park, and were less than happy about it. I started to collect resident car numbers, and through that I discovered that several strange numbers were appearing. Guiltily, I checked my list and found two numbers that I had been told to watch out for. However, there were many others not on the list. My suspicious hackles rose.

A call to Robin Lutterworth brought him round at the double. "I thought all was quiet here as we hadn't heard from you," he said, reproachfully. I wondered if the various departments ever spoke to each other.

"There haven't been strange cars before now," I said heatedly, "but there has been plenty else happening." I filled him in on the brothel, the strange bags and referred him to Sheila Vine.

He raised his arms defensively. "Sorry, sorry," he said. "I tend to have tunnel vision when I'm following a case. Tell me all."

I filled him in on everything that had happened since I last saw him; I found that the discussion the other night with the Gang had clarified my thoughts.

"It does seem extraordinary that so much has happened in a comparatively short space of time," he said thoughtfully.

"Do you think it's because I'm a woman and seen to be a soft option?" I asked bluntly.

He considered this. "It's possible," he said, "but on balance I think it's unlikely. Look, I would like to set up an observation post here for a few nights. Could you cope with that?"

I gulped. "I suppose so." I made a mental note to stock up on tea and coffee. Would they give me a catering allowance? I doubted it.

For the next week I was the reluctant hostess to a relay of thirsty police officers. In fairness, they weren't really any trouble, it was just that the cats and I were used to being on our own and we did not take kindly to sharing. Doubtless it was all character building, only I didn't want my character built any further and the cats were convinced that their characters didn't need it.... We compromised by departing to flat 1 where Ron and Julian were only too happy to hear all the gossip and all four cats became accustomed to sharing each other's space on a regular basis.

***

Nothing at all happened during the first week. The car park continued to be overcrowded, the tenants continued to complain to me but nothing dramatic. I wondered how long all this was going to last. I wanted my flat back. I should have remembered the old adage, beware of what you wish for, it might come true.

Ten days after the police took up residence in my flat, all hell broke loose.

The evening began quietly enough, then at about eleven o'clock, I was in bed but not asleep, when the resident officer, who was Robin himself as it chanced, came to call me.

"Come and look at this," he said. "Is it usual?"

As had happened once before, a silent crowd consisting entirely of men was slowly filing into the car park. No one seemed to be in command, though I did see a shadowy figure who seemed to be flitting from group to group. The silence was eerie and even in the flat, behind the window, I felt I could sense the fear. After a while no more seemed to be arriving, those present seemed to be waiting. I felt they had been waiting for things for a very long time.

"It might be worth having a word with Security," I whispered. There was no need to whisper, they couldn't hear me down there, but it was instinctive. "They will know if they are trying to come in, and to which flat." Robin made a gesture and an underling vanished. We continued to watch.

Then there seemed to be a movement rippling through the crowd. Robin jerked upright and spoke urgently into his radio. The main doors were opened and the crowd began to move into the block, still, apparently, in that eerie silence. They were going in by the stair doors too, I noticed. Someone must have let them in there, they were not controlled by Security. I pointed this out to Robin, who nodded abstractedly. He spoke into his radio again and I saw more figures slipping unobtrusively into the car park as it emptied and taking up positions close to the doors. He spoke again, then turned to me. "Stay in here, don't come out whatever you hear. There might possibly be shooting."

"Could I go to flat 1?" I asked. "They are very good friends and I don't exactly fancy staying here on my own."

By now Robin knew about Julian and Ron. "Good idea, if they don't mind you descending on them at this time of night," he agreed. I needed no further advice; scooping up an outraged cat under each arm – I wasn't going to desert them now, was I – I shot next door to the safety, as I saw it, of flat 1.

Not to my surprise, they were wide-awake and welcomed me with open arms. They had been glued to the window and were enchanted to be brought up to date with police activity. In fact, nothing much happened immediately. The car park emptied into the block, the police figures – presumably – guarded the doors. There was no sound.

Then bedlam erupted. There were shouts and yells in the block, running feet overhead and more yells coming from the stairs. The stair doors burst open and men poured out into the waiting arms of more police than I had ever seen together at one time. Then they came out of the main door as well, they could use the lift, they were coming from an even floor. Large police vans appeared and were rapidly filled. The noise died down, there were many men but they seemed curiously apathetic. They clearly realised there was nothing they could do, just submit to the inevitable. They were driven away very expeditiously. Then, after a pause, two figures that I thought I recognised as the tenants of flat 7, Richard Johnston and Mary White, were ushered out of the building and pushed, none too gently, into a police car.

"Well!" I gasped. "I never liked them, they were very dismissive when I tried to be helpful, but I never thought of them as criminals."

"Innocent until proven guilty." Ron was reproving. "There may be some perfectly valid explanation for hordes of silent visitors in the middle of the night."

"Like they have a lot of dumb relatives," suggested Julian helpfully.

There came a knock at the door. We all jumped, we had been so engrossed by the drama being enacted outside that we had been completely unaware of activities inside. Julian answered it.

"Can I come in?" Robin was outside. I had accompanied Julian to the door and I saw that Robin's face bore a grin so satisfied that it bordered on the smug. I performed introductions and Robin sank onto the sofa, his expression, if possible, becoming more smug by the minute.

"A very good evening's work, though I say it myself," he said, accepting coffee with the air of one that knows what is his due. "I think we may have discovered exactly what we have been looking for in the people-smuggling business." His face fell momentarily. "Though I doubt that we've got the man at the top. Those two -" "Richard Johnston and Mary White?" I interrupted - "Yes. I doubt that they are terribly important in the chain, though it's great that we have them and they may spill all sorts of beans. Let's hope so, it's a dirty business."

"What exactly is the business?" asked Ron.

"People desperate to come into this country for a variety of reasons; economic, fear, hoping for a better life, pay vast sums of money for the privilege of being crammed into dangerous vehicles and smuggled across borders. They are promised jobs, security, accommodation, for which they pay through the nose only to find, when they get here, that there is nothing, the promises are completely worthless. I've seen it again and again. They are sent back to their own countries, or they escape and become an underclass in this country and they have lost all their money and all hope, plus being separated from their families, whom they hoped would join them in this El Dorado. It's a filthy business, trafficking in human misery. Don't get me started, I feel strongly about this."

We made sympathetic noises, we were all somewhat taken aback by his vehemence. He got up.

"I must go. It's been a good night's work. You can go back to your flat now," he said. turning to me. "Thank you for your hospitality, one and all. Keep an eye on Frankie, she's valuable."

And he disappeared down the stairs.

"Well!" Julian sank into a chair. "That was a night. More coffee, Frankie, or do you want to go back home?"

"Back home," I said feelingly. "Some of us have to work in the morning."

"My God!" Julian looked stricken. "I've got to go to Leeds tomorrow at crack of dawn, I'd forgotten!" He hustled me out, then remembering that I had not come in alone, ushered two rudely awakened cats after me.

We were, all three, glad to be in our own, quiet, home.

***

Two days after this social services contacted me; June Williams had died in her sleep. I was grateful to them; they had promised to let me know how she was and they had kept their word. I had been to see June at the home a few times, but, while she was pleased to see me she was clearly completely unaware of who I was. She lived more and more in her own dream world, where Mary was with her. She was docile, doing everything that was asked of her, and was, presumably, quite happy.

I found it impossible to grieve over her passing, it would have been terrible if she had somehow been jolted back into real life. And I was quite determined, this time, to attend her funeral. I needed to say my good-byes to both the sisters. After all, they had been the first tenants to welcome me to the block. Accordingly, I rang the social service number I'd been given.

"Of course you must come to the funeral." The voice on the other end was cordial. "We don't yet know when it will be, the same relative that arranged Mary's is seeing to it, at least, we think she is. We'll let you know, anyway."

It was a week later that I was contacted again, I'd almost given up. But: "The funeral is on Monday afternoon, 2 o'clock at the Crem," I was told. "*Very* quiet, we were told. I'm glad you'll be there. The relative couldn't care less. Wouldn't be surprised if she didn't bother to turn up." The voice was disgusted.

Having cleared it with the Office I duly presented myself at the Arkchester Crematorium chapel. Quiet it certainly was; just me, a couple from the home and an acidulated female whom I presumed was the famous relative. I certainly didn't recognise her, I doubt that she had been to the block at all. She left as soon as the brief service ended, having spoken not one word from start to finish.

The rest of us lingered for a few minutes, saying the usual things one says on these occasions, then we too departed. I was glad I had gone, but it was a sad farewell to two such delightful ladies as the Williams sisters.

– Chapter Eleven –

Life remained quiet after this, as far as external alarms and excursions were concerned.

However, it was far from peaceful, the installing of the new lifts saw to that. I had expected it to be disruptive and possibly dirty, but I had never envisaged the reality.

To start with, the whole lift motor had to be dismantled and brought down to ground level; as it was on the roof this had to be done with a crane which took up residence in the car park, which was never too roomy at the best of times. This occupied the whole of one week, I was not quite clear why, except that what came down had to go up again, only new. I tried not to think that all this had to go on again with the second lift. This obviously could not be started until the first was finished, or some of our older residents would be completely stranded. Not a happy thought. What I did not expect, and still did not understand, was the amount of dirt that the operation seemed to generate. I was forever cleaning up. I had to admit, though, that everyone was remarkably patient, even the well-known grouches like my old friend Joan Foster. We met up, as we often did, in the foyer.

"I hope you aren't finding all this too trying," I said, civilly.

"Only to be expected, isn't it." returned Joan. "At least the lift won't break down when it's all done – I hope." And she stumped determinedly off to the even lift, leaving me, for once, speechless.

We did have our funny moments too. I was in my flat one afternoon when there was a knock on the door, which turned out to be Ronnie Jacobs, looking sheepish.

"Can you help me?" he asked. "I slipped on the landing, bashed into the gate round the lift and dropped my keys down the shaft."

"That shouldn't be a problem," I assured him. "I'll call the engineers out right away. You are on the 8th floor aren't you? The even lift?"

He looked more sheepish than ever. "Actually, I was visiting a pal on the 13th floor. They've fallen down the lift shaft of the new lift."

I hid my surprise. "Come on, then," I said. "We'll go up to the top floor and see if we can catch them before they go off work." Whereupon we proceeded down to the foyer and up again in the even lift and were lucky enough to find the workmen congregated on the landing, obviously about to go home.

"Sorry to pounce on you as you're about to go," I said, "but this gentleman has dropped his keys down this shaft. Could you possibly rescue them for him?"

The senior man, whom I knew as Tom, looked concerned. "How did that happen?" he asked. "The lift doors are supposed to be secure."

"I fell against the gate on the 13th floor," said Ronnie, looking more embarrassed than ever. "There was a gap and somehow my keys slipped through."

"I don't like this one bit." Tom was clearly perturbed. "Look, I'll come down and rescue the keys. Bill, go to the 13th floor and check out the gate. I'll meet you there."

Suddenly the incident didn't seem so amusing as we went down to the ground floor with Tom. He was obviously very worried about how the gate had been opened enough to let the keys through. He opened the gate at the bottom with a special key and quickly found the missing bunch. He handed them to Ronnie. "There you are, all safe and sound. And we'll check out all the gates for safety."

"Thank you. Sorry to cause all this bother." A somewhat chastened Ronnie walked swiftly to the doors and disappeared.

"I'll go up and check out the 13th floor," said Tom. "Thank you for bringing it to our attention, it's very worrying. Could you keep your eyes open? I believe you go round the block every day?"

"I do indeed, and I'll certainly watch out," I promised.

"How are you coping with all this?" he surprised me by asking. "We do seem to make an awful lot of work for you. I'm sorry, my wife would have my guts for garters if she had to clear up after us."

I laughed. "I'm used to clearing up after people," I assured him. "I keep reminding myself how good it will be when it's all done."

"Yes, it should be much better. These lifts are well past their sell-by date. I'm bothered about how that gate was moved, though. It needs looking into urgently." He went off, shaking his head.

Back at my own landing I was surprised to find Judith waiting for me outside my flat.

"What lies was that man telling you?" she asked me. "The one who called on you just now."

I stared at her in astonishment. "Whatever do you mean? None, as far as I know, he dropped his keys down the lift shaft. It was strange though, it was the odd side lift and he managed to move the gate on the 13th floor. He lives on the 8th."

"There's something not right about him." I was concerned, Judith could see farther into a brick wall than most. She said it was the result of "living visually".

"Come and have a coffee and we can tear his character to shreds," I invited, holding the door open. "It's well past signing off time anyway." We went in together.

***

The weather had turned colder, and I found the first "sleeping beauty" curled up in the chute room. As I shook him awake, after the first heart stopping moment of wondering if he *would* wake, I thought, not for the first time what on earth made these people choose an unheated rubbish room to sleep in. This beauty was a particularly malodorous specimen, clearly wearing all the clothes he possessed at the same time, and had done so for quite some time. I prodded him again.

A bleary eye, somewhat bloodshot, opened and regarded me. "I'm Jerry. Who are you? Wasser matter?"

"I'm the caretaker of this block. It's a tower block, not a hotel, it's morning and time you were on your way."

"No problimo." He heaved himself to his feet and stood, swaying slightly. "Thanks for 'osp – ospitolitee – tee." He gave me a surprisingly charming smile. "You go on with wot you've to do and I'll be on my way."

Returning the smile I retreated to allow him to leave under his own steam. I resolved to go back when I had finished my rounds, rather dreading what I might find.

Sure enough, there was a lot of cleaning up to do, he was clearly not a well man. Having cleared up and restored the chute room to normal I retired to my flat to restore myself to normal with a swift coffee. I was becoming all too accustomed to cleaning up revolting messes but it didn't mean I had to like it.

Hardly had I started to drink my much-needed cup than I heard shouting and running footsteps. I hastened out of the flat and down to the foyer where I found an appalled Tom unlocking the gate of the odd lift.

"Get an ambulance!" he cried as he saw me. "Bill has fallen down the shaft!" Horrified, I ran back to my flat to summon the required assistance, then raced back downstairs.

"Ambulance on its way," I said, somewhat breathlessly. "What happened?"

"Bill was repairing the gate on the 13th floor, but I don't know how he came to fall. He's unconscious at the moment. I don't know how badly injured he is but it doesn't look good."

Luckily the ambulance arrived just then so we moved back to give the paramedics room. Swiftly the injured man was placed tenderly on a stretcher and wheeled to the vehicle.

"I'll go to the hospital and let you know what's happening when I get back," Tom said hurriedly and vanished into the ambulance, which then drove off, its siren blaring. Thoughtfully I returned to my own quarters and, after a moment, and almost against my will, I went up to the 13th floor to see for myself how it looked.

There I found the gate open, with wood, obviously waiting to be used to close it off, lying on the floor close by. I made a mental note to check that it was made safe later, obviously only a temporary repair was so far envisaged. I also found Bonzo Ray standing beside the yawning gap and eyeing it dubiously.

"Don't like the look of that," he volunteered. "Don't know what happened. How's the bloke?"

"In hospital," I answered shortly, my earlier suspicions returning abruptly. Bonzo had always seemed to be a dodgy character, teetering on the right/wrong side of the law. After all, I remembered, it was from this floor that Ronnie had dropped his keys.

"Do you know Ronnie Jacobs?" I asked suddenly. "He dropped his keys down the lift shaft yesterday."

"No, no, not at all." Bonzo seemed strangely agitated and began to sidle back to his own door. "No, I'm sure I don't." And he vanished into his flat, slamming the door behind him.

I went down to have a chat with Phil. I hoped he was on duty; his opposite number, Fred, was not nearly as forthcoming, or as knowledgeable, added to which he was still not happy about me as a female caretaker. I often caught him shooting suspicious glances at me. Fortunately, Phil was on duty.

"Did you see all that?" I asked him.

"Did I. Health and safety will go spare. What happened? Do you know?"

"Bill was repairing the gate on the 13th floor, the one shutting off the new lift. Somehow, he seems to have fallen through. That was the gate that Ronnie Jacobs dropped his keys down."

"Seems a bit odd." Phil was thoughtful. "They're pretty strong, those gates. I don't see how that Jacobs fella could have dislodged it in the first place, then how Bill fell down, in the second."

"Bonzo Ray was out looking when I went up," I said. "He's a strange one. Do you know anything about him?"

"Not really," Phil said, regretfully. "He's been here for donkey's years, and in and out of trouble with the police –"

"Yes," I interrupted. "Last time I saw him he was being put into a police car. I didn't know he was back."

"Came back last week," Phil, as usual, knew everyone's comings and goings. "But I don't really *know* anything. He really does keep himself to himself."

And with that I had to be content.

***

Judith was sitting in her flat, deep in thought. Abruptly she stood up and made her way to flat 1. Ron answered her knock and was delighted to see her.

"Come in, come in," he said hospitably. "Coffee? Or something stronger? Sun's over the yard arm somewhere."

"Yes, I could do with a glass of wine. I'm worried," as Ron looked surprised. Judith was usually the most abstemious of the group. "It's this business of the keys being lost down the lift shaft, and now the workman falling. It doesn't add up."

"Explain," ordered Ron, handing her a large glass of red wine.

"Well, I saw this man who lost his keys talking to Frankie, then they went off to find the workmen. I don't think they saw me, certainly he didn't, nor could I see what he said, his back was towards me. But there was something about his body language that bothered me. I did mention it to Frankie but I don't think it really registered. And now this man falling. I can't help feeling there must be a connection, or am I just being fanciful?"

"I don't know." Ron was thoughtful, he had a great respect for Judith's acumen where people were concerned. "I know you can often see more than we can but how could the two incidents be related?"

"I don't know, but I don't like it. And I worry about Frankie."

"I would think she was well able to look after herself, especially with all her police cronies. But we'll all keep our eyes open, don't worry. Drink your nice wine."

A little comforted, Judith obediently did so.

"One thing I have been thinking about, though." Ron settled himself with his own wine. Furball, delighted, immediately leapt onto his lap. "I'm really intrigued with your lip-reading. Half the time we all forget you're deaf. How on earth do you do it?"

"It depends on the circumstances and who's talking." Judith was rather pleased to enlighten Ron, whom she knew was genuinely interested. "It needs a good light, and clear speakers, though you get used to how people speak. It's easy, now with you lot. And I do do a good deal of guessing. It also depends on the context. But I was lucky in having a really good teacher initially, and, it seems I am naturally observant."

"Hence reading that man's body language."

"Exactly. But signing is much easier, and less tiring to follow. It made all the difference when I learned that."

"Perhaps we should all learn sign language, then." Ron was only half joking. He'd been considering it for a while, and even trying a little. "How are you, Judith?" he signed, slowly and carefully.

"Wow!" said Judith. "I am well," she said, and signed. "I have to admit, it would be a help," she added, "we could make it fun, too."

"We'll try it," said Ron, firmly. "More wine?"

As Judith held out her glass, she reflected, not for the first time, how fortunate she had been to find a flat on the first floor of Tower Court.

***

A week later, with the lift motor finished and work started on the new lift car and entrances, I retired to the bin room to change the bins and generally tidy up. In order to move the bins safely I had to pull a plate across the bottom of the chute, and I was just about to do this when a package came down the chute, bounced on the edge of the full bin and burst open on the floor. I left the plate, and bent to pick up the package to put it in the bin. The light was quite dim in the bin room and to start with I did not realise what I was looking at. Then I started back in horror: reposing at my feet was a bloodstained *human hand!*

I stared at it aghast, not quite believing what I was seeing. I had often fantasized, while sweeping the stairs (after all, you have to think of something), about how I would feel, and what I would do if I found something like this. Now I knew what I felt: absolute horror, and rather sick.

What I did was to lock up the bin room, leaving the plate open, I had a dim idea that I should touch as little as possible, and high-tailed it back to my flat and the phone. I was shaking so much that it took several attempts to punch in Sheila's number. Thankfully she was on duty and in, I was in no state to remember whom else I could call.

"You must come at once!" I gasped. "I've found a hand!"

"*What?*" So much for police imperturbability.

"In the bin. In the bin room," I elaborated. "I've locked it in so it can't get away." Clearly hysteria was setting in.

"Yes, quite right, I'll come at once. Just sit tight in your flat and we'll be with you straight away."

I was only too happy to do as I was told (for once). I collapsed onto the nearest chair and tried to gather my shattered wits. Sophie, whom I had nearly sat on, so deep was my preoccupation, got up, stretched and moved ostentatiously to the windowsill where she surveyed the outside world, her back pointedly turned. For once I hardly noticed her.

Thankfully my macabre find was considered serious enough for a swift police response. Sooner than I would have believed possible a constable was knocking on my door and asking me what had happened.

"I found a human hand when I was sorting out the rubbish bin at the back," I informed him.

He looked sympathetic. "Not something you expect to find in the normal course of duty," he said.

"I should think not," I agreed with feeling.

"Could you take me down and show me?" he asked.

"If I must." I was not exactly looking forward to returning to the scene of the crime if that is what it should be called.

I escorted them to the soon-to-be-famous bin room and thankfully, left them to it. Though I was told to be ready to give a statement later. A strange WPC came with me back to the flat, I was glad of the company.

"I suppose I had better ring the Office," I said, thinking aloud.

"No, leave that for now, we'll report when we're ready." Then, predictably, "Any chance of a brew?"

I obediently went about my duties as hostess.

***

Having seen the caretaker back to her flat the constable set about surveying the area. He found that the packet, presumably containing the hand, was lying on the floor of the bin room, not far from the bin itself, which stood under a hatch. This was open, and even as he watched a couple of tins and a bottle came flying down and into the waiting bin. As carefully as he could he closed the plate shutting off the bin from the chute. He then used his radio to call for forensic help, this required far more expertise than he had.

By the time the crime scene investigator arrived, the constable, who knew that he would now be known as the First Officer Attending, had strung official tape round the whole of the bin area and re-locked the bin room door. He sighed, the title sounded good but he knew he was in for a lot of standing around and keeping people out. Indeed, here was the first one now.

"I'm sorry, sir," he said to a man who was approaching carrying a rather small bag of rubbish. "No one can come in here at the moment."

"Why, what's happened?" the man demanded. "I live here. Why can't I put my rubbish in the bin?"

"Sorry, sir. Not at the moment."

"Stupid red tape," the man snorted as he turned away. Frankie would not have been surprised to discover it was Jimbo, on the nose as usual. Not that he had achieved anything. He decided he would try again later.

The forensic scientist called the constable over. "What can you tell me about this?" he asked. He hoped the officer, who looked very young and inexperienced, had had his wits about him. At least the scene looked reasonably secure.

"The caretaker called us, sir," the constable replied promptly. "She was in the bin room when a packet containing a hand fell down the chute." He was pleased how matter-of-fact he sounded. Secretly, the stained newspaper package had shaken him rigid. He unlocked the bin room door. "The plate covering the chute was open, sir. I closed it because some tins and a bottle came down."

The scientist, whose name was Giles Howard, nodded. "Glad to see you used common sense," he said. He glanced at the constable's hands, yes, safely gloved. "Go out and keep people away. My lot will be here in a minute."

Left alone, he looked round the bin room. He saw that it was quite small with a bin in place under the chute and two others waiting to be filled, he presumed. He peered into them, both were indeed empty. The package was lying on the floor, he supposed where it had fallen. The caretaker would be able to tell him more. The bin under the chute was full, it looked as though the package had come down the chute and bounced off the rubbish already there. He sighed, this was going to be a messy business, if not as gory as some scenes he had attended.

"Hey, Giles, are you there? Want any holiday snaps taken?" George, the photographer and a close personal friend, was standing in the doorway.

"Why not," he replied, "though the light's pretty bad."

"I'll do a few with what there is, then set up proper lighting." George settled down to the painstaking photography that was his trademark.

Giles left him to it, he would study the package and its grisly contents later. He wandered out into the area behind the block where he found other large bins placed neatly beside the wall. He investigated, one was full, the other two were empty. He also found several police officers waiting, much to his relief. They would be needed. He called them over.

"We need to seal off all the entrances to the rubbish chute until we can study them," he said authoritatively. "That's not going to be popular but never mind. Put one of these bins outside the tape. The tenants can walk for once. Anyone know where the caretaker is?"

"In her flat, no 3 on the first floor."

"Good. Try and keep all this under wraps. We don't want to start a riot." He departed to see the caretaker and learn rather more about the set up and what she herself had seen.

***

However, despite any police desire to keep the episode quiet there was too much activity in the car park to hope to keep the thing "under wraps", and very soon Ian arrived hot foot from the Office demanding to know what was happening. He arrived on my doorstep at the same time as a figure clad from head to foot in protective clothing. I gaped at the pair of them in astonishment.

"You the caretaker?" asked this apparition. Dumbly, I nodded. "Good. I need you to tell me exactly what the arrangements are for rubbish in this block."

Ian interrupted. "What's going on?" he demanded. "Who are you?"

"I'm the Crime Scene Investigator, Giles Howard. And you are?"

"Ian Turner, block supervisor. What do you mean, crime scene investigator? What crime scene? Frankie, what *is* going on now?"

I opened my mouth to inform him but Giles got in first. "The caretaker – you?" I nodded. "- found a human hand in the rubbish." He made it sound positively commonplace. "I'm investigating. I suggest you go down and have a word with the police while I have a chat with this young lady."

Young! For heaven's sake! Still, he had managed to shut Ian up, he went off quite meekly to seek further enlightenment. I invited Giles into my flat.

Once there I took him through the waste system for the block in minute detail and showed him the chute.

"Ah, yes," he said. "These will have to be closed off, I'm afraid.

We want to find out where the package came from, if we can. We're putting a bin outside the tapes at the back."

I gulped, I could see trouble ahead there. "Come back down with me now and show me just what happened, if you would."

There we found absolute chaos, or so it seemed to me; not only was the offending bin empty, its contents being sifted through by white overalled figures (I didn't envy them the task, I knew what the bins could be like) but so was the other full bin. Luckily they had been emptied the previous day so it could have been worse from the mess point of view, but this also meant that any evidence was gone forever, chewed up by the bin truck and dumped. Guiltily I felt that that was the least of my worries.

One of the white-clad figures approached Giles Howard. "We've found three more packages," it said. I couldn't tell whether it was male or female but the voice seemed female. She indicated a forlorn constable standing by the wall, apparently guarding four ominous packages enclosed in paper bags and bearing official looking labels. He looked very young and slightly sick; I had the feeling that he was somewhat out of his depth in this scene. The white-clad female drew Giles away from me and started talking to him earnestly.

After a few minutes he came back to me. "I'm afraid we've found some other – parts," he said apologetically. I shivered, this was too gruesome by half for my stomach. "I suggest you go back to your flat, you can explain things to me later. Leave all this to us, we're trained for it." I was only too glad to leave them all to it and return again to my burrow, guardian angel in tow.

Having seen said angel ensconced in a comfortable chair and obviously only too happy to relax there indefinitely (lucky her, I'd never felt less relaxed in all my life), I retired to the window. I was far too tensed up to sit still, so amused myself watching the comings and goings in the car park below. Suddenly I stiffened. A nondescript van had turned into the only remaining space. It was a tired green in colour but its number plate was surprisingly bright, almost as if it was new. A heavily built man was extracting himself, not without difficulty, as he was large and the van was small, but I recognised him immediately as the snubbing "policeman" who had come round to collect the second lot of bloodstained clothing.

"Call Sheila *at once!*" I ordered the astonished WPC who appeared to be half asleep. "*Now*, not next week." She dutifully got Sheila on her radio, which I promptly snatched out of her hand. "Sheila, the fake cop is in the car park, getting out of a green van with a new number plate. It's in the last but one space on the right."

"Right." Thank goodness Sheila was quick on the uptake. "Stay there and watch. Oh yes, I've got it."

The angel and I watched enthralled as the "cop", who had got himself stuck on the hand brake (serve him right, he should have gone on a diet before starting to lead a life of crime), struggled to shed the van and/or his coat as several real police officers boiled into the car park from the back and surrounded him. He managed to escape from the van and started to sprint for the street, but I had the undoubted pleasure of seeing him "wrestled to the floor" as it will doubtless be described in the press – if it is judged to be of sufficient importance, that is.

"That'll larn you to be so snubbing," I murmured viciously, momentarily forgetting that he was, after all, a fake. But I was still delighted to see him firmly removed and stuffed unceremoniously into one of the waiting vans. I was also not surprised to see the ubiquitous Jimbo watching avidly from the sidelines. I wondered if he'd had the nerve to investigate at the back of the block, and if so, what reception he had had from the police.

By now, time was getting on and I was nearly off duty. I wondered where Ian had got to but was not disposed to go and find out. I also wondered what state the bin room was in by now. No prizes for guessing who would have to clear up ultimately.

***

Unsurprisingly, I soon had several visitors "on the borrow". The first was Tony, who didn't bother to ask to borrow anything.

"What's going on?" he demanded, almost before I had opened the door. Before I could answer my sheep dog was there.

"Who are you?" she asked, rather too brusquely for perfect politeness. "What's your name?"

"This is Tony Barnstaple from flat 17," I replied, as Tony just stood with his mouth open. "He's been very helpful to me in the past," I added sedately.

"There has been an incident in the block," my WPC used her best terminology. "Will you be in your flat if we should need to question you?"

For once bereft of words Tony nodded and withdrew.

He was followed in quick succession by various tenants, most of whom "happened to be passing". The WPC dealt with them in short order, sending them on their way more puzzled than ever. I drew her back into the flat.

"What do you want me to say if people ask what's going on when I'm working?" I asked her.

She looked surprised. "Just that, that there's been an incident. Don't go into details. If necessary say the police have told you to say nothing."

I tried not to imagine the effect of that would have on some of my charges. Perhaps the stairs needed a really good do, I was rarely troubled there....

***

At last, when I was officially off duty, and there had been no sign of Ian I asked if I could go to Magda's flat. "We had arranged that I should go there after work," I lied, hoping to goodness that Magda was in. "It's only across the way, flat 2. Anyone can find me if necessary."

The angel consulted her radio and agreed that, as long as I did not leave the block I could change flats. I thankfully departed, leaving her guarding the landing – I did provide her with a chair – and crossed over to Magda's flat. Ron was already there and he was dispatched to fetch Judith and Julian as they arrived home. We settled down to discuss the latest outrage. I had to be a bit careful what I said, though as I had already told them about everything except the fake policemen, I did say that I had found a hand in the bin. "But I am not supposed to say anything," I said warningly.

"Whatever is going on?" asked Magda. "Is this anything to do with those bags you've found?"

"Goodness knows," I sighed. Rather to my surprise no one asked me about the man arrested and bundled into a police van. Perhaps they thought I wouldn't know about it. I decided to keep quiet.

Judith came in. Due to the car park being full of large police vans she had had to park some way away. "I don't think I have ever seen so many police in so small an area. I wonder what mess they have made out the back. Are they still there? Ron said you found a hand, Frankie. Surely he was joking?"

"No such luck," I said gloomily. "The mess, when I last saw it, was frightful. And yes, as far as I know, they are still rummaging. Rather them than me, even if the bins were emptied yesterday."

We were all in complete agreement with this, also that the sun was sufficiently above the yardarm for something stronger than coffee to appear. I thought, not for the first time that it was extraordinary where all the wine came from when we have a serious get-together. Not that I was complaining.

Finally, at about eight o'clock Sheila, looking as though she had had a long day, called me out. "We're off now, but I'll be in to see you tomorrow."

"Why don't you join us, if you're off duty?" I suggested.

She hesitated. "No, I'd like to, but I've a load of paperwork to catch up on at the station. I'd better be off, but thank you."

We parted cordially and I started to go back to the wine fest behind me. Then I had a thought.

"Could I have a quick word?" I asked.

"Of course," said Sheila. "Fire away."

I drew her into my flat. "Lifts have ears," I said, "even when they're not working. Did one of the tenants come snooping round the back?"

"Yes, indeed," she said, promptly. "We sent him packing in short order. A right nosy-parker. Who is he?"

"Assuming it was who it usually is," I responded, not very clearly, "it was Jimbo Preston, who lives in flat 9. He invariably turns up if anything untoward happens. With so many odd things happening I can't help being a bit suspicious."

Sheila looked thoughtful. "I think he might be worth a visit," she said. "Leave it with us. Now, I must go. I'll see you tomorrow."

This time I did go back to the wine fest.

***

The next morning I nerved myself to inspect the bin area at the back. As I had feared, the bin room, and all the ground at the rear of the block, was a right mess. I supposed they'd done their best, but they seemed to have no idea of order. There were heaps of rubbish against the walls and the bins were just sitting about where they landed. The bin room was no better, plus the fact that the plate closing off the chute, which I had left open, had been closed. I trembled to think how much rubbish had built up above it.

I soon discovered the reason for this. At about ten o'clock, when I had at last brought some order into the bin room, had swept and hosed it and was beginning to re-fill the bins outside, a truck presented itself to my affronted gaze and its driver, not politely, demanded to know what the **** I thought I was doing.

"My job," I said tersely, carrying on.

"Well, you can stop right there. Don't you know this is a crime scene?"

"Why is it not cordoned off, then? And why did no one tell me to leave everything? And yes, I know what happened. I found it. And large blocks of flats create a lot of rubbish that has to be disposed of. Next question?" I felt quite proud of myself getting all that off my chest.

However, the driver was unimpressed. "There 'as got to be new bins, *clean* bins," he emphasised, looking disapprovingly at my admittedly elderly charges. "All the rubbish 'as to go in them and be checked every day and now you've contaminated everything with your interfering."

At this I fairly blew up. "I've got my job to do, keeping the block clean and hygienic, plus, no one told me not to do said job. Am I expected to keep all this rubbish lying around, attracting rats and causing disease and starting a cholera epidemic" - I was well into my stride now - "so you can swan in and alter my whole schedule? I found the blasted hand," I blazed, "so don't you start telling me what's been going on here. But that was yesterday and today I've got to clear up, being as how no one else will." I ran out of breath.

"Blimey, take it easy, luv. I've only brought you some nice new bins -"

"I am not six years old," I rapped, quite willing to re-enter the battle. "I shall continue to do my work until someone with authority"

- I stressed cuttingly - " tells me otherwise."

"Right. Yes." Clearly I was to be humoured. "Where shall I put these, then?"

"Put them over there by the wall," I directed loftily, "and see that they're tidy, not just dumped." And I watched, steely-eyed, as the driver and his mate, who had listened round eyed to my tirade and vouchsafed not one word from start to finish, obediently put three gleaming new bins against the wall. They then departed hastily, with obvious relief.

I was so pleased with this routing of the enemy that I decided to reward myself with an early coffee and retired to the flat. Revived, I could see the wisdom of providing new bins to receive any more unorthodox packages, but why in heaven's name had no one seen fit to tell me the night before that the bins would be replaced so soon? I couldn't let the rubbish pile up in the chute or I'd have to call out the builders to clear it. I decided to move the partially filled old bins and start using the new ones, though three bins would certainly not last the week unless half the block decided to move out en masse. Why did people not ask "them as would know", namely, in this case, me?

At least rage had burned up any fears I had about the bins and chutes. I had, after all, had to nerve myself to go out to the back in the first place. I went off again to put the new bins to work and to continue to clear up the back. But first I opened the chute plate and, as I expected, a mound of rubbish whooshed down. It nearly filled the waiting bin, but I judged it could wait till the next day before it was changed. And here, as I expected, I was visited by Mr Nosy-Parker himself, Jimbo Preston.

"What happened?" he asked avidly. "Did you really find a human hand?"

"Yes," I answered briefly. "But I've been told to say nothing by the police."

"Aw, you can tell me. I live here," he reminded me.

I regarded him with distaste. "Yes, I know," I said. "Flat 9." He looked a bit taken aback, clearly he didn't expect me to know where my tenants actually lived. "As I said, I've been told not to say anything. But while we're on the subject," I went on, seizing the opportunity, "how is it you always manage to turn up when anything happens? Particularly anything unpleasant? And anywhere in the block? People are beginning to notice." Well, I was noticing, anyway.

"Just coincidence," he said, hurriedly. "Nothing more. See you!" He hurried off, a good deal faster than he had arrived. I went back to work on my bins.

***

Here, Sheila and her boss, who turned out to be one Chief Inspector Johnson, found me. By the time they had admired what I had done, apologised for the mess and confirmed the use of the new bins I felt quite human again. I showed them the bin, already three quarters full, that I had put under the chute plate.

"So you see," I pointed out, "three bins won't be enough unless you only plan to use them for a very short time, or to empty them more than once a week."

"No, I can see what you mean," said Inspector Johnson, contriving to make me feel I was quite the most intelligent and helpful woman he had ever met. "You will keep this to yourself, but we have found several more – er – packages which we have removed for examination."

I felt a little sick. At least I hadn't found them this time. "We intend to monitor the rubbish for quite a while and try to gather more evidence. So far we have no idea where this is all coming from, though forensics will be going over all the chute rooms today. Your boss has given us a list of tenants, but your expert knowledge of who lives where will be invaluable." I purred. "We don't as yet know whether the block is involved, or whether it has just been used as a useful dump. Forensics will be checking the bins daily and we will be watching all comings and goings very carefully for quite some time, I would imagine. Thank you so much for your co-operation." He flashed me a smile that would not have been out of place in Hollywood.

"Not at all," I muttered inanely and watched as they departed, by now feeling quite mollified.

Sheila hung back a moment. "I'll try and get back later and… and bring you up to date. I'm off this weekend but I'll look in on Monday for sure. Johnnie's an old smoothie, isn't he?" She winked. She'd obviously noticed how my feathers had been expertly smoothed. "By the way, was that Jimbo rushing away as we arrived?"

"Yes," I said. "I was asking him how he managed to turn up every time anything happened and he vanished like smoke."

"I looked him up when I got back last night," Sheila said. "As I suspected he he's got a record as long as your arm, burglary mostly, some GBH, theft of motor vehicles, that sort of thing. Been at it from childhood."

"He was at the same children's home as Ron," I told her. "Though Ron doesn't know where he went after that."

"It figures. Was he a bully? I'll bet he was." I nodded. "All his victims have been noticeably smaller and weaker than he was. He was in for quite a long stretch last time, the judge was fed up. But he seems to have kept his nose clean since he moved here."

"I think Ron told him to behave, I laughed.

"Good for him. I must go. I'll look in when I can."

I waved her away and returned to my violated bin room.

***

In a small, rather dusty room in the College Road police station serving Tower Court and its environs, a conference was in progress. Leading it was Detective Chief Inspector Martin Johnson; with him were Detective Constable Sheila Vine, and Sgt Robin Lutterworth, PCs Jill Hammond and David Jones from the uniformed branch.

Martin Johnson went straight to the point. "First, congratulations, Robin, you're now in CID. Yes," as Robin looked astonished, "it's come through, and not before time, considering the work you've been doing at Tower Court. And, of course, it's Tower Court we have to discuss. One thing is worrying me not a little. Although we have been observing the block for several months now, it is only since the new caretaker took over that so much has happened. Is this coincidence, or is it down to her? I'm asking you as all of you have had a good deal to do with her. I've only met her once."

"I'm sure it is just coincidence." Robin was positive. "Though it might be a possibility that the fact that the new caretaker is a woman has brought various pans to the boil, as it were. I'm convinced that she herself is kosher."

"Here, here," Sheila agreed. "I've got to know her quite well, and though she is reticent about her past I don't doubt her honesty. After all, these last months have not been easy for her, and culminating in these body parts in the bin – well! But she has been telling me about one of the tenants who has a habit of turning up when anything is happening, particularly anything unpleasant. I've looked him up and we know him very well, Jimbo Preston."

"We do indeed know him," agreed DCI Johnson. "Remind me of his form. It's mostly pretty small stuff, isn't it? Quantity, not quality?"

"Yes, sir. But I did wonder if he might have cultivated some rather nasty friends?"

"It's a possibility. Look into it. Now, let's concentrate on what else has been happening in the block, starting off with the bins. How many parcels have been found?"

"Four, the hands and the feet. The feet are distinctive, one is missing two toes, looks like a birth defect, and the other has slightly webbed toes. Forensics says that all the parts come from the same body. It looks like an attempt to lose distinctive parts, they were meant to disappear into the bins and be crushed, not found." Sheila put away her notebook then continued. "So far there has been no report of a body missing its hands and feet anywhere. I am beginning to search other forces but no joy as yet."

"Any DNA?"

"Yes, but no match, not yet, anyway. And nothing so far on missing persons."

"Any connection with all the other things that have been going on in the Court?" Chief Inspector Johnson looked at Robin.

"Not that I can see," Robin returned. "It is possible that they are all connected but so far they *seem* only to have the Court in common. I am curious about Bonzo Ray, though. We have been watching him for a long time on suspicion of fencing, and have taken him into custody a few times, not very conclusively. But he has never been connected with violence. However, what does worry me is that at least one of the body part parcels seems, according to forensics, to have been 'posted', if that's the right word, in the rubbish chute on his floor. This could mean nothing, or it could be important."

"Where were the other parcels 'posted'? I like that word." The

Chief Inspector grinned for the first time. "Macabre, but appropriate."

"Quite," Robin agreed. "Forensics are working on it now, there are so many chute openings to check, and, of course, they were all in use. They think, though, that each package was posted down a different chute, not all down the same one. Apparently there are signs on several of them. Presumably that was to spread suspicion if the packages were found. The bins are being checked regularly but, if we are right that only readily identifiable parts are concerned, and we have those, I doubt that we will find any more."

"Right." The Chief Inspector got up. "You lot are the official team dealing with this, so get out of uniform and jump to it. Him upstairs wants a quick result. Bodies in tower blocks. Whatever next?" And he left, shaking his head.

Robin caught Sheila's arm. "What's this about Jimbo Preston?" he asked. "Frankie's not mentioned him to me as one to keep an eye on."

"She told me about it on the day the hand was found," Sheila answered. "I meant to mention it to you but it slipped my mind, what with one thing and another. She was irritated by him more than anything else, I think, always poking his nose in. As I said, I looked him up and there's nothing major, only a lot of relatively small stuff. He's kept his nose clean since he moved into Tower Court, but I suppose it is possible that he may have undesirable friends. I'll certainly check up, perhaps call in a favour or two."

"Do that," Robin agreed. "After all, if we are saying that things have happened since Frankie took over, it's also true to say that they've happened since Jimbo arrived too. When was that, by the way?"

"I checked the list at the Office and it seemed to be sometime before Christmas, round about the time of the fire on the top floor."

"So he's been around for most of the events."

"Precisely."

Robin looked grim. "He'll definitely bear watching, then."

"It will be a pleasure," agreed Sheila. "Do you think, perhaps, a nice visit?"

"What a good idea. I should enjoy scaring the living daylights out of him. He seems to be a right little squirt."

– Chapter Twelve –

The next day Ian came to see me, wanting details of the recent doings. I had reported them to him as a matter of course, but now he wanted chapter and verse.

"Where do you want me to start?" I asked him.

"You've had these strange bags in the rubbish chutes." He looked at me reproachfully. "Tell me about them."

"There's nothing more I can add," I answered, rather annoyed by his attitude. "I found these two bags on two separate occasions, well, one bag on the 12th floor and the bloodstained jacket on the 5th. Though that might have been part of the brothel set up, it was the same floor."

"Yes, there was the brothel business as well," said Ian, a little ominously. "Go on."

"Well, there is something connected with the bag, but I have been asked to keep quiet. You'll have to ask the police." I was hanged if I was going to tell him outright about the bogus officers but I did feel that I should say something. "Then the hand in the bin."

"The Committee is not at all happy about this."

I presumed he meant the Committee who were meant to be running the block.

"I really don't see how they can blame me for any of it," I protested. "After all, I'm not even responsible for security. You could just as well blame them for letting undesirables in."

"They're not happy," he repeated.

"What do they expect me to do?" I demanded. "Put the beastly thing back in the bin and pretend I hadn't seen it?"

"No, of course not," he said, a little too quickly. He sank, unasked, into a chair (we were in my flat, the "office" having been taken over by the police), having a go at me had been better accomplished standing up, it seemed. "I'm sorry, they've all descended on the Office and all hell's been let loose. I suppose I'm taking it out on you. They want to see you, by the way."

"Well, I don't want to see them," I said firmly. "If they want to know anything tell them to ask the police. And I want some time off, all this is well outside my job description." I had only just thought of this but some time away suddenly seemed like a very good idea.

"Yes, of course you must take some leave." Ian seemed relieved to return to such ordinary matters. "Do you need counselling?"

I shuddered, the last thing I wanted to do was to rehash it all again to a stranger. "No, thank you. Just some time off."

"Alright, so how much time do you think you'll need?" I repressed the urge to say forever, with pay, and we settled that I should take the rest of the week off and then see how I felt. "Will you go away?"

That brought me up short. "I don't know if I'll be allowed to. The police always seem to be on my doorstep at the moment."

"Oh well, try some girlish vapours." And Ian left, leaving me with a strong desire to hit him but also a prey to many disturbing thoughts. Was my job on the line? For activities that there was no way I could have prevented? I shivered.

***

Sure enough, I was summoned to the Office to explain how I had allowed suspect clothing, bags and body parts to turn up in my block. I was livid at their attitude; did they live in cloud cuckoo land? How the *hell* was it my fault? But it seems that it was.

"We put you into that block because we felt that your – er – seniority would be an asset," the most senior suit informed me portentously. Why couldn't he just say my age, I wondered savagely.

"How could you have allowed these things to happen?" demanded another. "Surely there must have been Signs."

Of what? A note through the door telling me that body parts etc. were due to be dumped on Tuesday next?

"The first jacket and knife were on the same floor as the brothel," I reminded the court (well, it felt like one, only rather less friendly). "I don't know whether they were connected with that or the bag, or the hand in the bin."

"Yes, the brothel." Another accuser decided to join in. "How did that come about?"

"I have no idea," I said, trying not to sound heated. "I understand that something similar occurred some years ago, before I came."

"Yes, that brings us to our main concern."

I wasn't off the hook yet.

"We cannot help but observe that all these things have happened since you took up your post. Have you anything to say to that?" The lesser suit sounded triumphant.

I took a deep breath. "Obviously, I cannot vouch for any events taking place prior to my appointment. But I can assure you that I am in no way responsible for any of these events. Perhaps you would like to speak to the police officers in charge of the investigations. They, at least, seem to trust me." I was perilously close to handing in my resignation there and then but I really couldn't afford that luxury. Making a huge effort I kept quiet after this last, rather high handed utterance and let the fury break over my demurely bent head.

At last they allowed me to return to the block where I prowled the stairs, daring anyone to approach me. Now I was definitely taking time off, as much as I could get away with.

***

Barbara Desmond looked hopelessly round her dismal flat, now almost totally bare of furniture, let alone the pictures and ornaments that had once made it such an attractive place in which to live.

Barbara herself was now gaunt and haggard, heroin had totally taken away her appetite; she knew she was probably dehydrated but no longer cared. There were no mirrors left in the flat, they had gone the way of everything else, sold for money for the precious drug.

For a long time she had managed to supply herself without resorting to crime but then the phone calls had started....

"If you want your next fix you must -" Small stuff at first, minor shoplifting, opportunist theft, then acting as a "runner", keeping look out on street corners for the pushers, though the first job, which had got her enmeshed, had been big. Her fee was drugs, in quantities commensurate with the deed. But she had a feeling that things were going to escalate. The voice on the phone had changed, become harsher, more menacing. What was the next chapter?

She shivered as she remembered the first time she had to commit a crime. The voice on the phone had said to her: "If you want your next fix you must go to the booze shop on the High Street at 11.30 am. You will be met there by two men who will tell you their names are Bill and Ben. Your name is Weed." What else? thought Barbara, rather hysterically. "Bill and Ben will tell you what to do next." The phone went dead.

Since she had no choice, Barbara went along to the "booze shop", a large off licence known locally as the Booze Cruise. Sure enough, two men were waiting for her, both wearing nondescript dark clothes with hoods pulled well over their faces. She got the impression that one was slightly built and white, while the other was a heavy weight and black.

"You Weed?" said the smaller of the two. She nodded. "Right. I'm Bill, this is Ben." He indicated the other figure towering over them both. "You're to go in, create a diversion. We've got a job to do." He looked at the other and sniggered.

"How do I do that?" asked Barbara, shaking.

"I dunno, use your imagination. Just get the staff away from the till. If you manage to nick anything it's a bonus. In you go, time's a-wasting." He pushed her towards the door.

Terrified, Barbara opened the shop door and went inside. She had no idea what to do, she hoped wildly if she delayed Bill and Ben would just go away. Then she saw they had entered the shop behind her. Ben prodded her, not gently. "Get a move on," he hissed.

Barbara looked round, frantically. She found she was standing close to a pyramid of beer cans; fear gave her inspiration. "Oh, I feel so ill," she cried out loudly, and fell, managing to knock the whole pile all over the floor. The only two staff members ran over to her, leaving the way clear for Bill, who pounced on the till and wrenched the drawer open. Ben vaulted the counter and dashed into the office. He clearly knew his way around as he went straight to the safe and spun the combination. The door opened, he seized the contents and raced back into the shop. By this time, Ben was pointing a handgun, holding up the staff and a couple of customers. Both he and Bill had put on masks before they went into action.

Bill and Ben backed towards the door. "Weed, with us," ordered Ben. Then taking deliberate aim he shot out the CCTV camera. "Out," he said, and the three of them dashed across the pavement and into a car, which appeared miraculously beside them. Barbara was thrown unceremoniously into the back, and the car roared away, almost before the doors were shut.

"Not bad for your first job," complemented Ben. He peeled off a few notes from the wodge he held in his hand and handed them to her. "Just remember. Your face wasn't covered. You can be recognised, and the police will know that you have been involved in an armed robbery. Just keep doing as you're told and you'll be fine. Get out of line and the boys in blue will find you in a trice." He smiled at her benignly. "Off you go, back to your nice cosy flat. You'll find a little present there, the reward for a good girl." The car drew into the kerb briefly and she was pushed out, landing sprawling on the pavement. The car raced away.

On her hands and knees Barbara looked round her. She found she knew where she was, and, in fact, she was not far from Tower Court. She struggled to her feet and trudged on.

Back in her flat she found a small packet of white powder lying prominently in the middle of the living room floor. She pounced on it: it was some time later before it dawned on her that someone had access to her flat.

As the voice had told her on the phone, she was now involved with crime and the police would find her, sooner or later. But as long as she did what she was told, did the jobs she was told to do, she would be "protected", and supplied with drugs. Gradually, she found this to be true; she was not asked to participate in anything big, no one came calling, she was even given some pocket money. But she was unable to buy her own drugs, her suppliers had mysteriously disappeared. She was completely trapped. And someone had access to her flat.

***

Defiantly I stayed away for two weeks, with police approval, and returned to find the block in urgent need of care and attention but no dramas. As usual I wondered what the relief cleaners had done, but at least nothing untoward had been found, though the bins were still under the charge of forensics. Rather them than me.

As always, I felt much refreshed by my retreat into my other life. Only Ron and Julian had my address when I went off, and then only because of the cats. Heroically, they refrained from questions; sometime I should tell them, it seemed only fair. Maybe. But not yet. Jealously I clung to my privacy.

I had a visit from Sheila soon after I got back. I was glad to see her, I was sufficiently recovered from the stress and its aftermath to want an update.

"Is this official or unofficial?" I asked. "Have you come to arrest me on the Committee's say so?".

"No, ignore that lot. They're looking for a scapegoat and we'll make sure it's not you. It's a bit of both. Bill, you remember, who fell down the lift shaft, has at last regained consciousness."

"Oh, that is good." I was relieved. "How is he?"

"Not too bad. The thing is, he now says he was pushed into the shaft."

"*What?* He must be mistaken."

"It seems not. At first, he couldn't remember anything. Then it started to come back in flashes and now he remembers pretty well but didn't see who it was. The thing is, what can you tell me about the tenants on that landing?"

"Just a moment, I'll get my list." I rummaged in my desk – I preferred to work in the flat when I could. "By the way, have your lot finished in the caretaker's office?"

"We still want to be able to go there when necessary but shouldn't get in your way."

"Fair enough." I returned with the list. "Our old friend Bonzo Ray, of course."

"Yes, we've questioned him pretty rigorously but can't make anything stick. Go on."

"He's in flat 51. Flat 49, next door to Bonzo – where did he come by that name, by the way? - is Charlie Wilkins, a retired joiner. He's well retired, seventy odd I should think, but does odd jobs for friends. Flat 50 opposite is Rosa Smith, also elderly, even older I shouldn't wonder, and very lame. I can't imagine either of them being physically able to push anyone down anything. Flat 52 is a student, Fiona Briony. She's young and presumably fit, but it seems unlikely."

"There certainly doesn't seem to be a suspect among any of them," agreed Sheila. "Oh well, it was a long shot. Did you enjoy your holiday?"

"Very much, thank you. I just hope the Committee leave me alone now. Have they been on to you?"

"Yes they have, and we shot them down in flames. Don't worry, as I said, they were looking for a scapegoat." She got up. "I'll be off, then. Hope things stay quiet for a bit."

So did I.

***

On a landing, Tom, the foreman of the lift engineers was chatting to another engineer, George, as they worked on the lift entrance. Having disposed of their football teams execrable performance at the weekend ("Five nil! I *ask* you!") George remembered something.

"By the way, how's Bill getting on? You've not said for a bit."

Tom, who was both friend and brother-in-law to the injured Bill, beamed. "He's doing really well. He's regained consciousness and is even beginning to remember what happened."

"That's good. I really thought he was a goner. Lucky, eh?"

"I'll say. Have you finished that bit? I reckon it's tea break."

"Yes, that's done. Let's go." And the two gathered up an assortment of tools and departed to the stairs, still reviling their football club.

Behind the door of one of the flats a tenant was looking extremely thoughtful. He moved to the telephone. The news he had to give was not good.

***

In a side ward in the William and Mary Hospital, Bill Edwards, lift engineer, lay sleeping peacefully for the first time since the accident. He was hooked up to various appliances and containers but the staff were well pleased with his progress. The police officer on duty glanced in, saw all was quiet and went off for a necessary reason.

The door of the main ward opened. A tall figure in the distinctive white coat of a doctor entered. Taking something from its pocket it moved quickly to the bed, jabbed a syringe once into the exposed arm, withdrew it, then jabbed again into the drip bag hanging on the stand above the bed. It left as silently as it had entered. It moved swiftly down the corridor and, reaching a door, tore off the coat and thrust it into the revealed cupboard. The whole episode had taken precisely three minutes.

The constable returned, glanced at the sleeping patient. All quiet. He settled down again.

***

David Jones, one of the plain-clothes team looking into the events at Tower Court was sitting in the police canteen with a mate, who had just come off duty.

"Tell me again about that robbery at Booze Cruise," he was saying. "It sounds a bit odd. Who was the girl? Do we know her?"

"Not until now," said his friend, grimly. "She seemed to be there to cause a diversion. The other two, who wore masks, scooped her up when they left. There's no CCTV footage, they shot up the camera before they left. We have a partial registration number of the getaway car from a bystander, but nothing's come up so far. There's talk of putting it on Crimewatch if we can only get a picture of the girl. It could be murder now, the manager had a heart attack at the scene and is critical in hospital. If he doesn't make it –" He paused, significantly.

"Oh well, it can't have any connection with our lot. See you around." He went off, whistling. He enjoyed his job but he was off for three days and it felt good to be alive.

***

I was busy in the foyer when Tom, the lift engineer came in. I was surprised to see him, usually the lift engineers were buried in the depths of the lift shaft long before I was ready to start on the foyer.

"Yes," he answered my startled look. "I'm late today. I've been at the hospital with Bill."

"How is he?" I asked, concerned.

"Doesn't look good. At first, when he regained consciousness, and especially when he began to remember what happened I thought he was going to be alright. Now it doesn't look good."

"I'm really sorry," I said, wishing there was more I could say. "You are friends too, as well as colleagues, aren't you?"

"Yes, been mates for years. Our wives are sisters. Oh well, best get on." And he moved slowly into the even lift and disappeared.

It was my day for surprising meetings in the foyer. A few

minutes later a stranger came in who did seem rather familiar, but I couldn't place him.

"Good morning," he said, with a slight accent I thought was French. "How are you? Do you remember me? Victor du Cros. My daughter, Vivienne, lives here, on the top floor."

"Yes, of course I remember you. How is Vivienne? She seems happy here."

"Yes, she likes it, in spite of all the excitements you have had, the fire and so on. And now the lifts are being renewed. That must mean a lot of extra work for you."

I warmed to him. "Yes, it's not easy to keep on top of it all but we manage. It will be good when it's all finished."

"Yes, indeed. How do I get to the top floor now? Not stairs all the way, I hope."

I laughed. "No, no, the even lift serves the top floor as well, I'm glad to say."

"Good. I'll be on my way, then. My daughter is expecting me." And he, in his turn passed into the even lift and vanished from sight.

I carried on working, pondering on the rather unusual couple. I wondered if he would approve of the way Vivienne had blossomed away from him. I grinned quietly to myself.

***

Barbara woke from a hazy sleep to hear knocking at the door. She buried her head under her single blanket but it persisted. Clearly, whoever it was, was not going to give up. She stumbled to the front door and opened it a crack.

"Hallo-allo. We're neighbours. Can I come in? Won't keep you a moment." A tall, well-built man she did not immediately recognise was on the other side.

"I – it's not convenient," she started to say but the stranger said, "Nonsense. I won't keep you a moment," and pushed the door so sharply that she staggered and nearly fell.

"Not much of a place, you've got here, is it. He looked contemptuously round the bare flat. "Now listen to me." He swung round and glared at her. His voice roughened and to her horror she recognised the voice on the phone that had so often made her do things she hated in order to get her drugs. He went on, as recognition dawned in her face. "Quite right, it's me. And you're not doing enough to earn your keep. And you muffed the last job. Yes," as she looked completely bewildered. "That – must – not – happen – again. When we tell you to do a job you do it when we tell you, how we tell you and you do it right. Or else." He grinned sardonically as Barbara started to shake.

"I don't know what you mean," she quavered. "What job?" Indeed, she had been left in peace for several days.

He ignored her. "We'll let you off this time," he handed her a packet, which she snatched, "but just remember in future. We're keeping tabs on you." He laughed shortly as slow tears started to roll down Barbara's face. "Just watch it, that's all."

He left, slamming the door behind him.

"Oh, hello, mate," he called out cheerily as the lift door opened and Derek Wood, the tenant in flat 32 emerged. "Nice day."

Derek, not a convivial character, grunted and opened his flat door. With a wave the heavily built man vanished into his own flat. He went to the phone and dialled a number.

"It's done. I've put the frighteners on her. Stupid little smack head." He listened. "Right, boss." He put the phone down.

***

Relaxing in my flat after another somewhat frustrating day trying to keep up with the cleaning, I was well pleased to be joined by Ron and Magda. They were suitably sympathetic about my woes and I very soon began to feel much better. I began to tell them about my foyer meetings of the morning.

"It's bad news about Bill," Magda agreed. "Especially as he seemed to be on the mend. Have you heard any more?"

I shook my head. "No, but Tom promised to let me know how he was. It seems that they are brothers-in-law as well as colleagues and mates."

"Have they any idea how it happened?" Ron asked.

"No, I don't think so." I had decided to keep quiet about the push theory until it was proved or disproved. "And I had another meeting," I said hastily, changing the subject. "Vivienne du Cros's overbearing father turned up. Very urbane. I wonder what he made of the change in her?"

"He should be pleased," said Magda severely. "She was such a little mouse." Vivienne and Magda often travelled into town together and had become quite friendly.

"Probably won't be if he can't boss her about," Ron snorted.

At that moment there was a well-recognised thunder at the door. Ron, who was nearest, got up and opened it to let a wildly excited Julian in.

"I've got them, I've got them!" he yelled as we all stared at him open mouthed. He collapsed into a chair. "Oh, sorry, Rudi, I didn't see you." Rudi glared and removed himself to safety. He liked Julian, but really! "I didn't tell you because I didn't think I could, but I have!"

"What in the world are you talking about?" I asked, soothing my affronted feline. "Got what?"

"Only tickets for the Gressington Ballet in the New Year," said Julian with pride.

"How on earth did you manage that? They're like gold dust," Ron demanded.

"My wheedling wiles, plus knowing what favour to call in," Julian replied smugly. "Anyway, I've got four tickets for their January tour so we can all go, though I think Judith's away. Though maybe she wouldn't want to go."

"When, in January?" Magda asked sharply. "I'm off to Florence on the 26th."

"It's before then, the 14th." Magda relaxed. "It's Ella Foster's farewell tour. They're doing *Sleeping Beauty* and she's playing her fabulous Carabosse. It's really creepy, and she's to be attended by bats who will be children from the local schools. That's how I heard about it. Are you all game?"

"You bet,"

"Try and stop me!"

"Yippee!"

I went to find the corkscrew. Celebrations were clearly on.

***

Barbara roused herself from the hazy state that she seemed to live in permanently these days Then the terrifying visit she had had from the voice on the phone rushed into her mind and she started to shake. What was the job she had muffed? Then she began to remember....

She became aware of voices outside, two men, probably lift engineers, talking as they worked on the lift. She listened vaguely, then something caught her attention.

"....yes, poor old Bill."

"How is he?" the other, deeper voice asked.

"Popped his clogs. Last night. Tom's wrecked."

"*What?* I thought he was getting better. Regained consciousness, remembered what happened and that."

"Well, he's dead now, poor old sod. Pass me that spanner, would you? Then we'll go up."

Another voice joined in, harsher and rougher than the first two.

"Hi, you two. Couldn't help overhearing. Who's copped it? Anyone we know?"

"Our mate, Bill, who fell down the lift shaft." The answering voice was curt. "Must go back up. See you." The voices faded as the lift moved off. Jimbo Preston was left staring after the departing lift.

Alone in her bleak flat Barbara was paralysed. What had she done? Now she remembered her last set of instructions. She was told that she must go to the 13th floor and that she must push a man who would be there into the lift, which would be waiting. She hadn't asked any questions, the voice on the phone didn't like questions. She had done exactly what she had been told; the man was crouched beside the lift entrance, doing something, she couldn't see what. Then she pushed him. She remembered being surprised that he didn't sprawl forward into the lift; she was aware of screaming that stopped abruptly, but it didn't concern her. She had done what she had been told to do and she would be rewarded. She had gone back to her flat, and sure enough, the little packet was waiting.

Was this really what the Voice had meant when he had said that she had muffed it? That she shouldn't have killed the man? Or that it was the wrong man, even? It was all beyond her. But the fact remained, she had killed a man.

Suddenly, all her accumulated doubts left her. She knew what she had to do.

***

Suddenly, it seemed, Christmas was upon us, and everyone seemed more cheerful. In the block, we greeted each other gaily when we met, and everyone seemed to be going to or coming from a party. The Gang had had a serious meeting and it was agreed that, since it had worked so well last year, that we should open up the landing again.

"And let's invite Judith's mother," I suggested. "She really seemed to enjoy it last time."

"She did indeed," confirmed Judith. "Thank you, she'd love it."

Since that memorable Christmas, and Belinda's surprise arrival she had visited the block several times and we all felt we were beginning to know her, so there was general agreement to my suggestion.

"She'll want to contribute, though," said Judith. "Any ideas?"

Julian thought. "Is there anything she particularly likes doing?" he asked.

"She's terrific at table decorations," Judith replied promptly.

"That's it, then. We'll hand over the decorating to her, give her all the things we've collected." Julian, very much in charge, decreed.

"Thanks, I'll tell her," said Judith, gratefully.

"And we'll hand over all last year's bits and pieces to you," I said, with relief.

But my festive spirit was severely strained when I had a phone call late on the night before Christmas Eve from Jacquetta Meyer, whose small son Magda and I had delivered. I remembered she lived on the 10th floor.

"I'm so sorry to trouble you off duty," she said, "but could you possibly help? It's Jacquetta Meyer, flat 37, here. There is the most dreadfully loud music coming from upstairs. I can't get hold of Security, Joshua is away," (he always seemed to be when needed, I thought, perhaps rather unkindly) " and John is yelling his head off. He's worn out but can't possibly sleep with that row going on."

"OK," I said, resigned. After all, this was why I had a rent free flat. "I'll see what I can do." And, reluctantly, I went off to calm things down – if I could.

On the 11th floor the racket was unbelievable; indeed, I had heard it growing in volume as I went up in the even side lift. I hammered as loudly as I could on the offending door – flat 43.

Eventually I heard heavy footsteps approaching and an apparition appeared as the door opened. The man was huge and seemingly covered with hair, I have seldom seen so much hair, and all of it wild. Further more, I didn't remember having seen him before. Surely I would have remembered?

"Could you turn the noise down?" I asked, trying to speak nicely, but it's difficult being polite when you are yelling at the full pitch of your lungs. "You're keeping the baby awake downstairs."

"Wasser marrer? It's my birfday. I'm cele – cele – having fun." The hair was reproachful.

I steeled myself. "It's very late," I yelled severely. Heaven knew what he was on but he seemed friendly enough. I had checked my list before I came up and had found that he was Malin Sterne, a student. Of what? Rugby? He was big enough.

Then the situation was taken out of my hands. Another student, Johannes Nilsen (how I blessed my list!), who was nearly as big as the hirsute Malin but not so hairy, erupted out of flat 44, stormed past me into flat 43 and yanked the player's plug from the wall. A blessed silence fell, tingling slightly from the memory of noise.

"I was lis'nin' to that." Malin was full of reproach. His friends, draped around the flat in various stages of inebriation, were goggling at the sudden change in circumstances but made no move to intervene. Nor did I, I was only too pleased to have the responsibility taken from me.

Johannes lifted the machine bodily, no mean feat as it was large, cumbersome and obviously not light, and carried it into his own flat. "You can have it back in the morning," was his parting shot as he shut the door, not quietly.

"And please have more regard for other people," I said austerely, as I too departed. I called in on Jacquetta on the way down, telling her to call on Johannes if there was any more noise, he clearly had the situation under control.

Next morning a very hangdog Malin, obviously much the worse for wear, hove to at my front door. He was full of apologies, saying over and over again, "It was my birfday, I was cel'brating." I told him firmly that that was no excuse for that amount of noise, and that he should apologise to Jacquetta. Then I shooed him away and went upstairs to thank Johannes for his timely intervention.

"That's alright." The lesser giant was forgiving. "I know him, he's fine until the beer reaches a certain level, then he can be impossible. But he's only noisy, never violent."

I thanked him again and went back downstairs, hoping that the whole Christmas period was not going to be as noisy.

***

Mercifully the rest of the Christmas festivities passed off peacefully and, for me, very happily.

As we had done last year so successfully, we opened up the landing and spent the time very pleasantly together, all five of us, and Belinda, with Ron doing the cooking and the rest of us sharing out the chores between us. Even the cats seemed to enjoy it and spent time in all the flats indiscriminately. Belinda surpassed herself with the decorations and we all had a very happy time, with no interruptions, pleasant or irritating, this time.

Once again, I blessed my good fortune at ending up here and finding such congenial companions. Fleetingly, I wondered how it was that we all "gelled" together so well, despite our very different backgrounds. I even felt that soon I would be able to tell them more about myself. I also realised, for the first time, that it would be a relief to do so.

– Chapter Thirteen –

Then one evening in the New Year, when I had just come off duty and was changing out of my uniform, there was a hesitant knock at the door. Resplendent in a dressing gown I opened it to find two Russian girls, twins, I believed, Ludmilla and Marika Orlova, hovering on the landing (now restored to its usual non-festive arrangement). I knew them quite well having sorted out some problems when they first arrived, when their English was, to say the least, scanty.

"Hello," I said. "Forgive the dressing gown, I was just changing."

They looked at each other. "We are so sorry to disturb you," said one, I think it was Marika (I always had difficulty remembering which was which), "But we are worried." Ludmilla (?) joined in. There was a pause.

"Yes?" I said helpfully.

"We are concerned with the girl in flat 30. We think there may be something wrong," they said together, in a rush. "We haven't seen her for several days now, and when we last saw her she looked dreadfully ill."

"We are not particularly close, you understand," said Marika.

"But we are always friendly when we meet." Ludmilla, this time. I wondered, irrelevantly, if they always spoke in canon.

"How long exactly is it since you saw her?" I asked them.

"We are not sure, but before Christmas. And there is mail sticking out of the letter box."

"Give me a moment to finish changing and I'll come up." This certainly merited investigation. I remembered that I had noticed post in the letter-box; usually I pushed it through. There was no need to advertise absence.

There was nothing to be seen outside flat 30, but there was indeed rather a lot of post on display. I had definitely slipped up this time. I knocked and listened, but I could hear nothing.

"She could just be on holiday, or away for some other reason," I pointed out. The girls agreed dubiously, they seemed unconvinced. I promised to have a word with Security, and with the people in the flat below.

"Please go on looking out for her," I asked them. "It's very good of you to take such care. Many people wouldn't bother."

"It is like that too, in Russia," said Ludmilla. "Too many people, not enough care."

I thanked them again and returned, thoughtfully, to my own quarters.

It had always been a horror in my mind ever since I started as caretaker that someone should die and be left undiscovered for weeks because of my negligence. It was because of this that I kept a special eye on my more elderly and vulnerable tenants. I was concerned about the Orlova girls' report but I did feel that it was perhaps rather too soon to take drastic action; after all, everyone was entitled to their privacy. It was at times like these that I was conscious of my relative inexperience and wished that I knew a caretaker of long standing with whom I could discuss the situation. Going to the Office was no good, Ian was even less experienced than I was. I decided to have a word with Security in the morning, any of them might have seen the tenant, my trusty list identified her as Barbara Desmond, since Christmas. After all, they did seem to have an almost encyclopaedic knowledge of the block. Somehow, it seemed such a solid, dependable name; surely someone like that couldn't have got herself into difficulties?

The next day I had a word with Ian, more in the nature of a report than a call for advice. We agreed that we should do nothing yet but keep on watching. I also had a word with Phil in Security.

"Barbara Desmond," he said in answer to my query. "No, I'm not sure that I call her to mind. Couldn't say for sure whether I've seen her or not. Sorry."

No help there, then.

***

I stood it for another week, then leaned on Ian. Reluctantly, he agreed that something should be done and promised to be there next morning with someone to drill out the lock and a police officer to make it all legal. I didn't care if he brought the town band so long as we could clear up the mystery and that we should discover Barbara fit and well, and surprised at all the fuss.

Promptly at nine the next morning Ian duly turned up with a stalwart police officer, who had the comforting appearance of having seen it all before, twice. The official man of all trades stepped up with his drill and proceeded to drill out the lock.

"Good thing you've got that drill, you'd never break that door down, else. It'd bring the whole wall down." The police officer was clearly experienced.

In a very short space of time the lock was drilled through and the door swung open. We listened, but heard nothing, not a sound, not a movement. It was viciously cold. We went in.

The first thing I noticed was how dark it was. No lights were on and the windows seemed to be covered, either with cardboard or with very thick curtains. It was absolutely silent, but strangely, the flat did not feel empty. Involuntarily, I shivered.

"Is there anyone there?" Ian took charge. He tried to switch on a light, but nothing happened.

"Here, try this." The driller of door locks handed over a large torch. "Never go anywhere without it."

With a word of thanks Ian took it, and led us into the living room. This, too, was totally dark; there were curtains, but on opening them we found that sheets of cardboard had been jammed into the frame, excluding all the light and imparting a musty, dusty odour to the room. On the 8th floor it was too high for this to have been noticeable from the ground. Between us, we managed to tug the cardboard free and let in some blessed light.

A dismal scene met our eyes. There was very little furniture; what there was, was dilapidated, shabby and covered with a layer of dust. The carpet was threadbare and dirty. Saucers, overflowing with cigarette ends littered surfaces and the floor, contributing to the dusty, stuffy atmosphere. I went into the kitchen; this too was blacked out but there was enough light from the living room to show that there were some dirty dishes in the sink, but very few, and, when I opened the fridge, it was completely empty.

I think we were all dreading what we might find for we lingered in the living room rather than pressing on into the bedrooms. The first one we tried was boarded up as before but otherwise totally empty, not so much as a box in it. This left the second bedroom. We girded up our collective loins and went in.

This was, as expected, boarded up but it was not empty. In the gloom we could see a shape on the bed, lying very still. The police officer went straight to the window, wrenched off its covering and we could see.

We could see a girl, seemingly in her late twenties, lying on a dishevelled bed. She was clearly dead, probably had been for sometime, though the extreme cold had preserved her. She was strangely peaceful; perhaps fancifully I felt that death had indeed been a release for her. Several pill bottles and a hypodermic syringe lay on a chair beside her that was evidently taking the place of a bedside table. The chair lacked most of its back and the bed was tilted, clearly minus a leg; there was nothing else in the room whatsoever.

As I stood beside the bed, looking down at its pathetic occupant I saw the corner of what looked like an envelope under the girl's hand. I drew it out and handed it to the police officer. There was a name on it but I couldn't see what it was.

"Looks like a suicide note. That'll make things easier for us." Authority, in the shape of the police officer, was relieved.

"What happens now?" Ian wanted to know.

"I'll have to call up reinforcements, make sure there are no suspicious circumstances. Can anyone identify the lady?"

We shook our heads, I realised I didn't even know her by sight.

"The Russian girls opposite know her as living here," I volunteered, hoping to goodness they were here legally, and not terrified of the police. "I had better go across and tell them what we've found, they have been very anxious, and, indeed, alerted us in the first place."

"Yes, do that. And see if they can identify the – girl."

I departed, not sorry to leave the dismal flat. But Ludmilla and Marika were both out, presumably at work so I had to go back. I found that nothing had changed in my absence.

As I went in I realised again how freezingly cold the flat was. The air was icy, with a chill that seemed to seep into your very bones. I also realised that a saucer on the bedside chair had contained the end of a candle. I had a thought and went to check the electricity cupboard. There was no sign of a meter, just a couple of loose wires. I fetched the constable.

"Whew! This is beyond my range of activities. This where I definitely call out the cavalry."

"Is it still likely to be suicide?" I asked.

"Probably, but now there is more to look at." He went out to the landing and spoke at some length on his radio. "Right," he said, coming back in. "Nothing more we can do here, just make the door secure and then leave it to the experts." He took the note I had given him out of his pocket and looked at it. "This is evidence, I shall have to keep it. Mrs Jean Desmond. Her mother perhaps?"

We looked blank, we had no idea.

"It would seem possible," Ian said at last. "I'll check our records. I can tell her you have a note if we can contact her."

"Do that. Now, let's go." He seemed not sorry to be away. I wondered how long he had been in the job; for all his apparent experience, perhaps it had been his first suicide, as it was mine.

"Sadly, no," he said when I asked him. "But it doesn't seem to get any easier. Still, I suppose that means we're human. Such a waste."

Meanwhile, a new lock had been fitted and the keys handed over to Ian. I was thankful it was not my responsibility. He locked up and we went down in the lift, all of us subdued and disinclined for conversation. I went to the ground floor with them and saw them off the premises. Ian was the last to leave.

"Try not to worry about this," he said, with rare sympathy. "There was probably nothing you could have done and you can't know everybody in the block. Probably she kept herself to herself. You're the caretaker, not their keeper."

Yes, probably.

But he was being kind so I roused myself to make a courteous reply. But I didn't tell him what was behind my silence. I was remembering the fun that Ron, Julian, Magda, Judith and I had had over Christmas, totally oblivious to what was going on not so far above our heads. I shivered.

***

Two days later Ian rang me; he had managed to contact

Barbara's mother and she would be coming to the block at the weekend. Would I make sure that I was there to see her.

Repressing an impulse to say that I was leaving for Outer Mongolia in an hour I agreed. "Though I don't see what help I can be. I can't say that I hardly knew the girl, not even enough to identify her formally."

"No, but you did instigate finding her body."

"Only because of the Orlova girls. They are the ones she should see."

"No matter. Be there." *That's an order* hung palpably in the air.

Various people had been in and out of the flat since poor Barbara's body had been moved to the mortuary; I had managed to be around for that and escorted the coffin into the hearse. It seemed to be the least I could do, somehow. No one seemed to notice as the hearse drove away, or so I thought. Then I saw Tom gazing sadly after it. I was surprised, I'd not seen him for some time.

"Hello," I said. "How are you? I've not seen you for ages."

"No," he said. "I've been on compassionate, helping my sister sort things out."

I looked a question. "Didn't you know? Bill didn't make it."

"But I thought he was on the mend. I assumed he was home convalescing by now."

"He did seem to do well then he had a heart attack and that was that. It was strange, but perhaps his heart was bad and no one knew."

I was very concerned. "Then it was not the fall that killed him?"

"No, not as such, though it couldn't have helped. The post mortem found natural causes. So no compensation. Oh well, I'm back now. Best get on."

"I'm really sorry," I said awkwardly.

"Thanks. That hearse brought it all back. See you." And he went on into the block.

I had been to see the Orlova girls to tell them what had happened. They were, of course, very shocked and sad.

"We should have done more for her," Marika said, distressed.

"You both did more for her than anyone," I pointed out.

"But it was not enough," she replied, unanswerably.

Soon after this conversation, Magda came upon me as I was putting the rubbish bins out. I hadn't seen any of the Gang since the finding of Barbara, I hadn't felt equal to explaining.

"What on earth's the matter?" Magda asked. Clearly I looked as bad as I felt. She confirmed it. "You look awful. Come along and explain All." Magda being masterful was as irresistible as a tank charge. Meekly I did as I was told.

It took a few minutes to get going, but once started I told her everything, finishing off with the guilt I felt at partying while Barbara was taking her own life.

"Are you sure that was when she died?"

"It seems like it," I said miserably.

"'But none of us could possibly have known," she said, reasonably. "In a place like this anything can go on, and probably does, but we are not responsible for what we can't know."

I had to agree with her, with a fleeting memory of some of the things that had gone on in the past eighteen months or so.

"I know you're right, but I still feel guilty. I feel I should have known. And I have to meet her mother on Friday. That will probably make me feel worse."

"Well, I certainly don't envy you that. Is Ian going to be there? He shouldn't leave you to face her on your own."

"I don't know. It is the weekend, after all."

"Yes, and it's your weekend too." Magda was nothing if not on my side. I began to feel better.

***

Barbara's mother duly turned up as expected, escorted by Ian with the keys. I had forgotten that little point. She was younger than I had expected, small and fair, and perhaps rather too used to being helped. I sensed a certain amount of the clinging vine. Ian unlocked the door and we all went in. If anything, the flat looked worse, and was even colder than when we had last been there. Mrs Desmond was obviously appalled.

"How could she have possibly lived like this? Where has all the furniture been taken? And what is all that cardboard?" I explained about the windows being blanked off. "But did nobody notice this? Are you all blind? You obviously don't care two straws for your tenants. And *where is* her furniture? Has it been stolen?" She rounded on me. "Have *you* stolen it? Is it all in *your* flat? Have there been looters? It should have been made secure. You have clearly been very negligent. I shall make an official complaint." She ran out of breath.

Ian, at last, spoke up. "Nothing has been stolen because there was nothing there. It is outrageous to accuse our caretaker of theft. When we came in it was because of her anxiety and concern for your daughter's welfare. It was just as you see, plus the fact that the electricity meter has been torn out. There is still no explanation for that. There was no light, no heat and your daughter had obviously been taking drugs, probably over a lengthy period. If you are complaining that your daughter lacked care you should look closer to home."

Not surprisingly Mrs Desmond dissolved into tears. I glared at Ian. I was grateful for the support, but he had been way too harsh. Obviously, the poor woman was distraught, and he wasn't helping.

I made soothing noises and she calmed down a little.

"There's something I don't begin to understand," she said, fishing in a capacious handbag. She pulled out a crumpled envelope. "It's in her note. Did you see it?"

We shook our heads.

"No, of course not, it's addressed to me. The police gave it to me. Well, in it she says she killed a man. That she didn't mean to, but she did. That's quite impossible. My little Barbara couldn't *possibly* kill anyone. What can she mean?"

"Perhaps she was hallucinating," I said soothingly. "You know, with the drugs." But I was thinking furiously. Two and two seemed to be making a totally unbelievable four. I put my thoughts aside for later. "Would you like to meet the neighbours who alerted us to the fact that they hadn't seen Barbara for a while?" I wanted to change the subject and prayed that Ludmilla and Marika were at home. Speechlessly, Mrs Desmond nodded and I shepherded her to flat 29. Mercifully, both the sisters were in, and once the identity of their visitor was made known they surrounded her with sympathy. I felt we could safely leave the poor mother in their hands.

Ian and I went down in the lift, both of us, I think, feeling a vast relief. It had been bad, but could have been worse. I asked him if he thought we should ever know what had really happened.

"Probably not." He was offhand. "Just one of life's little

mysteries." And to think I was almost feeling grateful to him. I bade him a somewhat frigid farewell, but I doubt that he even noticed. "Let him go back to his cosy weekend and cut the grass, or whatever," I thought viciously, forgetting it was January and hardly the grass cutting season. "If he plays golf I hope he gets stuck in a bunker and stays there *all night.*" Rudi opened an astonished eye at my vehemence – I had waited to relieve my feelings until I was safely in my own flat – stretched, and went back to sleep. Humans, and me in particular, were beyond his ken.

***

I did eventually learn a little more about Barbara. It seemed that, although the police were pretty sure it was suicide, it was drug related and that had got their antennae waving. She was known to be a user, and had turned to petty crime to fund her habit. They had hoped to find her supplier, but these hopes were fading. All her money went on drugs, they in turn had prevented her from finding work. Her mother's surprise at the empty flat was also explained. It had been beautifully and lovingly furnished by mother and daughter, and Barbara had a good job as a club hostess – "Respectable, I assure you," my police informant said hastily. "But perhaps that was how she became hooked on drugs. We think she may have been involved in an armed robbery, causing a distraction while the thieves got going, but that was, we think, her first crime, to get her hooked and too heavily involved to escape. Since then it's only been petty stuff, shop lifting, look out, things like that. But we can't be sure, and she was never charged with anything."

I had a visit from Mrs Desmond, full of apologies for her outburst. I assured her it didn't matter, that I quite understood, and that I wished I had known more about what had been going on. "Why don't you come in, have a cup of tea, and we'll see if we can work anything out." I held the door open hospitably.

"Thank you," said Mrs Desmond, gratefully. She clearly felt a need to talk about her daughter. I wondered what I was letting myself in for, but in common humanity I had to try to help.

Once settled with tea, and ignoring disapproving looks from the cats – didn't anyone realise this was siesta time? – the floodgates opened.

"You know, I don't think she allowed anyone to know," she said sadly. "I know I accused you of not knowing what was going on, but I was wrong, I'm sorry. She even kept me at arm's length, and we used to be so close. I couldn't understand it.

"We had great fun choosing things for her flat. She had been working as a hostess at a club at home, well, it was more of a manageress, really. She used to welcome people, see that everything ran smoothly, organise staff rotas, everything like that. She was really good, the members liked her and everything ran smoothly. I used to go in quite often for lunch or tea, the club was open from ten in the morning till midnight. It was a long day, but she loved it. As it was so near our home she lived there, which was so nice for me. She took over the top floor and made it into her own flat, with a separate entrance and everything."

She paused for breath, took a drink of tea and went on. "I was so proud of her when I went into the club, she looked so beautiful. She wore a black dress during the day, very simple, then something more dressy in the evenings. Then the club owners decided to open a branch here in Arkchester and asked Barbara to take it on and run it. We were thrilled, she came up here full of ideas to make it even better than the original one. She found this flat and everything seemed wonderful."

Here poor Mrs Desmond succumbed to a burst of tears. I waited quietly and presently she went on: "When she first moved here she used to like me to visit and we had great fun choosing the things for the flat. I had given her all the things from her old flat and we added to them, pictures, ornaments, things like that. I used to come up every couple of weeks at first, then every month. We used to go to auctions too, and find treasures, big and small. There was no shortage of money, the club paid her well, more when she moved here, plus a generous lump sum for her to find and furnish her own home.

"Then suddenly, all the shutters went up, it was never convenient for me to visit, I usually got the answer-phone when I rang, and she rang back less and less and finally stopped altogether. I've heard nothing for nearly six months.

"Then the club owners started calling, asking me what was happening, where she had gone. Apparently, no sooner had she got the club up and running than she disappeared. I didn't know what to think. And I couldn't get hold of her to ask. Even when I came up here, she never answered the door. I didn't know whether she was here or not, though your security man said that no one else was in her flat. I was frantic, but completely helpless."

I felt really sorry for her, and also less guilty. I began to wonder if Barbara had been supplied by the Smiths on the top floor, and resolved to mention it to the police. I said nothing to Mrs Desmond, it wouldn't help and would probably distress her further, and needlessly.

"What do you want to do about the funeral?" I asked.

"I am going to take Barbara's body south to her childhood home, when the police release it," Mrs Desmond informed me.

I was relieved, obviously I couldn't go all that way to a block funeral. I hoped it would comfort the bereaved mother. She got up. "I must go, I've taken up far too much of your time. Thank you so much, you've been so kind. I'm really sorry I accused you of theft. It was dreadful of me."

"Don't worry about it," I said soothingly. "You were upset, I quite understand."

"I expect you were upset too," she said unexpectedly.

"Well, yes, I was," I admitted. "I had a horror of something like that happening when I took on the job, but never really expected that it would. Thank *you*, for taking the time to talk to me."

We parted, with expressions of mutual esteem.

***

I wondered when the block grapevine would find out about the suicide. I didn't have long to wait.

I met Malin Sterne in the lift, still repentant over his Christmas Eve lapse from sobriety. He didn't beat about the bush. "Is it true that a girl topped herself in the block?" he asked.

I confirmed that a girl had died but that it was not yet certain whether or not it was suicide. I waited for the next question.

"When did it happen?"

"As far as we know, sometime over the Christmas period."

"So while we were having our party she was doin' it?"

"It's a possibility."

"What a bugger." He said no more until the lift reached the ground floor, then he looked at me. "We'd never have been so noisy if we'd known," he said sadly, and went off across the foyer, head drooping. As an epitaph it took some beating, and I had a feeling there would be no more noisy parties in flat 43. It eased my own guilt to have a companion in remorse.

– Chapter Fourteen –

In the cubbyhole glorified by the name of Junior Doctors' Common Room at the William and Mary Hospital, several members of the junior doctors staff were strewn in attitudes of exhaustion across sundry shabby chairs. Coffee mugs were much in evidence, and had it not been for a No Smoking policy in the hospital an onlooker would not have been surprised to find the atmosphere thick with smoke from the weed.

One of the recumbent figures roused himself. Clearly a long awaited moment had come. "Hey, Brian, whatever is eating you? You've been in the depths for days and we're fed up with having our noses snapped off if we dare speak to you."

Brian, who indeed was sitting a little apart and seemed to be sunk in thought, grinned. "Sorry, Pete. I know I've been impossible but I am seriously worried."

The assembled audience woke up and started to pay attention. As Peter Dennis had said, they had all suffered from Brian Somerville's uncharacteristic moroseness of late and had murmured about it amongst themselves.

"Come on then, cough it up. Or do you need more coffee as inspiration?" Susan Makepiece, a pretty redhead, started to uncoil herself to make the proffered brew.

Brian shook his head. "No, I think the time has come to see what you lot think." He settled himself more comfortably in the shabby chair. "Do you remember the lift engineer who came in shortly before Christmas? He had fallen down the lift shaft at Tower Court and presented with multiple fractures and head injuries."

His audience nodded. "Bill Edwards," said Peter. "Seemed to be doing well then suddenly had a heart attack and died."

"Precisely, that's the one. It was accepted as a perfectly ordinary natural causes; though there was an autopsy nothing was found. Now you remember how busy we were at that time with the mini flu epidemic? How we were only too happy to have a straightforward natural causes death?" His audience nodded. "Well,

I've been remembering. You may recall that I was the doctor on duty, and the nurses called me. It seemed straightforward enough, but I did see a small mark on the arm like a hypodermic puncture wound and couldn't imagine what it was doing there; he had a cannula for drug administration. Then the Prof called me so I scribbled on the form and fled. I forgot all about it until last week when I had that junkie with puncture wounds all over the place. And I've not been able to get it out of my mind."

"What are you saying?" demanded Peter. "That he injected himself with heroin which then vanished out of his body? Come on!"

Brian didn't smile. "No. First, remember there was a police guard on the patient because he had remembered that he was pushed into the shaft. What if someone needed to ensure that he didn't remember anything else?"

"But Brian, there was a police presence, you've just said so." Susan looked concerned.

"Even the police have to go to the loo sometimes. Perhaps he should have called someone, but it probably seemed safe enough, especially as the toilets are so close to that side ward. No, what could be injected that would leave no trace but would lead to a heart attack at some moment? And there was another point. Do you remember Sister having a right go at one of the nurses because a drip bag had leaked and made the floor slippery?"

"Do I," laughed Peter. "I thought the nurse was either going to burst into tears or faint, or possibly both. I remember wondering at the time why Sister was so het up."

"Which nurse was it?" asked Susan. "Was it the dippy one who never, ever gets things right till she's been told a minimum of three times? If so, no wonder Sister was in a strop. She's a disaster waiting to happen, that girl."

"Yes, as a matter of fact it was her." Peter blushed slightly. "She's not nearly so dippy when you get to know her, just nervous. Anyway," he added hurriedly, as the others started to show far too much interest for his peace of mind, "what about it?"

"What if the bag had been injected with something as well, to make certain?"

"Now you are in the world of make believe," scoffed Peter. "What substance, pray tell?"

"Potassium." His audience gaped at him. "Causes a heart attack if taken in excess? Not too fast acting so the murderer can be well away? Nothing left in the body? And, finally, what killed Bill Edwards, who was supposed to be on the road to recovery? I rest my case."

"And you've swallowed a medical textbook," snorted Susan

"Hang about." Another doctor, Henry Thomas, looked up. "You may not have heard, but two of the nurses were giggling about Bill Edwards after he died. They said he must have been having incredibly erotic dreams and no wonder he had a heart attack. Apparently he had a massive erection. I gave them a rocket for gossiping about a patient and for unprofessional conduct." He looked smug.

The other doctors burst into shouts of laughter. Henry was well known for doing precisely that, no one was safe from his busy tongue.

He had the grace to look sheepish. "Well, I've been hauled over the coals for it so often I can recognise it when I see it," he explained.

"That, too, can be caused by potassium." Brian called the meeting to order. "No, I didn't know about it. Could be a clincher. Now what the hell do I do about this.?" Brian looked round his audience in despair.

"You are seriously thinking that this could be – *murder?"* asked Susan, incredulously.

Brian looked at her. "I know it sounds weird, but yes, I think I am. There are too many questions. And I say again, what am I going to do about it? If I go to hospital management they'll start playing the blame game, and I don't think it's anyone's fault, not seriously. The patient was under police protection, for heaven's sake!"

There was a silence, then Peter leapt to his feet. "You do this," he shouted. "My cousin is one Robin Lutterworth, he recently joined CID and has been looking into things at Tower Court. The caretaker found body parts in the bins. I'll give him a ring and you can offload onto him. Then it will cease to be your responsibility!" He beamed round and sat down, well pleased.

"Pete, could you really do that? It would be a load off my mind." Brian looked greatly relieved.

"Consider it done, old friend. Consider it done!"

**

January 14th, the day we were to make use of our "gold dust" tickets for *Sleeping Beauty,* was surprisingly warm for the time of year. We had decided to make a day of it, and having had lunch in town, we sat outside with glasses of wine, making the most of the winter sunshine.

"This is the life," said Julian. "I could really get used to this, except that it should be champagne and the dress circle, or a box, this evening."

He was interrupted. "Julian Fry as I live and breathe!" The voice was only too familiar to me. I had a nasty feeling my cat was about to emerge from the bag. I was right. "I'd completely forgotten you lived in Arkchester. Who are – *Francesca!* What on *earth* are you doing here? And with Julian? Do you actually *know* him?"

"Hello, Ella. Yes I do know Julian, we're neighbours. And we're here because we're coming to see you tonight. How are you? How's the show? Am I going to grind my teeth or beam fondly?"

"Beam fondly, I hope. It's a good production." She leaned forward and hissed in my ear, "Do they know what you do?"

"No," I hissed back, "I'll tell them later."

My friends, in various degrees of bewilderment were waiting patiently for me to explain what was going on. Ron was holding tightly to Julian's arm, I suspected that it was only that grip that was keeping his volatile partner quiet.

"This is Ella Foster, formerly principal ballerina of the Gressington Ballet, and currently Senior Ballet Mistress and Artistic Director of the company." I performed the introductions with a wicked grin at Ella. She hated having her titles rolled out. "How I know her, and know her well, I might add, I promise I will explain later, with due apologies for keeping quiet about my past life."

"You're quite entitled to keep as quiet as you like," Magda broke in.

"Thank you, but I feel that you are now entitled to explanations, but later. Ella, do join us. You've got bags of time before the performance."

"Don't you believe it," said Ella feelingly. "It takes forever to make up. Fake everything, my dears, and the wig is very nearly alive. But I have some time. Can you get coffee here? No booze pre-performance, unfortunately. But afterwards, that's another story." She grinned fiendishly. So did I, recalling some memorable post show parties.

"I'll get you some." Julian leapt to his feet.

"Thank you, darling. Black filtered, please, and just a drop of milk. Well, this is nice. And are you going to introduce these other friends, or do I guess?"

"Sorry." Belatedly I remembered my manners. "This is Magda Benjamin, flat 2, and Ron Peters, Julian's partner. They are both in flat 1. We, with Judith English who is away at the moment, form the Gang that I've told you about."

"You have indeed, and I am delighted to meet you all. Francesca and I go back a long way. Oh, thank you, that's just right," as Julian placed a large cup of very dark coffee before her. "Now, where are you sitting? Oh, that won't do," as Julian meekly handed her the tickets. She scribbled a note on the envelope and signed it with a flourish. "Take that to the box office and see if Carabosse can still perform some magic."

"Th – thank you," Julian stammered. He still looked completely shell-shocked. Ella gave her wicked grin again.

"I do like being surprising," she said complacently. She drained her coffee. "Now, I must fly. Come round after the show and tell me what it's like. Though I shall *not* tell them you are in the audience," she added to me. She gave me a final hug, blew a kiss to the others and vanished down the street in a flurry of scarves.

"Well!" exclaimed Julian. "You certainly have some explaining to do, young Frankie."

"But only if you want to," said Magda with a minatory look which Julian blithely ignored. "Everyone is entitled to privacy."

"I know," I said, "and I do feel bad at not telling you more about my former life. But I will tell you this evening, after the show. Suffice it to say at the moment that I have had a great deal to do with the ballet world in general and the Gressington Company and School in particular." I looked at my watch. "Come on, let's go and see what Ella has cooked up with the box office. We can have more wine in the theatre bar."

***

Ella Foster did indeed like being surprising. The box office looked at the scribbled note and handed over replacement tickets. Although the auditorium was not yet officially open we were escorted to a box and ushered into its little anteroom like visiting royalty. Hardly had we taken off numerous coats and wrappings than there was a knock at the door and a waiter came in bearing what he clearly thought of as the Holy Grail, a bottle of champagne in an ice bucket, and followed by an underling bearing four champagne flutes on a tray together with a plate of miniscule sandwiches. These goodies were placed on a table; "With Miss Foster's compliments," murmured the first one reverently.

"Thank you," I said, everyone else being too shell-shocked to say anything. I turned to Julian. "Be careful what you wish for, it might come true," I said to him.

"It might, mightn't it," he agreed.

That was the start of an idyllic evening. Ella outdid herself in vengeful fury as the evil fairy Carabosse, wickedly shooting me particularly sizzling glances as I sat, I hoped regally, in the stage box. The lively wig proved to be, apparently, made of snakes, which were certainly impressive. The company indeed excelled themselves, with the Rose Adagio being particularly successful. I was relieved, I knew the young dancer concerned was far from secure in it. But this time she danced strongly, held the balances perfectly, and managed to look every inch the birthday princess as well. And I purred smugly during "Bluebird" – I had coached the young man myself! He was everything that I had hoped he would be.

At the first interval, with more goodies brought in courtesy of Ella, Julian looked at me. "I don't want to be a bore –" "then shut up" interrupted Ron "- but did you have anything to do with this production?"

"Not directly, but I have taught Alicia, who is dancing Aurora, and I coached Igor who is dancing the Bluebird in Act III. He was having terrible trouble with his brisés," I said wickedly, knowing full well they wouldn't have the remotest idea what I was talking about.

"Sounds painful. And for that you can point it out when he gets to it."

"Them," I murmured. "Didn't you say that the bats and so on

came from local schools?"

Julian was glad to change the subject. "Yes, I did, that's how I got the tickets, the original tickets, that is. They're doing well, aren't they?"

"They are indeed," I agreed, "and obviously thoroughly enjoying themselves. That little boy who turns somersaults whenever he can get away with it shows quite a lot of promise."

"I thought so, too," said Julian, looking gratified. "And he has *not* got a pushy mother. I've photographed him and she was really helpful. And managed to keep him in order. Not easy, I've never met a child with so much energy."

"Come on, you two." Magda called us to order. "The next act is starting."

We trooped round afterwards to see Ella. I was concerned that she was plainly very tired, it was obvious that this truly was her farewell tour. We stayed long enough to congratulate her, and I sent messages to Alicia and Igor. Then we started to wend our way home – and my overdue explanation.

***

I had first met Ella when we were both pupils at the Gressington Ballet School, though she was way ahead of me in ability. Even then, she showed exceptional talent; I was good, or I would not have been accepted as a pupil at the school, but Ella was going to be great. Events were to prove that this was true.

I very soon discovered that I was not cut out to be a performer. We had many opportunities to appear on stage during our training; at first I quite enjoyed it, but eventually I came actively to dislike it. On the other hand, I loved helping the younger ones with their work.

This did not go unnoticed by the staff. When I was sixteen, at a time when I should have been looking forward to entering a company, the Principal, Alexandra Gressington herself, called me in to see her. I was shaking in my shoes, she was a very imposing woman and we seldom even saw her.

She had danced in the Diaghilev company as a young girl and was unusual in that she had flatly refused to "Russianize" her name. Later she had founded the Gressington Ballet, dancing the major roles herself, and gathering round her a strong company from dancers she had met while touring with Diaghilev in her youth. This led to the foundation of the School attached to the company, which had, as Julian had said when I first went to Tower Court, a reputation on a par with the Royal Ballet School and the English National Ballet School today.

I went to Madame Alexandra's sumptuous office, knocked, entered and gave the obligatory curtsey, wondering what my fate would be.

"Come in, chèrie. Sit down. Do not be afraid, I am not going to scold you, or throw you to the wolves outside this ballet world of ours. But you do not like to perform, do you?"

"No, Madame Alexandra," I admitted. Surely this was heresy? Would I be shot at dawn?

Madame Alexandra (she had long ago decided that this was how she was to be addressed in the School, but of course I didn't know that – then. It was just tradition as far as I was concerned) laughed gently. "You students," she shook her head. "You always think we know nothing, that we, the staff, haven't experienced just the doubts that you feel. I assure you, we have. And we have decided, in your case, that you will stop trying to force yourself into the performer's role and concentrate on teaching." She sat back. If she wasn't the great Madame Alexandra I'd have said she looked smug. "Am I not right?" she asked. "Do you not, in fact infinitely prefer to teach?"

"Y – yes," I stammered. I did indeed, I loved helping the younger ones sort out their problems, but how on earth did she know?

"You thought your classes –"

"I wouldn't call them that," I protested.

"Your classes," she repeated, "were a great secret. Far from it. We, the staff, all knew about them and, I might add, applauded. You managed to help many of our younger ones achieve great things. You have the knack of finding the best way to approach their problems and put them right. Because of that, we want you to teach the new Saturday classes we are starting for local children. Oh, not completely on your own," she had obviously picked up my horrified expression, "you will, of course be supervised, but the classes will be yours to run as you please, subject to this supervision. What do you say? Will you do this thing for us?"

"*Yes!*" It was like having Christmas and a birthday together. "When do I start?"

Madame Alexandra laughed at my enthusiasm. "In September, at the beginning of the academic year. Instead of repertoire classes you will go to different staff members and be instructed in teaching methods. You will also receive tuition in anatomy and physiology, all teachers should know how the body works. One day, I predict, all dance teachers will need this. At the moment I know of only a few training establishments who include such things." She paused, apparently lost in thought. After a moment she went on. "Now, off you go, tell Ella the great news –" I blinked, did she truly know everything? It was just what I was longing to do! – "and be ready to start your new time-table on Monday."

I was so excited I nearly forgot to curtsey at the door, I could hear her laughing as I tore down the corridor. I shot into the studio where I knew Ella was practising.

"I'm going to be a teacher!" I yelled.

"Quite right too," she replied coolly. "Now you can help me. How in the world do I get myself into this arabesque without putting in a glissade?"

"Posé on the right foot instead of the left," I said, without thinking.

She grinned. "There you are. A natural born teacher as I am a natural born dancer. I knew it all along."

That was the start of my career as a teacher. The school put me in for my teaching exams – they didn't bother with exams normally, they taught their own syllabi, but I needed recognised qualifications. In fact, I was the start of the teaching side of the school, and in due course I was training teachers as well as performers there. As my reputation grew I started going to other countries to freelance in teaching in their schools and companies. It was a heady existence, and very exciting. But I always flew back to the nest to refresh myself and hone my teaching skills.

I was teaching in South Africa when I met my husband, Richard. I fell over him, literally. I was following him down a flight of steps when he suddenly stopped dead. I was miles away, as usual, crashed into him and we both fell to the bottom of the flight, with me, mercifully, on top. We picked ourselves up, assured each other we were not hurt in the least, and decided we needed coffee to make quite sure. I was lost the moment I looked into brown eyes fringed with lashes I would give my eyeteeth for. He told me it was the same for him, except that it was my laugh he fell for.

I discovered that he was a musician, leading almost as peripatetic life as I was, but conducting. We were even going to be leaving on the same day and returning to the UK on the same plane. If that wasn't fate, what was it?

One thing led to another and we found that with a little ingenuity our two professional lives could be made to work.

And so they did, very happily and successfully until I became pregnant. Even then, we managed pretty well, Philippa was such a good baby we found we were able to carry on nearly as before. We established a base in London, which we hadn't really needed until then, and I did stay closer to the UK with my commitments, but that was about all the adjustment we found we had to make. Then Justin was born and things began to fall apart.

It was in a mood of defiance that I accepted a prestigious – and very pressing – invitation to teach for six months in America. I had done very little work and was feeling intolerably house-bound; Richard seemed to think that I should be satisfied with the children and some teaching while he undertook conducting engagements all over the world. I was alone far too much and fell to brooding. The American idea was in the nature of an ultimatum. We parted on distinctly cool terms.

I could be said to have got my just deserts when I had a serious fall two months into my contract. One leg was badly broken and I had many other injuries, which necessitated prolonged periods of hospital treatment. On the plus side, it did bring Richard and me together again; he visited me several times before we decided that the sensible thing was to bring the children over and set up house in the States until my injuries were finally healed. Whether or not I would ever be able to work again we carefully did not discuss.

So it was that Richard was flying in with Philly and Justin when the plane fell out of the sky and there were no survivors. And no explanation as to what had happened.

That was the start of a very bleak period. I still needed massive hospital treatment, which ate up my money, as, not being resident, I had no insurance. At last, eighteen months later I returned to the UK, well, fairly strong – and penniless. Ella, who by now had taken over the Gressington, was able to give me some work but could not afford to employ me full time. So, in the fullness of time I came to Tower Court and took up my new career as caretaker, warden, detective and tea lady to the masses.

***

We retired to flat 1 with yet more wine and plates of Ron's nibbles prepared in advance for the post show wind down. As we settled I tried to arrange my thoughts; my whole life story was not sufficiently interesting to tell and some aspects were still too painful.

"Now!" said Julian. "Please?" as Magda glared at him.

"Now," I agreed. "I should first thank you for not asking me about my past life when I gave you the address when you were cat sitting for me. It is, of course, Ella's flat at Gressington Hall. I go there and do some teaching whenever I'm off, I have a room at the School.

"As you know by now I have been involved in ballet for years, virtually all my life, counting when I started dancing classes, soon after the end of the War."

"Were you a ballerina?" asked a slightly awestruck Julian.

"Good heavens, no," I laughed. "That is a definite, and very senior, rank in the ballet world. Even Alicia, who danced the princess this evening, isn't a ballerina, just a soloist. Yet. I think she has the talent, I just wonder about her temperament." I paused for a moment, lost in thought. Julian recalled me to my story. "Sorry. In fact, I never wanted to dance myself, but I did want, desperately, to teach. And teach I did, all over the place, freelancing in ballet schools and companies, in this country and in Europe, and even, for two years, in Australia. Now that was something. I loved that."

"Why did you stop?" asked Ron. "You must have been good, teaching in all those different places."

"Injury and finance, and the two went hand in hand. I was in America when I fell down a flight of stairs and broke my leg badly. That put paid to teaching for months, plus this was America, I had no medical insurance and the treatments ate up nearly all my savings. It was very good treatment though, I arrived back in the UK nearly as strong as ever but broke."

I took a reviving gulp of wine. I was afraid that I would not be able to leave it there. I was right.

"What about your family?" asked Magda. I remember, when we were doing our midwife bit that you said you had had two children."

I stiffened. I tried not to, it was an obvious question, but I couldn't help it. "Yes," I said. "I did, two, one of each. But they and my husband were killed in a plane crash when they were coming to join me in America. I'm sorry, it's still too painful to talk about."

There was a moment's sympathetic silence, which was broken by Julian.

"What happened next?" He was clearly enthralled.

"I had done quite a lot of teaching at the Gressington over the years, both in the School and taking company class. I had got to know Ella well when we were both pupils and then students at the School, so she was able to give me some teaching work, she had taken over the school and the company by that time, but they could not afford to take me on full time. Funding is pretty tight. So eventually I decided to break loose completely. I tried several jobs, then I saw the advertisement for this caretaker's job, went for it, got it, and the rest, as they say, is history. I still do the odd bit of teaching at the Gressington, I call it my other life." I grinned round at them affectionately. "And now you are part of it."

"And when I think how I told you all about the big companies," wailed Julian. "How you must have laughed."

"No, I didn't, not at all," I hastened to reassure him. "It was just that the memory of my old life and all I had lost through the accident was still too painful. I couldn't face explanations so it seemed better just to pretend I didn't know anything. I'm sorry."

"And now you feel able to talk to us?" asked Ron, a little anxiously.

"Yes I do, and I can't tell you how grateful I am. And can you tell Judith at some point? She shouldn't miss out on it." I got up. "And now I'm bound for my bed. Sophie and Rudi will give me hell for being a nasty little stop out."

Julian came across and gave me a hug. "Thank you for trusting us enough to tell us."

I hugged him back. "Thank you for trusting me enough not to ask questions. And after such mutual admiration, good night!" And I left, amid laughter.

***

"Didn't I say she looked like a dancer?" said Julian triumphantly as he and Ron set the room to rights.

"You did. And I am so glad she was able to tell us about her life at last. It can't have been easy for her."

"No. She skated over the accident and that but it must have been hell on wheels for her at the time, especially with the plane crash to cope with on top of it all. And then job hunting when all she's done is ballet. No wonder she's such a good caretaker, probably thinks Tower Court is a stage set!"

"Maybe. Well, I for one am going to exit. Tomorrow is also a day."

***

In her office beside the forensic laboratory attached to the police headquarters in Arkchester, Julia Yates was staring at her computer. It was very late but Julia had had a row with her boy friend and was in no mood to go home. She was trying to see if there was a DNA match for the body parts discovered in such a macabre manner at the tower block in Heathfield.

Earlier she had determined that the hands and feet belonged to one person. There had been a visual match but DNA had clinched it. Now she needed to know if the so far unknown had come to the notice of the police when alive.

She leant forward and gazed intently at the screen. There was no doubt about it, she had a match. The hands and feet had an owner: Theo Carson. The name meant nothing to her. She toyed with the idea of bringing his file up on her screen but was suddenly hit by fatigue. Instead, she lifted the phone and called the office where the Tower Court investigation was being carried out. She just hoped someone would be there.

***

Once again a conference was in progress at the College Road

police station. The atmosphere was somewhat despondent, very little seemed to have been achieved.

"Let's just recap," Chief Inspector Johnson said at last. "By the way, where's Robin? He should be here."

"He had a phone call just as we were coming up," Jill Hammond informed him. "It seemed to be important but he should be here in a minute."

At that moment footsteps were heard hurrying along the corridor and Robin burst into the room. "Sorry I'm late, but I've just had a very interesting phone call." He flopped into a chair, still rather breathless.

"Come on then. What's it all about? Is it a breakthrough?" The Chief Inspector sounded hopeful.

"No, I don't think so exactly, but it is definitely odd. You remember the lift engineer, Bill Edwards, who fell down the lift shaft at the Court?"

"Yes, but that was natural causes, wasn't it?" Sheila looked faintly disapproving.

"So they thought. But my cousin is a junior doctor at the William and Mary, and one of his colleagues, Brian Somerville, who was looking after Bill, started to put two and two together. He discussed it with the other young doctors, including my cousin Peter. To cut a long story short, they think Bill could have been murdered. You remember, Bill said he had been pushed down the shaft, when he regained consciousness. He was under police guard. Perhaps, when that didn't work, someone came to the hospital to finish the job with a shot of potassium before he could remember anything else."

His audience was transfixed. "This could put a very different complexion on things, but it sounds a bit of a long shot –"

"But, sir," Sheila interrupted. "It might explain that bit in Barbara's suicide note when she says she killed a man. We didn't think that meant anything, but suppose it was *she* who pushed Bill down the shaft?"

"That's an even longer shot. Why on earth would she want to do that?" David Jones was sceptical.

"For drugs?" suggested Sheila. "We know she did petty crime for supplies, why not something big? Especially if she didn't know what she was doing."

"It looks as though we might have something to go on at last." The Chief Inspector got up. "Bring in your doctor cousin and his pal, Robin, and Sheila, go and have a cosy chat with the caretaker about her tenants. We'd better know right away if there have been any other unnoticed odd happenings. David, you go with Robin, and Jill, go and lean on forensics. They seem to be dragging their heels rather more than somewhat."

Dead on cue, there was a knock on the door. An officer put his head round and waved a piece of paper. "This came last night," he said. "Sorry not to bring it sooner, it got covered up."

Hoping his expression said what he didn't trust his tongue to say, on the grounds that if he started he wouldn't stop (if there was one thing the DCI couldn't stand it was sloppy office work), he took the proffered paper. "We have a name for our body," he announced, with some satisfaction. "It's Theo Carson." There was a silence as he surveyed his team expectantly.

Then Jill's face lit up. "The banker?" she said. "Jailed for fraud and then escaped? Never been seen?"

"The very same. At least, I think so. Though how on earth his hands and feet ended up in Tower Court is anybody's guess. Still, it ties up a loose end, at least we know he's dead. Off you go, now, and see what else you can come up with."

Amid a general scraping of chairs the room emptied as they all scattered to their allotted duties.

***

I was rather surprised to receive an official visit from Sheila. Things seemed to have quietened down, even my bins had been returned to me, though I hung on to the new ones. We settled down in my flat with the obligatory coffee.

After some preliminary chitchat Sheila got to the point. "This is not a social call," she said. "I have been sent to talk to you about tenants. Do you have your list handy?"

"I can get it," I returned. "Has something new turned up?"

" Yes – no, a definite maybe," was her rather obscure remark. "We think that Bill Edwards may have been murdered in hospital, and that someone in the block, possibly Barbara, may have pushed him down the lift shaft. If it was Barbara, then it would probably have been at someone else's instigation."

I gaped at her. "Where has all this come from?" I asked.

"It's not what you know, it's who. Robin Lutterworth's cousin is a doctor at the hospital, a colleague of his was looking after Bill and started having second thoughts about the cause of death. Then we tied in a rather strange claim in Barbara's suicide note that she had killed a man. It's all rather a leap of faith but it's all possible, and, frankly, we've nothing else to go on. But it would be a big help to go through your list of tenants."

I got up. "I'll fetch it." On my return I remembered something I had intended to point out but had forgotten. "I know they're long gone, but do you think the Smiths on the top floor could have been Barbara's suppliers?"

"It's a possibility. Let's start at the top and work down."

I spread the list out. "Right. Flat 57, the one where the fire was, is now occupied by Elizabeth Giles and Janine du Pont. I think they're related, otherwise I don't know a great deal about them. They go off to work together at about 8.30, smartly dressed, office type clothes, and return at about 6.30. They seem friendly enough and Joan Stephenson says they have been very helpful during the lift renewal. Joan is in flat 59, she was badly shaken by the fire but seems to have recovered well. She's been in the block for donkey's years, from the beginning, I think. The Smith's flat is now occupied by Nobunaga Akio from Japan. He is mad keen to practise his English whenever he sees anyone but his progress is undeniably slow. Then there's Vivienne du Cros in flat 60, another student. She has blossomed since coming out of the shadow of a domineering father."

"I don't think we need go through the list in such detail," said a slightly stunned Sheila, "though I am very impressed at how well you know you tenants, or at least, about them. Could you give me copy of the list, and any comments you may have about them? Sorry to put extra work on you, but I think it might help."

"No problem," I said magnanimously. "How soon by?"

"As soon as possible, I'm afraid. As I said, we have so little to go on."

"Believe me," I said earnestly. "I'm almost as keen as you are to get this all sorted out. Then life can return to normal, or what passes for normal in this madhouse." We settled down for a quiet gossip over our coffee.

***

Straight after the meeting at the College Road police station Robin rang his cousin.

"You've really set the cat among the pigeons," he informed Peter. "I am instructed to give you and your colleague the third degree and wrest all your secrets from you. When can you come down to the nick to give a statement?"

"That could be a bit of a problem if you want us both together," returned his cousin. "I shall have to sort out duty rosters. Can I call you back later? It will give you time to prepare the thumbscrews and heat the branding irons."

Robin laughed. "You have almost as lurid an imagination as I have. Yes, see what you can sort out, and sooner rather than later, OK?"

A couple of hours later Peter came back to him. "Not as bad as I expected," he said. "We can both come to you tomorrow morning, around 10.30, if that suits you."

Robin thought rapidly. "Yes, I can do that. See you then."

Promptly at 10.30 the next morning Robin and David were sitting opposite Robin's cousin, Peter Dennis, and his colleague, Brian Somerville. Robin opened the proceedings by introducing David Jones to the two doctors. He then went on:

"First, do you mind if we tape this? We can type it up then for you to sign."

Peter glanced at his friend, who nodded. "Yes, that's fine."

"Right," Robin switched into official mode. "perhaps you could explain who you are and what you do."

"I'm Peter Dennis, and I am a junior doctor at the William and Mary Hospital."

"And I'm Brian Somerville, also a junior doctor, and also at the William and Mary Hospital." Brian spoke for the first time.

"You were looking after Bill Edwards. Is that right?" Brian nodded. "Tell us what happened.

"When Bill Edwards came in he was unconscious and suffering from several fractures and other injuries from falling down the lift shaft at Tower Court. He was operated on and his fractures set but it was very much touch and go, his injuries were extensive."

"At this time, did you have any idea that the fall might not have been an accident?"

"No, it seemed quite straight forward, though the foreman, who was Bill Edwards's brother-in-law, was extremely puzzled as to how it could have happened."

Robin made a note. "Go on."

"It was several days before Bill regained consciousness, we were all delighted that he did so, as I said, it was touch and go whether he would pull through."

David spoke for the first time. "Peter, were you involved at this time?"

"To a certain extent," Peter answered. "Bill was primarily Brian's patient but I checked on him when Brian was off."

David nodded. "Go on," he said to Brian.

"Well, as you know, when Bill came round he claimed that he had been pushed down the shaft and you people were informed at once. You put a police guard on him. Not that it seemed to do much good," he added bitterly.

"That was most unfortunate," said Robin smoothly. "Go on, Bill was on the mend?"

"It seemed so," Brian agreed. "We were extra busy at that time with an influx of flu patients and I was called to the side ward when one of the nurses found him. He had apparently suffered a heart attack. It seemed straight forward enough and, as we were so busy I perhaps didn't examine him as carefully as I might have done. And after all he had been through it didn't seem surprising, even though he had been improving. But I did see what looked like a puncture mark on his arm which seemed odd."

"Why?" demanded David. "Surely he was receiving medication? Wasn't some of that by means of an injection?"

"Yes, indeed, but that was given through a needle permanently in place in his arm. Otherwise he would have been a pin cushion."

"Which arm was it?" asked Robin.

"The right one, nearest the door, and nearest the bag of medication on the stand by the bed."

"We think that the bag might have been injected with something as well," Peter broke in. "Some nurses had got into trouble when a bag leaked on the floor. It could have been done at the same time, it fits."

"What was injected?" asked Robin.

"I suspect potassium," answered Brian. "There would be no sign of it in the body and the symptoms fit." He hoped they wouldn't ask him to elaborate on those.

"So we can have no proof," said Robin despondently.

"Not unless we can find someone who saw someone slinking around the ward a few days before Bill died. Just a minute, though." Peter was excited. "Brian, do you remember Sister going mad about the doctor's coat she found in the linen cupboard?"

"Sister's always going mad about something," said his friend gloomily. "Hang about, yes, I do. She blamed me. Fortunately it was several sizes too small." Brian played rugby and looked like it. "Not that that stopped her from tearing me limb from limb," he grinned.

"So, we do not have proof but we do have a strong possibility." Robin brought the session to a close. "Many thanks for coming in, you two. Let us know if anything else occurs to you or to any of your colleagues."

"Sure thing. If it was murder, I hope you catch the guy who did it sooner rather than later. Bill seemed a nice guy."

Robin and David looked at each other as the young doctors departed. "It hangs together," said Robin.

"If only we had some proof," responded David. "Hey, I'd better go after them, we need signatures." He vanished in pursuit of their witnesses.

Robin returned to his office in a pensive mood.

– Chapter Fifteen –

Bonzo Ray sat in his somewhat depressing flat and shook. He rather thought he had just done the stupidest thing he had ever done in a career not remarkable for good sense. If you are receiving stolen property (the police were perfectly correct in their suspicions but so far he had managed to evade them), it is less than wise to try and diddle the clients. Especially if you suspect that this particular client was a bigger fish than any you'd dealt with before. He was afraid that he'd been dealing outside his league. This was a mistake; he was a (fairly) large fish in a small pond and he'd have been wiser to remain that way.

He wandered restlessly round the flat. He was not particularly interested in housework and the flat in consequence was cluttered and grubby, with a musty, dusty smell of which he was totally oblivious. He did have some very nice pieces gleaned from a lifetime of acting as a fence for stolen goods; for example, a very pretty Sevres bowl stood on a shelf beside a Dresden shepherdess. But the beauty of both was obscured by a layer of dust, and the bowl was used as a receptacle for miscellaneous bits of tat. On a table on the other side of the room a magnificent candelabra displayed its delicate but badly tarnished branches. He often thought that had the fates been kinder he would have done well as a legitimate antiques dealer. He blithely overlooked the fact that a fondness for alcohol and drugs had given the fates a generous helping hand.

He sighed again. How was he going to get himself out of this mess? Not that he was in it – yet, he reminded himself. He remembered the pills his friend had given him the day before. The Big Fella had noticed that Bonzo seemed a little down. "Take these," he had said. "They'll make you feel better in no time."

Perhaps now was the time to try them. At least he had one friend he could count on.

***

I started on my rounds with a lighter heart than for many weeks.

The first lift was finished! And I was promised a couple of weeks' grace before the second one was started.

"That should cheer you up," Tom had said when he told me the good news. He was still noticeably quieter than he had been before Bill's death but seemed to be coping. I wondered if he had any idea of the police suspicions. It was certainly not for me to say anything.

I had reached the 10th floor in my rounds when I was pulled up short. I suddenly realised I was hearing a baby crying – in stereo. Flat 37 belonged to the Meyers and I well knew that Baby John had an excellent pair of lungs and believed in exercising them. But opposite, in flat 38, I could hear another child, whose feeble wail didn't sound anything like as healthy as John's triumphant bellow. Indeed, I thought, if the Meyers were not given a house soon there would be complaints from the neighbours.

I knew that flat 38 was occupied by Alec and Joanna Heron, who certainly did not have a child with them when they moved in a few weeks ago. Oh well, they probably had visitors staying. I went on my way, but resolved to keep an ear open.

***

Unknown to Bonzo, there was another anxious tenant pacing round his flat three floors below. Alec Heron, tall, thin and haggard from lack of sleep and worry, could not sit still.

The cause of his anxiety was held in his wife's arms. A baby, about six months old, was lying limply, breathing stertorously, seemingly too weak to move. Every so often she would give a little wailing cry, which made Joanna clutch her closer and gaze into the flushed face with ever increasing fear.

"Can't you keep her quiet?" snarled Alec. His wife looked at him hopelessly. "I'm sorry, I shouldn't take it out on you. I'm just so scared. After all we've been through to get her, not to mention the price we had to pay, I couldn't bear it if she were to be taken away now."

Joanna had to agree. "But I'm so afraid she's really ill," she said. "She should see a doctor, you know she should."

"We can't come out into the open until we've been given the papers, you know what Ronnie said. And as he lives in this block too, we'll get them as soon as he does."

At that moment there was a knock at the door. Joanna vanished into the bedroom with the child, closing the door behind her. As soon as the door was shut Alec went to the front door.

"Who is it?" he called.

"It's alright, it's me," a familiar voice answered and he opened the door to admit a big, thickset man who walked in briskly. He came straight to the point. "Not good news, I'm afraid. I've met the people who can supply the papers but the price has gone up. They want another grand."

Alec's already pale face blanched further. "But how on earth am I to find that amount of money? Going to Romania and paying the orphanage cost a fortune."

The big man shrugged. "Sorry, that's what they say."

"When do they need it by?" asked Alec, an edge of desperation in his voice.

"By next week or you can forget the whole thing. I'm really sorry," said Ronnie, sounding suddenly more human. "I did what I could to persuade them that you'd paid enough but they were adamant."

"Alright. I'll find the money somehow." Alec slumped into a chair.

"How is the little one? Settling in?"

"Not good. She needs a doctor,"

"But you can't see one till you have the papers." The other finished for him. "Do what you can as soon as you can. I'll see myself out." He left, leaving Alec still slumped in his chair, his head in his hands.

Outside the flat the big man's face twisted into a sneer. "Sucker," he said to himself. He was an old hand at extortion, apparently at one remove. He had nothing but contempt for those he dragged into his net.

Back in the flat Joanna peered out of the bedroom. Seeing no one in the hall of the flat she came out, shutting the door softly behind her. In the living room she stopped abruptly at the sight of her husband's despairing posture.

"Who was it?" she asked.

"Our friend. And they need more money before they'll do the papers."

"How much?"

"A grand. But we'll find it. I'm not giving up now we've come so far. How is Lara?"

"She's asleep. She's gone very pale, but she's still burning hot, and her breathing is really bad. She needs antibiotics at the very least, probably oxygen as well."

Alec got up, suddenly determined. "Stay with her, keep her quiet if you can. I'm going money hunting." He left the flat, suddenly purposeful, leaving Joanna to return to the bedroom to watch over her sick little Romanian orphan.

However, once outside the flat his purposeful attitude left him. He walked slowly to the little park nearby and sat on a convenient bench, sunk in thought. Where was he to find another thousand pounds? He had used up all his savings already, and cajoled every shilling he could from friends and relatives. It was remarkable how generous they had been, considering how little he could tell them. By the same token he could not go to a bank.

He had a sudden thought. Surely he had seen a shop, or an office, admittedly rather seedy looking, advertising something about " No amount too big or too small, we'll come to your rescue!" He cudgelled his exhausted brain. Think! Where had he seen it?

"I've got it!" he shouted, to the astonishment of an elderly couple walking their equally elderly dog. They looked after him as he leapt to his feet and made off down the path.

"Seems in a hurry," the old man remarked. "What about turning for home? It's cold, and I want a brew."

The trio turned and walked slowly after Alec, now out of sight.

***

From high up in the tower block the big man watched as Alec raced off in the direction that he had hoped that he would go. He went to the phone. He dialled a number and waited.

"I think the fish has bitten," he said, "and I didn't even have to suggest it." He listened. "Yes, boss." He put the phone down.

On an impulse he went up to the 10th floor and knocked on the door of flat 38.

He put on a caring face. "How is the little one?" he asked when Joanna came to the door.

"No better," she said. "I'm really worried about her. You feel so useless when something so tiny, who has been through so much needs help desperately and you can't do anything."

"I quite understand," said the other, who didn't, and cared less. "Where's Alec? I've had an idea which might help him."

"I don't know," replied Joanna. "He went out soon after you left, I think to find that thousand pounds your friends need."

"No friends of mine," denied the big man. "Bloodsucking leeches more like. But we need them. Look, could I wait till Alec comes back? I don't want to miss him. I really think I might be able to help. What about a brew? You look as though you could do with one too."

"I'll put the kettle on," responded Joanna listlessly. She went into the kitchen.

The big man sat himself down in the best chair. He had decided to come in case Alec had not trodden the path he'd hoped for. He knew all about the loan shark in the shabby office, indeed, he had "casually" pointed it out to Alec a few days earlier. The interest rates were exorbitant, but he knew very well whose pockets they were going into, and that he would get his cut. He settled down to wait. This fish was not going to get away if he could help it.

Some time later, when the big man and Joanna had long run out of conversation, they heard the lift arriving. At the same time Joanna heard a wailing cry from the baby and vanished into the bedroom without a word. The other was delighted, he much preferred to deal with Alec on his own.

Sure enough, Alec came into the flat, looking much brighter than when he had last seen him. "I've got the money," Alec said. "The interest rates are terrible but I've got it."

"I'm really glad," said the big man, truthfully. "How did you manage it? Where did you go?"

"Do you remember pointing out to me that tiny office promising loans, 'None too small, none too big'?"

"Did I? I don't remember." Inside, the other hugged himself. Everything was going beautifully to plan.

"Well, you did. So here it is, now you can get the papers, and we can get the doctor." Alec handed over the packet of money.

The big man got up. "I'll do it right away," he said, smiling benignly.

He left the flat, chortling to himself.

***

I still felt puzzled by the strange crying I had heard, though I couldn't put my finger on why. It was perfectly possible that the Herons had a child to stay. Thoughtfully I went down to consult with the fount of all knowledge, Phil in Security.

"I know who you mean," he said, in answer to my query. "Nice looking couple, moved in a few weeks ago. I certainly don't know anything about a child. Not seen any visitors, either. Seems a little odd."

I had to agree, and his remarks did nothing to reassure me. The next move was to contact Ian.

"No, definitely no children," he said. "They wouldn't have got the tenancy if they had. You know the ruling about children in tower blocks."

"Yes," I said, "but they could have a child staying with them, couldn't they?"

"I suppose so, but they would have to be careful as probationary tenants."

"True." I still felt very dissatisfied. I resolved to keep an eye on the setup. I wondered whether to have a word with Jacquetta Meyer but decided not to – yet. I didn't want to stir up a mare's nest.

True to my plan I made a point of visiting the 10th floor at least a couple of times a day, subjecting the electricity cupboard to a minute inspection. Sometimes there was nothing, sometimes I heard the thin wailing that had so distressed me when I heard it first. I was just deciding that I would have a word with Jacquetta when things were taken rather abruptly out of my hands.

I was up there, again gazing fixedly into the useful cupboard when the door of flat 38 burst open and Alec Heron stood there, glaring at me.

"Come in, then, you nosy bitch and see what doesn't concern you." He seized my arm and pulled me bodily into the flat, slamming the door behind us. He hauled me into the living room where Joanna was sitting on the sofa with a baby, aged about six months I thought, lying very still in her lap.

"This is Lara," said Alec, more quietly this time. "She's very sick and we don't know what to do."

I went and knelt down beside the child. She was deathly pale, but with two hectic spots of red in her cheeks, and seemed hardly to be breathing. She was also very thin. I felt her forehead, she was clearly running a temperature, I thought a high one.

"Let's make her comfortable on the sofa," I suggested, "and try and cool her down with water. But she should see a doctor urgently, possibly even call an ambulance."

But at this Alec blew up again.

"Not on, bitch face. You're not going to get out that easily. Now you're here, you're staying."

After a lot of argument and noise, Joanna having become as heated as her husband, they both calmed down. They told me that Lara was a Romanian orphan whom they had smuggled out of Romania and into Britain in a tapestry bag. I felt she must have been pretty weak then to have kept quiet all through border controls.

"How on earth did you get from Romania?" I asked. "Surely you didn't fly?"

"No, we drove," answered Joanna. "It was a nightmare journey. We went to Romania because we are desperate to have a child. I can't have children and it's the one thing I want in life. We can't afford IVF –"

"Though this has cost us nearly as much," Alec broke in.

"- and they won't look at us on the NHS, too old," Joanna went on. "We were promised a little boy, an intermediary arranged it all." Alec snorted. "We arrived at the orphanage but they told us he had died but that we could have a little girl instead."

I was silent. It reminded me horribly of buying a puppy or a kitten, but at least they would probably be taken to a vet. This child was clearly ill but they had done nothing. I decided that the best thing was to keep them talking.

"What happened when you reached Romania?" I asked.

"We met up with Grisha, a Russian who spoke perfect English," Joanna went on. "He had made all the arrangements at the Romanian end. We paid over part of the money to him straight away and he took us to the orphanage. He left us there. Then we were led into an awful, bleak waiting room with a table and two rickety chairs. There was no fire and it was very cold. We waited there for two hours, it seemed like forever." She shivered, remembering. "We could hear the occasional child's cry, but considering how many children there must have been in the building, as we discovered later, it was surprisingly quiet, and rather sinister.

"Eventually a door opened and we glimpsed a long, barn-like room with dozens of beds in it, lining the walls and in rows down the middle. They all seemed to have children in them, some even had two or three. And some seemed to be tied to them. It was terrible, we were appalled."

"Then the door was slammed," Alec carried on the story, "and we were bundled into an office where a stern-faced nurse was waiting. She was holding Lara, huddled in blankets. While we watched, horrified, the nurse stuffed Lara into a tapestry bag as though she was so much washing. It was awful.

"Then the nurse said, 'Here you are. You want baby, she want home. Now go. Grisha will give papers.'"

"And with that we were hustled out, with Lara, to where Grisha was waiting for us in a café in the square."

"But didn't you realise that all this was probably totally illegal?" I demanded. Alec scowled. I wished I'd kept quiet.

"We were desperate," said Joanna simply. "Do you have children?" I nodded. "Then how can you know the hunger if you can't have them?" I was silent.

"We drove all the way from Romania, the orphanage was just outside Bucharest." Alec seemed to have forgotten his former aggressiveness. Perhaps telling someone about it all had helped. "Then we went through Yugoslavia, skirting Belgrade, then Croatia, missing Zagreb. We didn't dare go too much into deep country in case we got stuck. On the other hand, we avoided the centre of the cities. Then it was north to Austria and back to the UK via Germany and Belgium. It was tough but we managed. Then I came on ahead to open up the flat; Joanna and Lara followed a few days later."

Since he seemed so calm I risked getting up. It was a mistake. There was an instant return of Alec's aggression.

"Oh no you don't. You'll only blow the gaff and ruin everything. You're staying here!"

"But Lara needs medical help," I tried to insist. "I promise I won't say anything but she needs help urgently. You all do."

"Rubbish, it's probably only teething or something. You and Joanna can cope. I'm not risking everything when we've got so far."

"You can't keep me here by force," I protested.

"Just try me. You poked your nose in where it wasn't wanted so you can take the consequences."

"I was only doing what I always do, as caretaker," I pointed out. "Then you called me in."

"Just sit down and shut up," was all the answer I got.

***

And so began a long, very trying time. Twice I tried to make a move to go but each time Alec barred my way. He was clearly on a very short fuse, which was getting steadily shorter. I felt he was beginning to lose all sense of reality. Lara was still alive – just - but she was growing visibly weaker, and Joanna seemed to be completely cowed, or maybe she was simply exhausted. None of us slept at all. Finally, I managed to persuade Alec to let me phone Flat 1 so that at least the cats could be fed. I had the germ of an idea in my head if only I could use the phone.

Alec thought hard for a moment. "Yes," he said, at last. "But wait a moment." He vanished into the bedroom and reappeared a minute later holding a small handgun. Both Joanna and I were horrified, she clearly had no idea he possessed such a thing.

"You may phone," he said, "but remember that I shall have this held to your head so don't try any clever tricks. Oh, do be quiet," he turned to the protesting Joanna. "Of course I had a gun. You don't really think that I would have gone all that way unarmed, do you? Heaven knew what we might have met. It was in the compartment in the car door all the way." He turned to me. "Now get on with this call, if you must make it."

Thinking furiously I dialled the familiar number, trying to ignore the gun inches from the back of my head. Julian answered.

"Oh, Julian," I said. "Could you do me a favour?" I tried to sound light hearted. "It's Francesca. I have to go to my Aunt Ada, you remember, the one who's a bit odd? Lives in 83 Back Street? Yes. Please could you feed the cats?"

"Francesca? Are you alright?" Thank goodness Julian was

quick in the uptake.

"No, no, not long. You can reach me at 83 Back Street if you need me. Must fly," as Alec waved the gun threateningly at me. I sat back, it was the best I could do.

***

On the first floor Julian replaced the receiver slowly.

"What was that?" asked Ron, who was combing an ecstatic Furball.

"I'm not sure, but I *think* Frankie is in some kind of trouble. She called herself Francesca, which she never does, and burbled on about her Aunt Ada who lives in 83 Back Street. Has she ever mentioned an Aunt Ada? Who was odd?"

"No. Wait a minute, Ada – *Aid.* Help? 'Odd' – strange, as in may not exist, reinforcing 'help'? Lives in 83 *Back* Street? 83 backwards is 38. Flat 38 here? 10th floor?"

"Could be. I'll go up and hunt for the 'caretaker', see what, if anything, I can find."

"Be careful. If she really is in trouble you could make matters worse."

"I'll be careful, don't worry." And Julian promptly departed on his mission.

Arrived at the 10th floor he was careful to knock at the door of flat 37, the home of the Meyers, first. Before he did so, he listened carefully but could hear nothing. Jacquetta answered the door, holding a beaming John in her arms.

"My goodness, he's growing," said Julian admiringly. "Jacquetta, have you seen Frankie? I need to see her rather urgently and she said she was coming up to the 10th floor. At least, I think it was the 10th. Something about a problem with the electricity cupboard." (When he told me about this afterwards I was amused that we had both thought of the same cover story.)

"No, sorry," replied Jacquetta. "I've only just come in. Perhaps the Herons in No 38 know."

"Thanks, I'll try them," said Julian, delighted that she had supplied his cue so neatly. He crossed the landing and knocked at the door. "Sorry to disturb you," he said to the exhausted looking woman who answered the door, "but have you seen the caretaker? I need her urgently and I think she said she was going to do some work on this floor."

"No, sorry. I've not seen her." And the door shut abruptly, but not before Julian had caught a whiff of the distinctive perfume that Frankie always wore. He went down in the lift in a very thoughtful frame of mind.

"I found out nothing definite," he reported to Ron. "But I'm darn sure that Frankie is in flat 38. I'm sure I smelt her perfume. Of course, the woman who lives there might wear it as well, but she didn't look the perfume type."

"Whatever that is," retorted Ron. "There's not a lot we can do just yet, is there? Except feed the cats, of course. And watch. If there really is an aunt she'll ring again."

"Hey, just a minute. When I asked her if she was alright she said 'No, no not long', as though I had asked her how long she'd be away. Surely that proves all is not well."

"I think you're right. Let's see if we can contact one of her police pals."

"Good idea. I'll go and feed the cats and see if I can find a number." Pleased to be able to do something constructive Julian departed.

***

Joanna came back from the front door. "One of those two men from the first floor," she said shortly. "He was looking for Frankie. He's gone now."

"So you can take that gun away from my head," I said tartly. "I work here, remember. Of course people want to see me."

"At the weekend?" Alec was sceptical.

"Problems don't restrict themselves to week days," I said wearily. "Are you going to let me go or not? How long do you think you can keep me here anyway?"

"As long as I want. Now stop talking. I want to think."

The next day things were even worse, tempers were getting decidedly frayed and Alec seemed welded to his gun. I was thinking desperately of ways to escape; I thought Julian had realised that all was not well but I couldn't be sure. Alec never seemed to sleep, it was three days now, and Joanna seemed to be too sunk in misery and fear to do anything. I was also getting very tired by this time, but worry and discomfort kept me from sleeping. We were all getting hungry too. Occasionally, Joanna would think to go to the kitchen, but she only supplied us with tea, a loaf of rather tired bread and a hunk of cheese that had definitely seen better days, and left us to help ourselves. She ate very little, being far to occupied in trying to persuade Lara to take something from a bottle. I don't think Alec ate anything at all. And certainly I didn't eat much. I did my best, though, I needed to have all my wits about me and they needed fuel.

Then, in the early evening, my chance came. At last, Alec, who must have been completely exhausted, fell into a deep sleep on the sofa. Joanna was still oblivious of anything except Lara. I rose from my chair, sidled to the door, watching Alec like a hawk and made it into the hall. Once there, praying that the quick release handle on the front door was working, I wrenched it open and fled down the stairs faster than I had ever run in my life, shaking like a leaf. I dared not wait for the lift and tore down ten flights of stairs and into my flat like a rabbit into its burrow, slamming and locking the door and thanking goodness that the front doors were so strong. I pounced on the phone, decided that this was, or could be, life threatening, and dialled 999. "Police," I shouted at the imperturbable voice at the other end. "And please hurry! I've just escaped from kidnap!"

"Where are you?"

"In my flat – oh," I pulled myself together and gave the address. "But he's a tenant in the same block and he's bound to follow me. And there's a sick child involved too, and he's got a gun!"

"The police are on their way. Just stay where you are and don't let anyone in." As if I would!

I put the phone down and almost immediately heard a key in the lock. For one hideous moment I thought it was Alec, then sanity prevailed. As I might have expected, it was Julian; what was not expected was that he was accompanied by Robin.

"Frankie! Thank goodness you're alright!" Julian exclaimed. "Er – was there anything wrong?"

"There most certainly was," I replied feelingly, "just as you worked out. I was being held at gun point."

Julian gasped. "What the dickens?"

"Tell you in a minute. But how did you get here so quickly?" I turned to Robin. "I've only just put the phone down."

"And here we are," Robin grinned. "Actually, Julian called me earlier, we were just working out how to rescue you when you rescued yourself."

"Might have known she would," grumbled Julian. "All that worry for nothing." He gave me a big hug.

The welcome sounds of police sirens resolved themselves into a small army of uniforms. Robin went down to meet them and bring the senior officer up to me. I was glad to see that they did believe me. I learned afterwards that mentioning the child and the gun meant that they could not take the chance of it being a hoax call, or hysteria on my part. I gave a heartfelt sigh of relief. As if echoing it, Rudi, unusually, hopped up onto my lap as I sat limply in our favourite chair, as though to offer both comfort and protection. I hugged him, he purred. Julian, after looking at me sharply vanished into the kitchen, I hoped to make coffee.

"What can you tell us about this incident?" demanded the senior police officer. I never did discover his name. I may have been told, but it certainly didn't register.

I paused, to collect my thoughts, which were somewhat chaotic. "I had heard a child crying in a flat on the 10th floor," I began, and related all the events as collectedly as I could. About halfway through the recital Julian came in with a tray of coffee, and some biscuits I had forgotten I possessed. Re-fuelled, I carried on and managed to complete the tale fairly intelligibly.

"What exactly was the situation when you left?"

"Alec was asleep on a chair, Joanna was holding Lara on her lap on the sofa," I said promptly.

"Where was the gun?"

"Alec was holding it on his lap, I think."

"Was it loaded?"

"I assumed that it was. I wasn't going to risk finding out. I was convinced that he would fire if he had to."

"Right. Thank you, you've been very clear." The brass departed, attended by Robin looking unusually deferential; the officer must have been *very* senior.

"You get that coffee down you," ordered Julian. "I'm just going to get Ron to organise some proper food. When did you last eat?"

"Goodness knows," I said wearily. "Joanna was too preoccupied to be the perfect hostess. We had stale bread, worse cheese and the occasional tea. You know how I *love* tea."

Julian laughed. "Never mind. Ron will rustle up a feast for the gods if I know him. Will you be alright on your own?"

"I should think so," I said. "But you might lock the door behind you."

"Certainly will. If you're bothered, bang on the wall or give us a ring. Won't be long." He departed, I was relieved to hear him lock up behind him.

***

As I sat trying to recover, I remembered the strength of the doors. I wondered how the police were going to get in. Oh well, that was their problem, not mine. Indeed, I found, when Robin came back to tell me what was happening, there was a full scale siege situation on the 10th floor, with the added complication of the danger to Lara if she didn't receive the medical attention she so desperately needed very soon. I could only hope that Joanna's maternal instincts would prevail, or that Alec, who genuinely seemed to care for the child, might let her go. On the other hand, I thought, he was very near the edge mentally, in my admittedly uninformed opinion.

"Do you think this is connected with the other happenings here?" Robin asked me. He seized the opportunity when we were momentarily alone, his boss still trying to sort things out upstairs.

"I wouldn't have thought so, do you? It seems rather far-fetched. Though the whole 'adoption' was undoubtedly illegal. And cost a fortune from what Alec said."

"Oh, it would." Robin was less than sympathetic. "I think you're probably right. I'm tending to think that everything is all connected in this block. What a place." He got up, but at that moment there was a knock at the door. I let him answer it, I did not feel like letting anyone into my fortress without an affidavit of probity and sixteen references.

"They want you to go up and see if you can persuade Joanna and the child to come out," Robin reported.

I swallowed. "I suppose I must, mustn't I? Have you got the whole of the Arkchester Police Force there to protect me?"

"Most of it," Robin laughed. Then he sobered. "Yes, I think you do have to if you possibly can. There is no danger to you, Armed Response officers are there as well as the others, and I'll come too, if you like. But we must get Lara and Joanna out."

I got up. "Let's go."

It was one of the hardest things I have ever done, going back to that landing. Arrived, I called to Joanna through the door as instructed.

"Joanna, are you there? Can you bring Lara out? You know how ill she is. She must go to hospital."

To my relief I heard her voice, apparently just the other side of the door. "You'll take her away, if I come out."

"No, no one will take her way," I reassured her, hoping it was true. "Look, look through the spy hole." Hastily everyone moved silently back out of sight. "There's just me here. Ask Alec to let you go."

There was a silence and we all held our breath. Then, very slowly the door opened and Joanna, holding Lara in her arms, moved out. As soon as she was clear it slammed shut again and I heard the key turn in the lock.

"Well done," said Robin. "Go down to the next floor and take the lift to your flat. Thank goodness both lifts are working at the moment. The ambulance crew can pick you up there. Off you go."

Only to glad to escape from that landing I shepherded Joanna down to my flat and the ministrations of the paramedics. She seemed to have given up completely and docilely did whatever she was told. Lara, to my eyes seemed worse than ever. I just hoped we were in time.

***

And that was the end of it, effectively. Lara did make it to the children's hospital in time; she was taken immediately to the Intensive Care Unit. Joanna was allowed to stay with her; while Alec was still barricaded in his flat; the rights and wrongs of smuggling a child into Britain were put on hold. I did find, though, that while Alec was around I did not dare leave my flat despite my army of protectors. Then that situation too was resolved. Evidently finally unable to cope, Alec shot himself.

The whole thing was very well managed, even I did not know anything about it until Robin came to see me the next day. It was a shock; apart from anything else it made me realise just how great was the danger I had been in. I didn't think that he would have hesitated to shoot me if I had really upset him. The other tenants on the landing had been evacuated as soon as the police arrived so no one except the police knew anything. I was sorry for Joanna, so tragically widowed, but I really felt that for Alec it was the best way out. He was clearly on the brink of insanity. I found I could feel sorry for him and not blame him too much for my ordeal.

"Will Joanna be able to keep Lara?" I asked Robin.

He shook his head. "I don't know," he said. "It will be up to the social services. If she can persuade them that she was completely dominated by Alec, and the gun should help that, they may let her. But it won't be easy. Now, are you alright? It's been a tough time."

"It certainly has," I agreed. "And not what I expected a caretaker's life to be like. Yes, I'm alright. I think I'll go next door and bring them all up to date."

"Good idea," Robin approved. "I'll escort you – as it's such a long way."

***

From afar, Jimbo Preston watched the commotion with interest. He had recovered from Ron's surprising attack and was his old, jaunty self once more. He wondered what would happen next. He wondered what he could do to provoke something.

– Chapter Sixteen –

I was annoyed to find that I was badly shaken by the siege and all its ramifications. "The Gang", as always, was very supportive and gradually I was able to settle down and carry out my duties normally without seeing a kidnapper round every corner. I was offered time off, which I accepted, but did not leave the block this time; I felt running away would only make things harder on my return. I spent a lot of time with Ron in flat 1; I found that sitting and reading while he was writing up his recipes, or tasting them when he was trying them out, was incredibly soothing. Magda, too, did her part, removing me forcibly to a fashion photo shoot as her "assistant". As this merely meant holding things for her, and once or twice acting as a body when a shot was being set up, this was not very arduous, but I found a different world incredibly soothing and gradually realised that I was no longer jumping out of my skin at any unexplained noise.

Once back at work I found myself absorbed into the tenants' lives as usual. Work was not due to start on the second lift until the following week, so I still had a respite before the noise, dirt and inconvenience started again. Then one day, on my rounds I met Lottie Maynard, who had obviously been lying in wait for me.

"Could I have a word?" she asked. "I won't keep you long."

"Of course," I said, not averse to a break from work, even if it was only rounds at the moment. "What can I do for you? How are you? How's the family?" I well remembered the fussy mother and the two delightful grandchildren. "Not been stuck in any lifts, I hope."

"No, but that is what I wanted to talk to you about. Sit down and I'll get you a – tea? Coffee?"

"Coffee, please. Strong white, no sugar." I settled down in a particularly comfortable chair as she bustled through into the kitchen. I looked round her living room; it was full of pretty pieces of china and family photographs, jostling each other for space on shelves and tables. It looked comfortable, lived in, and full of memories of a long and probably happy life. I could quite understand why she had not wanted to uproot herself and move closer to a daughter and son-in-law with whom she had so little in common.

Lottie came back into the room. "Here you are, I hope it's alright, I like it weak myself so I had to guess." She handed me a suitably dark looking brew.

"That looks fine," I said gratefully. Of all things, I hated weak, milky coffee, and this offering was clearly neither. "Now, what's the problem? And how can I help?"

"Well, it's the lift," Lottie said in a rush. "I know it's ridiculous, but I'm getting a 'thing' about it. First of all, the hullabaloo when Susan and the girls got stuck that time, then the accident when that poor man fell down the shaft when they were working on it. And now, they're going to start on this lift, aren't they?"

"Yes, next week, or so they say. Look, are you still against moving closer to your family?"

"Indeed I am," said Lottie firmly. "Nothing's changed there. It's just this stupid phobia about the lift." She shifted restlessly in her chair. I noticed that she did not look as well as she had when we were coping with the lift débacle; I thought she had lost weight, and she looked tired and strained. An idea began to stir. I drank some coffee to give myself time.

"Assuming you want to stay in the block," I put down my cup, "Would you be happier if you lived lower down, on the second floor, say?"

Lottie looked thoughtful. "It's certainly an idea," she said. "Is there one empty, do you know?"

"I don't, at the moment," I admitted. "But I'll ask around, and possibly see if someone might like to swap, move up here for the view, and the quiet, and let you move in on the lower floor where the lift isn't so essential. Leave it with me," I said, glad to have something so normal to think about. "I'll see what I can come up with."

"Thank you so much," Lottie looked very relieved. "I had a feeling you could help."

"I can't promise anything," I said hastily, "But I'll do my best."

***

I continued on my rounds in a very thoughtful frame of mind. Mentally I ran through the tenants on the second floor, I couldn't see any of us on the first floor consenting to a move, we were all too settled where we were. But the second floor now; that was a horse of a very different colour. I decided to try and get hold of Ian first, then do a little gentle prodding.

However, all that was to fly out of my mind when I entered the odd side lift.

The new lift was very fine and it was a matter of pride on my part to keep it shining. So I was not best pleased to find a crumpled piece of paper littering its floor. Being a conscientious caretaker I picked it up, but something stopped me from putting it in my pocket to dispose of later. I pressed the lift button to go to the 11th floor (the chute there had looked as though it might be blocked), and started to smooth out the scruffy piece. Then all thoughts of chutes, tenants and everything else flew out of my mind as a sentence, written in bold black ink met my astonished eyes: "so you see, Bonzo, you are undoubtedly a murderer."

The lift dutifully arrived at the 11th floor and opened its door. As I still stood there, staring at the paper, it closed again, then started to travel down, another client seemingly requiring transport. I came to myself with a slight click and pressed the button for the first floor, hoping it would disgorge me before picking up its next passenger. Sure enough, it stopped obediently for me and I was able to reach the sanctuary of my flat unobserved.

Once there I spread the crumpled page out on the table and studied it. It appeared to be part of a letter, written in a striking, well-educated hand, in very black ink. It was short and to the point.

"So you see, Bonzo, you are undoubtedly a murderer, it's only a matter of time before the police catch up with you and you get your just deserts. However, all is not lost, for a suitable fee we can get you out of the country and…

The rest of the page was torn off.

I sat at the table, reading the scrap of writing over and over again. I could not believe that Bonzo was responsible for Bill's death, or, indeed, the death of anyone. He was undoubtedly odd, but surely not a killer. Eventually, I sighed and reached the phone; thankfully, none of it was my responsibility, at least, not once I had handed the paper over to the police.

David Jones seemed to be on phone duty that day. I explained what I had found.

"Where was this? In the lift? Do you often find incriminating documents in your lift?"

"Not usually, but I'll believe anything of this block," I retorted. I was not in the mood for humour.

David obviously realised this. "Sorry, not funny. Put it in a paper bag and hang on till we come, we won't be long."

"Would an envelope be alright?" I asked. "It'll have my prints all over it, I'm afraid, I thought it was just ordinary rubbish."

"Of course you did. Not to worry, there still might be something. See you." He rang off, leaving me to unearth a suitable receptacle for the evidence, now no longer to be thought of as rubbish.

With an effort, to give myself something else to think about, I turned my mind to Lottie's problem. My trusty list informed me that the residents of the second floor were somewhat varied. In flat 5 was Stefan Klimek, a Polish immigrant who had the most amazing collection of embroideries executed by the women of his family. He had shown them to me and I had been enthralled. My folk dance experience had taught me that Polish costume was one of the most beautiful and varied in Europe and I was fascinated to see the truth of it. I thought it was unlikely that he would want to move; he had been in his flat for many years, and although his English was good, he was a little hard of hearing and the thought of explaining the situation to him made me quail. Then I remembered that the Williams sisters had lived in flat 6 on the second floor. Although it was some months since June died I had not seen any signs of new tenants moving in. Apparently the flat, although it had looked so spotless, had suffered from being occupied by two elderly ladies for so long and had needed a good deal of work before it could be re-let. It would be ideal for Lottie. I decided to speak to Ian at the first opportunity. Otherwise there was only Nancy Smith in flat 8, a totally unknown quantity, and flat 7, which had had a somewhat chequered career since the illegal immigrant brokers were removed. I wasn't sure what the situation was with that flat; surely the authorities had finished with it by now. Again, I would consult with

Ian as a matter of urgency.

At this point I was interrupted by Robin. I was only too pleased to hand over my discovery to him.

"Does it mean what I think it does?" I demanded.

"It could do," he replied cautiously. "Only I wonder, though, is it a find or a plant?"

"I hadn't thought of that," I confessed.

"Yes, well, that's our job, not yours. Thank you for it, anyway. We'll see what we can make of it."

And with that I had to be content.

***

On the 13th floor, in flat 51, Bonzo Ray, as yet quite unaware of the suspicions that were beginning to fall on him, was deep in restless slumber. He slept a good deal, these days, but it was not refreshing sleep. He had dreams that seemed to follow him into real life, so he hardly knew which was real and which was dream. It was sometimes terrifying, but mainly he was in a bemused but not unhappy state. The fear that had been with him when he started to take the pills supplied by his friend, whom he called the Big Fella to himself, had completely left him; he had totally forgotten that he had swindled some very big fish in his personal pond.

As he slept, tossing and turning in his rumpled bed, but quite unaware of what was going on around him, the front door of the flat opened softly. A figure slipped in, listened, then entered the bedroom. He stood looking down at the restless figure for a while, then started to search for something. He found it on the floor by the bed, a small bottle of pills. He put it in his pocket, then substituted it for another, precisely similar bottle which he placed carefully on the floor where the first one had lain.

"Sweet dreams, old chap," he sneered, and left, as softly as he had entered.

Back in his own flat he picked up the phone.

"It's done," he said into it. "I swapped the pills for hallucination jobs. He'll be flying all over Heathfield. Then I'll just pop him down the lift, I've got a key."

"No, you fool, not the lift again. Think of something else."

"But –"

"No. Think again. That's what you're paid for."
"Right, boss."

***

I managed to reach Ian on the third time of asking, almost a record.

"What is it?" he asked. "have the police some news?"

"Not that I know of," I replied. I had promised to keep the information about the crumpled paper to myself. "It's about Lottie Maynard in flat 55."

"Oh, yes? What about her?" Ian was not renowned for his interest in individual tenants.

"She's the one whose family was trapped in the lift," I reminded him patiently. "Because of that, and because of Bill's accident, and the work starting on the lifts again she's developed a phobia about them and can't bear to go in one. She's an old lady," I added.

"Yes, well, she can go on the re-housing list. That's no problem. She'll just have to wait. Or make other arrangements."

"She doesn't want to leave the block, she's lived here forever," I explained, wishing he didn't have to have everything spelled out to him. "I thought we might be able to move her down to the second floor, perhaps arrange a swap? Then I remembered flat 7, where the illegal immigrant set up was. Is it let? Could she go there? And there's flat 6 too, where the Williams sisters lived. Is that let?"

"I'm not sure. I know there was a lot of work to do there. But flat 7, that's a thought. Hold on a minute, I'll bring up the file." There was a pause. I crossed my fingers. "That's odd. The rent is still being paid. A direct debit from someone called Smith, would you believe? That's why we hadn't realised it's empty. I presume it is?"

"Empty? Oh yes, at least, I've not seen anyone near it. Would you like to check flat 8? The tenant there is Nancy Smith and I don't know anything about her."

"Yes, I'd better." Ian sounded far from pleased.

"And could Lottie have one of those flats when it's sorted out?" I pressed him.

"Yes, I suppose so. I'll let you know." He rang off.

I went up to flat 55 to tell Lottie before he could change his mind. As I expected, she was delighted by the news.

"I can't promise anything," I warned her again. "But I really can't see why you shouldn't have one of the empty ones, especially as your flat here would become vacant. It's a nice flat, the view is spectacular."

"It is a nice flat," Lottie agreed. "And if it wasn't for being silly about the lift I wouldn't think of moving. But the second floor would suit me very well, especially if I could have the Williams sisters' flat. I've visited there many times. Such nice people, I miss them."

"I'll see if I can lean on Ian," I promised again, mentally determining that I would move heaven and earth to get her into flat 6. It would suit her admirably and I could keep an eye on her. It would also mean that her daughter would have less of a lever if she tried to persuade Lottie to move away. I felt that Lottie was finding it ever harder to stand firm against the idea.

***

In flat 51 on the 13th floor, just below Lottie Maynard, Bonzo Ray awoke and sat up. He felt better than he had for quite a while. He shambled through to the kitchen to get himself a drink. Suddenly he could kill for a cup of tea. He opened the fridge. A gust of cold air reached him; the only thing in it, a carton of milk, was solid. Surprised, he looked at the sell-by date. It was nearly a month old. He shook his head. He had a feeling he had missed out on quite a lot of time. Finding a lonely can of beer lying forgotten in a cupboard he decided to make do with that.

Beer in hand, he wandered through to the living room and out on to the balcony. It was a beautiful evening, not too cold, with a feeling that spring was just around the corner. He drank his beer, at peace with the world.

The phone rang, making him jump. He had a funny feeling that he didn't want to answer it, but he did.

"Just what do you think you're up to?" demanded an angry voice. "Trying to diddle us? You've got one chance to pay up what you owe, then the heavies will come." The phone went dead.

Five floors down The Big Fella, not quite the friend that Bonzo imagined, grinned sardonically as he put the phone down. If that didn't put him back on the pills nothing would. Then they'd see some action.

Shaking like a leaf Bonzo nearly spilt the last of his beer. What to do? He remembered his pills. Oblivion would do for a start.

Sometime later, he had no idea how long, he woke with a start. He lay still on the untidy bed wondering at the unaccustomed state of euphoria he was experiencing. He looked round the dingy, cluttered room. Why had he never noticed before the pattern of angles and shapes made by the furniture? Why was the soft rose of the bed cover so alluring, suddenly? He floated up out of the bed, hardly feeling the floor with his bare feet, and drifted through to the living room. He saw that a marvellous yellow sun was pouring light on to the walls, making the flowers on the wallpaper pulsate with colour. They seem to stir in a soft breeze, he was sure he could smell them.

It came as no surprise to see his friend sitting in the chair, smiling benignly at him. Bonzo smiled beatifically and floated up onto the top of a cupboard.

"Look at me!" he cried ecstatically. "Come up here too! It's wonderful." He floated across to perch on the top of the door. "This is even better. Whee!" He spread his arms like wings and soared round the room before alighting gently on the floor. "There, I always wanted to fly," he added conversationally.

The Big Fella watched the little man bumble round the room, bumping into things but seemingly oblivious. With some difficulty he kept the kindly expression pinned to his face, it was no part of his plan to jerk Bonzo back to reality. The pills were working better than he had dared hope, but he wondered if a top up was needed. He decided to risk it, Bonzo seemed well away.

"You fly really well," he said enviously. "I wish I could. Can you fly outside?"

"Course I can," said Bonzo loftily. "I can do anything!"

"Would you show me?" Holding his breath, the big man opened the door to the balcony. This was crunch time. He need not have worried, Bonzo was well away in his delightful new world and he hurried outside. He climbed, not without difficulty, on to the balcony rail, poised himself, arms outstretched. With a triumphant cry he leapt out, thirteen floors above the ground.

Mercifully he lost consciousness on the way down and never knew when the dream died at the same time as he did, on the unforgiving ground.

Left alone in the deserted flat the big man smiled smugly. Very neatly carried out, he thought, the boss would be pleased. So perish all who seek to diddle their betters, he added piously. After making sure that there was no possible sign of his presence in the flat he locked up, carefully taking the duplicate key with him, and returned to his own abode. He made a mental note to dispose of the key down the nearest drain next time he went out. Then he had a sudden thought and made his way into the lift.

***

Down in the car park Jimbo Preston stared at the body that had narrowly missed him as it plummeted to the ground. He knew the little man, he had often seen him about in the block. He decided to make himself scarce.

***

In flat 1 we were all relaxing over tea and feather-light cakes provided by Ron. For once, we were all there, feeling content and pleased with life. Ron had sent his latest cookery book off to the publishers, Julian had been asked to compile a coffee table book about the dance world, Magda had just returned from a flying but particularly successful trip to Italy and we were waiting for Judith to tell us her particular piece of news.

"Well, what is it?" demanded Julian. "You've been listening very patiently to us but you obviously have news of your own. Spit it out!"

"I have indeed," Judith responded, "though I have enjoyed everything you lot have had to say. I'm getting a hearing dog – you know, like a guide dog for the blind, but these are trained to tell us deafies about sound."

"I don't think I've heard of those." Magda was intrigued. "Have they been going long?"

"Quite a while," said Judith. "Not as long as blind dogs, but the Hearing Dogs for Deaf People was launched at Crufts in 1982. So it's not really new either. A friend of mine has one," she blushed faintly, "and when I saw what a difference it has made to his life I thought I'd apply. There won't be any difficulty, will there?" She turned to me. "I know dogs are not usually allowed in tower blocks, but this is different, and we are only on the first floor."

"I don't see why there should be, " I started, when my attention was caught by something flying past the window. I only glimpsed it out of the corner of my eye. Then there was a sort of meaty thump. Julian jumped up and went to the window.

"Oh my God!" he exclaimed. "No, stay there, all of you. Some poor devil has fallen from – somewhere."

At that moment the Security buzzer sounded. Julian went into the hall to answer it. The rest of us sat as though frozen in our places. We heard his voice.

"Frankie? Yes, she's here. What's happened? OK, I'll pass you over."

He called me and I roused myself from shock and went to the intercom. "Yes, I'm here. What is it? Has someone fallen?"

"Looks like it." Phil was laconic. "I've called the ambulance, not that they can do anything, poor sod. The thing is, you stay out of it. You may have to be involved later but let the experts cope. You've had enough alarms and excursions lately."

"Thank you, Phil, I appreciate that. Just call me if I am needed, I'll stay here."

"I always know where to find you if you're not in your own flat." I could hear the smile in his voice. "You just let your friends look after you."

I returned slowly to the others. "Phil says I should stay here and let the experts cope," I reported. "But I do feel I should go out."

"What's the time?" demanded Magda.

I looked at my watch. "Just after 6.30," I said, surprised.

"Precisely. You're off duty. You could even be out. Let other people cope for once. They'll come running quick enough if they really can't manage without you."

"Meanwhile, a general pick-me-up. Break out the duty free, Magda," commanded Julian. Rather chastened, we resumed our interrupted evening.

"Tell us more about the Hearing Dog," I suggested to Judith, as much to take our minds off the tragedy outside as for any other reason. She visibly pulled herself together.

"As I said, my friend has one –"

"Yes, you can tell us about *him* in a minute," Magda broke in.

Judith blushed. "It really has made a difference to his life," she went on hastily. "The dog can tell him when there is someone at the door, when an alarm or a timer goes off, all sorts of things like that. And, of course, it's company, not that I'm short of that, thanks to you lot." She grinned at us.

"How will the cats cope?" Julian wanted to know.

"I tremble to think," I said, thinking of my two, who, as far as I knew, had never met a dog. "But I am sure that a well trained dog will take them in its stride. They'll just have to learn to live with it," I added, with an assurance I was far from feeling.

"Now, tell us about this friend," said Magda, "who just happens to be of the male gender. What's he like? Where did you meet? More important, when are we going to vet him?"

"Probably never, if you pressure the poor girl like that," I retorted. "There's no need to tell us anything," I assured Judith. "Unless you want to," I added hopefully.

Judith laughed. "There's nothing for you to vet,"

"Yet," said Magda *sotto voce*. I glared at her.

"We met at the library, we have similar tastes in books. We have been out for coffee and the odd drink, but nothing like a date, or anything. We just get on really well."

"It sounds very good," I said, before Magda could say anything. Considering how protective she had been with my revelations I was surprised that she was being so pressing. She evidently considered me to be a far more fragile flower than Judith.

"Will there be any problems over having a dog in the block?" Judith asked me again. "After all, we're not allowed dogs here, are we."

"I wouldn't have thought so," I said, "as it is a specially trained dog. And we are on the first floor, after all. Go for it, we'll fight if we have to." I got up. "I think I really had better go back to my own domain just in case I'm needed. Oh, I won't go down," I added, as Magda opened her mouth to protest. "I just feel I should be around. See you all, I'll let you have any news when I have it myself."

***

Back in my own flat I risked a look out of the window but everything seemed to be over, thank goodness. An ambulance was on its way out of the car park and a couple of police officers were conferring close to their car. Even as I watched, they got in and drove away.

I called Security, Geoff Wilson was now on duty. "Who was it?" I asked him bluntly.

"Bonzo Ray, I think," he replied. "I expect the police will be in touch in the morning. I should stay well out of the way for now, if I was you."

"Thanks, I will. Good night."

I was glad to give my thoughts a happier turn when Ian rang me the next day.

"About the Williams flat," he said without preamble. "I can see no reason why your Lottie shouldn't move in when she likes. I had got someone interested but I expect he'll be just as happy higher up. What floor is she on did you say?"

"The 14th. The views are wonderful. You needn't tell him they are starting work on the even lift next week," I added warningly. "Have you been told about our latest fatality?" I was determined that he should take responsibility.

"Er – yes, I had." He seemed reluctant to discuss it. "I must go, you tell Lottie she can pack up. I'll bring the paperwork round later today." He rang off.

As I went up to tell Lottie the good news I couldn't help wondering if the apparent suicide had had anything to do with Ian's sudden helpfulness. Could it be that he was afraid of a serial jump? Now, that would give the block a bad name.

As I expected, Lottie was delighted. "I shall start packing up right away," she said enthusiastically, looking brighter than she had for several weeks. "Do you think people here would give me a hand?" she asked me anxiously. "I don't want to tell Susan until it's *a fait acompli*"

"I'm quite sure they will," I said. "Just tell me what day you want to move down and I'll put up a notice. I know Ron and Julian will help, for a start, and there are plenty others I can ask."

***

In the end it turned into quite a party. As I had expected, Ron and Julian headed the list of helpers, with the two heavyweights on the 11th floor, Malin Sterne and Johannes Nielsen close behind. The two music students, Tony and Drew were up for it, and several others pitched in to help carry the smaller bits. It had to be done that weekend, before the lift was put out of action, and in an extraordinarily short space of time Lottie was ensconced in her new flat while the helpers sat around exhausted and feasting on nibbles provided – of course – by Ron. Cans of beer appeared from somewhere, I never did discover where, and music was provided by the two musicians who produced guitars as if by magic. We all sedulously avoided any mention of the recent happenings on the block and spent a happy evening, very much as a community.

It proved very helpful in taking my mind off a particularly unpleasant duty involving a hose and a stiff broom that I had had to carry out the morning after Bonzo's death. I was annoyed, but not surprised that Jimbo turned up. I'm afraid I was barely civil, I couldn't stand his avid interest in other people's misfortunes. I was also very relieved that he did not turn up to help Lottie, though whether it was me or Ron he was avoiding was hard to tell. Suffice it to say, he was not missed.

I went to see Lottie the day after her move in. "How are you?" I asked. "Settled in, alright?"

"Yes indeed," she said with enthusiasm. "Wasn't yesterday *fun*? Aren't people kind, particularly all those youngsters. And the music!" She grinned wickedly. "I'm looking forward to telling Susan later. Even she can't expect me to move again right away."

"Hardly," I said. I looked round the flat. To my amusement she had arranged it precisely the way her old flat had been.

"Yes," she laughed as she saw me looking. "Why change? I know exactly where everything is. Though I have managed to throw a few things out, though probably not as much as I should. But why bother? I'm happy."

"Quite right too," I said firmly. "It's your life."

I went off to work, devoutly thankful that at least something had worked out well.

– Chapter Seventeen –

Once again the police in charge of the "Case of the Manic Tower Block" as David Jones, a Sherlock Holmes devotee, had dubbed it, were racking their brains trying to make sense of the latest happening. Did Bonzo fall, or was he pushed?

"Has the body been formally identified?" the Chief Inspector wanted to know.

"Yes, just about," replied Robin Lutterworth, "though it was not easy. The poor devil landed on his head. One of the tenants, Ronnie Jacobs did it, apparently he recognised the coat, he remembered giving it to Bonzo Ray, and finger prints confirmed it."

"Did you have to ask the caretaker?" asked Sheila Vine.

"Mercifully, no. This Ronnie Jacobs happened to be on his way out just as we arrived and recognised the victim almost at once. I was relieved," Robin added. "I didn't want to ask Frankie if I could possibly help it. She's had quite a lot to cope with."

"Good," said Sheila. "She told me once that having to identify someone who had fallen off the block was one of her secret fears on taking up the job, that, and finding someone long dead in a flat. She's only just avoided that one," she added.

"What's the general conclusion?" the DCI brought the meeting to order.

"Probably accident," responded Robin. "We found a bottle of pills which have to be tested by forensics, but it seems that they could be some form of hallucinatory drug. The balcony door was open, perhaps he thought he could fly. There was no sign of anyone else in the flat, though some door handles seemed to be suspiciously clean. But with nothing else to go on it looks like a drug induced misadventure."

"What about that scrap of paper Frankie found in the lift, accusing Bonzo of murder?" asked Sheila.

"I'm still not convinced that that wasn't a plant," Robin answered. "Though it would tie everything up very neatly if it were found to be genuine."

"It would indeed." The DCI got up. "Keep on ferreting, but if you don't turn anything else up I think we can declare the lift murder as closed and Bonzo's demise as – what did you call it? Drug induced misadventure. Good luck."

"Good luck for what?" wondered Sheila. "To find or not to find?"

"Goodness knows," sighed Robin. "Let's hope we don't find anything, I'm sick of this case."

"Here, here," said David and Sheila in unison.

***

Jimbo Preston was having what he called "a little look round" on the 13th floor. He wondered if there was any significance in the number. He had greatly enjoyed the upheaval surrounding Bonzo's fall from, presumably, the balcony of his flat. Really, moving to this block had been inspired. To be sure, meeting up with Ron had not gone according to plan, who would have thought the shrimp would have developed so well? In spite of himself, Jimbo felt a grudging admiration. Though he still hadn't forgiven, or forgotten the blow that had given him the scar. Still, he had to admit, it did add a certain distinction. He had woven numerous stories as to how he had acquired it, all in his favour, naturally.

Disappointingly there was nothing to be seen on the 13th floor. He had hoped that something would show the drama that had occurred, but nothing. And no one came out of any of the flats, though Jimbo had made some noise, hoping that someone would come out who could be pumped for information.

However, just as he was about to leave, disconsolate, he heard a noise coming from the stairs. Almost at once the stair door opened and a large, thickset man came on to the landing.

"You!" he said. "You are being a nuisance." Jimbo gaped at him. "If you know what's good for you, you will make yourself extremely scarce. We are beginning to find you are getting in our way."

"Wha –" quavered Jimbo, completely floored by this unexpected attack.

"Perhaps this will help you to make up your mind." The big man allowed the snout of a handgun to show in the front of his jacket.

"Er – yes. Certainly. Right away," said Jimbo, prodding frantically at the lift button. The big man was between him and the stairs; there was no way he was going to push past. To his relief the lift arrived and he shot into it like a rabbit into its burrow. Thankfully, it was the new lift, and it descended swiftly and smoothly to the 3rd floor. He rocketed into his flat and started throwing clothes into bags as fast as he could. He was leaving right now, if not sooner.

On the landing of the 13th floor the big man smiled grimly. He had nothing against Jimbo personally, but he was becoming a nuisance. Hopefully he was the type of bully who would run the moment he was threatened.

***

A couple of days after Bonzo's death I was surprised, when I arrived at the 3rd floor to find the door of flat 9 wide open.

"Hello," I called. "Anyone there?" No answer. I peered in, there was no sign of life at all. I wasn't sure, off hand, whose flat it was. I decided to find that out first, then return.

Down in my own flat I found that flat 9 was the home of Jimbo Preston. I was intrigued, and went back up to investigate further. Greatly daring, after all, he had been a pest but hadn't seemed dangerous, I went in.

Inside the flat was in chaos. What furniture there was had been pushed in all directions, while drawers and cupboards bore all the signs of having been ransacked. There was no sign of Jimbo at all. Had he done a flit, or had his flat been broken into? I wondered. I decided that the Office could sort this out.

As I went out to the lift to go down and make my report I was surprised to meet a large, thickset man coming through the stair door. I recognised him as Ronnie Jacobs, who lived on the 8th floor.

Hello," I said. "Not lost your keys again, I hope?"

He laughed. "Oh no, they're quite safe. I was just coming to see Jimbo. Hello, why's the door open? Is he there?"

"Apparently not," I said. "The door was open when I arrived on my rounds. I'm not sure whether he's been broken into or –"

"Done a flit," Ronnie supplied.

I hadn't liked to suggest that if Jimbo was a friend of his.

"Well, yes. Excuse me, I must go and report."

"Don't let me hold you up. I'll just have a quick look round, shall I? As he's a friend. I'll let you know if I find anything."

"Thank you," I said, not sorry to hand over some responsibility. "I'll see you, then." I departed, in our nice new lift.

***

I was taking a break in my flat when there was a rather tentative knock at the door. I opened it and found Vivienne du Cros outside, looking rather nervous.

"Could I have word with you?" she asked. "I'm a bit worried."

"Of course. Come in," I invited, feeling that this was not a doorstep matter. "What's the problem?"

Vivienne came in and sat down, but to my surprise seemed to be unable to come to the point. Remarks about the weather jostled with comments about her college course, which in turn bounced off reflections on her flat. Eventually I broke in.

"Yes," I said. "But what is your actual problem? The one you think I could help you with?"

"Well," she said, and paused. I began to wonder if we'd ever get to the bottom of her anxiety.

At this point her mobile phone rang imperatively. She snatched it up and looked at it, suddenly turning deathly pale. "I must go," she said, "at once." And she fled incontinently from the flat, leaving me with my mouth open and no nearer to knowing what was bothering her. Thoughtfully, I closed the door behind her and returned to my interrupted break.

But she was not the only tenant with a problem that it seemed that only I could solve. I was going through the foyer en route to the rubbish bins when Ronnie Jacobs accosted me.

"Could you possibly come up to my flat for a moment?" he asked. "I have a problem with my electricity meter. It seems to be running backwards."

I hesitated, he was not a tenant I knew well and I found his breezy, hail-fellow-well-met attitude a little overpowering. Plus, after the Romanian incident I was very chary of entering any flat unless I knew the occupant reasonably well. Not that I had had much option then, I remembered; Alec had dragged me in bodily. I also thought that in this case the electricity company would be more help than I.

"You can bring a chaperone if you like." There was just enough veiled contempt in Ronnie's voice to make up my mind.

"I doubt I need one at my age," I laughed. "I'll come up right away."

"Good, I'd be glad to get this sorted." He chatted inconsequently as we went up in the lift to the 9th floor, the odd side lift; as work had now started on replacing the even side lift; we had to walk down one flight.

"Come in, come in," cried Ronnie hospitably. "Tea? Coffee? The kettle's just boiled."

Feeling it would be churlish not to accept I opted for coffee.

"Coffee it is. Sit down, make yourself at home." He departed into the kitchen leaving me to look round his flat. I was always intrigued to see what different people made of the identical flats. This was clearly a bachelor abode, and Ronnie, while liking his creature comforts, as indicated by large, squashy armchairs, was not a great reader, neither was he interested in personalising the flat with pictures. I allowed one of the squashy armchairs to envelop me and waited.

"Do you mind it black?" asked Ronnie putting his head round the kitchen door. "The milk's gone off."

"Not at all," I said politely and accepted the large mug of very black coffee he shortly brought to me. It was a little bitter, but agreeably hot and strong. Rather to my surprise Ronnie also seemed unwilling to come to the point. What was it with everybody today? I wondered. Was I really so difficult to speak to?

I pondered this knotty question for some time while enjoying the brew. Then I became aware that not only was Ronnie's voice coming from a strange distance but that the flat was wavering before my eyes. I just had time to put my mug down before everything went dark.

***

Ronnie threw a contemptuous look at the sleeping caretaker. Really, it had been too easy. He preferred more of a challenge. He picked up the phone and dialled the number he knew so well.

"Mission accomplished, boss," he said. "What do you want now?"

"Good. Did anyone see her go to your flat?"

"I don't think so, no. We didn't meet anyone on the way."

"Right. Bring her up here. I have a companion for her." The phone went dead.

Ronnie looked horrified. Had his boss forgotten that the even lift was out? How on earth was he going to get a zonked out caretaker into the odd side lift without being seen? He concentrated.

Shortly afterwards he was to be observed by anyone interested to be lugging a wooden crate, apparently containing books, down the stairs to the 7th floor and thence into the lift. However, he did not, as might have been expected, press the button to descend to the ground floor; instead the lift went up to the 15th. Holding the lift door open he peered out into the landing. All clear, which was surprising since the work had started on the new, even floor lift. Blessing his good fortune, though he did have a cover story ready, he heaved the crate to the door of flat 60 and knocked. The tall, thin man opened it quickly.

"Come in," said Victor du Cros. "At least you seem to have got this right. I presume she's in the crate?"

Puffing slightly, Ronnie nodded. "Yes, and she weighs a ton. Bitch!" He rubbed aching shoulders.

Victor ignored him. "Put her in the usual room and be quick about it." He went into the living room leaving his confederate to shift the heavy crate into the spare bedroom on his own. Which did Ronnie's shoulders no favours at all, but he knew better than to complain. He emphatically did not want a certain steely glint in the ice blue eyes to be turned on *him*. That meant serious trouble for someone, usually the recipient of the glare.

"Why do you want her?" he asked curiously when Victor returned. "She seemed harmless enough, even useful. She handed that bit of paper to the police, good as gold."

"She's getting entirely too nosy, and too friendly with the police," replied Victor coldly. "Plus Vivienne went to see her this morning, unscheduled. She's lost her nerve and can no longer be trusted. They must both be got rid of, but this time I'll do it myself. You are too unreliable."

An icy chill ran down Ronnie's spine. "I'll be off, then," he said hurriedly, "if that's all."

"For now. I'll call you."

***

I woke up slowly, with a raging thirst and a splitting headache. I couldn't at first work out where I was; the light was very bright so I shut my eyes, which did nothing to ease my other ills. A voice I didn't at first recognise asked me if I wanted a drink, I managed to say yes and a cup was held to my lips. I drank thirstily, which made me feel sick, but, with what felt like a colossal effort of will I controlled it and opened my eyes again.

I found myself in a room completely devoid of furniture save for the chair in which I sat. In fact, onto which I was tied. I moved restlessly and found that my hands were fastened, not too uncomfortably, behind my back and the back of the chair, and my legs were tied to the front chair legs. I was not pleased.

"You look better," remarked a voice which I vaguely recognised but could not place. Then a shape moved into my line of sight and I realised that I was looking at Victor du Cros. At the same time I realised that the groaning noise I could hear was in the room. I turned my head and saw, to my astonishment, that another figure was also tied to a chair, and whose mouth was covered with tape in addition. I was not absolutely sure, but it seemed to be Vivienne.

"Now you are beginning to realise what is going on," said Victor, pleased. "I see that you recognise me and probably Vivienne as well. No, she is not my daughter, as you supposed, but my niece and, sadly, she has proved to be a broken reed. She must therefore be got rid of," he added casually, with no more feeling than if he were commenting upon the weather. The bound figure of Vivienne wriggled wildly. "Do sit still. If you fall over I shall not trouble to pick you up so you will be more comfortable if you stay where you are." He turned back to me. "You are, as you may have realised, in a bedroom in flat 60, but I have made certain modifications so that it is virtually soundproof. But if you start screaming or any other foolishness I shall not hesitate to bind up your mouth too. Though I don't want to do that. We are going to have a nice chat, you and I, before you too are disposed of. I did not expect to have a tiresome caretaker interfering with my plans and I won't put up with it." He added viciously, "I don't often miscalculate but I did expect that a female caretaker would be less trouble that a male, if only because she would find the work harder. Well, I was wrong on that point. I congratulate you. And, after all, when I decided to set up my headquarters here you hadn't arrived." He sounded reproachful.

"Thank you," I said ironically if a little unwisely. I was hanged if he was going to see how terrified I was. But he went on as though I hadn't spoken.

"That, however, was my only mistake. Before I deal with the two of you I shall give myself the pleasure of telling you exactly what I have been doing in this large block of yours. But first I have a little errand to perform so I must leave you for the moment. Please excuse me," he added politely. "And do be quiet, no one will hear you if you do scream, and if I tape your mouth I will not be gentle when I take it off to talk to you." And with that he left the room.

I was glad of the respite, I was feeling far from well and could not imagine how I had come to be in this predicament. Then I remembered talking to Ronnie Jacobs and going to his flat, then drinking the rather bitter coffee. I guessed it had been drugged, and was responsible for the headache and nausea that now possessed me. Clearly he was in on this as well. I had been right to be wary of going to his flat, not that that made much difference now. I wondered what was going to happen, I couldn't seriously believe that Victor and/or Ronnie were intending to kill us; how on earth would they dispose of two bodies? But they definitely did not have our welfare at heart.

I wondered what the time was; my watch, of course, was behind my back. The sun was shining from the left side of the window, which I knew faced north, more or less, if we really were in flat 60. That made it early evening. Probably I should have clocked off by now but it was unlikely that I would be missed for many hours yet. I wondered if I could pull the same trick that I had with Alec and the siege. I rather doubted it, I felt Victor was a far tougher proposition than that desperate man.

I shut my eyes again and concentrated on easing my various ills away. I had a feeling I would need all my wits if I was ever to escape this situation.

***

Satisfied that his two captives were secure and sufficiently subdued Victor went to the lift. The workmen engaged on the renovations on the second lift were long gone, it was a nuisance that he had to take them into his considerations. He had decided that he needed to have Ronnie under his eye from now on, that gentleman knew too much, and was becoming less and less reliable. Confederates who panicked, or had too little resourcefulness in an emergency would have to go.

As the lift came to the 9th floor it slowed and stopped. He frowned, he did not really want too many people to see him. Ah well, he shrugged mentally, it couldn't be helped. He recognised the woman who entered as the deaf person who lived on the first floor. That pleased him, he and Ronnie could talk undisturbed. He needed to keep his control over Ronnie, who should be waiting for them on the 7th floor.

Obediently, the lift stopped at that floor and Ronnie got in. Victor grunted, then, as Ronnie looked anxiously at the woman said, "You needn't worry about her, she's stone deaf. Now, have you got rid of the pills as I told you?"

Ronnie nodded. "Yes, boss."

"And did she suspect anything, or say anything to anyone when you took her to your flat?"

"No, boss."

"And are you sure no one saw you carry her up to the top floor?"

"Quite sure, boss."

At this point the lift reached the ground floor and the two men left it to walk briskly to the main door.

***

Judith looked thoughtfully after them. She had been visiting Jacquetta Meyer on the 10th floor when she entered the lift on the 9th. She recognised Victor as being a fairly regular visitor to Vivienne on the top floor. In fact, that gentleman would have been surprised, and probably disconcerted, by how many people did know him, at least by sight. There was quite a lively student community in the block, of which Vivienne, following the instructions of her "father", had become an enthusiastic member.

Although Judith had not been facing them she had had an excellent reflection of the faces of the two men in the highly polished metal at the back of the lift, and had been able to lip-read what they had said almost in its entirety. And she had not liked what she had discovered. Nor had she appreciated the off-hand way in which Victor had dismissed her deafness. She decided other opinions were needed and consequently abandoned her plan to call at the local shop in favour of returning to the first floor and a consultation.

Unfortunately she wasn't able to have this; most unusually, everyone else in the first floor flats was out. She was not too disturbed by this; she decided to think it all through more carefully on her own. Tomorrow would do just as well. Taken in conjunction with all the events of the past months, the whole conversation needed serious and careful thought. She hoped she was not over-reacting, but remembering the siege, and Frankie's enforced incarceration in the flat, and particularly remembering her adroit message for rescue, Judith was not inclined just to let things go. She hoped the others would not be away for too long.

***

I had actually dozed off in my somewhat uncomfortable position when I was woken by Victor returning. Vivienne was also silent, perhaps she too was sleeping. He came into the room carrying a chair which he set down facing me, then he went out again, retuning with a glass of what I presumed was whiskey. Clearly he intended making a night of it.

"Well now," he said chattily. "I have been wanting to tell someone of my exploits for quite some time and you will do very well, especially as you have been aware of most of them, if not always involved."

"Delighted, I'm sure," I said. I was feeling a lot better for my unexpected nap and prepared to give battle whenever I had the chance.

"You should know that you have been entertaining, if not an angel unawares at least a man of considerable importance, not to say acumen." Modesty was obviously not one of his virtues. "Yes," he said, nodding sagely at the thought of his own brilliance, "I may say that I am a big man in my own world. And very, very rich," he added complacently.

"Good for you." But this was going too far. He frowned.

"And consequently not to be put off my plans by a pip squeak like you."

I decided this was not the moment for a smart retort and tried to maintain a cowed silence.

"I have a web of activities the immensity of which would surprise you," he said, returned to good humour at the thought, "but I will confine myself to those that actually affect this block.

"I decided to move here when I found I needed a base where I was completely unknown. You will remember that this place had a pretty seedy reputation when I arrived; I did not reckon on an insignificant female caretaker making any difference. I was wrong, I admit it, even the best of us make mistakes."

"Why did you move Vivienne in?" I asked curiously.

"As cover, of course," he said impatiently. "She had been wished on me when her father died so I thought she could be useful and would do as she was told. She did at first, then she started getting big ideas. She became a nuisance," he glared at the wilting figure of his niece, "and her crowning act of folly was going bleating to you when I had already decided that you had got in my way too often." The glare switched back to me.

"Where was I. Yes. First, the fire in flat 57. That, of course, was my doing. The Smiths had been in my employ for some time, one of an army of small dealers. They also earned their keep as caretakers for flat 57 which I used for storage and as a safe house when I needed it."

"Did you set fire to the flat deliberately, then?" I asked. I was becoming really interested by this time.

"Not exactly," he admitted. "But it's usefulness was waning, especially with you poking your nose in everywhere," he added viciously.

"Sorry."

"So you should be," he said with heavy humour. "To continue. I already had Ronnie installed in the block and his cover was intact. I could afford to lose flat 57 and the Smiths had definitely outlived their usefulness. They're in Spain now. If they should ever be rash enough to come back I'll find them before the police do, as they very well know." He seemed to dwell pleasantly on the thought of the retribution he would wreak.

"It was at about this time I enrolled Roger Knight. Now he was useful. I needed someone who could pull strings here when necessary."

"Was my predecessor one of yours?" I asked, remembering how Rich had tried to rope me in on his nefarious doings when I first arrived.

"No. I had hopes of him but he was too much of a fool. Roger was much better, he had more power. He was able to install Susan and her girls in flat 20 with no difficulty and even remove security when I needed it."

"So the brothel was yours, then?"

"Yes, indeed. All mine. And very lucrative it was too. Thank you for keeping the place so clean and tidy. We were able to go quite up-market because of that."

"A pleasure," I growled. "And I take it all the murders were down to you, too?"

"Oh, not me personally. I've not killed anyone myself. Wouldn't soil my hands, you understand. The body parts should not have been found, that was not as planned. You getting in the way again."

"Who was it?" I demanded.

"No one, no one at all, just a tramp. But he had rather distinctive feet, and, of course, fingerprints, and it didn't suit me that he should be recognised. I was the one who turned him into a tramp, you see. In fact, he was Theo Carson, the banker who embezzled millions, I expect you remember the case."

I did, he had escaped from prison and vanished. "Yes," Victor nodded. "I got him out of jail and safely away but he gave me the slip – *me*! And went on the streets. I couldn't afford to let him live, now could I? I discovered that he was calling himself Jerry and used to sleep in the chute rooms here, now and again. I couldn't risk him seeing and recognising me, and thus connecting me with the block so, of course, he had to go."

I remembered the "Sleeping Beauty" I had found in the chute room last year. I was sad, he had seemed pleasant, even polite. If he was the absconding banker it now made sense. I remembered the mysterious bags in the chute rooms.

"Were those bags in the chute rooms down to you? And the bogus police?"

"Yes." He scowled. "A lazy, or careless operator. He has been dealt with. The items should either have been put down the chute, or, if they were too big –"

"Which they were," I interrupted.

"Quite. Then they should have been put in the bins themselves. No one would have noticed them there. As it was, I had to use the bogus police to remove them and hack in to the police network to remove your report. You really are a nuisance, you know. But I suppose, on that occasion, you didn't really have any choice." He was forgiving.

" Not really. What about the lift accident?" I asked. "And Bill dying in hospital?"

Victor looked smug. "Yes, both down to me. Though in fact, it was meant to be Bonzo who went down the lift, that silly little smack-head got it wrong."

"*Barbara?* Were you responsible for her too?" This did shake me.

"Yes, of course. We got her hooked, then induced her to take an overdose. Well, I had to when she realised she'd killed someone. She was basically a nice girl. She had been quite useful too, in a small way, running errands and so on, and once or twice persuading other silly sheep into my net." He shook his head sorrowfully.

"And what about the missing electricity meter?" I remembered another minor mystery.

He looked startled. "I don't know anything about that. If she was starting to think for herself then it was definitely time she went. As I said, she was basically honest."

"Until you got your hooks into her," I couldn't help saying.

"Indeed. But as I say, she was quite useful. In dealing with the lift engineer – what was his name?"

"Bill Edwards," I ground my teeth.

"Yes, of course. It was meant to be Bonzo, not the engineer at all. He should have been killed by the fall, just as I had planned for Bonzo. I sent Ronnie to the hospital to finish him off."

"Why? And how?"

"He remembered being pushed when he came round."

"How did you know that?" I didn't really want to fuel his ego by asking, but I was curious.

"Ronnie overheard the lift engineers talking about it. As for how, potassium, injected into the arm and into the drip bag. Causes a heart attack. Very neat, don't you think?"

I was silent.

"Then Ronnie dealt with Bonzo, feeding him pills to calm him down and then switching them for hallucinatory ones and persuading him he could fly."

"But why? Surely the poor little man was relatively harmless?"

"He swindled me. I couldn't let that pass, now, could I? That was, in fact, my second attempt to get rid of him. I don't usually need two bites at the cherry." He scowled, clearly the memory annoyed him considerably. "You may remember the riot in the car park? When Bonzo's door was smashed in?"

I nodded; I was not likely to forget it, it could be said to have killed Mary Williams.

"Yes. I thought I had stirred up the ringleaders so that they would deal with the man properly. Clearly they were fools. I don't often make mistakes as I've told you, but, and I admit it freely, I was guilty of misjudgement there."

"Did you realise that the upset killed a frail old lady?" I demanded.

"Really? No, a pity." He dismissed it. I seethed, especially as it could be said that June's death was due to it as well, she had never recovered from losing her sister.

"And what about the first riot?" I pressed him.

He looked startled. "I know nothing about that." (Not so infallible then, I thought viciously.) "Could have been someone else Bonzo swindled." He paused, looking annoyed. Then he resumed.

"What else. Oh yes, the people trafficking. Another very lucrative line. Still is, for that matter, though I've had to shift locations. But I've kept on the flat," (another minor mystery solved, I thought), "you never know when it might be useful. That was down to you and your spying too. Same with the Romanian orphan. Though that went a bit pear shaped, I still made a mint out of it, and no one had a clue I was behind it. And the loan company that supplied the money at a somewhat uncompetitive rate of interest. That can continue."

I thought back over the various events. "What happened with Ronnie's keys? I asked. "How did you manage to open the lift gate?"

"I really don't know about that." He was dismissive. "One of Ronnie's little blunders, I suppose. He is becoming more and more unreliable." He frowned. I found myself feeling almost sorry for the hapless Ronnie.

"One drama in the block wasn't down to you," I said triumphantly. "Amrita!"

"Really? How did Haidar and Jahnu know where to come for her? And when? And who supplied the gun which put the idea into Jahnu's head?"

I suddenly remembered something. "You were at the trial," I said. "I saw you, but couldn't think who you were."

He nodded. "Yes, I was there. It was most entertaining. You gave your evidence very well," he patronised me.

"But why?" I asked. "What harm had they ever done you?"

"Jahnu had refused to join me when I needed him. And because I could."

I was silenced. I thought for a moment, then went on with the questions. "What about Ronnie?" I asked.

"What about him? Though you're right, I'm getting a bit concerned about him, he knows rather too much and he's a fool. When he's dealt with you two I think it will be his turn."

"But how will you get rid of all these bodies?" Mercifully for my peace of mind this all seemed unreal.

"Oh, down the chute, I think. It's calmed down now and there won't be a caretaker poking her nose in. It really should have worked last time." He yawned suddenly. "Lord, I'm tired. If you'll excuse me I'll go and have a nap then see about tying up these loose ends. Good night."

"Good night," said the loose end faintly.

***

Left to myself I looked round the room. I had been too woozy to pay much attention when I had first woken up, then too concerned by the conversation. I now discovered that the room had been completely lined with some hard material, wood or plastic or some other liner, to make a complete inner room. No wonder Victor had said nothing could be heard outside. Only the window was left, so I could see it was dark outside. Otherwise I had no idea of the time.

I wriggled restlessly in the chair. I was very cramped by this time, and other concerns were becoming increasingly imperative. I looked across at the chair where Vivienne was but I couldn't really see her, she was just outside my line of sight. At least the light had been left on, total darkness would have been hard to bear. Vivienne was quite silent now. I would have been worried about her, but my own discomforts took up too much of my energies.

The door re-opened and Victor appeared, bearing, joy of joys, a bucket. "I suddenly thought you would be needing this," he said, the perfect host. "I'll untie you, there's not much you can do." As good as his word he released me then left me to avail myself of the facilities, such as they were.

Considerably more comfortable, though I discovered I had somehow managed to collect a remarkable number of bruises, I made a tour of our prison. It was indeed an inner room, with a stout door with a secure lock. No help there. And of course, the window was out of the question, though I did try to see if we really were on the 15th floor. It was too dark to be sure, but I didn't seriously doubt it. Then I checked Vivienne; she seemed barely conscious, but I was able to untie her, and lowered her gently to the floor. I felt she would be better off there than fastened to the chair. Then I curled up beside her and attempted to sleep.

Surprisingly, I did sleep; perhaps the drug that Ronnie had given me was still working. When I opened my eyes it was daylight and I was stiff and sore from lying on the floor, and very hungry. I realised I hadn't eaten since yesterday morning.

I availed myself of the friendly bucket – everything seemed to be working even if I was half starved – and waited. Sure enough, after only a short time, Victor came in looking brisk and rested.

"I trust you slept well," he said politely.

"Not bad, thank you," I replied, equally polite. It was then, I think, that I realised that he had completely lost touch with reality. Not that that made him any less dangerous, probably more so. I waited for the next move.

"Ronnie will be here shortly," he said conversationally, "then we can get on with things."

What things? I decided I didn't want to know.

Sure enough, dead on cue there was a knock at the front door and a few minutes later Ronnie came in. He was looking pale and rumpled, as though he hadn't slept much. His usual bonhomie was well in abeyance.

"Right," said Victor, very much in charge. "This is the plan. You will shoot the pair of them, cut them up in here then put the pieces down the chute."

Ronnie looked as though he was going to be sick. Mercifully I was back in the state of unreality; I couldn't really believe this was happening.

"Come on, now," said Victor impatiently. "Get on with it. You did bring your gun with you, didn't you?"

"Y – yes," faltered Ronnie. I suspect that he had never been asked to shoot anyone in cold blood before, his killings were at one remove so to speak.

At that moment there was a crash of breaking glass at the window. At the same time there was the unmistakable sound of a shot. I closed my eyes and waited to feel the bullet, or oblivion, which ever was the sooner. Nothing happened, except a great deal of noise. I opened my eyes. Two men in dark coloured uniforms were swinging themselves expertly into the room through the smashed window. Victor was struggling in the enveloping arms of David and Robin – how on earth had they got here? Ronnie was sitting on the floor with a dazed expression and his hand pressed to a wound in his shoulder, while another figure in a dark uniform was pointing a gun at him with menacing intent. Realising that I really did not want to know anything more at this juncture, and that I was probably out of immediate danger, I closed my eyes and sank thankfully into oblivion.

– Epilogue –

Several days later we were all congregated in Flat 1 to discuss the dramas of the last few weeks and months, and to fill in very many gaps. Robin and Sheila had joined us to give the police perspective, as we were all involved to a greater or lesser extent. Ella Foster was also with us as she had announced her decision to take me down to Gressington for a long rest as soon as I was allowed to go. I wasn't complaining.

"How did you a) manage to find me, and b) know I was in trouble?" These questions had been nagging at me ever since I had recovered consciousness in hospital.

"Ah, there you have Judith to thank," replied Julian. "Come on, Judith. Tell All."

"It was a bit of luck, really," said Judith, "good for us and bad for them. As you know, I had suspicions of Ronnie Jacobs for quite some time, purely because of his body language when I saw him talking to you, Frankie. I just didn't trust him at all. So when I travelled down in the lift with him and Victor, not that I knew who Victor was then, I was prepared to take note. I'd been visiting Jacquetta and John, and Ronnie was very perturbed when I joined them in the lift on the 10th floor. I saw Victor make some disparaging remarks about my being deaf so my hackles were well up," she grinned. "And because you keep that mirror in the lift so highly polished, Frankie, I was able to watch the whole conversation."

"It's a matter of pride to keep that mirror sparkling," I agreed. "I didn't know it was going to save my life, though. Go on."

Judith continued. "They started talking about getting rid of pills, and whether 'she' had been seen going to Ronnie's flat, or whether anyone had seen 'her' being carried to the top floor. None of which made a lot of sense until we couldn't find Frankie, or any message from her. We started to feel suspicious then, after the Romanian orphan thing. So we started putting two and two together, and called Robin and Sheila in." She turned to me. "How did you cope, Frankie? You were incredibly brave."

"Not really," I replied. "I was woozy from the drug Ronnie had fed me most of the time and it all seemed totally unreal. I don't think I ever thought he genuinely intended to kill me. Go on, what happened next?"

"We were able to have a look in your flat, Frankie," Sheila took up the tale, "and found your list of tenants. It's a good thing Ron and Julian have a key, it made things much easier."

"You can thank the cats for that," I said, "and our reciprocal feeding arrangements. Not that it seems very reciprocal, I've hardly ever fed yours."

"*We* don't have to go away to relax," said Julian loftily "We're happy to stay here."

Sheila, who was waiting patiently to continue her tale, called us to order. "When you've quite finished scoring points off each other I'll go on." Obediently we subsided.

"We checked up on the top floor for any strange events in the last few months, also with tenants on the floor below, and had several reports of apparent building work coming from flat 60. We also checked up on Ronnie's flat, 31. We managed to get some prints from the front door of flats 31 and 60 without being spotted and they gave some very interesting results. Victor, Vivienne and Ronnie are all very well known to us, under other names, of course, and we expect to clear up a good many crimes, and put several gangs behind bars because of all this."

"Glad to have been of service," I murmured.

"Yes, well, we didn't for one moment think you would be in danger when we first asked you to keep your eyes open," Robin was apologetic, "but it has been extremely valuable and we do owe you a big debt of gratitude."

"How did you manage to get in through the window? It's fifteen floors up." This question had been occupying my mind for quite some time.

"Easy – for the experts," Robin laughed. "It was all a question of timing, though that was tricky, thanks to all that sound-proofing. We had called in Armed Response of course, when we knew whom we were dealing with, and those with SAS type training. They simply abseiled down from the roof. A doddle, for them. Only one floor." He grinned.

"It was amazing when they crashed through the window," I remembered. "I couldn't believe my eyes. I thought I was dreaming at first, with everything being a bit unreal anyway." I shivered, and hoped that I would never remember too clearly what had happened.

"What has happened to Victor, Vivienne and Ronnie?" I went on. "Particularly Vivienne? He was all set to kill her, as well, his own niece. If she is his niece," I added.

"She isn't, of course, just an addict he coerced into doing what he wanted. He was a supplier in a big way, handling drug networks worldwide with an army of villains in on it. Most of whom we expect to pick up," Robin added complacently. "In fact, we, or at least the drugs boys, were a lot closer to him than he realised. We were just about to pick him up for people trafficking too, thanks to the raid here. I think the orphans scam was fairly new, we've not had much on that – yet. Give us time. Meanwhile, he's sectioned in a mental hospital, he went completely off his head when we got him back to the station and he realised how much we knew. Ronnie, of course, is still in hospital with a hole in his shoulder, and under a very strict police guard. We don't want another episode like Bill."

"What about Vivienne?" I asked. "She seemed really ill."

"She is," returned Robin, soberly. "She may or may not recover, physically or mentally."

"That's an awful thing." Magda spoke for the first time. "She showed real promise at her studies at Uni. I think it was the first time she had been let off the hook, as it were, and had a life away from that Victor. If she does recover I'm going to see what I can do for her."

"Do," Robin was full of approval. "We've nothing on her that was not totally attributable to Victor so there shouldn't be a problem, so long as she recovers, physically and mentally. Which is by no means certain, as I said. And I guess she'll probably have to go to rehab for drug addiction as well."

"I'll see what I can do," Magda repeated, looking determined.

"What about Ronnie?" I demanded. "How badly was he hurt? I remember seeing him clutching his shoulder, and there being a lot of blood. You say he's in hospital?"

Robin laughed. "Yes, but luckily, Victor was such a rotten shot that's all there was. A wound in the shoulder, lots of blood and pain, doubtless, but very little damage. He was so furious at being shot he's singing like a canary. We're very happy. Not that it'll help him much; he's been involved in four deaths here –"

"Four?" Magda broke in, surprised. "I'd not realised it was so many."

"Yes; there were Bill Edwards and Bonzo, of course; it's pretty clear that it was he who went to the hospital and killed Bill, and that he fed Bonzo hallucinatory drugs and persuaded him to 'fly' from the balcony. He was definitely implicated in Barbara's death, inducing her to commit suicide, and in Alec Heron's - the Romanian orphan man who shot himself – did you not realise that?" as we looked surprised. "Yes, not only had Victor and he organised the whole scam but Victor owned the loan shark business that was the final straw. And, of course, friend Ronnie had a rake of from that in return for turning the financial screw, and hounding Alec into committing suicide as well."

"You could include the deaths of the Williams sisters." It was my turn to interrupt. "Mary died as a result of the troubles engineered by Victor and Ronnie and June never recovered from her sister's death. But I suppose you couldn't prove it in court."

"Sadly, no," said Robin regretfully. "They didn't have a duty of care towards them and I doubt that there is a strong enough chain of causation to keep the legal eagles happy. But the four we know of should be enough for several life sentences and they are probably only the tip of the iceberg. He was Victor's number one hit man. Largely because Victor couldn't shoot for toffee and liked his violence at first remove. Didn't want to get his hands dirty." He took a large gulp of wine as we all waited expectantly. "And, of course, there was Theo Carson. We don't know quite when he was killed but we do know that Victor was responsible for it, over and above his boasting to Frankie. It might have been Ronnie who killed him or it might not; he denies it, but he certainly knew all about it and was responsible for disposing of the body parts. Though there again, he may have got others actually to drop them down the chutes. He is somewhat selective in his admissions.

"Yes, Victor did say he didn't like getting his hands dirty," I remembered. "What a poisonous specimen."

Robin laughed. "But you needn't worry. You'll not see either of that pair for a very long time – if ever."

"Just one more thing. How did you get there just at the right time?" I wanted to know the details.

"Well, Julian rang us as soon as he and Ron had heard Judith's story and we alerted and mobilised the troops. Then it was just a case of liaising via the trap door to the roof. We didn't even have to be particularly quiet, the soundproofing worked both ways. Then Armed Response shot the front door lock out at the same time as the others abseiled down from the roof, and the rest, as they say, is history. Really, it was just like the fillums." He grinned.

"I'm very thankful it all worked so well," I said feelingly.

He got up. "Our pleasure. Come on Sheila, I think we had better get going. We've got massive reports to write up for the CPS. Goodbye, everyone, and many thanks for clearing up our crime statistics practically single handed!"

"Pleasure!"

"Don't mention it!"

"Any time!" we chorused, escorting them ceremoniously to the lift.

"Now, Frankie, what about you?" asked Julian as we settled ourselves once again, plates and glasses replenished.

"Yes, well, I have got some news," I admitted. "I'm retiring as caretaker at the end of the summer, it's rather too exciting an occupation."

"Can't say I blame you," grunted Ron. "We'll miss you, though. Where are you going? Back down south?"

"No, you'll not get rid of me that easily. I'm staying put. Here. In my flat." I elaborated. "Assuming I can persuade the Office to take me on as a tenant, of course. Go on, Ella, tell them the rest."

"The Gressington School is opening a branch here at Heathfield, and a junior company. We have asked Francesca to head it," Ella announced with suitable gravity. "Work will start in September, renovating and altering Newton Hall, do you know it?"

"Yes," said Julian, "It's a big, sprawling, Victorian place. It's been empty for years. Isn't it just about a ruin?"

"It's pretty bad, but not hopeless. It's structurally sound. We've got planning permission to do more or less what we want to it inside, also to build boarding houses, and accommodation for adult dancers in the grounds. I've been wanting Francesca on the staff for a long while, and she is ideally suited to start, and to run this, especially after her experience here."

"What, at catching criminals?" demanded Magda. "What are you running, a dancing school or an academy for villains?"

"One thing I still don't really understand," I said, soberly. "It's nothing to do with all the crime. But how is it that we all seem to 'gel' so well on this floor? We couldn't be more different, but we all seem to fit, somehow."

Ron took this up, he had always seemed to be the most thoughtful out of us all. "I've been thinking about that quite a lot too," he said. "I think it may be because we have all had it pretty tough at some part of our life." He took up a school masterly pose. "I spent my early life in a children's home, I never knew who my parents were or anything about them. I was bullied too, by our friend Jimbo." He broke off. "By the way, where is he? I've not seen him for a while, and I would have expected him to be around with all this hoo-ha."

"Done a runner," I said tersely. "Possibly owes rent, I don't know. Or maybe he got too nosy for his own good and fell foul of Ronnie and his mates. I saw the flat, he took hardly anything with him."

"That explains that, then. Then I was adopted from the home, or so I thought, but when my adoptive mother died my 'father'," he indicated inverted commas, " threw me out to sink or swim. I was in the process of sinking when I met up with Julian."

"We met in hospital," Julian took up the tale. "My twin brother was killed in a car accident in which Ron was also involved. Although I wasn't driving my father blamed me and turned me out. Then Ron and I joined up" ("At the hip," said Magda *sotto voce*) "and both managed to haul ourselves up, get training in our respective careers and came here." He ran out of breath.

"Magda, your turn." Ron pointed an imaginary ruler.

"I was abused by my uncle in Israel and escaped to London," Magda started her story. "I was taken on by a magazine and was doing well, but I was raped by the owner, who was also the editor." We all gasped. We had none of us known about that. Magda smiled grimly. "Well, I managed to cope with that, all the girls in the office were marvellous and gave the bastard a really hard time. Thanks to them I could cope with the rape, but then I found out I was pregnant."

We gave an appalled murmur. "Yes. There was no way I felt I could keep the poor little thing, or even carry it for adoption. Wendy helped me through a termination. I shall never forget that. I think it's one reason why she and I make such a successful team. Helping with John's birth did me so much good. I felt I had given a life to replace the one I had taken away, even though I felt there was nothing else I could have done. That, and all the support I've had from all of you, even if you didn't know I needed it."

I got up and hugged her. "I fully understand that," I said. "I expect telling us now will help too, I know it helped me."

She hugged me back. "It already has. I've never been able to speak of it to anyone, not how I felt about it, not even Wendy. Now you know, you will have to meet her. I think you'll get on."

"Judith." The schoolmaster called on the last pupil.

"You know most of what happened, I think. In many ways I was far more fortunate than the rest of you. Yes, I lost my hearing but I was not abandoned, nor did I lose my family. In fact, I was smothered. But I did escape, and now my mother and I are really close. *And* I shall be getting the dog I told you about."

"And the boyfriend," Julian chipped in, wickedly. Judith blushed.

Ron kicked him. "You mind your own business." He turned to the rest of us. "So, we have all had our battles, and I think it has made us more sympathetic towards each other, if you see what I mean."

"Just one thing," I said. In all the fuss I'd almost forgotten." I turned to Judith. "I haven't said anything because I wasn't sure I could swing it, but now it's definite. You are to get a video link to the main door. So you will know who is trying to contact you." I grinned wickedly. "I actually used all the trouble we've been having here to persuade them that it was unsafe for you *not* to have one! Talk about an ill wind." I sat back, feeling smug.

"Frankie, that's marvellous. I'd given up all hope, they were being so sticky." There was no doubt of Judith's pleasure. "And it really does make me feel safer. When will it be fitted?"

"That's another matter," I said regretfully. "The impossible I can do at once, miracles take a little longer. They wouldn't commit themselves. Is there any chance you could come by a doctor's certificate? Get him to say he fears for your mental health? Yes, I know," as the others gave a shout of laughter at the idea of the level-headed Judith having mental health problems. "Or saying you are contemplating moving if they don't secure your safety? You could threaten to claim compensation, or something. There must be someway you can bring pressure to bear."

"I'll certainly try," said Judith firmly. "There are so many gadgets on the market now for us," she added.

"Not before time," interrupted Julian.

"Yes, but they are there. And I mean to make the most of them."

"*And,*" I added portentously, "There will be no difficulty with the Office over a Hearing Dog. I checked, while they are so het up over the troubles and over whether I am going to sue over lack of care. I'm not, of course, but there's no harm in keeping them hopping," I ended, smiling seraphically round the assembled company.

"That's a great relief," said Judith. "I suppose you suggested that we all needed a guard dog."

"I didn't think of that," I said, crestfallen. We all laughed.

Suddenly Ella spoke up. We all jumped slightly; she had been silent for so long I think we had all almost forgotten she was there. As I knew of old, she had this ability to disappear into the woodwork when she wanted to. "I think you are all exceptional people," she said. We preened. We weren't going to disagree. "Let me propose a toast. Are all your glasses charged?"

"One moment!" Julian rectified the omission. We all stood up, the occasion seemed to demand it.

"To the Future!" said Ella, showman to the last.

We drank to it with acclaim.